MW01134250

This book is a work of fiction. Any references to historical events, real people, or real places are used fictitiously. Other names, characters, places, and events are products of the author's imagination, and any resemblance to actual events or places or persons, living or dead, is entirely coincidental.

Contact the author here:
ScribeSammyScott@gmail.com

contents

*For Michele, who doesn't like being scared,
doesn't understand those of us who do, and
read all these stories nonetheless.*

what we have here

"Ugh, I ate too much," Emily said, and slightly reclined her seat, which eased the pressure on her full stomach. Elliot was driving, eyes focused on the dark road ahead, hands firmly on the wheel. He didn't respond.

She closed her eyes and sighed. "My salad was good. What was that cheese called again? Rock—"

"Roquefort," Elliott interrupted, still not taking his eyes off the road.

"Right," she said. "Good food. Pretentious restaurant. I don't know why Lynn feels the need to eat at such fancy places. I can just as easily make myself feel this miserable on less expensive food."

Silence. Emily glanced sideways at Elliott.

"How was your steak?"

"Good," he responded, but his tone didn't sell it. Headlights from passing cars illuminated his face. His expression was stone.

"Okay, what's going on with you?" she said, bringing her seat back to a fully upright position.

He took a breath and glanced over at her briefly, then returned his gaze to the road. "I don't understand why you said what you said. About Walt."

"What did I say?" she asked.

"You've got to be kidding me," he said, glaring at her. "You don't remember?"

She felt irritation beginning to rise, but pushed it down. She was too tired and full for an argument. There was no need to stoke the fire. "I know we talked about the office some. I don't specifically remember what I said about Walt."

"You were telling Greg and Lynn about my presentation last week. And how Walt shot the whole thing down in front of my entire department."

"Should I not have told them about that?"

"It was embarrassing, Em. I'm not sure why my workplace woes needed to be brought up at all. This was supposed to be a fun evening."

"I didn't think it was a big deal," she responded, shrugging, finally allowing her irritation to affect her tone. "Greg and Lynn are our best friends. They care about what's going on with us. I thought they could lend some moral support."

"You made it sound like I'm completely whipped there and can't stand up for myself."

"No I didn't."

"Yes, you did. I believe you used the phrase 'grow a pair'?"

"I was joking."

"It wasn't funny."

"Oh, lighten up."

Silence. Elliot tightened his grip on the steering wheel. "Tonight was supposed to be about old friends catching up," he finally said. "Relaxing and having a good time. I didn't want to talk about work. I wanted to *forget* about work."

"Greg talked about work!" Emily argued.

"Of course he did. Because his business is booming. Why you then decided to segue into my embarrassing presentation is beyond me. It had nothing to do with anything."

"You really do need to stand up to Walt," she responded. "You put a lot of work into that presentation and he sabotaged you. It was uncalled for and you have every right to call him out on it. I don't care if he is your boss."

"It's not that simple and you know it. There are a lot of politics involved. Confronting Walt would, at best, lead to a very uncomfortable work environment and, at worst, cost me my job."

"You're just making excuses."

He stared at her briefly. "Em, you don't know what you're talking about. And regardless, none of this has anything to do with why you decided this was a necessary topic of conversation."

"Well, I thought Greg and Lynn might back me up. Encourage you to take a stand. They both said you have every right to be angry with

Walt."

"I do not need my wife and my friends to tell me what to do. I am fully capable of dealing with this on my own."

"I didn't say you weren't. I just thought you could use some support."

"Support?" He laughed mirthlessly. "No, you wanted someone else to back *you* up so that I would do what *you* think I should do. The fact of the matter is, if you were in my place, you would've been fired years ago because you think it's okay to spout off whatever pops into your head."

"You're right," she responded. "I probably would get fired. But then that would mean that I'd have the opportunity to move on to a better job and still have my dignity."

"You did *not* just say that," Elliot said, his face livid. He took another deep breath; he was clearly trying to calm himself. "See? There you go. You say whatever you want and think you don't have to live with any kind of consequences. You don't stop and ask yourself if what you're about to say does more harm than good or might just leave me feeling emasculated in front of my friends."

"You care way too much about what other people think," Emily said.

"And you care way too much about what *you* think," he responded. "And you make certain that everyone knows exactly what you think at all times."

Neither of them spoke for a moment. Emily looked out the window at the dark world passing outside. Her irritation slowly defusing, she turned to Elliot and began to speak. But before she said anything, he reached over quickly and turned on the radio. Music filled the car.

"Elliot?" she said.

"I'm done talking," he said, flipping through stations.

"Scientists are baffled as—" [click] *"You're listening to 99.5 FM—"* [click] *"—still reluctant to label it an epidemic as medical professionals—"* [click].

Elliot settled on a rock station and turned up the volume until the song was blaring. Emily shook her head and turned away from him. It was a relief to her when they finally pulled into their driveway and the radio died with the engine. Her ears rang in the quiet.

Elliot exited the car and slammed the door behind him. She followed, and they walked in silence to the front door. Elliot opened it and gestured impatiently for Emily to enter. They stood briefly in the foyer before two open staircases: one leading to their finished basement where they both had home offices (and Elliot a small workout area), the other leading upstairs to the bedrooms. To the left of the foyer was the dining room, beyond which was the kitchen; to the right was the living room.

They hung their coats in the foyer closet. Emily dropped her purse on the closet floor, closed the door, and trudged up the stairs. Elliot followed, head down. It was late. They undressed in tense silence and then stood side-by-side at the bathroom sink while they both brushed their teeth. Emily's stomach churned audibly, and she turned sideways toward the mirror, noting that her belly looked bloated. She glanced at Elliot and saw that his did as well.

"Something isn't sitting well with me," she said, rubbing her stomach, unsure if Elliot would be willing to entertain a different topic of conversation or was planning to continue to give her the silent treatment.

He eyed Emily's stomach in the mirror and then looked down at his own. He pulled up his t-shirt, exposing his white belly. His stomach, normally flat, was swollen. He grunted. "I do feel a little queasy," he said through a mouthful of toothbrush. "Something we both ate?"

"Maybe," she said, relieved that he had responded.

Elliot bent over, spit, and then went to use the toilet. Emily left the bathroom and got into bed. After a moment, Elliot came out of the bathroom and stood at the foot of the bed. He didn't say anything.

"What is it?"

"I don't like it when we fight," he said, locking eyes with her. His eyes looked very tired. Defeated. More so than usual. "But I don't know what the solution is."

She patted the mattress beside her. "Come to bed," she said. "Let's talk about it in the morning."

"No," he said, shaking his head. "Don't tell me what to do." His tone was determined but gentle. "We fight too much anymore. I know

I'm sensitive about work. Too sensitive. But I really need you to stop and think about your words before you accuse me of over-reacting."

She bit her lip, thinking over her response before making it, just as he'd asked. It struck her as oddly funny and unnatural. "You would think after eight years of marriage we would be better at this whole communication thing," she finally said.

He nodded, dropping his gaze. "You would think."

The silence was awkward.

"Look," he finally said, "I'm sorry if I over-reacted in the car. Whether you intended to or not, you embarrassed me tonight, but I shouldn't have lost my temper. So I'm sorry about that."

Emily nodded at him slowly, acknowledging his apology, smiling slightly. He stood silently, anticipating her response. She knew exactly the words he needed to hear, words that would diffuse the tension between them and allow this miserable evening to quietly die. But her pride stood like a block in the way of those words and she couldn't will herself to say them, knowing that they would not be entirely honest. Her mouth felt suddenly dry, her lips sticking aridly together.

Elliot looked once again in her eyes and nodded almost imperceptibly. He knew she was not going to give him what he wanted, and the disappointment visibly deflated him. Finally he turned his gaze to the bedroom door. "I'm not sleepy," he said. "I think I'm going to go downstairs."

"Seriously?" she asked him in disbelief.

"Yeah," he nodded. "I just need to be alone for a while."

She watched him walk to the door. In the doorway he paused and looked back at her. "I do love you," he said.

She broke his gaze and looked down, her heart warring between guilt and pride.

He shut the door behind him when he left. Moments later, she heard the TV come on in the living room downstairs.

Sometime later, Emily wasn't sure how much later, she woke up. The bedroom was dark and completely silent. Eerily silent. She moved one hand gently to her left and felt the mattress beside her. It was cool and vacant.

She sat up and swung her feet out of bed. Immediately she realized something was terribly wrong. Her movements, though slight, had produced no sound. Not even a whisper. She did not hear her feet as they slid across the sheets, did not hear the covers as she threw them off her legs.

She reached to the bedside lamp and turned it on. As the light stung her eyes, she realized that there was no clicking sound as she had turned the switch. She sat still on the edge of the bed for a moment, trying to yawn in an effort to get her ears to pop, but found herself unable to.

She raised her right hand to the side of her head and snapped her fingers.

Silence.

She brushed her hair back and touched her ears. Her heart clenched at what she felt: her fingertips rubbed against soft, smooth skin where her ears should have been. It was as if they had been covered over by patches of satin.

She rubbed at them, gently at first and then more forcefully. She heard nothing. Not even the muffled sound one might hear through earmuffs or silenced headphones.

Panic began to overtake her. Her hands shook as her fingertips prodded at the smooth mounds of skin. She jumped from the bed and raced to the bathroom, flipping on the lights. The switch made no sound. She pulled back her hair once again, clenching it in a ponytail in one fist and looking into the mirror, turning slightly to better see the sides of her head.

The reflection horrified her. She would have screamed if she could have, but she could not. She dropped her hair, spilling it onto her shoulders, and stumbled backward until she hit the wall behind her.

Her mouth was gone. Instead there was flawless, completely featureless skin extending from her small nose all the way to her chin. She put trembling fingers on it and found that it was smooth and soft, like the skin of a baby.

She was overcome with horror, terrified by the Halloween mask that stared back at her in the mirror: hair disheveled, mouth and ears missing, eyes wide with horror.

She took a deep breath through her nose and attempted to scream but could not. She tried opening her mouth. The skin over what had once had been her mouth stretched but did not break. She struggled to move her tongue, to push it against the back of her teeth or the roof of her mouth, but she had the odd sensation that it was no longer there. Her mouth was not simply hidden by this veil of new flesh: it was altogether gone.

She panicked and sank to the bathroom floor, covering her face with her hands. She began to weep. Heart pounding in her chest, she found herself unable to take a full breath. Without her mouth, she was forced to inhale only through her nose, which was now flowing with mucus as she wept with fear. It was like breathing through a thin straw after a long run.

The panic then gave way to terror, like a dam bursting. She fell to one side on the cold floor, one hand slapping the tile silently. She realized she was hyperventilating but was unable to draw in the air she so desperately needed. Her peripheral vision went black as her lungs burned for oxygen. Sideways on the floor, she brought her knees up to her chest, curling her body into a fetal position, and the world went suddenly dark.

Sometime later she woke up. She pushed herself up off the floor, immediately noting once again the absence of even the slightest of sounds, not even the subtle ringing in the ears that one experiences in a completely quiet room. Standing, she glanced only passingly at the mirror, willing herself not to panic again. She met her own red-eyed gaze and then looked away quickly.

She left the bedroom and went quickly down the stairs. She forced herself to breathe slowly, but her heart was racing, and she could not keep her hands from shaking on the railing. In the foyer, she looked over to the dining room on her right and the kitchen beyond, both covered in darkness, both vacant. To her left, the TV was on in the living room, but the sofa was empty. Elliot was not there.

There was a reporter on the TV screen. For a brief moment Emily thought the reporter's mouth was missing, but then she realized he was wearing a surgical mask. His jaw movements indicated that he was speaking, but of course she could hear nothing. The bright red news ticker across the bottom of the screen read: "Nationwide panic as bizarre epidemic sweeps the country and beyond."

The newscaster's image was replaced by footage of a hospital room. A short-haired woman, obviously gripped by fear, was being restrained on a hospital bed by medical staff, their faces also covered by surgical masks. The woman was crying, her hair matted with sweat. Her mouth and ears were gone.

Emily stepped back from the television and turned back to the foyer. She needed to find Elliot. She took a deep breath and attempted to scream, hoping that she could at the very least emit a loud groan that would alert his attention.

But she could not. Deaf as she was, she knew she was making no sound. She put one hand to her throat and tried again. There was no vibration, no sensation at all except her racing pulse against her pressing fingers. She was incapable of making noise. In her mind she screamed his name.

She ran to a window and pulled back the curtains. The car was still in the driveway. Elliot hadn't left.

Her mind raced. She could run to the kitchen and bang on a pot. If Elliot was still in the house, he would hear that. But then she had another idea. She raced to the foyer closet and grabbed her purse, retrieving her phone.

With trembling fingers she punched out a text: "WHERE ARE YOU?"

She stood and waited, staring at the bright screen. No response. She had to keep looking.

Intending to go back upstairs, she took a step forward, but then glanced down the stairs toward the lower level. Through the darkness she perceived a dark shape on the floor below. She flipped the switch beside her and light silently flooded the stairwell. There, at the bottom of the basement stairs, was Elliot. He was lying face down on the floor, legs splayed at uncomfortable angles, one foot propped up on the bottom step. There was a dark circle under his head, blood soaking into the thin carpet.

Emily raced down the stairs toward him, her mind screaming his name. She could barely breathe. She knelt beside him and placed one shaking hand on his back.

He reacted instantly, pushing himself off the floor in a panic, sitting up. Emily recoiled from him, his sudden movement startling her, immediately realizing that she was unable to gasp. She felt fleeting relief that he was alive, but then she found herself reflexively placing her hands over the place where her mouth used to be, stifling the scream that she could not emit.

Elliot faced her, trembling, his hair matted with blood from a gash above his right eyebrow. He reached out toward her with one unsteady hand. Though she could not hear him, from the movement of his lips she could tell that he was saying her name. But the name was a question, not a statement, because he could not see her.

Elliot had no eyes.

She grabbed his shoulders and pulled him toward her in an embrace. He hugged her tightly, almost violently squeezing her. Instinctively she tried to talk. She could feel Elliot's breath against her neck, the vibration of his vocal chords as he spoke, but she could hear no words. He trembled so violently that his body shook her own.

He pulled away from her, holding her at arm's length. He was speaking, his eyeless face contorted in confusion. He put his fingers to his eyes, touching the smooth skin there, and continued to talk to her, his face pleading. He looked agitated and afraid. He was speaking rapidly, but his words fell into the void. She knew if she could hear him that he was asking her what was happening and why she wasn't saying anything.

She reached down and took one of his hands into her own and slowly brought it up to the side of her head. She rubbed his fingertips against the satiny skin where her ears used to be. Then she touched his fingers to her nose, trailing them down slowly to her chin, across the flawless epidermis where her mouth used to be. She allowed his fingers to see what his eyes could not.

The confusion on his face slowly gave way to realization and then to horror. He spoke again, and Emily could tell he was shouting, trying to get her to hear him, trying to get her to understand. But she heard nothing and understood nothing. She placed his hand on her cheek and shook her head, crying, telling him *no, I cannot hear you.*

She pulled him toward her again and they embraced. Sobs shook his body, and in the silence she felt the vibration of his voice against her shoulder.

They sat there, clinging desperately to one another at the bottom of the steps, physically together but separated by silence and darkness.

I'm so sorry, Elliot, she thought. *And I love you too.*

theresa

This is not my story; it is my daughter's. Her name was Theresa. She died two weeks ago, a suicide by overdose. She called me just prior to the act, informing me of her intentions and the reasons behind them. I of course pled with her, begging her through tears not to go through with what she had planned. But she was resolute in her decision, and with growing horror I realized that this was no bluff, no desperate cry for attention or reassurance. As she hung up the phone, I knew with certainty she was already as good as dead. I knew it from the moment she had said, "Daddy, Ray is here."

I immediately phoned the police, knowing that they would be able to reach her well before I ever could. But I also knew they would be too late. They found her in bed, by all appearances in a deep and peaceful sleep, one hand draped across her stomach, the other outstretched to the side, palm up, fingers curled as if clutching something – another hand perhaps – but the other side of the bed – Ray's side – was empty.

This is also Ray's story. He died a little more than a year before Theresa did. He was shot twice, once through his right hand, which he had held out defensively, the bullet piercing both his cell phone and his palm before lodging in the tile of the wall of the bathroom in which he had made a final desperate attempt to hide. The second bullet found his neck, and he bled out quickly, alone on the cold floor. He was one of nine people who died in his office building that day. Eight of those people had thought it was simply another Monday at work, unaware that they would not be walking out alive at the end of the day. The ninth to die – the shooter – never had any intention of walking out again at all.

Ray had called Theresa on his morning break. She was at home, and the sight of his name lighting up her cell had made her smile. Married only three months, the pair was still in that young, fleeting honeymoon stage of marriage, and Ray would frequently find an excuse to phone his bride from work if time allowed.

"Hello?" she answered, a smile in her voice.

"Why did the man always get hit by a bike on his way to work?" Ray said.

"I don't know," Theresa responded. "Why did he?"

"Because he was stuck in a vicious cycle."

Theresa chuckled. The joke wasn't really all that funny, but Ray had always delighted in corny humor, and his joy in telling awful jokes brought Theresa more pleasure than the punchlines themselves. Case in point, he had used a ridiculous pick-up line to win her over when they first met. "Feel my shirt," he had said to her, a stranger in a sea of people crammed into a mixer at one of her girlfriend's apartments two years prior. "Do you know what it's made of? Boyfriend material."

Theresa had laughed out loud. One, because the pick-up line was genuinely funny. And two, because Ray, tall and attractive in a goofy kind of way, was so ridiculously happy to use it on her, his smile contagious and immediately endearing. And as bad as the line had been, it had worked. They had been together ever since.

"How is your day?" Theresa said, sitting down at the kitchen table.

"Living the dream," Ray responded with a note of sarcasm. "Actually, my presentation went well this morning. I'm supposed to present it again to senior staff on Wednesday. It's looking promising."

"That's great news," Theresa said.

"It really is," Ray said, satisfaction in his voice.

"You know, if this proposal goes through, we should celebrate. Go away somewhere."

There was a pause on Ray's end. "That sounds like a wonderful idea," he responded, only now he sounded slightly distracted. "Do you have some place in mind?"

"I don't know," Theresa said, thinking. "Sheryl has that cabin that she said we're always welcome to use. We ought to take her up on that sometime. She and Brad will end up selling it before we ever use it. It would be nice to get away."

Ray didn't respond.

"Babe?" Theresa said.

A moment's hesitation. "Did you…hear that?" Ray asked.

"Hear what?" Theresa said. But before he could respond, she did hear it. A loud report, a distant bang, coming over the phone. "Ray, what was that?"

"I don't know," he said, and from the sound of his voice, he was walking. His tone was shaky.

"Ray?"

There was a second loud report, still distant but closer, and Theresa felt her hands go cold when she heard a woman scream.

"I'm going to find out what's going on," Ray said. "I'll call you back."

"Ray—" Theresa said, but he was gone.

She set the cell phone down on the table and stared at its black screen. She got up suddenly from the kitchen table, walked to the sink, and filled a glass with water, which she downed. Staring over at the phone, she willed it to ring again, to show Ray's name. It did not.

Theresa rushed over and picked it up. She called Ray's cell phone. It went to voicemail. She called his desk phone. It too went to voicemail. She called reception at his office. No answer. She slammed the phone back down on the table, hands trembling. She found it hard to catch her breath, to not imagine the worst, to convince herself that what she had heard did not mean what she thought it meant.

An interminable moment later, her phone rang. She snatched it up. "Ray?" she said.

"Baby," he said, whispering, his tone urgent. "There's a man with a gun."

Theresa sank into a chair. "Where are you?" she asked, whispering too without realizing she was.

"I'm in a bathroom down the hall from my office. Reese, he killed Mark. I saw it happen." His voice was trembling, on the verge of panic.

"Ray, hang up and call the police," she said.

"I *did*," he insisted. "They're on their way."

"Okay," she said. "Just be calm." She said this as much to herself as she said it to him. "Where is he?" she asked.

"I don't know," he said. "I saw him at the end of the hallway. I saw him shoot Mark. I came in here because it was the closest door. I don't know if he saw me."

"Did you lock the door?" she asked.

"The door doesn't lock," he said, a small sob hitching in his voice. "I'm in one of the stalls. It's locked."

Theresa began to cry silently, the hopelessness of Ray's situation sinking in.

"Who is he?" she asked.

"I don't know. He's wearing a mask. A ski mask. I think he's—"

Ray stopped talking suddenly at the sound of a loud bang, disturbingly close. Ray hesitated and took a long, shaking breath.

"I love you, Reese," he whispered, his voice even quieter now, barely audible.

"No," she objected, and she slid from the chair to the kitchen floor, the phone pressed tightly to her ear.

There was another loud noise, but this time it wasn't the report from a gun. It was the sound of a door being kicked open and hitting a wall. Ray took a sudden, gasping breath.

"Ray?" Theresa whispered.

Bang. The sound of the door of a bathroom stall being kicked.

"No!" Ray cried out, and the sound of his desperation made Theresa's entire body go numb, jolts of electricity coursing just underneath her skin.

"Ray?" Theresa said, louder.

Bang. The sound of the stall door crashing open.

"*No!*" Ray screamed.

"Ray?" Theresa yelled.

Bang. The sound of a gun.

And then, everything was silent in the house for several seconds as Theresa struggled to take in a breath. Finally, she gasped. And then she screamed.

The shooter was a man named Vincent Holland. He had worked in the Engineering department just one floor down from Ray's office in Marketing. He had been a textbook disgruntled employee with manic depressive issues; at least, that was the story that the press reported. Vincent had managed to kill eight of his coworkers, and then had turned the gun on himself at the first sound of approaching sirens.

The following 24 hours were a blur for Theresa. Through a haze of shock, she had answered police questions, had identified her husband's body, his face pale but still unmistakably his own, and had made necessary phone calls to friends and family. And in the moments between, Theresa had wept, her body crushed under the weight of a grief that was nearly unbearable, the physical pain of it enough to make her welcome the thought that perhaps it might end her own life. *What a mercy that would be*, she thought.

The night of Ray's death, she had slept the deep and artificial sleep of the drugged, her body succumbing to whatever cocktail her best friend Sheryl had insisted on giving her. Theresa had not asked – did not even care – what the pills were, but had taken them all and quickly slipped into the warm embrace of sleep, where her grief at least briefly could not reach her.

When she woke the next day, her body almost crushingly heavy, she wondered briefly why her chest hurt so badly. It took but a moment for her to remember, and the tears were immediate. She rolled to her side and put her palm on Ray's side of the bed, where the mattress was cold and empty. Behind the sound of her crying, she could hear voices down the hallway: Sheryl and Theresa's mother were speaking in somber tones. Theresa looked at the clock. It was shortly after noon. Sheryl's sleeping pills had caused her to sleep for more than eleven hours.

Theresa sat up in bed and wiped the tears from her cheeks, consciously pressing the sorrow down deep into her stomach. She picked up her cell phone from the nightstand, more out of habit than necessity, and shuffled toward the bathroom, flipping a switch. The light assaulted her eyes, and for a moment she absorbed her own pitiful reflection: eyes swollen, cheeks splotchy, nose red. She took in a long, shaking breath.

Then her phone buzzed in her hand and she jumped. The screen said: RAY.

Theresa stared at it, a mixture of disbelief and confusion coursing through her brain.

She answered it. "Hello?" Her voice was barely a croak.

"Why did the man always get hit by a bike on his way to work?"

Ray said.

Theresa struggled to take a breath, and when she was finally able, it came in a rattling gasp. She took an involuntary step away from the mirror, as if retreating from what she was hearing. Her mind raced as she felt a sudden surge of hope warring against her lingering sorrow, and she wondered if perhaps the events of yesterday had been nothing but an incredible dream.

"Because he was stuck in a vicious cycle," Ray concluded.

"Ray?" Theresa said.

"Yeah, baby?" he responded. "What's wrong? The joke wasn't *that* bad."

"Ray, where are you?" she asked.

"I'm at work," he said with a slight chuckle. "Just got out of a meeting. My presentation went well. I'm supposed to present it again to senior staff on Wednesday. Things are looking promising."

Theresa didn't respond.

"Reese, are you okay?" he asked.

Theresa looked at herself in the mirror, at her visible grief. The floor felt like it tilted under her, and her head, still kicking off the last remnants of Sheryl's pills, was a quagmire of conflicting thoughts.

"Reese?" he said again.

"What day is this?" she asked.

"What? It's Monday," he said. "What's going on? What's wrong?"

"It's Tuesday," she said.

"No it's—" Ray began, but then he stopped. There was silence on both ends of the phone for a moment. Then Ray said, "Did you hear that?"

"Hear what?" she asked. And then she heard it, and a sick feeling of déjà vu swept through her. There was a loud report, a distant bang, coming over the phone.

"What *was* that?" Ray said.

"Ray, wait," Theresa said.

There was another loud report, still distant but closer, and a woman screamed.

"I'm going to find out what's going on," Ray said. "I'll call you back."

"*Don't!*" Theresa said, but he was gone.

Theresa put her phone down on the bathroom sink and stared down at it, her hair cascading in front of her eyes. She shook her head violently, trying to shake off the confusion that made it difficult for her to focus. She ran shaking fingers through her hair and then pulled at it in frustration.

She picked her phone back up and called Ray's cell. Voicemail. She called his desk phone. Voicemail. She called reception at his office. The outgoing message informed her that in light of yesterday's tragic events, the office would be closed for the remainder of the week. Theresa furrowed her brow and put the phone down on the sink again.

Seconds later, it rang again.

The screen said: RAY.

She answered it without saying anything.

"Reese?" Ray said, his voice whispering panic. "Listen to me. There's a man with a gun."

Theresa began to sob, and her hand shook so violently that she could barely hold the phone to her ear.

"I'm in the bathroom down the hall from my office. Baby, he killed Mark. I saw it happen." Ray's voice trembled, on the verge of tears.

Theresa said nothing.

"I called the police," Ray continued. "They're on their way." He took a long, trembling breath.

Theresa sat down on the floor and brought her knees up to her chest. She began to rock back and forth.

"I don't know where he is now," Ray said. "I saw him at the end of the hallway. I saw him shoot Mark. I came in here because it was the closest door. I don't know if he saw me. But the door doesn't lock. I'm in one of the stalls."

There was a long moment of silence.

"Reese, *talk* to me," Ray demanded desperately.

"Ray," she said through her sobs. She could manage no further words than that.

"I don't know who this guy is," Ray said. He's wearing a mask. A ski mask. I think he's—"

But Ray stopped talking suddenly at the sound of a loud bang, disturbingly close. He hesitated and took a long, nervous breath.

"I love you, Reese," he whispered.

Over the phone, Theresa heard the sound of a door being kicked open and hitting a wall. Ray gasped. Theresa heard again the sound of the bathroom stall door being kicked open, the sound of Ray's desperate objection, and then the final sound of a gun being fired.

And then, in the ensuing silence, Theresa relived the grief of her husband's death for the second time.

She told no one about the call. Not Sheryl, and not her mother. She couldn't explain it to herself, much less to anyone else. The two had continued to keep her company throughout the day, answering phone calls, dealing with concerned well-wishers, attempting to get Theresa to eat, and managing the details of Ray's viewing and funeral, which were scheduled for Saturday evening and Sunday morning, respectively. But mostly, the two of them were there simply to make sure that Theresa was not alone. In her waking moments, they treated her like an antique porcelain doll, delicate and fragile.

Theresa slept for most of the day, even without Sheryl's chemical help. She ate hardly at all, a fact that distressed her mother.

She had still been in bed at noon on the following day, Wednesday, two days after Ray's death, when her cell phone rang.

The screen said: RAY.

Her body went numb and she quietly began to cry. She answered it. "Ray?" she said quietly.

"Why did the man always get hit by a bike on his way to work?" he said.

Theresa ended the call immediately, and then shut her phone off and tossed it aside. She lay in bed and wept.

On the third day, Thursday, Theresa was alone in the house. Sheryl and her mother had other things to attend to and hadn't been outside the house since Monday evening. Theresa had showered, brushed her hair, and even put on a bit of makeup. Her arms felt weak and heavy as she did so. But she attempted a tired smile as she insisted that she would be fine if her mom and best friend left her alone for a few hours.

When her cell phone rang shortly after noon, she was sitting at the kitchen table, the bright sunlight through the windows making her head ache after so much time spent in the darkness of her bedroom.

She answered it, her voice weak: "Because he was stuck in a vicious cycle."

There was silence on the other end, and for a moment Theresa wondered if Ray was really there.

Finally, he laughed and asked, "How did you do that?"

"I'm not sure," she said.

"Are you okay?" he asked. "You sound strange."

Theresa took a deep breath. "Do you know who Vincent Holland is?" she asked.

"Yeah, he works down in Engineering, I think. I don't know him real well. I do know that every day at lunch he eats an onion like an apple. Never seen anything like it."

"Ray, he has a gun," Theresa said.

"What? How do you know that?"

"Don't ask me that right now," she responded. "He has a gun and he's going to start shooting people. You have to get out."

"Reese, I don't—" But then Ray stopped as they both heard the sound of a gun being fired. "What was that?"

"Listen to me," Theresa said. "You have to get out of the building."

Ray was silent for moment. Then he said, "Okay. Okay. I'm going." And then the phone fell silent.

Theresa put the phone on the table and stared at it dully. Dust floated silently through a sunbeam that cascaded through the window and landed with warmth on the back of her hand. She wondered how the sun continued to shine, as if the entire world wasn't enveloped in a grief as thick as her own.

Her phone rang again. Ray.

She answered. "Baby?"

"I saw him," Ray whispered.

"Where are you?" she asked.

"I'm in the bathroom down the hall from my office. Baby, he killed Mark."

Theresa ended the call and slammed her phone back down on the table. She put her hands over her eyes and cried.

Friday, shortly after noon, Theresa sat at the kitchen table with

Sheryl and her mother. The three of them were quietly nursing cups of tea, the kitchen counters and nearly every other available surface covered in gift baskets and flowers. Theresa's mother and Sheryl made quiet small talk as Theresa sat silently, her eyes intently focused on her cell phone, which sat like a dumb blank slate on the table in front of her.

12:03 came and went without a call. Theresa chuckled mirthlessly to herself. She had intentionally made sure she was not alone for today's phone call from Ray. If he did call again, this time she wanted witnesses. But part of her knew that he would not call her if she was not alone.

"Is everything okay, Reese?" Sheryl asked.

Theresa peeled her swollen eyes away from the silent phone. "Yes," she whispered, and sipped her tea.

I flew in from across country for Ray's viewing and funeral. Theresa's mother and I were cordial toward each other, but also avoided one another as much as possible for Theresa's sake. I was shocked at how she looked – tired and haggard and grief-stricken, of course, but also troubled in a way that did not look like mourning. I held her tightly several times over the course of those two days, always at a loss for words, wishing there was anything in the world I could do to remove the weight of sorrow pressing upon her shoulders.

Theresa told me later that she had tucked her phone away during those two days. She had thought that maybe going through the ceremony of remembering Ray's life, seeing his serene face as he lay dead in his casket, and then watching with surprising detachment as his body was lowered into the ground, would bring a final end to his daily calls.

But on Monday, alone at home for only the second time in the week since Ray had died, her phone rang again. She considered not answering it, but could not resist doing so, a sense of both longing and hopelessness in her chest.

"Ray?" she said.

"Why did the man always get hit by a bike on his way to work?" Ray said, and Theresa burst into tears.

For the next several days, Theresa lived in a fog. She always took

Ray's call. Some days, she let the conversation play out like it had on the first day, relishing those first fleeting seconds when Ray was still happy and alive. Other days, she interrupted his joke in order to ask him a question, like where he had put the key to the safety deposit box, or where he had filed insurance papers. Confused but cooperative, Ray always answered her questions. Some days she had used those initial seconds to convey her deep love for him, and she had sobbed as he had expressed his love for her in return. But then, all too quickly, the sound of a gun would bring their conversation to an abrupt end.

And then one day, several weeks on, the phone had rung, and Theresa had said, "Hello, baby," and waited for Ray to launch into his bicycle joke.

There was a pause, and Ray had said, "Reese… did, did I call you earlier today?"

A coldness spread through Theresa's chest. "What? No, you didn't."

"It's so strange," Ray said. "I picked up the phone to call you and got this sudden sense of déjà vu. Like I already called you today."

A tear slid down Theresa's cheek. She couldn't find words.

"Is everything okay?" Ray asked.

"I miss you, baby," she whispered.

Ray chuckled. "I miss you too?" he responded, more of a question than a statement. "I'll see you in a few hours."

"No you won't," she said.

"Reese, what—" and then he stopped. "Did you hear that?"

Theresa hung up the phone. Her thoughts stirred with confusion and an odd feeling of hope. Every prior conversation had been laden with a heavy sense of the inevitable; no matter what Theresa said to him, Ray would always end up dead on the floor of his office bathroom. But today, today he had seemed to remember something, and their conversation had taken a different course at Ray's direction. And Theresa began to wonder what would happen if she tried pushing harder, made more of an effort to get Ray to make different choices.

The next day when Ray called, Theresa immediately took charge of the conversation. "Ray, I need you to listen to me carefully and answer me as fast as you can. How many different ways are there out of your office? Out of your department, I mean."

"What?" he said.

"Answer me!" she insisted.

"There's the main door. Straight through goes to the IT department, and to the left takes me down the main hallway. There's a second door that goes through HR, but that just meets up with the main hallway at the other end. And then there's the door to the balcony. Why are you asking me this?"

"Grab your keys. Don't grab anything else," Theresa insisted. "Go through the IT department. Do *not* go down the hall. Get to your car and *come home. Now.*"

There was a pause, and then Ray said, "Okay. Okay, I'm coming." And the line went dead.

Theresa found herself out of breath while she waited. She paced. Moments later, her phone rang again.

"Reese? Listen to me. There's a man with a gun."

Theresa screamed in frustration and threw her phone across the room, where it hit the carpet and slid across the floor.

The next time he called, Theresa asked, "Ray, the balcony outside your department. Does it have steps that go down to the courtyard?"

"Yes," he said. "Why do you ask?"

"And you can get to the parking lot from there?"

"Yes. What's going on?"

"Go," Theresa insisted. "Don't ask me anything. Just go out the balcony doors and to your car. Do it now. Come home."

"Is everything okay?" he asked.

"*Go!*" she yelled, and hung up the phone.

A minute passed, then two. Theresa barely breathed as she stared at her phone. Five minutes passed without a call from Ray. She was finally able to take in a slow, shaking breath.

Theresa was seated on her bed. Her back ached as she sat arched over her phone. For the first time since the day Ray died there was no second phone call, and Theresa had no idea what to expect next.

She was lost in a nearly thoughtless daze when she heard the front door open, causing her to jump and gasp. The door closed and she heard footsteps. She slipped from the bed, walked cautiously from the bedroom and down the hallway to the foyer.

And impossibly, there he was – his tall, gangly, goofy-looking-yet-handsome self, although his skin was deathly pale to the point of almost being blue. He smiled at her, although his brow was furrowed in concern. His mouth formed the beginnings of a question, but she ran to him and leapt into his arms. He was cold, deathly cold, and Theresa gasped.

"Is everything okay?" he asked, and his voice sounded like it did on mornings when he had first woken up, rattling and unused.

"Everything is okay now," Theresa said, weeping into his shoulder, holding him tighter than she ever had before.

And in return, Ray held her tightly as well, but his hands were like ice on her back, his body stiff against hers, and although her ear was pressed firmly against his chest, she could not feel his heart beating, a fact that she dismissed just as quickly as she realized it.

She decided to tell him everything. Sitting at the kitchen table, she held his hands in both of hers as she recounted everything from the initial shooting at Ray's office, his death, and his funeral, to his daily phone calls. He stared at her blankly, his face registering no alarm, confusion, or even recollection as she spoke. When she finished, she sat back in her chair and considered him for a moment. *Tabula rasa,* she thought dully as she stared at him.

He wasn't hungry. He wasn't thirsty. He was content to sit quietly until Theresa gave him directions to move. Her heart ached with the dueling emotions of relief and terrible confusion, and she studied him closely, unable to hide the obvious bewilderment on her face, and yet Ray never asked her what was wrong.

That evening, Theresa led Ray to their bedroom, where he stood dumbly by the foot of the bed and looked around as if he had never been in the room before. She undressed him, and as she did so she realized he was wearing his work clothes, not the suit he had been buried in – the suit he had worn on their wedding day. She pulled back the covers and told him to lie down. He did so with silent obedience.

She slid in beside him and kissed him. His kiss was both familiar and foreign to her. His lips were soft and passive where they had always been firm and insistent before, and there was no warmth there. But the texture and the taste of him was the same, and Theresa held back tears as they embraced again. They made love, Theresa initiating and leading where Ray had always taken charge before, and while her heart overflowed with the joy of being held by her husband once more, her body shivered at the iciness of his touch.

When Theresa awoke the next morning, sunlight touching her eyelids, she reached to her side without opening her eyes. But her fingers encountered nothing. Ray's side of the bed was empty, the covers pulled up as if he had never been there. She sat up abruptly.

"Ray?" she called out. But there was no answer. She searched the house, calling out for him several times. But he was gone.

She returned to the bedroom, feeling both confused and sorrowful. Where had he gone? And would he come back?

And then, shortly after noon, her phone rang. The screen said: RAY.

She answered it. "Ray?"

"Reese," he said, his voice sounding even more raspy and unused than before. "Don't worry. I know there's a shooter. I'm coming home."

The line went dead and Theresa set her phone down. Her chest knotted in such a cacophony of emotions – sorrow, hope, frustration, and even fear – that she realized she could hardly feel anything anymore.

But come home he did. And this became their new pattern – the new vicious cycle they were stuck in. Every day he would come home, every day looking even more pale and feeling even more cold to the touch, his personality receding even further into the empty shell that he was becoming, a vacancy behind the eyes that had once been so passionate and full of life. Theresa had to tell him to sit, to eat, to bathe himself. He was like an elderly man who was losing use of his faculties, and Theresa evolved into his loving but confused and somewhat terrified caretaker.

And every morning, Ray's side of the bed would be empty again, and he would call Theresa from work shortly after noon to tell her that he was coming home. Theresa noticed that each time, his voice sounded more worn, like it was being dragged over stones. As if his vocal chords were decaying. It was not long before his countenance began to catch up with his voice. He began to look more physically withered, his tall frame beginning to bend, his eyes large in their sockets as his face became even more wan and his cheeks more sunken.

Theresa allowed this pattern to continue for months, her love for her husband locking her in a living hell, but she was rapidly reaching the point of collapse herself, her emotional and mental well-being withering right along with Ray's countenance.

"I'm coming home," he had said to her over the phone, his voice like dusty rocks being rubbed together, barely recognizable to her.

"Wait," she had said. "Ray – don't. Don't come home. Stay there. It's okay. Stay there."

"No," he responded, slowly and without emotion. "No, if I stay here I'll die. I'm coming home."

Theresa had hung up the phone, wept, and waited once more for her husband to return. She wept because her husband was dead. She wept because he was alive and yet dying a little bit more every day before her very eyes. She wept because she felt bound to him in whatever repeating loop that his death and their love had created. And she wept because they were together again and yet she felt entirely alone.

Finally, on the day that Theresa took her own life, she made a decision, a decision that came to her easily and without fear. The idea gave her the first comfort she had felt in the year since Ray had died. Perhaps, she thought, the key to escaping this living hell was to die herself. More precisely, to die beside Ray as they slept together in bed. And in the morning, when he was gone, perhaps she could be gone too. Gone, but together with her husband.

She called me that afternoon to tell me her story, to tell me her plan, and to tell me good-bye. I listened with terrified disbelief as she recounted the details of her miserable life in the months since Ray had died. Her story was one I could not accept as fact, and yet I also knew from the sound of her tired yet determined voice that my daughter was telling me the absolute truth.

"Is Ray there now?" I asked her.

"Yes, Daddy," she said tiredly. "Ray's here. Do you want to talk to him?"

I didn't answer, but then I heard Theresa say distantly, "It's Dad. Talk to him."

There was a shuffling sound, followed by raspy breathing.

"Ray?" I said, barely managing a whisper.

He didn't respond, but I could hear as he attempted to. All I heard was the sound of his laborious breath and the vaguely recognizable tones of his voice as he attempted to speak. But his words were garbled, his voice wasted.

Theresa took the phone back. "I have to go now, Daddy."

"Baby, don't do this," I said, crying but trying to hold myself together. "I love you. Your mother loves you. Let us help you. There has to be some other way."

Theresa began to cry. "There is no other way, Daddy. This is the only way."

"No," I insisted. "You still have so much to live for. Let me take you away from there. You can come here. Maybe Ray won't come to you anymore if you're not there." I felt myself playing along with her, even though I wasn't sure I even fully believed her.

"Daddy, there's something else," she said, taking a long and exhausted breath. "I'm pregnant."

"You're—" I started, then stopped. A hard lump lodged in my throat. I couldn't breathe. My mind pieced it together. Theresa was pregnant. And Ray had been dead for more than a year.

"It's Ray's," she said, answering the question I hadn't asked. "But it's…" She didn't finish the statement. "I don't know what it is. I just know I can't, Daddy. I just can't." She wept.

She said her final goodbyes to me, ignoring my pleading. And then the call was over.

I already told you how the police found her. The autopsy revealed that she had died consuming a large number of sleeping pills left helpfully behind by her best friend Sheryl. It also revealed that she had been several months pregnant. I insisted that this detail never be revealed to her mother. Estranged and distant though we are, there are some horrors a mother should be spared when it comes to her own child.

So this, as I said, is Theresa's story. And the story of her husband Ray. And you may not believe me, but it's an absolutely true story, as fantastical as that might sound. I believe Theresa now, although two weeks ago when she told me her story for the first time, of course I had doubted her. I don't doubt her anymore, not a single detail. Because every day, she calls to tell me her story all over again.

blackbird

Molly's appointment with Dr. Masterson was at 9:00 a.m. on a Monday morning. He called her into his office, smiling warmly as she stepped by him. He smelled lightly of an unfamiliar cologne, and his thin frame, high forehead, and wire-rimmed glasses reminded her very much of her father, which was why she had felt at an immediate ease with him. The tone of his voice was deep and warm as he greeted her, almost melodic.

The black leather chair threatened to swallow her as she sank into it. It was placed in front of Dr. Masterson's desk, a huge black beast standing guard in front of a row of impressive, orderly bookshelves. Molly placed her purse in her lap, hugging it like a pillow as Dr. Masterson sat in an identical leather chair across from her. She appreciated the fact that he did not sit behind his desk, which would have served as a literal separation between him and her. Instead, there was nothing between them except open space and an ornate rug. The room's layout invited conversation.

He flipped open a notebook and clicked a pen, smiling lightly at her. "And how are you doing this morning, Molly?"

"I'm doing...ok," she said, returning his smile with a slight reluctance.

He made a note on his pad. "Good," he said. "You do seem a little lighter today, I have to say."

"I am, a bit," she confessed.

"Any particular reason why?" he asked.

"Yes," she said, breaking eye contact with him and looking at the bookshelves to her right. "It's a little silly, I guess. But I had this dream last night. It was so vivid and peaceful. You know my dreams are usually upsetting or frightening. But this one was nice. And it was particularly special because it was about my mom."

"Ah," he responded, making another note and nodding once with approval.

Molly's cell phone buzzed in her purse. She pulled it out and silenced it in one quick motion. "Sorry," she said, dropping it back into the bag. "But yeah, the dream was great. It was like she was with me again, and we could just talk. It was so real. I was actually a little sad when I woke up and realized it was all a dream, but mostly it made me feel… really peaceful. I can't remember the last time I woke up feeling even a little positive. Before the accident, definitely. It was nice having a chance to talk to her again. In a way."

Dr. Masterson continued to write in silence. Molly shifted in her chair while she waited for him to respond, her left index finger tracing the spider web of scars along the back of her right hand. She curled her fingers, feeling a familiar ache. "It made me wish that that would happen more often, you know? I mean, I know I can't bring her back. But even just seeing her again in a dream like that more often would be… you know, nice."

Dr. Masterson stopped writing and regarded her for a moment, a nearly imperceptible smile on his face. He studied her. Eventually, he took a deep breath and said, "It's very interesting that you brought this up this morning, Molly."

"Why?" she asked.

"I have recently introduced a new program to my practice," he answered. "I call it dream therapy. It's essentially a combination of mild sedatives, hypnosis, and a controlled sleeping environment, as well as a few other proprietary procedures. Together, they allow the subject to enter into a deep dream state, but one that allows for more control over the content of the dream itself."

Molly sat forward slightly in her chair, her thumb still rubbing the back of her aching hand.

"Like I said, it's a new concept. But I've used it to allow patients to revisit moments in their past that bring them particular happiness, or to relive, if only for a moment, an event that they wish could have had a different outcome. Lame patients can dream of running or even flying if they want to. It provides a temporary, controlled respite from reality. In your case, it would allow you to see your mother again whenever you would like to."

"I'm in," she said without hesitation.

Dr. Masterson chuckled lightly. "You need to understand that this is a new procedure, not covered by insurance. And it's still in its experimental phase. But I think you would be an ideal candidate."

"Dr. Masterson," she said. "I'm in. Please."

About an hour later, Molly walked to her car feeling lighter than air, a glossy brochure clutched in one hand. On it, a pretty blonde woman with perfect teeth smiled from the front panel, the words "Dream Therapy" above her head. The tagline "Dream of a Better Today" appeared at the bottom.

"Right now, we only offer dream therapy sessions once per week," Dr. Masterson had explained to her. "I want to be careful about my patients becoming too reliant on the therapy itself, not to mention the drugs involved that induce sleep. The last thing I want to happen is for the patient to enter the controlled dream state so frequently that they begin to lose their grip on reality. As inviting as it might be to sleep and dream whatever you'd like to dream on a nightly basis, one must stay grounded in reality. Otherwise it could do more harm than good."

Molly's first session was scheduled for Thursday, a frustratingly long three nights away. She was told to arrive at Dr. Masterson's office at 8:30 p.m. with an overnight bag. The morning after, she would have a brief follow-up session with the doctor to see how the dream had gone. Assuming all was well, future weekly appointments could be scheduled from there.

The evening of the first session, Molly pulled her car into the dark parking lot of Dr. Masterson's office building. It was empty save for three other cars. She stopped the engine, grabbed a duffel bag from the passenger seat, and walked toward the front doors. A woman Molly recognized as Dr. Masterson's receptionist, Iliana, approached from the other side of the glass, smiling warmly and unlocking the doors, pushing one open to let Molly in. Once Molly had walked past her, Iliana pulled the door closed and locked it once more.

After a short walk down a dimly lit hallway, Iliana opened another door for Molly, revealing a small room with a full bed, a desk with a chair, and a coat rack in one corner. There was a painting on the wall, a small house with a white picket fence and a nicely manicured lawn, a black and white puppy romping after a large rubber ball.

Molly tossed her duffel bag on the bed and turned to face Iliana, who had stopped in the doorway. Molly noticed a small camera tucked into the top left hand corner of the room.

"Dr. Masterson is on his way down," Iliana said. "Go ahead and change into whatever you would like to wear to sleep. There is a bathroom across the hall if you need to use it. The camera is off."

Iliana ducked out of the room and shut the door. Molly shed her clothes quickly and slipped into a pair of gray sweatpants and a soft black t-shirt. She rolled up her other clothes and stuffed them into the duffel bag, which she placed on the desk, and then sat on the bed and stared at the picture on the wall. Soft music began to play in the room — dulcet tones that were soothing but lacking any kind of perceptible melody.

There was a light knocking at the door, and Dr. Masterson walked in, smiling, leaving the door open behind him. He handed Molly a small plastic cup that was three quarters full with a clear liquid.

"Drink this," he said softly, his voice even quieter and more soothing than usual.

She swallowed it without question and handed the cup back to him. The concoction was both slightly bitter and cloyingly sweet.

"Go ahead and lie down," he said, and she turned, pulled back the covers of the bed, and slid in. Dr. Masterson sat on the bed beside her. Iliana entered behind him, pushing a small metal cart topped with an electronic console covered with dials and buttons. Dr. Masterson retrieved several electrodes that were attached to it – half a dozen clear suction cups connected to white wires – and gently applied them to Molly's temples, forehead, neck, and wrists.

"We will be monitoring your vitals while you sleep," he said. "And we can also keep an eye on you." He pointed over his shoulder at the camera, which now sported a glowing green light.

Molly nodded her understanding.

"Now there are a few things we need to go over before you sleep," he said. "You will be dreaming more deeply than you ever have before. But you will always remain somewhat aware of the fact that you are dreaming. This allows you some measure of control over the dream itself. You can choose to be a passive observer in the dream, or you can be an active participant. It's your choice. But keep in mind that just like regular dreams, not everything will always make sense. I call this 'dream logic.' Most of the time you can just ignore it or even will it to go away if you want. But if something disturbing happens, something that upsets you and you want to exit the dream, you need a safe word. It's a word of your choosing that will end the dream immediately and break the sedation."

Molly furrowed her brow at him.

"It's nothing to worry about, trust me," he said, patting the back of her hand. "You are going to be under fairly heavy sedation, and in the rare instance that the dream takes a turn that you don't care for, you need an exit door."

"Blackbird," she said.

"Blackbird?" he repeated.

"It's what my dad calls me," she said. "Since I was little. Because of my hair. Blackbird."

"I've been meaning to ask you how your father is," he responded, beginning to fiddle with some of the dials on the console. "Any progress there?"

"Not really," she said. "He still isn't the same since losing Mom. He's very distant. But I don't see him much. He works all the time. I wish he would retire."

"Well, *blackbird* it is," the doctor said, and Molly wondered momentarily if he had even been listening to her or simply keeping her distracted. "If you want to end the dream, just say, 'blackbird,' and you'll be safely awake again in this room. Now, give me your forearm."

She obediently pulled her left arm out from under the covers. There was a sharp prick, and she inhaled softly through her teeth.

"Hush now," Dr. Masterson said, smiling down at her. "It will help you sleep."

She nodded again, and her head felt suddenly incredibly heavy, as did her eyelids.

"Just relax," he said. He waved his hand in a slow circular motion above her face. Something silver – perhaps a coin of some sort –

dangled from a thin chain that wrapped once around his middle finger, once around his hand, and then disappeared into his sleeve. It caught the faint light from the hallway and reflected strange colors into her eyes.

"Sleep and dream, Molly," he said soothingly. "Your safe word is 'blackbird.' Sleep and dream. Now tell me – what would you like to dream about?"

"My mother," she said, the words coming out in a mumble.

"Dream about your mother, Molly. Your safe word is 'blackbird.' Dream about your mother. Sleep and dream."

Dr. Masterson repeated these words, his hand continuing to move in a slow circular motion above her head, the disk of silver dangling and reflecting light, and just as her eyes fell closed, a man, his features hidden in shadow, entered the room behind him.

* * *

Molly found herself seated on the front step of a house. She was wearing a polka-dot dress with white lace along the hemline. Her knees were chubby, one of them adorned with a band aid barely covering a nasty scrape, the bright light of a spring sun illuminating the fine golden hairs on her legs. She looked at her hands, small and soft, with short fingers devoid of scars, the knuckles dimpled, the nails painted with a cheap and flaking glittery polish.

The yard before her was framed by a white picket fence, and she gasped and giggled as a black and white puppy raced across the front yard in pursuit of a large rubber ball, tripping over his own feet and tumbling over.

She looked beyond the puppy to the gate at the end of the sidewalk, and there she saw her mother. She was young – mid- to late-20s at most – her skin smooth and darkened by the sun. She was walking toward Molly, humming as she shuffled through the handful of mail she had just retrieved from the mailbox. She was wearing a small white t-shirt and tight jeans, looking more trim and healthy than Molly had remembered her ever being, and for a moment Molly found herself confused by her mother's youth and beauty. Suddenly a large maple tree in the corner of the yard bent over, folding as if made of paper, its high branches tickling the grass. Its unnatural movement startled her.

Dream logic, she thought, and blinked her eyes hard. When she opened them, the tree stood upright again.

Molly's mother sat beside her on the front step, resting the stack of mail on her knees.

"Whatcha doing, babydoll?" she asked.

Molly smiled up at her. "That puppy is silly," she said.

Her mother laughed. "That puppy *is* silly," she agreed. Then she curled up her eyebrows in exaggerated confusion. "Whose puppy is that, anyway?"

"It's our puppy, Mommy!" Molly exclaimed, leaning one shoulder into her mother's arm. The skin there was warm and smooth.

"Okay," she chuckled, "if you say so." She leaned her weight into Molly, pushing her gently, playfully threatening to topple her over. "Do you want to sing a song?"

"Yes!" Molly said.

"What do you want to sing?" she asked.

"'Hush Little Baby.'"

They held hands, and together they sang, a gentle spring breeze playing with their hair and carrying their notes out into the neighborhood. The sky was cloudless, the puppy ran tirelessly through the yard, and across the street, hidden mostly in shadow, a man watched and listened as they sang.

* * *

The following morning, Molly was dressed and seated in Dr. Masterson's office, holding a hot mug of coffee he had poured for her. The warmth eased the persistent ache in her hands. He was studying a chart in his lap. Molly yawned hard, the effects of whatever chemicals she had been given still lingering in her muscles, which were heavy with exhaustion.

"By all external measurements, the night went well," he said, flipping over a paper. "You slept for a solid nine hours. All of your vitals remained well within healthy parameters and you barely moved. So that's all good. But now you tell me – how did last night go?"

"Excellent," she said, smiling. "Perfect." She took a sip of coffee and then set the mug down. She rubbed one thumb against the raised scars of her left hand, sleepy but also excited.

"And you dreamed about your mother?"

"Yes," she said. "I was a kid again. I wasn't expecting that. And she was young too. It was wonderful. It really was like being with her again."

"So… same time next week?" he asked.

Dr. Masterson gave her a key card. He explained that it would grant Molly access to his office building on the nights of her appointments, which meant it would no longer be necessary for Iliana to be there to let her in.

The following Thursday evening, Molly walked across the dark parking lot, empty save for her car and one other and entered the building. Dr. Masterson had instructed her to use a different room for this dream session, one that was located next door to the one she'd used the week before. It was identical to the first one, save for the picture on the wall, this one of an idyllic kitchen scene that would have made Norman Rockwell proud.

She had already changed clothes and slipped under the covers when Dr. Masterson knocked lightly and entered the room, pushing the small metal cart in front of him. Molly sat up and took the cup he extended to her, downing its contents, and then offered her left arm to the needle in his hand.

"Tell me again what your safe word is, Molly," he said as he attached suction cups to her temples.

"Blackbird," she said, lying down.

"Relax," he said, extending his hand until it hovered inches above her face, the silver coin dangling from a chain wrapped around his finger. She tried to make out the details of the engraving upon it, but in the dim light of the room could decipher nothing.

"What would you like to dream about, Molly?" he asked.

"My mom," she whispered.

"Dream about your mother, Molly. Your safe word is 'blackbird.' Dream about your mother. Sleep and dream."

As sleep overtook her, Molly looked beyond Dr. Masterson to the door behind him, mostly blocked by his shoulder. A man lingered in the hallway.

"Who is that?" she mumbled, and for the briefest of moments she felt herself becoming dully alarmed.

"Sleep now," the doctor said.

* * *

She found herself seated at a kitchen table. The room was unlike any room of any house she had ever lived in, and yet at the same time it felt warmly familiar. There was a steaming bowl of oatmeal in front of her, smelling sweet with brown sugar and blueberries. Her mother was standing at the stove, stirring the contents of a large pot, her back to Molly.

"Good morning, Mom," Molly said.

"Good morning, babydoll," she replied, not turning. "Did you sleep well?"

"The best," she said. She realized her voice wasn't as small and childlike as it had been in the previous dream. She looked down at her hands. The fingers were longer, as were the nails, which were polished and shining. She was a teenager, and her hands were free of scars. "How did you sleep?" Molly asked her mother.

Her mother turned, a puzzled look on her pretty face. She too was older than she had been in the last dream. Mid-30s, the age she was during Molly's early teenage years. "It's funny," she said, gesturing with a large spoon dripping with steaming oatmeal. "I had this dream. I mean, I remember dreaming. But now I can't remember anything about it." She shook her head dismissively.

"Dreams are funny that way," Molly said.

"They can be," she responded. "Eat your oatmeal. You'll be late for school."

Molly raised the spoon from the bowl in front of her, its contents steaming but suddenly black like tar. "Why is my oatmeal black?" she asked, chuckling.

"What?" her mother responded, glancing at the bowl before her daughter.

Dream logic, Molly thought, and blinked, and immediately the oatmeal returned to its normal beige. "Never mind," she said, devouring the spoonful. It was hot and perfectly sweet. Her mother returned to stirring the pot.

"Hey Mom, I have an idea," Molly said.

"What's that?" she asked.

"How about I ditch school today and we go to the mall?"

"Oh Molly," she chastised.

"Aw, c'mon," Molly pleaded, getting up from her chair and walking over to the stove. "We haven't done a Mom-n-Molly day in *forever*. We could shop, get lunch at some greasy spoon, have onion rings and strawberry milkshakes, and go to a matinee."

"Your father would kill me," she said, but even as she spoke, Molly could tell her mother was considering it.

"*Pleeeeeeease?*" Molly said, pulling on her arm.

Her mother laughed, and for the briefest of moments she looked so vibrant and alive that Molly felt a terrible sinking feeling in her chest, her present reality encroaching upon the dream, a small voice in the back of her head telling her *no, she's not alive, she's dead now*, and suddenly the floor began to tilt. Molly stumbled sideways, but her mom caught her arm and held her upright.

"Did you feel that?" she asked.

Molly threw her arms around her mother and hugged her tightly. *Don't wake up*, Molly thought. *Don't wake up, don't wake up, do not wake up*.

"Okay, okay," her mother said, laughing and pushing Molly away gently. "Go get your coat. We'll have a Mom-n-Molly day. Just *don't* tell your father."

* * *

"Dr. Masterson?" Molly said. She was seated in his office the next morning, her knees pulled up under her chin, watching him as he studied a chart. Molly hadn't sat like that since she was a teenager, more than a decade ago, but the dream had left her feeling incredibly childlike again. She had just finished telling him the details of her dream, which had ended up being longer and more vivid than the first.

"Hmmm?" he responded.

"Did someone come into the room last night?" she asked him. "Right before I fell asleep, I thought I saw someone outside the room."

"No, of course not," he said, not looking up from his clipboard. "There was no one else here except for you and me."

* * *

One week later. Night number three.

"Tell me again what your safe word is, Molly," Dr. Masterson said.

"Blackbird," Molly responded, studying the painting on the wall to her left, a pretty picture of a busy playground. "That's a different picture than last time. Last time it was a kitchen."

"The pictures are different in each room," he said. "That is intentional. The pictures aid the patient in filling in the details of the dream while also providing some variety. If you found yourself in the same setting with every dream, you might more easily recognize that you are dreaming and then wake up involuntarily. Now, relax. Tell me, what would you like to dream about?"

"My mom again," Molly said.

For a brief moment, Molly tried to resist the sleep-inducing cocktail that was coursing through her body. She fought it long enough to catch the slightest of details in the coin that Dr. Masterson dangled in front of her. It was a symbol, something that looked vaguely like Greek lettering but also a little like ram horns.

"Dream about your mother, Molly," said Dr. Masterson. "Dream about your mother. Sleep and dream."

He repeated these words over and over again as she drifted off to sleep. And then, just as reality faded into a dream, his words changed into something foreign, a language she had never heard before. It sounded almost like an incantation.

* * *

She was seated on a park bench, her mother beside her. Both of them had bag lunches on their laps. It was autumn, and as children ran and played in front of them, there was the pleasant sound of dead leaves being crushed under running feet. Molly was wearing a suede jacket that was soft and warm, a favorite of hers when she was in college that she had long forgotten about ever owning. Her mother took a bite of her sandwich, watching the children run and play in front of them, lost in thought.

In the dream, Molly was a young adult; early 20s. Her mother was in her 40s. They were not much younger than they had been on the day of the accident. This was a thought that Molly shoved away immediately, squashing it like a bug.

"How's Dad?" Molly asked.

"He's good," her mother responded. "Working too much, of course. But good."

"I wish he could've joined us," Molly said, and for a moment she considered wishing him into the dream.

Her mother didn't respond.

Molly's cell phone buzzed in her pocket. She pulled it out, silenced it, and put it back.

"You and that phone," her mother said, staring out over the playground. A few moments passed with nothing but the sound of squealing children and the occasional scolding duck.

"What are you thinking about, Mom?"

Molly's mother chewed slowly, not answering. Finally she swallowed and said, "It's a gorgeous day." Then a tiny tear ran down her cheek.

"Mom, what's wrong?"

She put down her sandwich and shook her head slightly. "I'm not sure," she said, sniffing. She brushed crumbs off her fingers. "This is going to sound ridiculous, but honestly, Molly, sometimes I think I'm losing my mind."

"What do you mean?" Molly asked. A rubber ball bounced against her shoe. She picked it up and handed it to a smiling child who had run over to retrieve it.

"It's like," she paused, thinking, watching the child run away. "I remember spending time with you. We've been spending a lot of time together lately, and it's been wonderful, but… I'm having a hard time remembering anything else but that."

"You have no other memories?" Molly asked her.

She shook her head slowly in response, deep in thought. The effort to remember was etched on her face.

Molly turned on the bench to face her mother more directly. "Do you remember marrying Dad? Or me being born? Or moving to Shreveport?"

"Yes, yes," she said emphatically, "I do remember. *All* of those things, now that you mention them. But I have such a hard time remembering much of anything else at all."

"What is the last thing you do remember?" Molly asked her.

She sat silently, pondering. A rubber ball bounced against Molly's shoe. She picked it up and handed it to a smiling child who had run over to retrieve it. *Dream logic,* she thought as the child ran away. In the distance, beyond the play equipment that was swarming with colorfully-dressed children, a man sat alone in the shadow of a tree, facing them.

"I remember… going to the mall with you. Shopping. Onion rings and strawberry shakes and a matinee. Stirring oatmeal in the kitchen. Singing 'Hush Little Baby' on the front step. A black and white puppy." As she listed each thing, her voice trailed off.

Molly shivered. "Anything else?"

"I remember… a terrible loud sound. Like metal being crushed. Glass shattering. And…*pain*." She took a deep breath, then turned to face her daughter. "Molly, why did you bring me back?"

The rubber ball bounced once again against Molly's shoe. She leaned over to pick it up, but the child who had come to retrieve it had a face that was covered with blood, hair matted and dark against his scalp. Shards of glass glittered in his hair. Molly stared in stunned silence, and suddenly her mother began to scream, grabbing her arm and shaking her. Molly tried to pull away from her, but her grip was too tight. Her mother stared at her, her eyes wide with fear and her face drained of all color.

"*Why did you bring me back?*" she screamed.

"Blackbird," Molly said.

* * *

"How did last night go?" asked Dr. Masterson.

"Not well."

"You woke up with the safe word," he responded.

"How do you know that that?"

"You said it out loud," he said. "The camera caught it."

"I dreamed that my mom was losing her memory," Molly said. "And then she started talking about the accident."

Dr. Masterson made a note. "Did you try to change the course of the dream?" he asked. "You do have some control over what happens."

"I was too frightened," Molly said. "I didn't even think of it. I just wanted it to end."

"If you think the dreams are proving to be less than therapeutic, perhaps we should take a break from them?"

"No," Molly said quickly. "I don't want to do that. It was just last night. The first two were good. Maybe I can make the next one good too."

"That's entirely your decision," he said.

"Dr. Masterson, can I ask you something?"

"Yes, of course," he responded, finally looking up from his notes.

"The dream therapy. I know you use drugs on me. Probably several. And hypnosis. But is there more to it than that?"

"Like what?" he asked.

"Like… I don't know. Something spiritual?" She didn't want to use the words *voodoo* or *occult*, afraid that they would make her sound silly and paranoid, but they were the only words coming to her mind. "That coin you use, it has a strange symbol on it. And it sounded like you were speaking in a foreign language before I fell asleep."

He chuckled and shook his head. "Dream logic," he said. "You were falling asleep and confused the dream for real life. My methods are completely proprietary, but I can assure you, the procedure is purely medical."

"Toward the end of the dream, my mom asked me why I had

brought her back," Molly said.

Dr. Masterson's mouth fell open just slightly before he caught himself and shut his lips tight again. He cleared his throat, then made an act of shuffling the papers on his lap. He smiled. "Molly, that was simply the real world encroaching upon your dreams. I promise you, your mother exists now only in your dreams and in your memory. That is all. But I will also remind you that if I begin to suspect that you are having a hard time differentiating between the dream therapy sessions and real life, I can stop them at any point that I deem necessary."

"No," she said, putting up her hands in protest. "No. I don't want to stop. I'll just try better next time to control it. Make it nice like it was the first two times."

* * *

The fourth dream began with Molly behind the wheel of a car. She was driving down an open highway. The windows were down, hot summer wind whipping through her hair. Pop music was blasting from the radio. She looked over at her mom, seated beside her. She was singing along to the song, smiling, one hand out the window, surfing the wind.

"Where are we headed?" she yelled over the music.

"Anywhere you want to go!" Molly responded, laughing.

"Hawaii!" she yelled, and they both laughed. She bopped along to the music and pushed her sunglasses up against her brow.

Molly's cell phone buzzed from the cup holder beside her. She picked it up and looked at the screen, but it was blank.

"Eyes on the road, kiddo," her mom scolded.

Molly put the cell phone back and blew a raspberry at her. "I'm thirty years old, Mom. Not a kiddo."

"You'll always be my kiddo," she said. "Keep your eyes on the road."

"Well, I hope you're ready to swim," Molly said, changing the subject. "It'll be an underwater drive to Hawaii." Trees whipped by in a blur as they sped along. "Didn't Dad want to come?" she asked.

"He's working," her mother said so quietly that Molly barely heard her over the music. She reached forward and turned off the radio, the smile falling from her face. "On second thought, I've changed my mind about Hawaii."

"Why?" Molly asked.

"There's nothing but darkness there."

"What?"

"There's nothing but darkness there, Molly. There's you and there's me, and then there's darkness." Even though the windows were still down, the wind abruptly ceased and everything went silent. Molly couldn't even hear the car's engine running as they sped down the road.

"What are you talking about?" Molly said.

"Why did you bring me back?" her mother asked, a sob in her voice.

Molly closed her eyes, gripping the steering wheel tight, her knuckles whitening. *Control the dream,* she thought. *Control the dream. Happy thoughts.*

"I can't remember anything, Molly," her mother said. "It was quiet for awhile. Like sleeping. It was peaceful. There was no pain. And then suddenly we were together again. And it was wonderful to see you, baby. It was like reliving my happiest memories." She began to cry. The road in front of them cracked loudly and the car shook as they ran over the small fissure.

"But then, when we're not together, there's nothing but darkness." As she spoke, panic began to rise in her voice. "It's like being in this huge room with no walls and no light, all alone. And it feels like an eternity passes. And no one will answer me when I scream. Days go by, it feels like. Months even. And there's nothing but being alone in complete darkness and silence." She began weeping. "Why did you bring me back?" she screamed. "Why didn't you let me be? Why didn't you just let me *rest*?"

The car swerved, and for a moment Molly almost lost control of it. "Calm down, Mom," she said, mind racing. *Control the dream,* she thought, closing her eyes again. *Picture a beach with palm trees and a sunset. The sound of seagulls. Warm sand under our feet. Picture paradise.*

Her mother grabbed her arm and the car swerved. "Don't wake up!" she screamed. "If you wake up, I'll be in the darkness again, Molly. Don't make me go back to the darkness again. Please, stay with me!"

Molly jerked her arm away. "Let go!" she yelled. Her mother stared at her, panic stricken, her eyes wide and pleading.

Molly's cell phone buzzed again. She looked down at it.

What happened next occurred in a slow instant. Molly looked up and saw, reflected in the rearview mirror, a man sitting in the back seat, looking directly into her eyes. She screamed. Then she saw a telephone pole, sickeningly large as it tore through the hood of the car, and she saw her mother careening forward and through the windshield, the broken glass tearing at her skin and clothes. The bones in Molly's hands shattered painfully as she involuntarily punched the dashboard, and before her head hit the steering wheel, she screamed, *"Blackbird!"*

* * *

She rocked herself quietly in the leather chair in Dr. Masterson's office, knees tucked up under her chin again. She was crying. She dabbed at her eyes with a sodden tissue.

"I don't want to do it again," she said. "I can't control the dream anymore. And it's too upsetting. I dreamed that my mom thinks that I've brought her back from the dead, but in between each dream she's lost in some kind of limbo. It's a nightmare."

"Molly," a soothing voice said.

"I don't want to risk having another dream like that," she said, sniffing, and she wiped her nose, then the tears on her cheeks with her palms. "I can't stand it. It's worse than not having her here anymore. The idea that her soul is lost in darkness between each dream."

"Molly," he said again.

She looked up. Through her tear-filled eyes she saw, seated across from her, not Dr. Masterson, but her father. She blinked. He too was crying.

"Dad?" she said. "What are you doing here?"

"There's something I need to say to you, Molly," he said. He got up from the chair and knelt in front of her, taking her hands in his. He gazed at her with warm, loving eyes.

"Why are you here?" she said.

"I wanted to tell you that I forgive you," he said. "Those aren't easy words for me to say, but I know that I need to say them. I forgive you, Molly."

"Forgive me for what?" she asked.

"For the accident," he said. "For taking your mother away from me. For the longest time I resented you for that. But I know you didn't mean to. It was so stupid, but it wasn't on purpose."

Molly looked back into his eyes, lost for words. She felt a deep sadness, but also a creeping terror of realization.

"But I've been seeing this really good therapist. His name is Dr. Masterson. He convinced me that the pathway to healing was forgiveness. I needed to forgive you. Not just for taking your mom away from me, but for taking *you* away from me too. It took me awhile, but I'm finally ready to let it all go, Molly."

"The accident was… my fault?" she asked him, stunned, her mind racing, digging for a memory that was eluding her.

"It's been really nice," he said, reaching up and touching her cheek. "Dreaming and watching you and your mom again. Together. It was very healing. But the dreams have started to become upsetting. So it's time for me to get back to real life again. It's time for me to let you both go for good."

Still kneeling, he took both of Molly's hands in his own and raised them to his lips, kissing them. Molly stared down at him, heart pounding, not fully comprehending. Tears fell from her father's eyes. One of them splashed against Molly's right hand. She looked at it and saw that her skin was flawless, without blemish, free of scars.

"Goodbye, my baby girl," he said, dropping her hands and standing up slowly. "I hope that, wherever you are, you and your mom are together again."

"Wait… Dad!" she said, beginning to rise, panic filling her chest. She reached out toward him. "Don't say it!"

"Hush now," he said, backing away from her. "Hush now. Blackbird."

And suddenly, everything was darkness.

the sisters

The house sat like a fading yellow cube among similar houses on its block. There was no landscaping to speak of, no flowers or bushes, no lawn ornaments or trees, nothing to ground it or give it any kind of personality. Its shutters and front door were a dark, unattractive brown, and the sidewalk leading to the front door was cracked. Grass and weeds poked through every fissure. The metal fence that framed the property was rusted and bent in random places, and the roof had bald spots where shingles had been plucked away by the wind. It was neglected and unwelcoming.

Andrea parked the car at the curb and stopped the engine. She picked up the manila folder on the passenger seat beside her, flipped it open and reviewed the file inside. "Dolores Cartwright. Age, 82. Early onset dementia." Andrea was the fourth in a line of homecare nurses who had been sent to take care of her. The previous three had quit without notice. Her daughter Julie had contacted Andrea, warning her in advance of the impossible job ahead. Andrea's task was to convince Dolores to move into convalescent care where she could be supervised and cared for 24/7, but even Julie admitted this would likely never happen. The house — plain and unwelcoming as it was — was Dolores's childhood home, and she adamantly refused to leave it. And so, barring that option, Andrea's secondary goal was simply to persuade Dolores that she needed in-home care — someone to cook, clean, and tend to her health. These were all tasks that Julie was willing to do herself, but her mother had forced her out, verbally abusing her until Julie had had no choice but to leave.

"She's not well enough to be alone," Julie had said to Andrea. "The stairs are steep and she refuses to move her bedroom down into the living area. She has a hard time getting around and spends most of her time in bed. She sometimes forgets to eat..." Julie's voice had faded at this point as she fought tears. Clearly, if Andrea was not able to successfully interject herself into Dolores's life, more drastic measures would have to be taken. She would have to be forcibly moved. Andrea fully understood the unpleasant task at hand.

"There's something else I need to tell you before you go," Julie said. "Her sister, my Aunt Edna, recently died."

"Oh, I'm so sorry to hear that," Andrea had replied.

"No, no," Julie continued with a sad chuckle, waving a hand dismissively. "They were estranged. Hadn't spoken in years. Edna was a terrible person. She had been since childhood. I didn't even know until I was a teenager that I had an aunt. The family never spoke of her. My grandparents couldn't control her. And she was abusive to my mom from the very start. On the day that my mother was born, they handed her to Edna. You know, 'Look at your new baby sister.' Edna dropped her on the floor. And that was just the beginning.

"She once pinned my mother down and cut her forearms with a piece of broken glass. Tied her to the bed and left her there for an entire day while their parents were away. Drowned my mom's kitten in the bathtub. Just... terrible things. My grandparents tried all kinds of measures to deal with her. They grew up in a generation where corporal punishment was the norm, and according to my mom, my grandfather even resorted to whipping with a leather belt. He would leave welts on Edna's legs and backside. But she never cried. Mom said Edna would walk away from these whippings completely stone-faced.

"When she was a teenager, they shipped her off to a school for troubled youths. Mom said at first they would visit her there every weekend, although Edna refused to talk to them at all except on certain occasions when she would unleash a loud verbal assault that left them no choice but to turn around and go back home. And so the weekly visits became monthly, the monthly visits became holiday visits, and eventually they stopped going to see her at all. Mom said that in her teenage years, she felt like an only child, and she loved it. She said that she and her parents eventually behaved as if Edna had never existed.

"One day, my grandfather got a call from the school telling him that Edna had run away. He simply said, 'Thank you,' and hung up the phone. They never bothered trying to track her down. The family assumed that she was likely to have gotten caught up in a bad lifestyle. Drugs, prostitution. It was hard for them to imagine any other course for her to have taken. But these were all assumptions on their part. Certainly none of them thought she would have gone on to live a long or normal life.

"Still, my mom said that there were things that happened over the years that made them think Edna was still around. Sometimes they'd come home to a shattered window. It was a nice neighborhood at the time and that sort of thing just didn't happen. Another time, the house had been ransacked. The place was a mess, but nothing had been stolen. The worst was the time they came home and found a leather belt curled up on the kitchen table, at my grandfather's chair. Mom says that grandpa simply picked it up and put it away, not saying a word. Everyone was thinking *Edna*, but no one spoke her name.

"Eventually, my mom grew up and moved out, of course. Struck out on her own. Got pregnant, had me. She suspected that Edna continued to make herself known at the old house, but grandma and grandpa of course never spoke of it. For my mom, it had been so long since the last incident that she had mostly forgotten about her. But then there was this." She held up her hand for Andrea to see, and for the first time she noticed that Julie's left ring finger was missing. "This happened when I was an infant. My mother had taken me to the park for a walk. I was in a stroller. She was distracted by a little boy who had fallen down near a duck pond. She helped him up, dusted him off, and pointed him to his mother. She said she was watching him walk away when I began to scream. When she got to me, I was covered in blood, and my finger was gone. She panicked, of course. It all happened in an instant, and although she never laid eyes on her, my mother knew it was Edna."

"That's just terrible," Andrea said.

Julie shrugged, a motion of acceptance and sadness. "My grandparents died about twenty years ago. They left my mom the house and she moved back into it. I was on my own by then."

"Did anything else happen?" Andrea asked. "After your mom moved back in?"

"I've always wondered," Julie said. "But like I said, my family didn't speak of her. And I didn't ask. Anyway," Julie offered a tired smile and sighed. "You're probably wondering if there's a point to all of this. The point is, Edna died a couple of months ago. She had lived to the age of 86. And now, my mom is convinced that..." Julie paused, taking a deep, shaky breath. "My mom is convinced that Aunt Edna is haunting her house." She averted her eyes from Andrea's, clearly uncomfortable with this admission.

"Oh," Andrea replied, pursing her lips thoughtfully. "Okay."

"I know what you're thinking," Julie said, holding up a palm. "You don't have to say it. A delusion like that is common for someone with dementia, and that's probably all that this is. But what concerns me is this: we didn't know that Edna had died until after Mom began insisting that her ghost was haunting the house. It was only after Mom refused to let go of the idea that I began digging into Edna's whereabouts. It took a lot of effort, but I finally tracked her down. She had lived close to the family her entire life, which I guess shouldn't have been surprising, all things considered. And she had died only a single day before my mom claimed to have seen her for the first time, standing in her kitchen."

Andrea let silence linger for a minute, allowing Julie's words sink in. "If she is so certain that her sister is haunting the house... isn't that reason enough for her to leave?"

"One would think," Julie laughed. "But she insists that the house is hers and she will not leave it."

"And what do you think?" Andrea asked.

"I don't believe in ghosts," said Julie. "I think my mom is sick. And it's because of my refusal to play along with her that she kicked me out of the house. My mom is not the evil seed that Edna was, but she's still a hard, stubborn woman. Always has been, and the dementia has made it worse. So I'm sorry to ask you to go in there, and I understand if you want to pass on this particular job, but she needs help. Please... help her."

The neighborhood was completely silent as Andrea exited the car, the sound of the slamming door echoing down the deserted street. She was acutely aware of the sound of her steps as her soft-soled shoes scuffled on the concrete and the high pitched squeal of the gate as she pushed it open. Approaching the house, she glanced upward and caught sight of a figure standing at one of the upstairs windows, staring down at her. She raised one hand in a timid greeting, attempting a pleasant smile, and the figure retreated.

The front door opened slightly before her knuckles even touched the wood. One eye, framed in wrinkles, peered out.

"Miss Cartwright?" Andrea asked.

"Yes," said the woman, the word sounding somehow defensive. Her face was deeply creased, her eyes the color of ice. Her white hair was pulled up in a severe bun on the top of her head. She was a stern-looking woman with a large, sharp nose that Andrea's own mother would have described as "proud." Her posture was amazingly straight for a woman of her age, and Andrea was surprised to note that this woman was actually an inch or two taller than her.

"My name is Andrea. I'm a nurse with Home Health Services. May I come in and talk to you?"

The woman's gaze drifted downward suspiciously. Andrea felt suddenly very self-conscious and wondered if perhaps her sweater was a tad too tight or her skirt just a hair too short. It was a childish reaction that she quickly squashed. After a moment, Dolores backed away, opening the door further, and Andrea stepped inside.

She was hit by a sudden chill that made her arms break out in hard goosebumps. The temperature outside was warm and humid, an early autumn day still stubbornly holding on to the remnants of summer. But it was uncomfortably cold in the house, and she immediately thought of how unhealthy such low temperatures would be on an elderly body.

The old woman extended an arm, inviting — or more accurately, demanding — that Andrea step into the living room. She took a seat on a couch that felt worn and dusty but soft, and felt herself sink uncomfortably into the cushion, the springs beneath it having long ago collapsed. Andrea set her briefcase on the floor and removed a pen along with Dolores' medical folder while the old woman took a seat in a rocking chair across the room. The chair faced the front bay window, the afternoon sunshine the only source of light in the dim room. She rocked slowly, her face in profile, not bothering to look at her guest.

The chair creaked.

"Your daughter sent me," Andrea began.

"I don't have a daughter!" she snapped, looking at Andrea harshly.

The suddenness of her response combined with her icy glare startled Andrea, and her immediate instinct was to chuckle slightly at the outburst. "She said you'd say that," Andrea responded. She tucked a lock of hair behind her ear nervously. "How are you feeling today, Miss Cartwright?"

"I'm *fine*," she responded, almost spitting the words, and returned her gaze slowly to the window.

"Julie is concerned," Andrea continued. "We know you value your independence. But you do have some pretty serious health concerns. I wanted to talk to you a little bit about the facilities we have at —"

"I'm not leaving," she interrupted. "This is my house. I grew up in this house. I'm not leaving." With each sentence she slapped one palm down on the arm of her chair.

"I understand," Andrea said. "Then perhaps we can talk about making your situation here a little more ideal. Having someone come in to take care of you. To cook, clean, monitor your health. Even provide some companionship."

"No," she said, continuing to rock.

"You can still maintain a lot of your independence," Andrea offered. "You should look at it more like a partnership. I'm not here to take over, but to assist. And you'd still be able to keep your home."

"No," she said again.

Andrea found herself momentarily at a loss for words. "Miss Cartwright, you need to understand —" She was interrupted by a noise. A low, quiet moan from upstairs. The sound sent an electrical charge down Andrea's spine. She looked up at the ceiling for a moment, listening. When she looked back down again, Dolores' face was unchanged, her gaze locked steadily on the window before her.

"You need to understand," Andrea continued, "that we must come to some sort of agreement today. A compromise. You have some pretty serious health concerns that need to be addressed, and if in my assessment I determine that it isn't safe for you to be here by yourself, then it could lead to a situation that you would find less agreeable than simply having home health care."

The old woman rocked, not responding. Andrea stared at her silently and shivered. She looked over at the thermostat on the wall.

"It doesn't work."

"It's colder in here than it is outside," Andrea said, pulling down at her sweater sleeves in an effort to cover more of her arms.

The woman rocked.

"Miss Cartwright, can we just discuss —" Again Andrea was interrupted by the moaning sound, louder this time, coming through the ceiling right above her head. She listened intently, but then there was only silence.

"I'm sorry," she said, pointing at the ceiling in a way that she hoped seemed casual and didn't betray her nerves. "Did you hear that?"

"Yes," she said. "I heard it. Every day and night I hear it. It doesn't stop."

"What was that?" Andrea asked.

"My *sister*," she hissed.

Andrea closed the medical folder and sat forward on the couch. "Can we talk about her?" she asked.

The old woman rocked.

"So you believe that your sister is... that your sister lives here now too?"

"I know she does," she responded.

"And you do understand that she died several weeks ago?"

At this, she let out a chuckle, a deep rattling sound that bordered on a cough. "She's been dead to me since we were children."

"So you believe in ghosts?"

"Oh my yes," she said.

"Have you always believed in ghosts?"

She hesitated. "Not until very recently," she said, and for the first time her tone was colored by melancholy.

"Can you see her or just hear her?" Andrea asked.

"See, hear, smell," she spat. "She walks around like she owns the place." She waved one bony hand dismissively. "I can't get a moment's peace for all of her shouting."

"What do you think she wants?"

"She wants me to leave. Just like you do! *Ha!* But this is *my house.* This has always been my house. I'm not going anywhere."

Andrea sat back on the couch, thinking. In the silence, she heard a new sound. A slight, shuffling sound, like something scraping against the floor above her. For the first time, Dolores looked up as well, acknowledging the noise. An impatient look fell across her eyes.

"Do you own a cat?" Andrea asked, her mind grasping for a logical explanation for the noise and silently chiding herself for not exhausting some reasonable explanations first.

"No," she said. "I hate cats. It's *her.*"

"Are you sure?" Andrea asked.

She looked at me. "You ask stupid questions," she said. "Of course I'm sure."

"Okay," Andrea said, pasting a determined smile on her face. "If you can be blunt, I can be blunt too. You have three options, Miss Cartwright. You can accept home health care, you can move to assisted living of your own volition, or you can be removed against your will. Those are your choices. Staying here on your own isn't one of them."

"Don't talk to me about choices, you ignorant little girl," she said, planting her feet flat on the floor, stilling her chair. She leaned sideways toward Andrea, the wood of the rocker creaking anciently under her weight. "Don't you dare come into my home and tell me what my choices are. Who do you think you are?"

Andrea's heart clenched nervously, and she took a moment to suck in a deep breath. Swallowing the words she wished to say in response to the insults and forcing herself to relax her face, she adopted the kind of calm, professional demeanor that warred against how she was actually feeling.

"Miss Cartwright," Andrea said, leaning further toward the old woman. "There are no such things as ghosts. You are a sick woman in need of continued medical assistance. I understand why you are angry, but you are not angry at me. You are angry about the cards you have been dealt. But you do have choices and not all of them are as disagreeable as you think that they are."

"Go and see," she said slowly, raising her eyebrows and flicking one wrinkled hand toward the stairs.

"Excuse me?" Andrea said.

"Go and see," she repeated, lifting her chin. "If you don't believe me, go upstairs and see her for yourself."

Andrea felt suddenly, stupidly scared. Biting her lip, she fidgeted nervously with the folder on her lap, bending one corner with her index finger. Her bluff had been called. She opened her mouth to speak but couldn't muster a word in response.

The old woman laughed, sitting back in her chair and rocking. She shook her head, continuing to chuckle. "Stupid little girl."

Andrea stood up quickly, turned, and marched toward the stairs, the movement instantly making her feel like an impudent child. When she looked back at the woman in the rocker, she had a surprised look on her face, her eyebrows raised in amusement. "First door on the right," she said, chuckling without smiling. "I found a way to keep her there. For now, anyway. Tell her I say hello." She dismissed Andrea with a gesture.

Andrea ascended the stairs. The stairway was steep and narrow, each step creaking as she made her way upward. It was impossibly, inexplicably even colder on the upstairs landing than it had been below. Soon she found herself in a dimly lit hallway. Off-white walls with no pictures anywhere, dusty beige carpeting. There were four closed doors before her, one on the left, one at the far end, and two on her right.

She approached the door on the right. As she reached for the knob, she once again heard a low moaning sound, and her heart lurched. She had for some reason expected the door to be locked, but the knob, ice cold against her hand, turned freely, and the door swung open.

There was nothing in the room except a single bed, lit by a dusty beam of light coming in from a lone window whose yellowing shade was drawn. And upon this bed was a woman. She was wearing a tattered nightgown. Her hair was long, white, and wild. Her eyes were wide and the color of ice, fixed firmly upon Andrea from the moment she stepped into the room. Her hands and feet were bound to the bed. Her mouth was gagged. She had cuts on her face and arms, and there was dried blood on the sheets and her gown.

Andrea raced toward the bed. She slipped trembling fingers under the gag, pulling it down with some effort. The woman had no teeth, and her mouth hung open in a silent, straining scream. She took a deep breath, her head rolling unsteadily in an effort to lift it off the pillow. She looked into Andrea's eyes, her face full of fear. "Edna," she croaked. "*Edna.*"

Andrea reached for the fabric restraining one of her wrists. The knot was tight and she saw that the woman's hands were blue, the veins bulging. Andrea's own hands were shaking terribly and she had trouble loosening the knot.

"Dolores?" Andrea asked, surprised to find herself breathless. "Are you Dolores?"

The woman in the bed nodded quickly.

Eventually Andrea was able to free her. Putting one of the old woman's arms over her shoulder, Andrea lifted her out of bed. She was disturbingly light, and when Andrea placed one hand on her side to steady her, she could feel ribs through the nightgown. Dolores groaned as they walked from the bedroom, and it was with much effort that they made the tortuously slow journey down the narrow stairs, Dolores' labored breath stinging Andrea's nostrils with its acrid aroma.

When they reached the foyer below, Andrea took one hesitant look toward the living room. There was the rocking chair, empty and pale in the dim afternoon light coming from the bay window. Looking away again, from the corner of one eye Andrea sensed that the chair rocked slightly, but she dared not look back to confirm it.

She became winded, and getting the old woman out the front door took so much effort that she did not bother closing it behind her. Ultimately it didn't matter, as she heard it slam shut behind them, its loud report startling her and sending a chill that numbed her fingertips. She did not know if anyone could see them as they made their way down the cracked and craggy sidewalk, but if they did, they might have wondered what their story was, Dolores in her thin, dirty nightgown and Andrea, pulling her forward more quickly than she could ably move.

Andrea deposited the old woman in the passenger seat of her car and carefully shut the door. She turned and faced the house once more, that fading yellow cube with its ugly shutters and cracked sidewalk, its forbidding iron fence standing guard against anyone stupid enough to lay claim to whatever waited within. Her keys clutched tightly in one hand, she looked to every window, expecting to see a solitary figure at one of them, looking back at her. But each one was empty — shadowy rectangles that hid whatever lurked behind them.

peeping tommy

It started innocently enough. Honest.

I was walking home from school, which is only about five blocks away from home. Most days I enjoy the walk, particularly in the fall and spring, when the air is comfortable. Add in a calm breeze, and the walk is something I actually look forward to. Rainy days suck, and winter days can be brutal. But it's not a long walk, and Mom's work schedule doesn't allow her the time to pick me up, so what choice do I have? Especially since Dad is, well… Dad's no longer in the picture.

Most of the time I spend the walk looking down at my feet. I'm shy. I don't like making eye contact with people. It irritates me in a way I can't explain. Needless to say I don't have many friends, but I'm okay with that. I look at other kids in their little groupings, usually laughing about something inane, sometimes casting a collective glance in my direction, and I don't see the appeal at all. No thank you, I'm fine all by myself.

Besides, the sidewalk on my route home is cracked and uneven. I have to look at my feet or I could easily trip. There's this one huge tree in particular where the roots have grown under the sidewalk and kicked up the slabs in places. It's a stubbed toe or a broken nose just waiting to happen.

So there was this one day that I was walking home and realized that I was about six yards behind Jenny Aldritch. I recognized her by her long blonde hair that fell in wavy locks down to the middle of her back. She sits in front of me in homeroom, so I probably know the back of her head better than she does. I'd never seen her on my walk before. She was one of the popular girls, always accompanied by two or three other pretty girls while being stared at by a cluster of pathetic 12-year-old boys in our class who are stupid enough to think Jenny would ever give them the time of day.

Moments after I'd recognized her, Jenny made an abrupt turn through a gate to her left, continuing on down a sidewalk that led to one of the nicer houses on the block. I reached the gate in time to see her open the front door and enter. The house was beige with gray shingles and shutters, a wide front porch with a quartet of plants in hanging baskets, and an ornate oak front door. The yard was dotted by a handful of trees and framed by a pristine white fence.

So this is where Jenny lives, I thought, *when she's not at school hypnotizing my fellow classmates.* The idea that she existed outside the seven hours of school struck me as odd. Of course she did, but at the same time I had never considered it.

Without making the conscious decision to do so, I turned and began walking down the sidewalk toward her house, placing my feet carefully enough that my footsteps were silent even to my own ears. I studied the house's windows as I approached to make sure no one was looking out at me. When I reached the porch, I set my backpack on the ground in front of some hedges, then tiptoed up the steps. I ducked over to a window on my right, crouching, and peeked inside.

There was no one in the living room. Floor to ceiling shelves burdened with books and an assortment of framed photos covered most of the walls. A huge black leather sofa faced a massive flat screen TV that was off. A glass coffee table held a stack of large picture books and a bowl of carved wooden fruit. There was a painting on the wall of a man in safari clothes, binoculars held up to his eyes.

Still crouched down, I passed by the front door and peered in another window to the left. I was greeted by the sight of a large wooden dining room table surrounded by matching chairs that had black leather backs and seats. A buffet held a vase of flowers and several ornate candles, over which loomed white framed photos of the family. By studying the pictures I learned that Jenny had two sisters – one younger, one older, also blonde.

There was movement beyond the dining room door, and I ducked slightly, my heart skipping. I could see the kitchen, and Jenny's mom – I recognized her from the family photos – was standing at a counter. She appeared to be sorting mail into two piles. *Keep, junk, junk, keep,* I imagined she was thinking. Jenny entered from the right, and the two of them talked, although I couldn't hear their voices. They both smiled at times, and from their body language it appeared that they had a good relationship. Jenny then turned and left the room, a more childlike bounce in her step than the way she typically cat-walked the hallways at school. By craning my neck and pressing my cheek into the glass, I was able to watch her as she began ascending a set of stairs. And then she was gone.

What am I doing? I thought with some urgency. *Someone else could come home, or a neighbor could see me.* I felt the sudden need to pee. Racing from the porch as quickly and quietly as I could, I snatched up my backpack without pausing and ran the rest of the way home.

Alone in my own dark kitchen, I poured a glass of milk and ate a stack of Oreos without even tasting them, staring vacantly across the room. What I had just done was stupid, but strangely thrilling. And it wasn't at all about Jenny Aldritch specifically or even her house. It was about seeing people – *really* seeing people – for who they are, absent the fake airs we all put on in public. "You are who you are when you are all alone," my mom had once told me. And suddenly I wanted to know more, because looking into the windows of Jenny Aldrich's home was exciting to me. But not in a pervy way. This isn't that kind of story.

***

I passed her in the hallway at school the next day. She was book-ended by two girls almost as attractive as her, the three of them deep in a conversation that, from the looks on their faces, likely centered on the degradation of some lesser classmate. She looked over at me as I passed her by, our eyes locking for the briefest of moments, and she pretended she didn't see me.

In an instant, I was on my butt on the cold linoleum floor, my books sliding away like hockey pucks. I had collided with Arnold "Butch" Gray, who was two years older but in the same grade as me, a 14-year-old with the body of a man but without the brains to match. He had responded to my distracted collision by shoving me away, and I heard scattered laughter as my tailbone made hard contact with the floor.

"Watch where you're going, mouse," he said. On top of his massive frame, Butch sported a melon-shaped head, a sneer-like smile that surrounded a mouthful of braces, and the most unfortunate orange buzz cut. His skin would have been sickly pale if it wasn't mostly covered with a mass of freckles the color of dog poop.

"Sorry, Butch," I muttered, sliding my books toward me. You know how in every class there's this one kid who's a bit smaller and less developed than all the others, a kid who's mostly quiet and socially awkward but frequently gets good grades? Yeah, that's me. And that's why Butch called me mouse. But I don't care. There are worse animals to be compared to.

"Sorry, Butch," he repeated in a mocking, high-pitched tone. He glanced over his shoulder to where I had been looking when I had run into him, and he saw Jenny and her entourage. He chortled derisively. "Not a chance, mouse. Not one chance in a million years."

I had been the object of Butch's disdain for two years and for reasons I could not begin to fathom. It was like my very presence had caused him great offense, and my first awareness of the existence of Butch Gray had been his immediate and relentless mockery. I avoided him as much as I could, but he seemed pulled toward me like a magnet.

I stood up, books in my arms, my head down, and walked around him, my body tensing for a second shove or perhaps for Butch to reach around with one of his ridiculously long arms and smack the load out of my hands. Neither happened. Instead, I continued my walk of shame through a hallway of kids who opted for one of two choices: silent stares or quiet laughter.

I don't understand people.

On my walk home from school, I found myself behind Jenny Aldrich again, but this time when she made a left turn toward her house, I did not follow. I wasn't interested in Jenny, no matter what Butch said. Instead, I continued to the house next door to hers. I observed it from the end of the walk. The windows of this home stared back at me quietly, its black front door like a mouth gasping in surprise. I approached it quietly. I couldn't tell if anyone was home, but should I be spotted and asked what I was doing, I planned to ask, "Does Franklin live here?"

and then shrug an apology when they said no.

Impressed at my own ability to mount the front porch and slink under a window without making a sound, I peered inside. I was greeted by another dining room. The table in this room was set for four, with plates, napkins, and utensils placed with militaristic precision in front of each chair. The rest of the table was empty save for a pair of tall salt and pepper shakers on top of a white lace runner.

At first I felt disappointment that there appeared to be no one at home, but then, in the kitchen (which, like Jenny's house, was situated just beyond the dining room), I saw a woman preparing food at the counter. From the way she subtly swayed her hips while working, and the occasional movement of her lips, it appeared she was listening to music while she busied herself over a cutting board that was covered with cucumber slices and the remnants of other vegetables.

She was a pretty woman, about my mom's age. Her auburn hair – dyed – was done up in a clip, and she was wearing full makeup as well as a red dress covered by a white apron devoid of stains. I was reminded of a younger, hotter version of the mom from *Leave it to Beaver*, one of those old black and white shows my mom likes to watch. I couldn't imagine that this woman dressed this nicely for a typical dinner at home, and I wondered if perhaps she was preparing for company. But it was a Tuesday, late afternoon, so that didn't really make sense to me.

She smiled as she dumped a handful of cucumber slices into a large wooden bowl that was already brimming with lettuce. She continued to sing and sway her hips as she tossed the salad using large tongs, and I wondered if she had a pretty voice. Then cradling the bowl in both hands, she swung around and approached the dining room door.

I ducked down quickly, making sure to stay as much out of her view as possible while still being able to see her. She set the bowl down in the center of the dining room table, stepped back and studied it for a moment, and then reached forward and turned the bowl ever so slightly. She smiled with satisfaction and wiped her palms on her apron, smoothing it in the process.

She was a picture of poise and grace, and I was thinking about how she looked just like an ideal mom from a vintage television commercial, when suddenly she jammed one red-painted pinky nail up her left nostril and began to dig.

I ducked down under the window and covered my mouth with both hands, stifling laughter. This action was so incongruous with her otherwise perfect demeanor that I found myself both incredibly shocked and overwhelmingly amused.

Crawling on my hands and knees to the porch stairs, I jumped down, skipping all the steps, grabbed my backpack, and booked it down the sidewalk and out of the yard, laughing all the way home.

What I was doing was stupid. I could get caught. I could get in trouble. But I was hooked. People were a mystery to me, and mostly I didn't like them, but observing them when they were alone was strangely appealing. Seeing them, observing them in their own habitat, was fascinating. It was like going to the zoo or the museum, only infinitely better. Tomorrow, I decided, I would check out the third house.

***

I had an arithmetic test the next day. It was simple enough, as far as I was concerned. Math has always been easy for me. Mr. Blumenthal, a skinny, balding man with a penchant for argyle sweater vests and a stupidly massive mustache, had told us to bring our tests up to his desk when we were finished. I was the first one done, so I walked quietly up the center aisle, my head down, my test paper pinched between the thumbs and index fingers of both hands.

Butch sat in the front row, right in front of the teacher's desk. This meant his massive bulk was a visual obstacle for anyone unfortunate enough to sit behind him, but it was the only way for Blumenthal to keep a constant eye on him. As I passed by Butch's desk, he whispered, "Squeak, squeak, mousey."

I placed my test on Mr. Blumenthal's desk.

"Done already, Tom?" he asked, sliding the paper toward himself and turning it around.

"Yes," I said.

"That was fast," he responded with a tone of skepticism, not looking at me. "Did you double-check your work?"

The question was offensive. I always aced math tests. Why would he ask a question that insinuated carelessness? From behind me, there was a high-pitched but quiet squeaking sound. I felt myself blush.

"Yes," I said, and turned around to go back to my desk.

I should have known it was coming. Butch stuck out one giant foot and before I knew it, I was flat on my face in the center aisle. The classroom erupted in laughter. Two days, two public pratfalls courtesy of Butch Gray.

My face burning crimson, I got up and returned to my desk. Butch was sent to the principal's office, saying as he walked out the door that he had only been stretching – a claim that elicited even more laughter, and Mr. Blumenthal proceeded to scold the class. But he never asked me if I was okay. Whatever. People are stupid.

***

Initially, I didn't have much success with my new hobby on the way home from school that afternoon. There was no one home in the first house I looked into. There was an old woman watering the yard of the second house, so I didn't stop there. I was halfway down the sidewalk of the third house when a man that I had somehow not seen over by the hedges called out, "Can I help you?"

I jumped, startled. "Sorry," I said. "Does, um, Franklin live here?"

He looked at me, puzzled. "No."

"Sorry," I said again, "wrong house," and made a hasty exit.

The next few houses were more interesting. I was able to observe a woman on the phone – a landline, no less – crying and holding a tissue up to her nose as she talked. She wept so hard that her pale face had erupted in red blotches. Next door, a teenage couple was getting hot and heavy on a living room sofa. Gross, no thank you, moving on. At another house, I watched a woman quietly reading a book, a pleasant smile on her face as she turned pages. At one point, she even put her hand on her chest and took in a long, satisfied breath, completely lost in another world. As soon as she put the book down, however, the smile evaporated into a default grimace as she looked around the room. Reality didn't sit well with her it seemed.

I looked at my phone. If I went home immediately, I'd be opening the door an hour later than usual. Not that it mattered. Mom wouldn't get back from her second job until around 9:00 or so. So it wasn't like anyone was missing me. I was getting hungry, though, so I decided that I would only look into one more house before being done.

At first, I was struck by how pristine the property was. This wasn't incredibly unusual for the area, but this one was particularly immaculate. The hedges surrounding the yard were trimmed to perfectly sharp angles. The grass was cut with precision, and there was not a weed in sight. Colorful flowers blossomed from dark brown mulch in front of the flawlessly painted porch. The house itself was a glowing white with royal blue shutters, and the windows were so clean they were practically invisible.

The first window I looked into revealed yet another dining room. A table, large and polished, was set for what looked like a Thanksgiving meal. Ornate placemats held shining silverware and gleaming plates. Stemmed crystal glasses were filled to the brim with translucent gold liquid — wine, I assumed. Numerous serving dishes held green beans, mashed potatoes, and stuffing. A basket with a checkered cloth was overflowing with rolls. And in the center of it all was the most massive turkey I had ever seen, a large two-pronged fork on one side and a gigantic carving knife on the other.

The scene struck me as supremely odd. The setting looked like a picture right out of a magazine. What was additionally strange was that there were no lights on in the room, even though dinner was clearly ready. It was then that I noticed that there was an unnatural shine to the food – the rolls, mashed potatoes, and turkey were all dully reflecting the light coming in through the windows. They were plastic.

I turned around and looked behind me into the yard, expecting to see a "For Sale" sign that I had missed. There was none. But that was the only explanation. This house had been staged for sale.

Feeling confident that the house was empty, I stood up and looked into the window again, cupping my hands on either side of my eyes. I could see past the dining room into the kitchen beyond – the houses on this block were nothing if not nearly identical – and saw neatly organized countertops, their surfaces shining. The refrigerator was devoid of magnets or a calendar. The stainless steel sink reflected sunlight from the window above it.

I walked past the front door to the set of windows on the right. I didn't even bother to duck down as I looked in, predicting correctly the living room that sat before me. Generic photos hung on the walls, gleaming polished shelves held fake flowers in narrow vases, and a thick, rust-and-beige rug covered the hardwood floors, on top of which rested a sofa.

And then, I saw *him*. How I had not noticed him at first I do not know, other than the fact that I had assumed the house was empty and the man was completely still. He was seated on the couch, a thin man, and apparently quite tall because even though his feet rested flat on the floor, his knees were higher than his lap. He was dressed in a white button-up shirt with a sharp collar, a burgundy cardigan, dark denim jeans, and polished black shoes. His hair was black and so thick with product that it was shining like plastic. I saw him in profile. He was facing a television set on the other side of the room, a large smile plastered on his face, his eyes wide. Although he was motionless, he was pointing with his right hand toward the screen.

I ducked down quickly, afraid that he might look over and see me. My heart was pounding. One, because surely I had almost been caught, and two, because the scene in front of me was unsettling in a way that I couldn't reconcile. The man didn't move. He sat frozen. His suspended arm didn't tremble in the slightest, and his face was locked in that overwide grin. Was he fake too, like the Thanksgiving food? That didn't make sense. They don't put prop people in model homes… *do they*?

Peeking in again, I observed the man for a moment more, his crystal blue eyes never moving, the skin of his face a completely even tone that looked almost painted. I felt a cold shiver creep down my spine even though the air around me was warm. I glanced over to the television to see what he was pointing and smiling at.

The screen was blank. The TV was off.

I looked back at him. He hadn't moved, but his eyes had shifted. He was looking at me. Still smiling, still pointing, but looking at me.

I ran home as fast my legs would carry me, hoping against hope that I didn't pass anyone along the way. I had wet my pants.

Back home, I took a shower and changed clothes. Then I turned on all the lights and counted the hours until Mom got home.

**

I promised myself I wouldn't go back, but the next day after school I found myself pausing in front of that house again, a house that I had been mentally referring to as "the model home" all day, even though I wasn't sure that's what it was. It sat, still and silent at the end of its immaculate walk. I hesitated, my thoughts a tug of war between dread and curiosity.

The latter eventually won, and I tiptoed quietly up the walk. I dropped my backpack at the bottom of the steps, thinking that I could be stealthier without its bulk, and ascended the porch steps before ducking under the dining room windows. I peeked. It was the same scene: fake food on an elaborately laid-out dining room table, that massive plastic turkey with its giant fork and carving knife like sentinels on either side.

I crawled past the front door until I was under the living room windows. I would look, just from one bottom corner of the window, to see if the man was still there. Just a quick glimpse and I would be done. Just enough to satisfy my curiosity.

I took a deep breath, pushed myself up into a squatting position, and, with my left eye closed, peeked through the bottom corner of the glass with my right eye, the rest of my body hidden to the left of the window.

At first I thought I saw my own reflection staring back at me from the glass. But with horror I realized that the man was squatting on the other side of the window, looking back at me, our faces mere inches apart. He was smiling.

I don't even remember running home, but I do remember that I was making an odd, terrified groaning sound the entire way. It was all I could do to keep from screaming.

I was running so fast that I nearly slammed into the front door of my house after leaping onto my own front porch. I turned around to study the street behind me, making sure I hadn't been followed. It was empty. My lungs were on fire. Breathless, I reached around for my backpack to retrieve my house key. Terror gripped my chest when I realized it wasn't there.

I had left my backpack at the model home.

I turned around and faced the street behind me, back pasted to the door. My chest heaved as I tried to catch my breath, but fear was leaving me even more breathless than running had. Everything I carried – my house key, my cell phone, my school books – was in that pack.

I couldn't go back. He had seen me. He would be waiting for me. But it would be at least four hours before Mom got home, well after dark. I couldn't sit on the porch that long. And what if he found me here?

I thought I heard footsteps.

Suddenly I remembered the Hide-a-Key, a hollow ceramic frog that Mom had hidden within the flower beds for occasions such as this. I could have kissed the stupid thing when I found it. With trembling fingers I let myself in the house, slamming the door and locking it behind me. I stood in the entryway for awhile, the key gripped firmly in one hand, the ceramic frog in another, still trying to catch my breath.

The evening hours passed slowly. My stomach was in too much of a knot to eat. I sat in front of the TV with the volume turned down. Every noise from outside made my heart leap.

By the time I heard Mom open the front door at 9:15, the sky outside was dark and I still hadn't figured out how to solve the problem of my backpack. None of my homework for tomorrow would be finished, and I could only hope that the pack would still be sitting in front of the hedges of the model home when I walked by it in the morning. I would have to work up the nerve to do a quick snatch-and-grab on my way to school and hope against hope that I didn't see the man. And that he didn't see me.

I was still sitting on the couch watching TV — but not really watching it — when my mom entered the room. She came up behind me and kissed me on top of the head.

"How you doing, kiddo?" she asked, tussling my hair. Her tone was pleasant but tired.

"Okay," I said, trying to sound casual.

"How as your day?" she asked.

"Okay," I repeated.

"You forget something?" she said.

"Huh?" I asked, turning around to look at her. "What are you talk—"

She was holding up my backpack.

"You left this on the porch," she said.

***

No more. Done. My new hobby was now my former hobby. No more looking in windows.

I found myself in detention at the end of school the next day. I had ended up with incomplete assignments in two different classes. Even though Mom had found the backpack, by the time I had gotten around to actually doing my homework for the evening, I found it impossible to focus and had overlooked two worksheets. None of my teachers had bought the lie that the contents of my backpack had spilled out on my way home from school. Even I knew that that story didn't hold water. The solution was that I was to stay after school for however long it took to finish the missing homework.

Mr. Blumenthal would be residing over this particular detention – he of the sad comb-over and gigantic mustache. He always made me think of another thing my mom liked to say: "A mustache says a lot about a man, and none of it is good." I smiled to myself. It made sense to me that a man like Blumenthal would have nothing to do in the evening but spend extra hours at school supervising detention.

I thought it would just be him and me for the duration when two figures entered the room, and my heart plummeted into my stomach. One was Butch. The other was one of his cronies, Ayden. Or was it Jayden or Braiden? *Who cares?* Regardless, while this kid wasn't as hulking as Butch, he had just as much of a mean streak to him as well as a vacant face to match his intelligence.

Both wore dour expressions as they entered, but Butch lit up the moment he saw me and elbowed Ayden-Jayden-Braiden with a grin. The boy's dumb face turned into a malevolent smile.

"Have a seat, gentlemen," Mr. Blumenthal said, and he neither noticed nor objected when Butch sat down in the desk immediately behind my own, his friend to his left.

"Squeak, squeak, mousey," Butch leaned forward and whispered in my ear, his breath hot and smelling of Cheetos. I sat forward, away from him, my eyes on the paper in front of me.

The four of us continued on in silence for a time. Occasionally, I felt a poke in my ribs as Butch would stick the eraser end of a pencil into my back. The two boys laughed quietly as I shifted in my seat. I looked up at Mr. Blumenthal, but he was looking down.

Then I felt a prick as Butch pressed the sharp end of the pencil into the back of my neck, not hard enough to break the skin but enough to cause discomfort. I swatted it away and placed my hand on my neck, hissing, "Stop it!"

Mr. Blumenthal looked up. "Is there a problem, boys?"

"No problem, sir," Butch piped up, and Ayden-Jayden-Braiden laughed. I made eye contact with the teacher, and while I knew that he knew that there was indeed a problem, *thank you very much*, he returned to his grading.

When Butch inevitably poked me again, I turned and swatted the pencil away hard enough that it flew from Butch's hand and clattered across a neighboring desk before hitting the floor. Butch glared at me.

"What's going on?" Mr. Blumenthal said with a sigh of irritation.

"Oh nothing, sir," Butch said, his voice full of mock respect.

Mr. Blumenthal looked at him with skepticism. "Mr. Gray, please take a seat in the front row. Braiden, you may stay right where you are."

I heard Butch gathering his things from his desk, muttering under his breath. Before he stood, he leaned forward and whispered hotly into my ear, "Squeak, squeak, mouse."

As he walked past me, my foot, as if with a mind of its own, stuck out into the aisle, and Butch lunged forward, his giant feet tangled, and he fell hard on the floor, his cargo of books and papers sliding away from him.

He stood up quickly and towered over me, fists clenched, his face pinched with rage. He made as if to move on me, right fist rising, and I shifted back in my seat, wincing. Preparing for the inevitable pain.

Mr. Blumenthal stood up. "That's *enough*, gentlemen," he said with more authority than I knew he could muster. "Unless you want to spend the next month in here with me, Mr. Gray, you will take a seat up here. *Now.*"

Butch stood frozen, then lowered his fist. Squatting down slowly without taking his eyes off me, he retrieved one of his books from the floor and said, "You're a dead mouse."

***

By the time I finished my outstanding assignments and began walking home, it was later than usual and the sun was low in the sky, covering the neighborhood in long shadows. There was nothing but the sound of my scuffling footsteps over cement as I made my way home, my head down, not even daring a look at any of the houses I passed.

When I reached the edge of the yard belonging to the model home, I paused. The windows were dark. I felt a shiver in my spine as I stared, wondering if there was anyone inside. I felt no desire to approach it.

Then I heard a voice and jumped. From the sidewalk behind me: "Whatcha lookin' at, mousey?"

I spun around and saw Butch, standing on the sidewalk maybe three yards away. He was smiling at me but his brow was angry. His empty hands were balled into fists and his body was tense.

"You're dead, mouse," he said, his smile fading, and began running toward me.

I knew I could never outrun him. I bolted into the yard in front of me, hoping to find a place to hide. But there was nothing, nothing between the front hedges and the house itself, and with horror I realized the foolishness of my decision. There was nowhere for me to hide from Butch, and even worse, no one could see either of us from the street.

I made it all the way to the porch steps and stopped. I was cornered.

Butch rounded the corner of the sidewalk and slowed. His smile returned. He knew I was trapped and was relishing my predicament.

He lumbered slowly toward me. "Caught like a mouse," he laughed. He stopped in front of me, looming over me, that stupid smile on his freckled face. "I've been wanting to do this for a looooong time," he said. He cocked one fist.

I closed my eyes and winced.

There was the sound of a door opening behind me. The sound was quiet, but it still made me jump. I opened my eyes and looked up hesitantly at Butch, but he was looking over my head, behind me, a puzzled expression on his face.

The man was there, standing in front of the door, motionless. He was still wearing his cardigan over a pressed white shirt, dark denim jeans covering his impossibly long legs, his shoes polished to a reflective shine. His slicked-down black hair crowned a flawless face with its huge, staring blue eyes and an impossibly wide, unwavering smile decorated by two rows of perfectly white teeth. His arms were down at his sides, a large carving knife held casually in one hand.

The man didn't move at all. He was like a mannequin. Butch's smile faded. He looked at the man, and the man looked at him, his paralyzed smile wide with joy, his eyes huge and unblinking. Butch's face then shifted from puzzlement to fear. His lip quivered. Everything was silent.

I ran. My shoulder collided with one of Butch's arms as I bolted past him, but he didn't move at all. My footsteps slapped on the sidewalk as I tore toward home. For a few seconds, it was the only sound to be heard in the darkening and quiet neighborhood. But then it was joined by the high-pitched sound of Butch's screams.

***

Mom woke me in the morning to tell me that school was canceled for the day. She had received an e-mail that a classmate had been killed last night on the street just a couple of blocks away. "The boy's name was Arnold Gray," she said. "Did you know him?"

I shrugged. "Not really."

"That poor child," Mom said, shaking her head. "I feel so sorry for his mother."

Poor child, I thought derisively. *Butch Gray was no poor child.*

"Will you be okay here if I go to work?" she asked.

"Yes," I said.

"I'll be calling to check on you." She left, a concerned look on her face as she went. "Keep the door locked. And don't go anywhere."

But I did. When I got to the house, the front door was unlocked. I went inside. The man – I've decided to call him Franklin – was sitting on the sofa, his eyes as wide as his smile. He looked as though he was on the verge of laughter, pointing at the television. It was off.

I took a seat beside Franklin and stared at the blank screen, our faint images staring back at us from its reflective darkness.

Then I smiled too.

becca

It was the middle of the night. I was on my way back to bed from the bathroom, placing my feet carefully on the cool hardwood floor in an effort to keep it from creaking and waking Becca. The moon was so full in the sky outside that I hadn't had to bother turning on the light in the bathroom as I emptied my bladder, our bedroom and bathroom glowing a soft yellow from the rays of light falling through the windows.

I was nearly back to the bed when I happened to glance out of the large bedroom window to my right, which looked down onto our front yard and the row of trees that lined the west side of our property, marking the beginning of thick woods that covered the untouched acres all around us. We had no neighbors for miles unless you counted the residents of the woods themselves, their occasional hoots and howls reaching our ears in the dead of night, sometimes startlingly close. But we gladly tolerated these noises over the sounds of car horns, engines, or late night, curbside conversations disturbing our sleep.

So bright was the moon that the trees were casting soft shadows over our yard. There was no breeze at all, and the still glow of the scene outside was both beautiful and haunting. I had barely given it a passing glance, trying to get back to bed before my brain was fully awake, when I saw him: a man near the edge of the woods kneeling in the grass. He was cast completely in shadow, a solid black figure by the edge of the trees. I stopped and stared. He was looking down at something on the ground in front of him, then he reached out carefully and picked it up. Whatever it was, it was too small for me to see. He pondered the object for a moment, then brought both hands close to his face, palms upward, studying them. He then curled them into fists.

Standing quickly, he looked directly up at the bedroom window. At me. I felt my toes go immediately numb with a stabbing rush of fear. Instinctively I took a step to my left, hiding myself from his view. I looked over at the cell phone resting on my bedside table, then at Becca, still sleeping peacefully. I waited. Then I peeked my head around, trying to remain hidden while attempting another glance at the figure below.

He was gone.

I stepped fully to the window again, looking down at the empty spot where he had stood. Shaking off a chill that tickled its way up my spine, I slid silently back into bed. I lay on my back, which I never do, folding my hands over my stomach. I closed my eyes, but I couldn't go back to sleep. I listened. All was quiet.

***

In the kitchen, next morning:

"Were you up last night?" Becca was dishing dry scrambled eggs onto my plate at the breakfast table.

"Had to pee," I replied. "Strangest thing…"

"Your pee?" she interrupted playfully.

"No. When I was coming back to bed, I thought I saw someone in the yard."

Becca's face fell, no longer playful. "You did?"

"Yeah, a man." I poked at my eggs, regretting that I had mentioned it. "I'm second-guessing myself now, though, because when I looked back again, he was gone. Now I'm not even sure I was completely awake," I lied.

Becca's face went from concerned to cautiously reassured. I changed the subject.

The next night, I was awoken from a dead sleep by a sound I could not identify, coming from outside. In our eight years in this house, we had gotten used to the occasional random, wild cries emanating from the surrounding woods. The sound that wild animals could make while fighting or afraid could be bone-chillingly startling at times, especially when it yanked me from the depths of sleep, but this was different. This noise, which was something between a scream and a yell, was not just wild. It had notes of fear and anger in it. And insanity.

I sat up quickly in bed. Surprisingly, Becca did not stir. I slipped my feet to the floor, crept to the window, and peered out, trying my best to stay hidden in the process.

He was there again, standing silhouetted by the edge of the trees, the full moon casting his shadow long in front of him. Once again I could make out no details. He was nothing but a solid black figure. And even though I couldn't see his face, I knew he was facing me. He was looking up at the window, standing perfectly still in the darkness. I felt cold pins of fear rush through my toes.

He was a big man. More than six feet tall and standing straight as an arrow. And muscular. Even from this distance and in the dim light I could see the definition of the muscles in his shoulders, arms, and upper legs, and suddenly I realized the man was probably naked. But I couldn't tell for sure. He certainly wasn't built like a typical vagrant or homeless person, and my mind boggled at how he could survive being out in these woods in the chill of October with no clothing to protect him.

There was a sound at my feet, the pinging of metal falling on hardwood. My wedding ring had slipped off my finger and fallen to the floor. Over the past 10 months I had managed to do something unprecedented in my life: I had successfully kept a new year's resolution. Through a combination of a consistent diet and daily exercise, I had managed to shed more than sixty pounds. I had whipped my body back into the shape that it was back in my college football days, almost fourteen years ago now. Becca, who was just as slender and beautiful as she had been on our wedding day, was certainly appreciative of the changes I had made. But one minor negative side effect was that my wedding ring was now too big for my finger and would occasionally slip off, especially if my hands were cold. And just now, standing in my boxer shorts by our bedroom window, I was certainly chilly. I needed to get it resized.

"You need to get that thing resized," Becca said in a sleepy voice.

I picked up the ring and gave a quick, hopefully imperceptible glance out the bedroom window. The man was gone.

I put the ring back on my finger, curling my fingers into a fist to keep it from falling off again, and slipped back into bed, once again lying on my back. Becca rolled toward me, draping her arm across my chest and her leg across both of my own. She was a snuggler; I was not, but I didn't mind. She sighed contentedly, her breath sweet and warm against my shoulder. I stroked her arm, hoping she could not feel the pounding of my heart.

"I wish you loved me," I said.

"Mmm… I wish I did too," she whispered, then poked a finger into my ribs.

She slept. I didn't.

***

Breakfast the next morning. "Dare I ask?" she said.

"What?" I responded over my plate full of bacon and, yet again, dry scrambled eggs.

"Any particular reason you were up again last night?"

"Thought I heard something," I said in a tone that I hoped sounded casual.

"What?" she asked.

"Not sure." I pretended for a moment to be preoccupied with my phone, which was resting beside my plate, but knowing that Becca would never relent until I gave her a satisfactory answer, I put down my fork. "I saw that man again in the yard."

"Seriously?"

"Yeah. Just standing there by the trees."

"Who do you think he is?"

"Homeless, maybe? Maybe living in the woods? I honestly have no idea. But he's … he's a big guy."

"Well… so are you," she said, squeezing my upper arm and giving a small grin. I could tell she was trying to calm herself by being playful. "Do you think we should call the police?"

"Maybe. Yeah. We'll see." I continued eating my eggs.

"Bryan," Becca said, completely serious again. "Do you still keep that baseball bat under the bed?"

***

Night three.

Sleep was thwarted by growing curiosity. After a couple of frustrating hours, I attempted to slide out of bed and take a look out of the bedroom window. I nearly jumped when Becca took hold of my hand, pulling me back toward her. "Stay," she whispered against my mouth as she kissed me. I eagerly returned her embrace and we made love in the darkness.

Afterward, I managed to fall asleep rather quickly, so quickly that I barely remembered much after my head touched the pillow again. I don't know what woke me up. There was no sound, no urge to use the bathroom. Suddenly awake but determined not to lose another night to sleeplessness, I turned my back to the window, facing the middle of the bed. I reached out, hoping to steal some of Becca's warmth.

She was gone.

I sat up, a bolt of fear running through my entire body. I patted the covers on Becca's side of the bed to be certain. I began to reach for the baseball bat under the bed when I saw her. She was standing at the bedroom window, looking down on the yard below, motionless.

"Becca?" I said.

A pause. "He's there," she whispered, her voice barely audible.

"He is?" I said, getting out of bed. I knelt down and pulled the baseball bat from under the bed.

"I thought I heard a noise outside, so I went to see, and… Bryan, I think he's looking at me."

I came to Becca's side. I put my arm around her waist and looked down. The man was there, as he had been the past two nights, standing by the edge of the trees. For the length of a heartbeat, he looked at the two of us, and then suddenly he was running. Toward the house. Toward the front door.

Becca gasped. Bat in hand, I raced from the room. It took me an eternity to run the length of the hallway and down the stairs, skipping a few steps and almost falling along the way, my bare heels painfully raking the edges. I reached the foyer and was shocked to find the front door standing wide open, a gaping hole into the darkness outside. The realization made me freeze in place. But then the sound of rapidly approaching footsteps from the front lawn brought me to my senses and I slammed the door quickly, locking the deadbolt and taking an immediate step back.

There was a sudden pounding from the outside, followed by a rattling of the doorknob. I backed further away. A loud, guttural sound that I immediately recognized as the scream that had woken me the night before penetrated the door. There was a brief pause, and then the violence against the door resumed, too loud and hard to be fists. He was hitting the door with something solid, something hard enough to do damage. I heard wood splintering.

I was frozen on the spot, fear coursing through my body like cold electricity. I was startled when Becca put her hand on my shoulder. "Bryan?" she pleaded. I turned and looked at her, wide-eyed. Her face was full of fear. It felt like my throat was closing off.

"We need to call the police," she said.

The assault against the door suddenly ceased, and all was quiet. There was a slight clattering noise, and then the man screamed again, an almost inhuman sound filled with rage. I had never heard anyone make a sound like this.

"*GO AWAY!*" Becca screamed at the door.

The man's scream gave way to words, and once again my fear left me paralyzed. "This is my house!" he yelled. "*Get out of my house!*" Fists met the door once again, pounding. Kicking. Slamming his body against the door.

Becca was backing down the hallway behind me, toward the kitchen. "Bryan?" she pleaded. And when I didn't move, she screamed my name. "*BRYAN!*"

The final notes of her scream were met with silence. I finally managed to turn away from the door and face Becca, who stood at the opposite end of the hallway just inside the kitchen, her face pale and terrified. I took a step toward her, and she reached a hand out to me.

The man screamed a final time. A loud, growling, possessive, unnatural tone.

"*MMMMMMBECCA!*"

***

We called the police. By the time they arrived an eternal 22 minutes later, the man had long since stopped assaulting the front door. Of course they did not find him, nor did they find any evidence of him during their cursory and all-too-quick peek into the woods at the west side of our property. We sat with the pair of officers at the kitchen table, trying through our fear and exhaustion to recount the events of the past three nights. They took notes. They offered unconvincing words of encouragement. One of them, the officer with the surname Hamm, told us to get an alarm system. A dog. A gun. And he told me to call if it happened again.

It was when I was showing the officers out, their breath visible in the 3:00 a.m. October night as they said their goodbyes, that I took notice of the front door. It was undamaged.

***

Night four.

I didn't sleep at all. Eventually I dared a peek out the window, careful not to be seen from below. Then I slipped back under the covers.

Becca, awake. "Is he there?"

"No."

"Bryan?"

"Go to sleep."

***

Night five.

I didn't have to get up to see if he was there. I could hear him screaming, that horrible sound penetrating the still darkness, this time with words:

"*WHERE ARE YOU?!*"

Becca lay awake beside me.

***

In the kitchen the next morning:

"Do you believe in ghosts?"

"Becca," I quietly scolded.

"No, seriously, Bryan."

We were at the breakfast table, tired hands holding limply to forks. Eggs again. I'm a creature of habit, even in stressful times. Routine brings comfort, and by nature when I set my mind to something, I follow through with it. I put down my fork. "No," I sighed. "Not normally, anyway."

"It makes no sense, but it's also the only thing that makes sense," she said, her breakfast untouched. "He was hitting the door. Hard. But there's not a mark on it. He's out there every night, just standing there. With no clothes. It's cold and what kind of shelter is there in the woods? What does he eat?"

"I don't know, Becca," I said, allowing impatience to creep into my voice. I hadn't slept well in more than a week. Even when the shadowed man didn't make any noise, my anxious heart kept me awake. Sometimes I looked. Sometimes I didn't. But I never bothered to call the police a second time, nor did Becca ask me to. Without conversing we had agreed it would do no good.

"He opened the front door but didn't come inside —"

"I know."

"He said my name. He knows my name." She shivered. Paused. "I think it's a ghost."

I started to reply, then shut my mouth. I don't believe in ghosts. But at the same time, I was certain that this man, whatever he was, was haunting us.

"I think it's a ghost," she said again. "And he wants in."

We went away for a weekend. Two nights at a cheap motel. Just to see. He didn't follow us there. I obsessively looked outside the hotel room window both nights, expecting him in the parking lot below. He wasn't there. Somehow I found that more unsettling than if he had been there. I actually stood at the window for more than an hour both nights, waiting for him, restless. Becca pleaded with me to come to bed. I ignored her. And thus surrounded by the sounds of horns and engines and curbside conversations, we didn't sleep. But not because of the noise.

* * *

Back home. In bed. Night fourteen. Two solid weeks of interrupt-ed sleep.

"We have to move," she whispered, and started to cry.

"You love this house," I said. "We love this house."

"I used to love this house," she said. She propped herself up on one elbow, facing me as I lay on my back. Her face was shrouded with darkness. "We can't continue like this, Bryan. We haven't slept in weeks. I feel like I'm losing my mind."

I looked at her tired face. I knew I should say something comfort-ing, but no words came to me. I had nothing to offer her. Exhaustion had drained me of all feeling, all feeling except anger and frustration, to the point that I was beginning to feel a divide between me and Becca. I no longer wanted to comfort her; I wanted her to feel as wrung out and terrible as I felt.

But she was right. We needed to move. Not just to escape the shadowed man, but to save *us*.

I brought my hand up to her cheek and brushed away a tear with my thumb. "Okay," I said, and dropped my hand. "We can —"

That scream, so foreign and yet now so familiar, split the night. We both jumped, and Becca crumbled into exhausted sobs, defeated. But the scream triggered something in me that I hadn't felt in the past two weeks: *rage*. Without a single thought, I was out of bed, snatching the baseball bat from where it leaned against my bedside table. I was out the bedroom door, barely registering the sound of Becca shouting my name after me, terrified.

I flew through the hallway, down the stairs, and flung open the front door, stepping into the night. I felt fear, but I had buried it some-where underneath my anger. Off the front porch and into the grass, I looked to the spot where the man always stood, night after night, star-ing up at our bedroom window.

He wasn't there.

I felt my shoulders and arms lose strength as a sense of defeat washed over me. In my blind fury I was certain that I would finally face him, finally fight him, finally beat him into submission. Whatever he was. The bat fell from my grip and made a soft noise as it settled in the grass.

I walked over to the place where he always stood, that place near the edge of the tree line, the bright moon casting its dim shadows over the yard. There was no breeze at all, but I was suddenly aware of the coldness of the night as it kissed my bare torso and legs. I stared into the woods, my eyes pleading with the space between the trees, hoping and fearing to catch a glance of him. I saw nothing, and yet… he felt terrifyingly near. I wished I hadn't dropped the bat.

"Where are you?" I yelled at the trees. "*WHERE ARE YOU?*" I then let out a yell, full of pent-up frustration and fear and rage and hours upon hours of sleepless anxiety.

Something glinted in the moonlight at my feet. I knelt down and plucked it out of the grass. It was a wedding ring. A man's wedding ring.

My wedding ring.

I quickly looked at my left hand, palm facing upwards. There, on my fourth finger, was my ring. I looked in my right hand, where an identical wedding ring rested in my palm.

I stood abruptly and looked up at the bedroom window. A figure stood there, looking down at me. A familiar female shape: Becca. I stared at her, not comprehending, when suddenly a second figure was at her side: a man, large, his arm moving around her waist.

My entire body went immediately numb with a rush of fear. I ran the length of the yard to the porch, the cold night biting at my exposed skin. As I neared the gaping front door, it slammed shut in front of me, and I heard the unmistakable sound of the deadbolt locking.

I pounded on the door with my fists, then tried the doorknob. I screamed, a guttural sound that I never knew I was capable of making, borne of both terror and rage. I retreated swiftly to the yard to retrieve the bat and immediately resumed my assault on the door.

Then I thought I heard a voice, soft and low, coming through the door. "Bryan?"

I stopped pounding. I dropped the bat, which made a clattering noise on the front porch. "Becca?" I whispered, I pleaded, my voice betraying me. I knew she didn't hear me. I heard her voice again, saying something soft and low, full of fear.

He was in there. With her.

I screamed again, overflowing with rage, not knowing how such a sound could be coming from me.

"*GO AWAY!*" Becca screamed.

I heard my own scream give way to words. "This is my house!" I yelled. "*Get of out of my house!*" My fists met the door once again, rapidly pounding. I rammed it with my knee. I threw my body against it. I heard it cracking.

Then my wife, my beautiful, loving wife, screamed my name. She needed me to protect her. She needed me to save her. From *him*. But I could not. I was outside. Powerless. And she was in there. With him.

I fell to my knees at the door and screamed a final time. A loud, growling, possessive tone.

"*MMMMBECCA!*"

***

And now, in the daylight, I sleep. I cease to be. The woods envelop me. I welcome the rest, which has been so elusive for too many nights.

But at night, I wait.

At times, yes, rage overcomes me, hopelessness and jealousy and sorrow are all I can feel, and I howl like the beasts in the woods surrounding the house. *My* house.

I see him there at times, in the window. He's scared of me. He can't sleep, knowing that I am here. Good.

I'll find a way in, and she will be mine again.

Becca.

sleeptalker

The meteor shower had been breathtaking. The news had spread beforehand that the development of Riverview would be one of the best for viewing the event, and it ended up turning into a neighborhood party. Neighbors up and down the block had set out lawn chairs and coolers on a bank behind a row of houses, where the view wouldn't be washed out by street or house lights. The night was crisp, cool, and clear, and the stars were bright.

Daniel held Naomi's hand, which was small and cold in his own, as they reclined and watched the night sky. Their immediate neighbors, Randy and Pam, had joined them, bringing over a blanket and a cooler overflowing with beer and wine coolers.

"You know," said Randy, grinning mischievously, "I heard that when there's a meteor shower, Chuck Norris grabs a bar of soap."

Daniel chuckled and clinked his bottle of beer against Randy's. Both wives groaned and shook their heads in mock disapproval, refusing to laugh.

The meteors came in rapid succession, a truly amazing sight to behold, and when one of them fell surprisingly close, blazing overhead and lighting up the sky, the neighborhood released a collective gasp.

* * *

"You talked in your sleep last night." Naomi was sitting across from Daniel at the kitchen table, warming both hands against a large mug of steaming coffee. Her hands were always cold. She looked tired.

"I did?" Daniel asked. "What did I say?"

"Nothing I could understand," she said, stretching her back and squeezing her shoulder blades together. "But you woke me up." She yawned widely without bothering to cover her mouth.

"Sorry?" Daniel offered with a shrug. "That's so strange, though. I don't think I've ever talked in my sleep before."

"Yeah, well, you do now," she said with impatience in her voice before raising her mug slowly to her lips and taking a cautious sip.

"It's a beautiful day outside," Daniel said, looking out the kitchen window. "Looks like spring."

"If you say so," she mumbled.

* * *

Two nights later as they readied for bed, Naomi handed Daniel's phone to him. The screen was filled with a logo he didn't recognize. An app was loading that was called "Sleeptalker."

"What is this?" he asked, although he had already pieced together a good idea of what it was.
She slid into bed beside him. "It records any noises you make while you're asleep," she said.

"Hmm," he said dully.

"Just put it on your nightstand on the edge closest to your pillow," she said. "You've talked in your sleep for two nights now. I want you to hear it." She gave him a peck on the cheek and turned over. He did as instructed and, turning off the light, gave his pillow a punch and fell promptly asleep.

The next morning, Naomi was already in the kitchen when Daniel came downstairs, wiping the counters. She gave him a dirty look as he entered the kitchen.

He raised both hands in mock surrender before going to the refrigerator for orange juice.

"Again?" he asked.

"Again, Chatty Cathy," she said. "Do you have your phone with you?"

He handed it to over. She turned it on, launched the Sleeptalker app, and tapped on a file. The first sounds to be heard were a series of random grunts and groans. There were no words, yet Daniel's voice was recognizable. At one point he made a sound like he was clucking his tongue, and they both chuckled.

Daniel sat down across the counter from Naomi and they looked at each other, continuing to listen. There was the sound of stirring, of bed covers being shifted, and then there was his voice, speaking clearly and slowly.

"Yes," he said.

He gave Naomi a bemused smile. She returned his gaze but not his smile.

The recording continued: "No... No... Yes, I tried... Maybe three more days. You? ...Okay." His voice was thick with sleep, but the words were clear.

The recording ended. Naomi and Daniel stared at each other. "So you heard all that last night?" he asked.

"No," she said. "As soon as you started talking I put a pillow over my head."

"I don't remember saying any of that," he chuckled. "It's so weird."

"Weird and annoying. Do you remember dreaming anything? It sounded like you were having a conversation."

"No," he said. "I don't remember dreaming at all."

* * *

On the fourth morning, he once again found Naomi at the kitchen table nursing a mug of coffee, her face sagging with exhaustion.

"Another bad night?" he asked with some trepidation.

"You could say that."

"Did I talk in my sleep again?"

"I don't know," she responded. "I'm not sure. I actually woke up because of a nightmare. It scared me so bad that I sat up in bed."

"Wow," Daniel said, sitting down across from her. "I slept through that. Do you remember the dream?"

She paused, thinking. "No. When I woke up it was so vivid I thought I'd remember it. But it's gone now."

Daniel pulled his phone from the pocket of his sleep pants and set it on the table between them. Launching the Sleeptalker app, he hit "play" on the newest recording. They listened to the recording of his voice. The words were slow and monotonous.

"Yes… No… No… Yes, a shifting of the hands and feet… Two more days… You? …Okay."

"That sounded a lot like what I said the night before," he observed.

Naomi nodded but said nothing.

* * *

That night, Daniel was awakened from a deep sleep by the sound of Naomi screaming. She was making jerking movements in the bed beside him and ripped the covers away. He rolled over toward her, spooning her back. Rubbing her shoulder, he made shushing sounds in her ear, whispering her name. Slowly she calmed down and became still while his heart continued to pound.

After a few moments, her breathing became steady. He assumed that she had fallen asleep. But then he felt her shift her legs and press the soles of her bare feet against the tops of his own.

She groaned. "Your feet are cold," she said, her voice sleepy.

Daniel touched his right big toe against his left foot. Normally his body radiated heat while he slept, but tonight his feet were as cold as ice.

"No," she said, abruptly sounding more awake. "Your feet are *wet*." She jerked her feet away from his.

Daniel reached down with one hand. She was right. His feet weren't just cold; they were wet, the cuffs of his sleep pants soaked through. He got out of bed and slipped them off, leaving them in a heap on the floor.

Daniel didn't sleep much the rest of that night. In the morning, just as the sun was beginning to rise, he sat up in bed, picked up his phone, and tapped on the Sleeptalker app. He wasn't surprised to see that there was a new recording.

Naomi stirred beside him and opened her eyes, staring up at the ceiling as he hit "play."

"Yes… Yes… Yes… Almost completely now… Tomorrow… You? …That is unfortunate… I understand."

He put his phone back down and yawned. When he looked back at Naomi, her eyes were wide and she was staring at him. The look startled him.

"What?" he asked.

She sat up reached for his phone. She turned the volume up completely and hit "play" again. Daniel's voice filled the room as the recording played again at full volume, surrounded by the hiss of ambient noise. He was confused, unsure why Naomi was playing the recording again, but then he heard it. A quiet, barely discernable sound between each of his recorded statements. He looked at Naomi.

"Daniel," she said. "There's another voice on that recording." They played it a third time. There was indeed another voice, but it was too quiet and muffled to be understood.

"Is that you?" he asked her.

"I'm not sure," she said.

* * *

When Daniel walked out of the front door after breakfast, the morning light stabbed his tired eyes. He walked, briefcase in hand, toward the car in the driveway, the soles of his shoes scuffing the concrete, and unlocked the driver's side door.

"Good morning, Daniel!"

He jumped and turned around, then laughed at his own reaction. He was greeted by the wide smile of Randy, who was standing on his front step dressed in a white terrycloth bathrobe, a cup of coffee in one hand, the morning paper tucked under one arm.

Randy chuckled. "Sorry, I didn't mean to scare you."

"It's ok," Daniel responded. "Good morning."

"Rough night?" he asked.

"You could say that," Daniel responded, turning back toward the car. He paused, then turned back to Randy. "Wait, why do you ask?"

"I saw you last night," he said. "Out here on your lawn."

"What?"

"Yeah, must have been about 2:00 in the morning. Really strange. You were just standing there, looking up at the sky. What were you doing?"

Daniel shook his head. "I have no idea. I don't remember doing that."

"Really?" he said. "Do you sleepwalk?"

"Not that I know of," Daniel said. "But I have been talking in my sleep lately. Naomi's about ready to kick me out of bed."

Randy raised his eyebrows and smiled.

"Well, I guess neither one of us had a good night's sleep then," Daniel said, opening the car door and tossing his briefcase inside.

Randy's smile faded. "What do you mean?"

"If you saw me out here that early in the morning, I guess you weren't sleeping so well either."

Randy furrowed his brow and dropped his eyes. He looked like he was thinking, trying to recall a memory. "Huh," he said, looking slightly amused. "I guess I didn't."

* * *

Work that day was a blur. Daniel fought to keep his eyes open, and found himself making frequent trips to the employee lounge, quickly losing count of the number of cups of coffee he consumed. He existed on the edge of sleep as he sat at his desk, his computer screen a blur through half-lidded eyes.

Near the end of the day, about an hour before he would have gotten off work, his phone rang.

It was Naomi. "Daniel," she said, her voice full of panic. "You need to come home."

Within the hour he pulled into the driveway. The neighboring house, the one that belonged to Randy and Pamela, was surrounded by yellow police tape. Two patrol cars were parked at the curb, as was an ambulance. The front door was open and several uniformed people were taking turns going in and coming out. Two officers watched Daniel closely as he parked and exited the car.

Naomi burst from their own front door and ran toward him.

"What happened?" he asked her.

"Pam is dead," she exclaimed, and began to cry, collapsing into his arms, nearly knocking him over. She rested her chin on his shoulder.

"What?"

"I went over to ask her if she wanted to come over for tea. The door was open." Naomi's voice hitched in her throat and she swallowed hard. When she spoke again, her breath was hot against his ear. "Daniel, she was in their bed. There was blood…"

"Shhhh," he said.

"…everywhere," she sobbed. "And they can't find Randy."

"Daniel Bingaman?" said a voice behind him.

He turned around and faced a uniformed officer. His name badge said Hamm, and for a fleeting moment he imagined the field day that Randy could make with that name. "I need to ask you a few questions," said the officer.

Daniel opened his mouth to speak, but then he was distracted by the sight of two more officers leading Randy, still dressed in a white bathrobe, out of the door of his house. His head hung low and his hands were cuffed behind him. As he was led down the sidewalk toward one of the patrol cars, he looked over at Daniel, raised his eyebrows, and smiled brightly, like one neighbor happy to see another. Naomi gasped.

* * *

That night in bed, Daniel and Naomi were both lying flat on their backs, staring up at the ceiling in the darkness.

"I don't want to go to sleep," she said.

He reached over and held her hand. "I know."

"I just can't believe it."

"Me either," he responded. "I just talked to Randy this morning. He seemed fine. He looked happy."

"Daniel, he was somewhere in the house. When I went in there and found Pam, he was still in there somewhere." Her voice trembled. She turned toward Daniel, burying her face into his chest. A hot tear fell on his skin, creating a warm spot. He consoled her, and eventually she slept, but her sleep was restless.

Despite his own exhaustion, sleep eluded him. Eventually he gave up and went downstairs. He turned on the TV and stared dully at the screen, not at all focusing on what was playing. At some point during the night, He was startled by the sound of Naomi screaming. But when he ran upstairs to check on her, she was sound asleep.

* * *

He was at the kitchen table the next morning when Naomi came downstairs. She looked at him with trepidation, then glanced at his phone, which was resting on the table in front of him.

"There isn't a new recording," he said, answering the question she didn't ask. "I didn't sleep at all last night."

She said nothing, but walked toward the coffeepot on the counter. She poured a cup. "I had another nightmare last night," she said, her back to him as she set the coffeepot back down. "I remember it this time."

"I know," Daniel said. "I heard you scream."

She added sugar and cream to her coffee. When she turned and looked at him, her eyes were bloodshot and red-rimmed.

"What was it?" he asked.

She shook her head, stirring her coffee. She didn't answer the question. Instead she said, "I think I'll sleep in the guest room tonight."

That night, Daniel pled with Naomi to join him in their room. She quietly refused. She would barely look at him when he spoke, and eventually he relented. After changing into her pajamas and brushing her teeth, she shuffled across the hall into the guest bedroom. She shut the door behind her, and then he heard a click as she locked the door.

* * *

On the final morning, he woke up seated at the kitchen counter. His neck was stiff from sleeping there, and the bright light of the morning sun blazing through the windows stung his eyes.

The first thing he noticed was that he was dressed in a bathrobe. He had no recollection of taking off his pajamas and putting the robe on. The next thing he realized was that his palms were pink and raw, as if he had just scrubbed them thoroughly.

His phone was in the pocket of the robe. He turned it on and launched Sleeptalker. There were two new recordings. He tapped on the first one and it played.

"Naomi?" he said. This was followed by the sound of knocking on a door. "Naomi?" he repeated. "Let me in, baby. Let me in. I promise I won't hurt you. I would never hurt you, baby. Just let me in." There was a pause, a click, and then the sound of a door opening. The recording ended.

He sat back in his chair, puzzled. He had no recollection of any of this.

He tapped on the second recording and was surprised to hear not his own voice, but Naomi's. Her words were slow and flat. Her voice was low and almost unrecognizable.

"Is the process complete?" she asked. Her speech was slurred, her tongue sounding heavy in her mouth. Even her words were oddly pronounced, the emphasis ever so slightly on the wrong syllables.

"Yes," Daniel responded.

"You now have full control?" she asked.

"Yes. Full control during the unconscious hours. By morning it will be total. You?"

"No," she said. "She is too resistant. This is proving to be true among all of the females. We can do no more than infiltrate the sub-conscious. Physical control is limited to speech alone."

"Most unfortunate," Daniel said.

"We have no choice but elimination."

"I understand," he responded.

The recording ended. Daniel looked over toward the bottom of the stairs. He considered going up but already knew what he would find if he did. Images flickered suddenly through his mind: a shining blade, a voice raised in horror, a splashing of red, all of them the remnants of a fading dream. Panicked, he began to dial 911, but then his thumb froze, hovering just above the screen.

His heart clenched with the terror of realization and his body shuddered. He stood up abruptly, knocking over the chair behind him. It clattered noisily onto the tile. But just as quickly as the sensation of terror had overtaken him, it drained completely, leaving him feeling oddly numb. He found himself moving, one shaking hand placing his phone on the counter in front of him, and then he walked to the front door.

He opened it and stepped outside. The warmth of the morning sun spilled across his face. The sensation felt comforting yet oddly unfamiliar. His bare feet touched the cold, wet grass as he walked across the lawn and stopped. It was a gorgeous spring day. Up and down the street, as far as Daniel could see, other men stood likewise on their lawns, regarding one another benignly.

Daniel looked up at a crystal clear blue sky and smiled. His ears were filled with the foreign songs of birds. A pleasant breeze moved his hair across his forehead, tickling the skin. And when he attempted to scream, nothing happened.

.

re-birth

"Son, come outside with me. Let's have a talk."

Jeff's father catches him in the hallway outside his bedroom – or what used to be his bedroom before he went away to school. Weeks into his freshmen year, his mother had converted the room into a home office for herself, his father already having one of his own in the basement. Jeff had expected her to turn it into something akin to a scrapbooking station, but then again his mother had never been the sentimental type. Anything Jeff had left behind, like the posters on the wall and most of his furniture, was promptly removed – relocated to the attic as far as he knew – and replaced with a beautiful oak office set. She did allow enough space, however, for a small cot tucked away in one corner for his occasional weekend visits, those times when he got a little homesick or his laundry had become mountainous.

Jeff follows his father through the screen door and out onto the porch. The morning sun assaults his eyes. His father sinks down into a rocker with a sigh and gestures for Jeff to do the same. There is a bite to the fall air, and Jeff finds himself wishing he was wearing more than a thin blue t-shirt and jeans. His father has donned a thick coat, which, Jeff muses, is probably providing more warmth than necessary. Jeff considers ducking back inside for a sweatshirt.

His father reaches down to the left of his chair, and there is the subsequent rattle of ice and the clink of glass. He pulls two bottles of beer from a hidden cooler with one hand, uncaps them, and offers one to his son.

"Happy 21st birthday, Jeffrey," he says, and Jeff takes a bottle with a smile. It is cold and wet against his already chilly fingers. They clink the necks together and take a swig, both of them turning to face the expanse of yard before them, acres of unblemished land that ends in a line of distant trees. The only thing between them and the woods is a giant solitary elm. Jeff used to climb that elm. He kissed his first girlfriend under that elm.

"Thanks, Dad," he says

"How is it?" his father asks.

"It's good," Jeff lies. This isn't his first taste of beer, and he is certain his father knows this. But he doesn't care for the taste and isn't sure he ever will. Somehow Jeff thinks his father knows this as well. But 21 is a milestone, and he figures that there is no better way to celebrate it than sharing a cold one with your old man on the back porch.

"Where's Mom?" Jeff asks. The morning is late and Jeff realizes that he didn't see her on their way through the kitchen. A sad but intelligent and caring woman, Jeff's mother was also prone to depression and slept in a lot. Her absence isn't necessarily unusual.

"She ran out while you were still sleeping," his father replies, placing his beer on a small table between their chairs. "Be back in a bit."

Father and son sit in silence for a moment, the only sound the breeze rustling through leaves that will soon be relenting their grip and making their final bed collectively on the ground.

"Jeff," his father says with a sigh, not looking at him. "You're 21. A man now. There's a conversation I've been needing to have with you, but it needed to wait until today."

"Dad, I know where babies come from," Jeff says, grinning widely.

Jeff's father gives him a sidelong glance and, after a pause, grins back, but it's a tired smile born mostly of obligation. Jeff suddenly wishes he could retract his comment.

Jeff's father looks away from him and out over the yard. He looks suddenly old to his son, much older than his 55 years. His hair is gray and thin and mostly gone except at the temples – a fate that Jeff wonders may someday befall his currently thick brown locks – and in the overcast autumn sunlight there are deep shadows in the creases of his eyes and mouth. He looks forlorn.

"You don't know this, Jeffrey, but twenty-five years ago, I worked for the CIA."

This is not the opening line Jeff had expected, and he considers for a moment whether or not his father is joking. All of Jeff's life, his father has worked as a banker. A successful one at that, but certainly not a job with either the prestige or intrigue of a CIA agent. It's unbelievable to Jeff, and yet in the same instant he can totally picture his father in the role – suit, tie, dark glasses, 25 years younger and in full agent mode. It's something Jeff never would have guessed but can somehow easily imagine. His father certainly has the intelligence and demeanor for the job.

"Okay," is all Jeff says, prompting his father to continue.

"My friends and family knew I worked for the government, but not in what capacity. I couldn't even tell your mother a lot of what I saw or even where I was going at times. I was let in on a lot of secret stuff that most people have no idea about. A lot of it, you don't want to know." He shakes his head quickly as he says this, as if trying to shake off a memory. "Ignorance is bliss and all that."

He picks up his beer and takes another swallow. Jeff clutches his own tightly but doesn't drink it. He's watching his father; his father is staring down the yard.

"About a year or so before I was hired, the government became aware of a doctor in California. Albert Kimball. He was the most successful plastic surgeon in the state. He was making millions of dollars performing amazing work on some of the most famous faces in Hollywood. Before he came along, there were plenty of starlets who saw their careers ruined by botched plastic surgery. This was before your time, but back then, actresses in particular would have work done in order to salvage both their looks and their careers, and in the end they'd end up looking… not natural really. They'd have no wrinkles, but they'd also be left with a face that just didn't belong in nature. Not completely. And then their careers would suffer. Ironic, really.

"Anyway, along comes Kimball and he quickly gains quite the reputation as a plastic surgeon with the miracle touch. His work was nearly undetectable. He could take ten to twenty years off a person's face and none of it looked artificial. He was almost like an artist in that regard. It was no wonder he became hugely successful. He became the most sought-after surgeon in town and could demand just about any price.

"But Kimball wasn't satisfied. He knew deep down that all he was doing was putting a shiny new coat of paint on cars that had 200,000 miles under the hood. The outsides looked young, but they didn't have the insides to match. He could make a sixty-year-old man *look* 40, but that man would still run, punch, and walk like he was sixty. That just wouldn't do, as far as Kimball was concerned.

"As it turned out, Kimball was brilliant beyond plastic surgery. He knew chemistry. Physiology. Biology. DNA. There are those who ultimately came to believe he might have been the most brilliant mind of his time. He began working on a formula... a process, that didn't stop at the appearance of restoring youth. He wanted to *actually* restore youth.

"And wouldn't you know? He figured it out." Jeff's father shakes his head morosely and takes a drink. Jeff studies him, part of him wondering if his father might still be pulling his leg.

"It took him awhile to really perfect it," Jeff's father continues. "He came up with this process, this series of injections and ingestions combined with external chemical applications. Needless to say, it was a very complicated formula, but the results literally turned back the hands of time, all without ever touching a blade to skin.

"He wasn't even fully aware of the power of what he had created. Not at first. He applied it very sparingly. Small doses that would erase wrinkles from faces, tighten up sagging skin, eliminate age spots. These weren't very exciting results, of course. He could achieve much the same thing with a scalpel. But as he became more confident in his formula and its absolute lack of any negative side effects, he began to slowly increase the dosage and potency.

"He knew the results went beyond the surface when he watched gray hair turn dark again. Soon he had patients whose eyesight and hearing improved. Bone density and muscle mass increased. Rattling old voices began to sound young again. Post-menopausal women became fertile. He had truly discovered how to turn back the hands of time within the human body.

"He called it the FOY Formula. F-O-Y. Fountain of Youth. And once he began offering it to his richest clients, there was no keeping it a secret, no matter how many non-disclosure agreements were signed. He went from servicing Hollywood A-listers to treating every billionaire entrepreneur and high-ranking political official in the country. Not only because he could restore youth, but because of the unintended but incredible side-effect: he could cure disease.

"Think about it. Alzheimer's was eradicated. Osteoporosis. Arthritis. Heart disease. Were you diagnosed with cancer in your forties? No problem, Kimball could de-age you to your thirties and the cancer would disappear. This was a world-altering discovery. Dr. Albert Kimball was on his way to becoming one of the most famous and celebrated men in history. And yet, you've never heard of him, have you?"

Jeff shakes his head, *no*. He was never the best student, his grades often a cause for his father's disapproval, but he was certain he would remember a man like this.

"Of course you haven't. In 2022, right around the time I was getting my security clearance, Kimball became the U.S. government's number one POI. What Kimball had at first seen as a breakthrough in cosmetic surgery and later as a medical miracle, the government saw as a Pandora's Box, an imminent threat that needed to be immediately regulated, controlled, and concealed. The government saw a goldmine, but they also saw a minefield."

"Why?" Jeff asks.

"One simple reason, and it wasn't the expense of it. It didn't take long for the country's top scientists to synthesize the formula until it became shockingly cheap to reproduce. No, the danger was something else. The FOY Formula reversed the aging process and restored youth, but it didn't stop aging from resuming once again. A sixty year old woman could become twenty, but in forty years, she'd look sixty again – even though she would actually be one hundred years old. But there would be nothing stopping her from taking the treatment again and again. Barring external circumstances like a car accident, a murder, or a suicide, the entire treated population would become essentially immortal.

"If the government were to subsidize the FOY Formula and offer it to everyone, nearly the entire U.S. population would become eternal twenty-somethings. Death rates would plummet and, simultaneously, birth rates would skyrocket. Within a generation the planet would die from overpopulation. A world of vibrant young people would all perish at the hands of famine and war.

"There were months of closed-door conversations within the government on how best to regulate Kimball's discovery. Most of these conversations revolved around the issue of morality. In an effort to offer the life-saving benefits of FOY without running the risk of overpopulation, it was suggested that all those who enrolled in some kind of government-run FOY program would have to necessarily agree to be sterilized in the process. If you wanted youth and immortality, you had to agree to never bear children.

"But that really wasn't a solution at all. You see, people aren't meant to live forever. There was a fear that a never-ending cycle of youth restoration – all the while being surrounded by the same people who also never aged or died – might lead to a worldwide depression the likes of which we had never seen and would never recover from.

"Similarly, there was the question of whether it was morally right for those who were fortunate enough to be alive at the birth of Kimball's discovery to essentially snuff out the existence of future generations. Was it selfish for the adults of 2022 to permanently lay claim to their place on this planet at the expense of the children of tomorrow who would never come to be? And what future discoveries, what future creations, what future progress would never come to fruition because we never allowed for the birth of future scientists, future artists, or future visionaries? These were the questions elected officials were volleying behind closed doors.

"In the end, the government took full control of the FOY Formula, not only its uses and applications, but also the dissemination of information. Those who had become aware of FOY early on – those clients of Kimball's who were lucky enough to buy into the process before Uncle Sam sunk his fingers into it – were given substantial payoffs to keep their mouths shut. Those that refused to comply were summarily *disappeared*. If you were to look back at some of the biggest box office stars of 2022, you'd note a good number that dropped off the radar completely in 2023. Retired overseas, died mysteriously, etcetera, etcetera. Those were the ones who flatly refused to keep their mouths shut over a sense of liberal goodness – the idea that recyclable youth should be made available to the hoi polloi.

"For the rest of the public, the FOY Formula was considered a conspiracy theory for awhile. Any journalist worth their salt who dug into the rumors that an LA plastic surgeon had somehow created the fountain of youth was humiliated or, at most, given the official line that while at one time it appeared that scientists were on the brink of a groundbreaking anti-aging cocktail, in the end the side-effects had, regrettably, proven to be catastrophic. A lie, of course.

"Eventually, any fires that Kimball had lit were snuffed out. The government's disinformation campaign was successful, and soon any inkling of the FOY Formula completely disappeared from the public consciousness."

"Whatever happened to Kimball?" Jeff asks.

His father shrugs. "I honestly don't know. I was told that he was shipped off to a private tropical island staffed by a hundred beautiful women and an unending supply of his own formula to live on for as long as he so chose. Sounds wonderful, doesn't it? But I can't help but wonder if Kimball himself was one of those fires that the government decided better not stay lit. I'd like to imagine he's on a white beach somewhere, sipping a bright red drink and looking at crystal blue water, tanning his twenty-something body. But who knows."

Jeff's father sips his beer. Jeff does the same, not really tasting it.

"Anyway, that's not the end of the story by any means. Over time, the government discussed how best use Kimball's discovery. Firstly, they decided to continue to make it available to the richest people across the world. Money still talks, of course. Those with the deepest pockets were allowed to turn back the clock in exchange for huge sums of money, absolute secrecy, and their own fertility. If you wanted to live forever, you weren't allowed to be adding to the population. Those were the terms. And those with famous faces had to agree to retire from public appearance before any suspicions rose. Celebrities were allowed to de-age five or ten years in order to extend their careers by a decade, but after that they had to go away. We couldn't have fifty-year-old actresses vying for the roles of twenty-year-old starlets. People would ask questions. So the choice was either extended youth or lifelong celebrity. You could not have both.

"Secondly, there was a select group of people – the world's greatest minds, the most prominent and influential leaders, those who had, in the government's flawless and unbiased opinion, contributed the most to society in their lifetime. These people were offered the treatment if they wanted it. Some accepted and were given access to an island like Kimball's. Somewhere out there in the tropics is a secret place populated by a who's who of the world's past elite, all of them young and ostensibly immortal. But it should be noted that some of those great minds passed on the opportunity. Some of them recognized that mortality is a necessary facet of life itself. A noble decision, if you ask me."

Jeff nods in thoughtful agreement.

"Thirdly, the government has selectively continued to offer the formula for its curative properties. Again, it's an exclusive list, one our names would never appear on. If a member of royalty comes down with Alzheimer's, or a lifelong member of the Deep State gets cancer, small doses of FOY are administered – just enough to regress the patient back a sufficient number of years before the disease first took root. But it's not for the masses. It's all who you know."

"That's just wrong," Jeff says.

"Of course it is," his father agrees. "But imagine being the person in position to decide who does and who does not have access to the fountain of youth. Would you deny it to your own mother if she had cancer? Of course not. But don't act like you'd make it available to every single person alive, knowing full well the global impact an undying population would have."

Jeff thinks for a moment. "I don't know. It sounds to me like the government made a lot of decisions based on projections. Maybe their projections were wrong."

"Maybe," his father says. "But I've had many years to mull it over, and in the end I feel it's best that if they erred at all, they erred on the side of caution." He then falls silent.

The breeze picks up and Jeff's skin breaks out in gooseflesh. He crosses his arms and, for a moment, considers again going inside for a jacket. But then his father gets up suddenly from his rocker, his hands in his coat pockets, pulling it tighter against his body.

"Let's walk," he says, proceeding down the porch steps before Jeff has a chance to respond.

Jeff follows without objecting. Out from under the shade of the porch, he is hit by the rays of the late morning sun, and his skin warms. His father walks in a straight, slow line toward the distant trees. Jeff can just barely hear the breeze whispering through the branches, the trees swaying in a lazy dance.

Jeff's father takes a deep breath through his nose. "But now I'm getting to the real point of our conversation. There was a fourth application of FOY, a use that the government has managed to keep completely secret for more than two decades now. And it's a subject you would never even begin to guess would be tied to a veritable fountain of youth."

Jeff is, of course, immensely curious, and perhaps that's why his father draws out a long pause. Jeff doesn't even wager a guess.

"Capital punishment," he finally says.

Jeff is puzzled, and smiles in confusion. "What?" he asks, a chuckle in his voice.

"It started off as just an interesting suggestion, an off-the-wall comment in the midst of many closed-door conversations concerning the morals of the application of FOY.

"See, in the end, Kimball and the scientists who synthesized and improved upon his formula didn't just stop at the erasure of a few decades. They continued to push the limits of how far they could go. At first, yes, they discovered that senior citizens could become twenty year olds again. But then, adults could become teenagers. Then children. Then infants. Eventually, young enough to no longer be able to survive outside the womb. Apply enough of the formula, prolong the process, and in the end they learned there was no limit to the de-aging process."

"You're kidding," Jeff says, incredulous.

"I am dead serious," his father responds. "They could literally turn an octogenarian into a fetus. Into a fertilized egg. Into nothing. The process was a long and painful one, requiring the removal of tissue and bone. But it could be done."

Jeff's jaw drops and he stops walking. The pair have reached the giant elm in the middle of the yard, and Jeff is cold again in its shade. There is a bald spot underneath one great branch where a tire swing used to be – a tire swing he spent many an hour on during childhood summers – but all that remains of it now is a broken and rotting rope. He pictures himself swinging there, waving to his mother as she sits alone on the distant porch, watching over him. Sometimes she didn't wave back, even though he was sure she had seen him.

Jeff's father has continued to stroll, so Jeff has to jog to catch up.

"In one of many spit balling sessions, it is suggested that perhaps the FOY formula could be given to criminals on death row. Ridiculous, right? Why restore youth to the nation's worst criminals? Well, the thought is that perhaps the FOY formula would render the question of whether or not capital punishment is moral null and void. Are we in fact killing a man if we simply de-age him from existence?

"It was an interesting question. But of course, one of the main purposes of capital punishment is deterrence. We execute criminals in an effort to de-incentivize possible future criminals, right? But since the FOY formula was top secret, we couldn't tell the world we had come up with a different way of executing criminals. If we went down that particular road, we would have to outwardly communicate that execution was still happening, while secretly de-aging the worst offenders into non-existence. In essence, it would only work to assuage the consciences of those who have to flip that fatal switch, or administer that lethal injection. It was a minor difference at best.

"But soon the conversation switched to something else. Soon we began having debates concerning nature versus nurture. What if, instead of either executing death row inmates or de-aging them from existence, we simply returned them to childhood? And then what if those children were placed in adoptive households handpicked by the government? Households run by parents who could provide these children the kind of positive, balanced upbringing that might put them on the correct path not offered to them the first time around?

"It's an interesting idea, right?" Jeff's father asks him, and Jeff has to agree. He nods.

"And that is exactly what we began to do. Men on death row, thinking they were about to receive a lethal injection, were instead given a general anesthetic to put them to sleep. They were then administered heavy doses of the FOY formula, de-aging them to infancy. These children were then placed with adoptive parents, parents who had been pre-screened as prime candidates for being able to provide a healthy, steady upbringing. Of course, these parents had no idea we had just given them a son – or in very rare cases, a daughter – who was a convicted murderer. But imagine looking into the beaming faces of these young new mothers and fathers as they embraced with joy these baby monsters. It never sat well with me.

"Eventually, we took it even further. We began regressing the criminals to the fertilized egg stage and implanting them in women who had sought out in vitro fertilization. We'd find a couple who looked like a physical match to these killers – a blonde-haired, blue-eyed criminal would go to a blonde-haired, blue-eyed couple, for example – and instead of implanting the mother with her own egg fertilized by her husband's sperm, we'd give them the fertilized egg that was actually once a death row inmate."

He shakes his head. "I still can't believe we did that. But there was no shortage of couples willing to participate. It was a government-funded program. Free adoption or free in vitro fertilization to a select group of couples that we thought might put these criminals on the right path, beginning all the way back at childhood again.

"We didn't leave these couples to flounder, of course. The children were given the best education, the best health care, and regular psychiatric evaluations, all on the government's dime. The couples were none the wiser. They were so happy to either finally give birth to a child of their own or be able to adopt one, all free of charge, that they didn't ever question *why* we were making their dreams come true. And the children themselves never had any memory of their former wretched lives."

"But as the children got older," Jeff says, "didn't any of these parents ever look at their kid and think, 'Wait, he looks exactly like that serial killer I read about years ago?'"

"Of course not," his father responds. "Nobody sees what they don't want to see. And honestly, aside from some of the most famous serial killers in history, how many death row inmates would *you* recognize on sight? We were smart enough to relocate these children to states where they were never likely to run into someone they knew in their adult lives. So there was never any recognition."

"It's all so hard to believe," Jeff says.

"We called it Project Re-Birth," his father continues. "Even the name was designed to make us feel better about what we were doing. We were giving children to childless couples, we were giving society's worst a second shot at life, and we were not, as some people argued, exacting merciless revenge by executing criminals. It all sounds wonderful, and I know it gave some of my colleagues the warm-and-fuzzies, but I didn't like it. Not from day one. I knew deep down what we were doing was placing monsters into the hands of oblivious couples.

"And I know we don't agree on this, Jeff, but I still believe in justice. The minute a man devalues another person's life to the point of taking it, he has given up the right to his own life. It's that plain and simple."

"Eye for an eye," Jeff offers.

"Exactly," his father says, his voice filling with sudden emotion. "I believed that even before that scum killed your grandmother and grandfather in cold blood. For seventy-five dollars and a gold necklace. Those were two wonderful people that you never knew because a junkie decided that money for his next hit was worth more than some random couple whose names he didn't care to know."

Jeff finds himself speechless. His father had rarely ever spoken to him about the murder of his parents. Jeff could probably count on one hand the number of times the subject had been brought up.

The pair reach the tree line, and both stop walking. The house is a tiny box in the distance behind them. Jeff's father sniffs, and Jeff pats him on the back. His father wipes his nose on the cuff of his coat.

"I only kept that job for about two years after Re-Birth was introduced. I couldn't stomach it. It went against everything I stood for. I got paid really well, and I worried about what I might do next, how I might support your mom without it. But then my mom and dad got killed, and that rat that pulled the trigger got convicted. He was publically put on death row but covertly put on the list for the Re-Birth program, and I walked away. I couldn't take it anymore. There I was, robbed of two of the most important people in my life, and that… that *monster* was given a second chance at life. A second chance at youth. A second chance at happiness. Where was *their* second chance at life? Where was *their* second chance at happiness? Or mine? I wouldn't stand for it. I walked away."

A sob hitches in his throat, and Jeff puts his arm around him, pulling him closer. But his father is stiff and resists the embrace, still facing the trees, and Jeff drops his arm.

"In the end, though, wasn't some of it worth it?" Jeff asks. "I mean, those kids in different households, with different parents… did they turn out better? Did nurture win over nature?"

His father nods, clearing his throat. "Most of them, yes. I mean, I didn't work there anymore, but I still had buddies on the inside who would tell me things. Guys who agreed with me that the system was wrong but kept their jobs because the pay was so good. They would tell me how things were going. Most of the kids turned out better. Much better. A few of them, particularly ones with genetic predispositions toward mental problems like schizophrenia, still had some issues. But the doctors were able to watch out for it and deal with them early. With medication and therapy. Only a few of the children had to be removed for the parents' safety. Most of them, though… most of them turned out okay on the second go-round."

"So it's not all bad, right?" Jeff says. "You did a good thing. Turning these criminals into good people was a good thing."

"Yes," his father agrees, nodding again slowly. "We did a good thing. Which is what makes this next part so much harder."

Jeff's father takes a step away from him, almost casually, and faces him for what Jeff realizes is the first time in almost their entire conversation. It takes Jeff a moment to notice his father is no longer holding his coat tight against him, but instead has drawn a pistol from a pocket and is pointing it directly at Jeff's chest. His hand is trembling. Jeff's entire body goes numb with a chill that is coming from deep inside of him. He can no longer feel his hands and feet.

"Dad?"

"Even though I quit that job, there were those still working within the program who agreed that it wasn't right. It wasn't right for a man to take someone else's life and their punishment – if you want to call it that – is to be given a literal start-over in life. Where's the start-over for the people who died? Or for the loved ones they left behind?"

"Dad?" Jeff says, and his voice is shaking. "What are you doing?"

"Those buddies of mine stood with me when my parents got lowered into the ground. And they knew the right thing to do. Sure, they argued with me at first. They tried to reason with me, to talk me out of it. But they came around eventually. And if anybody knows how to do things covertly, it's the boys in the Re-Birth program."

Jeff puts up his hands and takes one step away from his father, a man who was always such a good provider, but emotionally distant. A familiar presence and yet in so many ways, Jeff realizes now, a stranger to him. "Please don't do this," he pleads.

"They gave you to me and your mom 21 years ago today. Your *re-birthday*. I wanted to end you then and there. Quick, like a Band-Aid. But your mother. She insisted. 'He's just a baby,' she said. So I agreed to wait. I agreed to wait until I could look into the eyes of the man who murdered my parents."

Jeff shakes his head rapidly, searching his thoughts, trying to conjure memories. But he comes up empty. "Dad, don't. You can't do this."

"Yes, I can," he says. "An eye for an eye. I want you to know. Their names were Wallace and Elinor. They would have been amazing grandparents if your mom and I had ever had children. But you killed them. For seventy-five dollars and a necklace, you pitiful excuse for a human being." He spits this last sentence and glares at Jeff with an anger he has never seen in his father's eyes before.

"Dad, please," Jeff says, heart pounding in his throat. "I – I don't remember anything."

"But I do, and I always will," he says, and he aims the gun between Jeff's eyes, his hand suddenly steady.

"Your mother said to tell you that she loved you."

katherine

The first time she ever saw him, he was standing in the corner of her living room, a shape more so than a clear figure. She almost didn't see him at all. Like a dim star in a dark sky, he was more visible in her periphery than when she looked at him directly, but he was definitely there, still and shadowy, and she was so badly startled that she dropped the armload of books she had been carrying, the edge of one hammering painfully into the top of her right foot.

She left the books where they fell and fled hastily up the stairs to her bedroom, locking the door behind her with trembling fingers. She slept very little that night. She knew that the logical thing for her to do would be to call the police and let them know that a man had broken into her house. But she already knew it would do no good. Because it wasn't a man she saw.

At least, he wasn't a man anymore.

* * *

The next morning she crept as quietly as she could back down the stairs. The bright light of morning revealed nothing more than the mundanity of the living room. She almost dismissed the entire event as a figment of her imagination, an illusion brought on by a mind and body exhausted from days of moving, unboxing and organizing her belongings into a new home.

The house itself was not new, but it was new to her. A moving company had placed all the furniture. All that was left to do was to unpack, decorate, and organize. She found herself perilously close to filling the house's ample closets with boxes, leaving precious little room to spare. She needed to purge. A task for another day.

It was on this second day of unpacking that she came across two boxes in particular – one marked *Josiah*, the other marked *James*. Their contents would need to be dealt with eventually, but certainly not today, not on a day when she was finding homes for such humdrum items as guest towels. These two boxes deserved more thoughtful consideration. She didn't want to stash them in the attic, and she refused to go in the cellar again. She decided upon the small closet beneath the stairs, so far untouched by her.

She opened the door and knelt inside, pulling a string to turn on the overhead lightbulb. The walls were an explosion of Crayola, the masterpieces of a previous owner's child. Dogs, rainbows, trees, and a decent recreation of the house itself. A boy and his mother stood hand-in-hand; a dour-looking father watched from some distance away.

She pushed *Josiah* and *James* into the closet and regarded them, briefly succumbing to a familiar tug of loneliness that pulled gently at her chest. She extinguished the light and shut the door with a quiet click.

That evening, just as the house grew dim, the figure was there again, hovering in the same corner. She spotted him as she passed through the living room on her way to the stairs, planning to retire early, her body once again exhausted from the chore of unpacking. She was startled, but notably less so than the day before.

She paused and looked at him directly. He was still and yet not still at the same time, his silhouette dark but translucent. Looking at him was like looking through a shadow. He was taller than her, but just barely, and thin. Based on the size of his frame, the rounded yet clearly defined jawline, and the narrowness of his neck and shoulders, he appeared to her much like a teenage boy or a very young man.

Although his face had no features of any kind, she could tell that he was returning her gaze. And she couldn't help but feel that, as mildly alarmed as she was of him, he was also uncertain of her. It was as though he was holding back from her, shrinking away from her slightly, like an abused dog that doesn't want to be struck again.

They regarded each other this way for a few moments, he from his side of the room and she from hers. Eventually she walked slowly by and up the stairs, pausing partway and looking down at him. Hard as it was to tell from his nearly featureless shape, she was certain he had turned his head and was watching her go. She continued on to her room, shutting the door quietly behind her. She didn't lock it this time.

* * *

The third night, she sat in the living room, an unopened book on her lap, and waited for the sun to set. As the light through the windows died and the shadows in the room deepened, he was there again, not in an instant, but slowly coming into view like a developing photograph.

"Can you hear me?" she asked him in a timid voice.

He neither spoke nor moved. Not exactly. There was a tiny shift, like a tremor or vibration. She could not be certain, but this nearly imperceptible motion felt like a response to her question.

"My name is Katherine," she said. "What is your name? Can you speak?"

Again, there was a tiny tremor, accompanied this time by a slight darkening of his hue. His outline became more clearly perceptible. She was confident that he was trying to communicate with her, but that doing so was taking considerable effort on his part.

She sat forward in her chair. "Are you trying to talk to me?"

The shape trembled, darkened, and seemed to rise ever so slightly off the floor. She sensed his excitement, the simple joy of communication. This same excitement welled in her own chest. She stood and took a slight step forward without consciously deciding to do so, and there was movement from him as well as he emerged ever so slightly from the darkness of the corner.

There they stood for a long moment, once again regarding each other. Her mind raced with questions. She chose the obvious one.

"Are you dead?" she whispered.

There was a small, barely visible tipping of his head. A nod. *Yes.*

"How did you die?" she asked.

He remained still. His silhouette vibrated slightly and darkened again. It registered to her as frustration.

"Can you speak?"

A slow turn of the head to the side and back again. *No.*

"Did you live in this house?"

A nod, stronger and more perceptible this time. *Yes.*

"Were you ill? Is that why you died?"

No. The silhouette grew more opaque.

"Did you die in an accident?"

No. The silhouette darkened further, shivering, and she sensed that he was growing frustrated. She was on the wrong track.

She considered for a moment before asking the question that she had been avoiding. "Were you murdered?"

The shape dimmed and became still. Then he nodded, the movement clearer than ever before. *Yes.*

She took one step back and sat down hard in the chair behind her. He likewise retreated, very slightly, back into his corner. She could sense his relief, but she could also feel his exhaustion, as if the act of communicating with her had drained him. He began to fade until she could no longer distinguish him from the shadows of the room. He was gone.

* * *

The next day as she continued the seemingly never-ending task of unpacking, her thoughts frequently drifted to her visitor. A not-unpleasant anticipation occupied her thoughts. Every time she walked through the living room, she glanced furtively into the empty corner, not expecting to see him there but wanting to nonetheless.

That evening she planted herself in the living room chair, a photo album on her lap, a glass of wine at her side. She looked at pictures to pass the time and waited for the sun to lower in the sky. James smiled at her, handsome as he ever was, in a picture taken at the Grand Canyon, the sky so blue behind him it shouldn't have been real. Her fingertip grazed his face. He would have loved this house.

When the sun was extinguished, the corner of the room remained empty. After several impatient minutes, Katherine walked over and hesitantly entered the space. There was nothing there. Disappointment clenching her chest, she collected her album and her glass of wine and retreated to her room.

That night she was awakened from a deep sleep. There was no

noise that had disturbed her, simply a soft sensation that something in the room had shifted. She sat up in bed, fully awake and yet not frightened. At least, not entirely. Her eyes, already accustomed to the darkness, found him, standing in the corner near the door. The moonlight cascading through the window passed right through him.

"Hi," she said weakly.

He didn't stir.

"Do you want me to help you?" she asked him.

His nod was clear. *Yes.*

"Can you still not speak?"

A pause. *No.*

"Do you know who killed you?"

The shape trembled. *Yes*, he nodded.

"Who?" she asked, and she bit her lip, frustrated by the limitations of their communication. The ghost remained still, awaiting the next question. "Was it someone in your family?" she asked.

The shape lurched suddenly forward, approaching the foot of the bed. He was a blur of motion as he shivered with excitement. His advancing startled her and she shifted backward, unexpectedly frightened, pulling the covers of the bed up to her chin. A breeze of cold air touched her face in his wake.

The ghost stopped moving just as suddenly as it had started, and she sensed his remorse, his regret at having startled her. He seemed to shrink and back slightly away.

"It's okay," she said, lowering the covers from her face and extending one cautious hand. "It's okay. So the person who killed you was in your family?"

Yes, he nodded.

"Was it one of your parents? Your father?"

Another tremor, followed by another nod. *Yes.*

She swallowed hard. "Did he kill you in this house?"

Yes.

Her mind spun with questions, but most of them required more than a yes or no answer. She sorted through them as quickly as she could, searching for one that the ghost could actually answer. He was leaning in toward her, anticipating her next question with impatience.

"Okay," she finally said. "My guess is that the reason you're here is because something is unresolved."

Yes.

"Is your father in prison?"

No.

"Did he get away with your murder?"

Yes.

"And you want me to… avenge you?"

No. He shook his head quickly, furiously.

"No? But you want people to know the truth?"

Yes.

"And you need me to help you." It was less a question than a statement.

Yes.

"And if do… will you be free?"

Yes.

With this answer, the ghost's vibrations, which had been growing more intense with each response, abruptly ceased. His countenance relaxed and his shoulders fell.

"How can I help you?" she asked him. "Can you show me?"

He paused, almost as if he was catching his breath. The ghost lifted his hands, palm-upward. He looked down at them, studying them, watching them as they faded. Soon his entire figure began to dissipate. He dropped his hands and looked back at her. She knew he wanted to stay, but their exchange had depleted him.

"It's okay. I will help you," she called out, and he nodded slowly before disappearing completely.

* * *

The next night, she found him at the door to the cellar. "You want me to go downstairs?" she asked him.

He nodded.

She hesitated. She had only been in the cellar one time, four weeks ago when she was given a full tour by her realtor. It was dark, damp, and claustrophobic, with not even the smallest of windows to let in enough light to scatter the shadows. As much as Katherine had loved the rest of the house, the cellar had given her such an uneasy feeling that it almost singlehandedly made her change her mind about buying the house. She had decided then and there to never use the space, not even for storage.

Yet there she was, her hand on the knob, contemplating going into that dead space again, only this time at night and at the beckoning of a ghost. It was all so ridiculous she almost laughed and backed away, but curiosity got the best of her. She turned the knob and opened the door. Before descending the steps, she looked back at her ghostly friend, but he was gone.

She used her cell phone's flashlight to light her way. The steps were narrow, and the dank boards bowed ever so slightly under her weight. She felt her heart begin to race slightly. *What am I doing?* she thought.

She reached the concrete floor and stopped. "Now what?" she said out loud, the sound of her voice swallowed by the thick, wet darkness. She shone the light around the cellar, wishing it was brighter and better able to penetrate the shadows. Stepping further into the room, she continued to pan the dim light around her. The beam eventually settled on one of the far corners, and it took her a moment to realize that one of the shadows wasn't broken by the light. The dark figure stood there, waiting.

Startled, she screamed and dropped her phone. Hand on heart, she knelt and picked it up again, shining its light once again toward the corner. The ghost was still there, only now he was pointing at the wall beside him.

She approached slowly, hesitantly. His finger, dark and still, was indicating a single brick. Upon closer inspection she realized that this brick did not sit quite flush with the others, but protruded slightly, the mortar around it cracked and broken.

With some difficulty she gripped the edges of the brick and pulled. The rough material abraded her fingers. The block finally gave way and was heavy in her hand. She dropped it with a thud to the floor.

Mild trepidation in her heart, she reached into the cavity before her and felt around. She encountered two objects. One was flat, smooth, and cold: a cell phone. The second was a gun.

The phone, of course, was completely dead. She plugged it into a receptacle in the kitchen and left it there on the counter. She filled up a glass with water from the tap, and sank into a chair at the kitchen table. She drained the glass of every drop, and when she lowered it back down again, she realized she was not alone.

"It will take a few minutes before it'll have enough juice to turn on," she said. "I'm guessing there's something on it you want me to see?"

Yes.

She nodded back, thinking, amused by the fact that she had so quickly become accustomed to talking with an apparition. "I wish I knew your name," she said. "I guess I might in a few minutes."

The ghost was still.

"You were young, weren't you?" she asked. "Like, sixteen, seventeen?"

Yes.

"Hmm," she said, sitting back in her chair. "My son would be sixteen now."

The ghost shifted ever so slightly.

"He was eight when he died," she said. "Such a simple thing too. He fell from monkey bars during recess. Probably not even a four foot drop. But he fell just the right way." She chuckled morosely. "Just the *wrong* way.

"I was at home when I got the call from his school. They told me there had been an accident and Josiah was on his way to the hospital. Said I should get there as soon as possible. They wouldn't give me any more details than that.

"My husband's name was James. I called him on the way out the door. I didn't get an answer on his cell, so I called his office. His secretary told me he'd gotten a call from the school and was on the way to the hospital too.

"I got there first," she sighed and took a deep breath, trying to calm herself, her emotions beginning to well. She turned the empty water glass distractedly on the table with her fingers. "It took an eternity before anyone would tell me what was going on. Josiah's skull was fractured and his brain was swollen. The doctors were still working on him. I wasn't allowed to see him. They let me sit in a chair in the hallway outside his door. That was as close as they would let me get.

"I was an absolute mess, of course. I kept looking down the hallway, waiting for James to come in. I needed him so badly. I'd never felt so alone and scared and desperate in my life. It was probably only a few minutes, but it felt like forever.

"Eventually, the door to Josiah's room opened and a doctor came out. His eyes told me everything there was to know. I couldn't even feel my feet as I took a step toward him. They were so numb. Or maybe there was nothing to feel because the entire earth had just dropped out from under me.

"But I never reached him. At that moment a whole team of EMTs came down the hallway, pushing a gurney. They were shouting. I could barely see the man on the gurney as they rushed by me. It was all a blur of bodies and yelling and blood and…"

Her breath caught in her throat, and twin tears rolled down her cheeks in a warm race toward her jaw. "He was terribly mangled, but I saw enough to recognize him. When you know somebody well enough, when you've studied those features you love with all of your heart for that many years, all you have to catch is a sliver, the tiniest glimpse, to know that it's them.

"Who knows how fast James had been driving, but I know he had been just as desperate as I was to get to the hospital, to see Josiah. He had flown through a red light and a tractor trailer hit him on the driver's side. It split the car completely in half.

"They put him in the next room, right next door to Josiah. Father and son in neighboring rooms, without even knowing it. Time of death was declared within minutes of each other."

She tipped the water glass to her mouth before remembering it was empty. She gave a tired glance at her spectral guest and set the glass back down. "That was eight years ago. Eight very sad, very lonely years ago. So yeah, Josiah would be about your age now. It's hard to imagine."

The ghost tipped its head slightly to one side in a motion that she translated as one of sympathy, his shoulders slouching under the weight of sadness.

She stood up and pushed her chair away with the backs of her knees. Slowly she approached him. He recoiled slightly but then was still again.

They stood inches apart. This close, she could feel the cold air that surrounded him. She could see the rest of the kitchen behind him, bathed in darkness as if she was looking through tinted glass. The edges of him vibrated in anticipation.

She lifted one hand and placed it on his cheek. Her fingers felt suddenly cold and damp, like she had just passed her hand through a thick mist. The dark shadow of his countenance shifted, and she caught little sparks of color dancing through his shadow – little glints of blue, yellow, and green. They swirled and glowed and dimmed. It was beautiful.

When she pulled her hand away, for the briefest of moments his face flickered, and she caught a sudden glimpse of his visage. It was young and fair and free of blemish, blonde locks falling down across his forehead, his eyes blue and full of a deep sadness that she easily recognized. She gasped quietly.

"It's nice to have someone to talk to again," she said.

* * *

She held the phone in her hands at the kitchen table. The home screen prompted her for a pin. "Obstacle one," she said, looking up at her guest.

He nodded twice in succession. She momentarily thought he was simply agreeing with her, but then realized he was telling her something.

"Two?" she asked, and he nodded once in response. "Two." Using this method, in short order he had given her his entire pin number.

"Open sesame," she said as the phone unlocked its contents to her. She tapped on various apps until one of them – Facebook – revealed his name.

"Your name is Abel," she said, smiling up at him, and he practically shimmered in response. She scrolled through his pictures. He had been a beautiful boy, ready with a smile, even if there was a pervasive sadness behind his eyes in every photo.

In some images he was wearing a football uniform, which surprised her given his slender frame, but then she could picture him being quite fast on the field, weaving his way through the offense. *It doesn't matter how slight you are if they can't catch you,* she thought.

In other pictures he was surrounded by friends, teenagers with friendly faces, all of them smiling and vibrant with life. Party pictures, school field trips, the beach. He was with a pretty brunette in several shots, her eyes wide with adoration for him; Katherine felt a sudden pity for this girl that she had never met.

Scrolling back through his online history, she was able to put pieces together in reverse. A large man was in a scattered few images, his eyes the same vibrant blue as Abel's, but his physical presence much larger and more intimidating, his face not welcoming but harsh, his brow perpetually furrowed. This would be Abel's father. One shot of the two of them by the side of a football field, post-game, was noteworthy in the obvious distance between the two of them even as they stood side by side, arms around each other.

A woman, blonde and pretty, appeared only in older pictures when Abel was younger and smaller. Abel had her face, minus her eyes, which were a rich brown.

"Your mother?" Katherine asked.

Yes.

"She died?"

Yes.

"I'm sorry, but I have to ask. Did your father kill her too?"

No.

"Okay," she said with some relief.

She scrolled for a while longer until her curiosity was mostly satisfied. She had a pretty good idea of the kid Abel had been, or at least the kid he presented himself to be on-line. She set the phone down on the table and looked up at him. "What am I looking for?" She asked him. "E-mails? Other pictures? Videos?"

At this final guess he nodded quickly, enthusiastically. She picked up the phone again and found a video app. There were dozens of clips. "This could take some time," she said.

And it did. Hours later she was still at the table. Most of the videos were innocuous and innocent, and many of them didn't feature Abel at all. This was, of course, to be expected. It was his phone, and he was therefore frequently the cameraman, heard but not seen.

She had begun to nod off a bit when Abel's face suddenly filled the screen. He looked tired and sad, his eyes puffy as if he had been crying.

"I don't even really know where to start," he said, and the image trembled a bit. His voice was deep but young. "I feel stupid recording this. But I think I should. Just in case.

"I love my dad. Really I do. It's just… he's not happy. He never has been. I was scared of him as a kid. I loved him, but I was scared of him. On the worst nights, I would hide in the closet under the stairs and just hope that he would leave me alone in there. He usually did. I would stay in there until he and Mom stopped arguing, and then I'd sneak up the stairs to bed. That closet was my sanctuary for many years. Mom let me draw on the walls to pass the time. I felt safe in there.

"Things got worse after Mom died. She helped to balance him. But now he gets drunk a lot. Like, more even than he used to. Most of the time he just passes out at night. But sometimes he gets really mad about stuff. Anything can set him off. And sometimes he hits me."

Abel sniffed and looked away from the camera for a moment. "I've never told anyone. Sometimes there are bruises but I blame those on football. I don't want to get him in trouble. He's all I've got."

A tear fell from Abel's eye and Katherine felt her heart clench. *The poor kid*, she thought.

"It's just… lately it's gotten a lot worse. He drinks almost every day, and he hits me almost every day. He can be fall down drunk and yet… he knows well enough to put the bruises where they can stay hidden. My arms, my back, my chest. Never my face. He knows what he's doing." He said this last statement with more than a hint of sourness.

"Last night, he forced me into the cellar," Abel said, and fresh tears began to fall. "He left me down there overnight. This morning he was all apologetic and he kept hugging me and stuff. But I just… I don't know. It's getting so much worse that sometimes I wonder if one day he'll go too far. I've already hidden one of his guns, in case I need it. He has so many he hasn't missed it. But I don't know if I could ever use it.

"I should probably tell someone," he continued, nodding. "I really should. But… he really is all I've got. And I do love him. I don't know." Abel wiped his nose and sniffed simultaneously.

"After school today, he gave me a new phone. 'Just like you've been asking for,' he said, and when he smiles at me like that, you know, it makes me hope for the best, like maybe today things will start to get better.

"It's probably stupid, but I thought, you know what, why not? I'd use my old phone to record this video. It feels better just to know I've said it. And if the day comes that he does go too far, maybe someone will find this and will know what happened. So this is how it is."

At this point Abel took a deep breath and looked deep into the camera. "If you're watching this and I'm dead, and if there's any question about how I died, know this: my father killed me."

The video ended, and Katherine sat back in the kitchen chair. "Oh Abel," she said, looking up. But he was gone. It was 3:20 in the morning.

* * *

She went to the library the next day. It was her first time visiting the local library since moving into the new house, so it was unfamiliar to her. It was large and impressive. A short, squat woman with a large, welcoming smile and a nametag that said "Beth" approached.

"Can I help you?" she asked.

"I need to get on the internet," Katherine said, "And maybe look at some old newspapers."

"Follow me," she said, and with a little bounce she led Katherine deeper into the library.

It didn't take her long to find Abel's obituary. He had died only three months ago, preceded in death by his mother and survived by only his father, Henry. There were no siblings and no surviving grandparents. All extended family was not local. He had been sixteen years old. The obit mentioned his love of football, friends, and writing. It did not give the cause of death.

Within an hour Katherine had found what she needed. The article was titled "Teen Dies in Home Accident." Abel had died from injuries sustained in a fall down the cellar steps of his home. He had been found by his father. The article was accompanied by a high school photo of Abel, looking handsome and smiling.

"Found by his father," Katherine whispered out loud.

She made copies of the article and the obituary, folded both, and put them in her purse.

* * *

"I went to the library today," she said to Abel that night. "I looked up your obituary and the article about your… accident."

They were back in the living room. She was seated in the same chair as before, across the room from Abel's corner, but this time he stood directly in front of her, over her, looking down on her. He radiated anticipation.

She had copies of his obituary and the article in her lap. She smoothed out the folds. "It just occurred to me that you don't know what they say," she said. She picked them up and read them to him.

When she was done, she looked up at him. "So your father told everyone it was an accident." This wasn't a question, nor was it something Abel had been alive to witness, but she knew both of them had drawn the same, obvious conclusion.

Yes.

"But he pushed you."

Yes.

She shook her head, biting the right side of her lip. She looked up at him. He was still standing over her.

"Can you sit?" she asked.

No.

"Okay," she responded. "Abel, how did your mom die?"

Abel stood still.

"Right," she said. "Was she ill?"

Yes.

"Cancer?"

Yes.

A few moments passed silently. Abel continued to loom.

Katherine drew in a deep, hesitant breath. "Abel," she said. "How do you know? I mean, if I take that video to the police, and they arrest your dad, how do you know that will set you free?"

She knew Abel couldn't answer, but she saw him tremble, a slight vibration that looked, best she could tell, like irritation.

But there was also a stirring in her heart, a deepening sadness that was bringing her nearly to tears. "I was just thinking, you know, what if it doesn't work?" she asked him. "I mean, I know about that whole un-finished business thing with ghosts, but that comes from stories, right? Fiction. How can we really know? Maybe you're meant to be here for some other reason."

Abel's silhouette continued to hum with movement as he stood over her. The blackness of his shadow deepened.

She started to cry. "I have been so lonely, Abel," she sobbed. "You have no idea how lonely. And then you came into my life in this most unusual way. And I've been thinking, maybe you're here because we were meant to be together. Like, maybe you're like the son I lost, and maybe I'm the mom you lost, and maybe we're just supposed to be here for each other."

She dropped her head and wept, clutching the papers in her hands, a few drops hitting the pages. She didn't want to look up at him, afraid that she would see disappointment.

"I just," she sniffed. "I don't think I can do it, Abel. When I left the library today, I went to the police. I just sat in my car. I had your phone with me and everything, but I just couldn't do it. I couldn't go in. It sounds so stupid and selfish, but I don't want to let you go."

She looked up at him through tears. He stood large over her, black as night, blocking the entire room behind him. Katherine sat back slightly in her chair, recoiling. She felt oddly afraid of him for the first time since the night he first appeared to her. "Abel, please," she whispered. "Don't make me do it. We can be together."

He reached out suddenly, swiftly, striking the pages in her hand, sending them flying off into the air before floating slowly to the floor. She gasped and drew up her knees, her hand stinging and cold where he had grazed her, her eyes wide with fear.

Abel retreated quickly, across the room and into the shadows of the corner. His head hung low, and she could see the remorse in his countenance. He raised his head briefly, regarding her penitently, and then faded away.

* * *

The next evening, after the sun went down, Abel did not return. Katherine looked all around the house for him. It felt distinctly like he was hiding from her. She contented herself by sitting at the kitchen table with his cell phone, looking at his pictures and watching some of his videos. She marveled at the fact that he had somehow managed to touch her, and she imagined that her hand still tingled from the contact. She wondered if perhaps his anger had been the key to allowing him some interaction with the physical world, brief as the moment was.

She was startled by a knock at the front door. She stood, putting the phone in one pocket. On the counter was the gun. She considered stashing it into a cabinet before slipping it into the other pocket. She walked toward the door, the words "Who is it" balanced on her lips, when she heard the deadbolt unlock, and the door swung open.

Katherine froze. She was greeted by bright, penetrating blue eyes – Abel's eyes – set in the middle of a stern, frowning face. *Henry.* He stepped inside almost casually, one hand dropping a set of keys into his jacket pocket. "Mind if I come in?" he asked. He was massive, his height and girth swallowing the room as he entered.

Katherine backed away from him. "Can I help you?" Her throat felt suddenly thick, her tongue a dry rug, and she found herself unable to swallow.

"I used to live here," he said, glancing around and smiling slightly. "And I see you haven't gotten around to changing the locks." He paused, studying her. "I think you might have something that belongs to me."

"What?" was the only word she could choke out. She took another step back.

"A cell phone," he said, shutting the door behind him with the kick of one heel.

She didn't respond.

"My son and I both had a GPS app on our phones," he continued. "Family Tracker. It let me know where he was all the time. So I was surprised when I got a notification that his old cell phone was back on-line and fully charged. It even took a trip to the library yesterday. And to the police station."

She stood there, staring at him, mouth open, words failing her. She was trying to piece together a story, a lie that she could sell him. But her mind was frantic, panic was freezing her thoughts. Suddenly she felt something cold beside her and glanced over. Abel was there, shaking like a leaf. He wasn't looking at Katherine but at his father. And he was angry. She looked from Abel to Henry and back again. But the man's eyes remained locked on her. He could not see Abel.

Henry gave Katherine a curious look and stepped forward. "I don't know what you found on that phone, or what you think you know," he said as he approached. "But I'm going to need it back."

She continued to retreat until her back was against the cellar door. She was steps away from the kitchen and a possible escape. But Henry was huge and she knew she would never get away if he managed to catch her. He was so far into the room now that he was standing next to Abel, who hadn't moved.

"I don't know what you mean," she said. "I don't know anything."

Henry took another step toward her, his right shoulder and arm passing through Abel, and Katherine saw his skin break out in goose-flesh. He ignored it. Then he was standing over her.

"Where is it?" he asked, and she could smell his breath. It was bitter and foul with alcohol.

"Down there," she said, and she tilted her head backwards against the cellar door.

Henry looked incredulous. "In the cellar?" he asked.

She slinked out of the way and turned the knob, opening the door in front of him. He looked down into the darkness.

"Yes," she said. "I didn't have the pin to unlock it, but I could still make the flashlight work. So I was using it as a flashlight and I left it down there." Her words came quickly and nervously and sounded overtly like a lie.

She looked beyond Henry into the living room. Abel was still there, watching them.

Henry looked away from her and into the cellar. She peeled herself away from the doorframe and stepped behind him, Abel behind her. She could feel both the damp coldness of the ghost and the chill wafting up the cellar stairs and shivered.

Slowly, incredibly, Henry took a step forward, through the door, one foot on the top step leading down to the darkness. She felt a faint trill of hope. If he continued down the stairs, she could lock him down there. But he hesitated, turning back again toward her. "Where did you –" he began.

In an instant she pulled the gun from her pocket, stepped forward, and fired. The sound was deafening. Henry's side blossomed red and he looked downward in shock. Katherine's ears were filled with an incredible, terrible sound, and she realized she was screaming.

Henry lurched backward, one hand grasping for the railing and missing, the other hand reaching out for Katherine, who saw Henry's eyes, huge and blue and full of both anger and fear, as he fell backwards and down the stairs. A loud, cracking sound echoed from below as he made his first contact with the steps, and the din continued until he finished his decent on the cellar floor below.

She raced forward and flicked on the basement lights. There at the bottom of the steps was Henry, limbs painfully askew, a pool of blood forming under his head on the concrete floor, blue eyes staring up at her but seeing nothing. She gasped, backed away, and shut the door, locking it instinctively even though she knew Henry was dead.

Katherine turned around and looked at Abel. She was out of breath. She put her hand on her chest, closed her eyes, and inhaled slowly through her nose. Fear was replaced with a blooming relief. "Abel," she said, stepping toward him.

Abel pulled away suddenly. He returned Katherine's gaze, but was shaking his head with despondence. She thought at first that he was retreating to his corner of the living room, but he was in fact moving toward the stairs – not the cellar stairs, but the ones leading up to the second floor. He stopped outside the door to the closet. Then he turned and disappeared inside.

"Abel?" Katherine said. "I did it, Abel. He's gone." She walked to the closet door and felt the lingering cold remains of his presence. She touched the knob and found it locked. "Abel?"

And then there was a loud moaning sound, startling her. When Katherine turned she saw, standing in the room just outside the cellar door, a new shape. She blinked in an effort to clear her vision. Horror enveloped her body as she realized that it was a man, staring at her. But no, that was not quite correct. Not anymore.

It was not a man but a ghost – the tall, dark silhouette of the man who used to be Henry. She gasped and backed away as he slowly approached her. A bitter coldness filled the room as he loomed over her, black as night and vibrating with rage.

scared mary

I had nearly completed my daily run. The trail through the woods below our property had been cool on this early autumn evening, a hint of a breeze rustling through leaves that were just beginning to surrender their green. My exposed shoulders and legs had been chilly at first, but my skin was covered with a fine layer of sweat as I completed my five miles and left the trail for the macadam along Brookshire Road. I paused briefly to look both ways for any oncoming traffic and, seeing none, jogged onto the asphalt. The remaining quarter mile to the house was at a slight incline, and my legs, already tired, began to burn.

I waved to a neighbor as I jogged by; he nodded a greeting in return. The lights were on in most of the houses I passed, and I imagined that dinner was being either prepared or served in some of them, given the time of day. This reminded me that I hadn't given any thought yet as to what I had planned to make for my own family, nor had I remembered to discuss it with Ted before I had left for my run. I often feigned surprise whenever my 18-year-old boys would inevitably tell me they were hungry as 6:00 approached, playfully responding, "Didn't I just feed you yesterday?" There might a meatloaf in the freezer that I could thaw. Or perhaps Teddy would surprise me by making dinner for myself and the twins, and I would open the door to the pleasant aroma of baked chicken or spaghetti. It wasn't likely, but stranger things had happened.

Ahead of me, a rusted brown pickup truck was parked crookedly on the berm, the nose of it cutting a slice in the road, and I casually cursed at the inconvenience of having to jog around it. Overhead, a bird squawked at me, as if scolding me for running in the middle of the road. I looked up to see what kind of bird was making such a racket, and saw nothing but leaves and branches.

Veering right, I stepped quickly over the edge of our lawn and onto the sidewalk that leads to the front door. The mailbox lid was open, revealing nothing inside. I flipped it shut. Looking to the house, I saw that there were no lights coming from any of the windows, which was odd. When I had left for my run, the boys had been in their rooms, supposedly working on homework, while Ted had been in his office, editing. But now, no light came from any of the windows at all, and my mind immediately went back to the idea of dinner. Maybe my boys had run out to pick up a pizza. But no, if pizza was the order of the evening, delivery was always Ted's go-to. Plus they *never* remembered to turn off lights before leaving the house.

The driveway was empty, but that meant nothing. Ted and I both parked our cars in the garage.

As I made my way down the sidewalk, my jog having devolved into a stroll, my mind then came up with another explanation for the darkened house, and my heart, still pounding from my five mile run, sank.

Two words: *Scared Mary*.

"Scared Mary" is the name of a YouTube video, a video that went viral a little more than two years ago. The whole thing started because of one of those here-today-gone-tomorrow internet trends, the kind that inspires people with too much time on their hands to eat Tide Pods or dump buckets of ice on their heads. This particular trend, which not coincidentally rose to prominence around Halloween of that year, was really simple and not the least bit original: men scaring their wives or girlfriends, catching their mortified reactions on video, and uploading the clip to YouTube or TikTok for all the world to see and laugh at.

Teddy had found the whole idea ridiculously delightful, laughing gleefully at each new clip he discovered, often playing the choicest ones for me and the boys. I had to admit some of them were quite funny. But at the same time I felt a fleeting sympathy for each of these briefly terrified women, then relief for them when they eventually laughed at their own reaction.

It should not have surprised me at all when Ted conspired to create a video of his own. Not that he put much thought to it. He simply stepped into the bathroom one evening following my run, yanked back the shower curtain where I was rinsing off my sweat, and, phone at the ready and digitizing every moment, yelled, "Boo!"

I turned toward him and screamed. I had never screamed like that before in my life, nor knew myself capable of making such a sound, both loud and guttural, as if it originated in my toes and gained momentum as it erupted its way to my mouth. The sound filled the room and reverberated off the tiles. My hands, covered in soap, came up to either side of my face and shook violently, flinging tiny suds like spit. My eyes bulged wide. The sides of my mouth pulled down in a mortified frown as if tugged by invisible fish hooks. My entire face was frozen in terror, framed by my long black hair, which was plastered by hot water against my head.

Ted at first was so incredibly startled by my reaction that he jumped backwards, but then was so overcome by laughter that he sat down on the bathroom floor, his back against the wall. Tears streamed down his cheeks, which had begun to turn red.

My heart pounding, I snatched a towel from the rack and covered myself before stepping out of the tub. I wanted to yell at him, shout at him for scaring me so badly, but knew it was no good saying anything until he had quieted down and was actually able to hear me speak. As I waited, my fear gave way to anger, and as Ted continued to laugh uncontrollably on the floor, my anger began to melt away as well, and soon I was surprised to find myself smiling and, eventually, laughing right along with him. Laughing out of relief, and laughing simply because Ted's own howling was so contagious.

I sat down on the floor beside him. Wiping tears, he held up the phone and played back the video he had just taken. I was relieved to see he had only captured me from the shoulders up. At least my modesty was still intact, if not my dignity. And when I heard my own scream again and saw the circus mask of terror that I had managed to contort my face into, both Ted and I dissolved into a second fit of laughter that left our sides in stitches and our cheeks tear-stained.

Later that evening, after playing the video for our boys, who watched it at least a dozen times and laughed uproariously every single time, Ted asked me if he could put the video on YouTube.

"You don't know anything about putting videos on YouTube," I said.

"I'll figure it out," he insisted. "Can I do it?" He was like a child asking his mom to buy him a shiny new toy at the store when he has no allowance saved up and Christmas is still months away. His absolute glee swayed me, and I reluctantly said yes.

And I have regretted it ever since.

As I stepped toward our front door, the security lights sensed me and came on. I squinted as my eyes adjusted to their glare, and then I saw that the window beside the door was shattered inward, the glass spilling into the kitchen on the other side.

My shoulders slumped with disappointment. "Ted," I whispered, shaking my head and scolding him under my breath even though I knew he couldn't hear me. I guessed that the door was unlocked, and sure enough the knob turned easily in my hand. I stepped inside, flipping on the kitchen lights. Glass crunched quietly under my sneakers. The room was empty. And there was no aroma of supper. But my disappointment at the lack of dinner was slight compared to the idea of having to replace what had been a perfectly good kitchen window.

"Ted?" I called out. "Just come out, please. I'm in no mood."

Silence responded.

Ted had titled the bathroom video clip "Scared Mary." He read enough to figure out that he needed to create a YouTube channel of his own before he could upload the clip and, in a moment of zero inspiration, he likewise named his new YouTube channel "Scared Mary." And so "Scared Mary" the video was uploaded to "Scared Mary" the YouTube channel, and in short order, Ted began texting and e-mailing the URL of the clip to his coworkers, his brothers, his golfing buddies… pretty much everyone he had ever gone to school with, worked with, or hung from the same family tree.

Within the week, the video went viral. Who knows why these things happen. Ted's video was one of literally hundreds of clips of husbands scaring their unsuspecting wives, but for reasons neither of us could ever explain, Ted's video took root and grew like a virtual weed. Hundreds of views became thousands, thousands became hundreds of thousands, and hundreds of thousands became a million and more. Friends of mine texted to say they had seen the clip, not because Ted had sent it to them, but because a friend or family member had shared it with them. A woman in the grocery store recognized me, stopping me to say her husband had nearly had a heart attack from laughter after watching the clip. My mom, who had likewise come to view the video from an indirect source, called to ask me if I was okay. Soon parody videos began to appear like an acne outbreak, one of them auto-tuning my scream to a techno beat, the resulting song a catchy ear worm that itself garnered thousands of views and was later available to download from iTunes or stream on Spotify.

Ted became obsessed. Before long, the video had so many views, and his YouTube had so many subscribers, that he was qualified to monetize any future content he uploaded. I could see the light twinkling in his eyes as he planned how best to build upon an opportunity that had presented itself to him seemingly out of nowhere. But doing so would mean creating new content.

Over the next few weeks, Ted scared me. A lot. He hid behind doors. In the shower. Under the bed. Outside of windows. In the basement. He once hid in the woods along the trail that I ran, jumping out behind a tree as I jogged by. He captured every single reaction on video. A handful of the clips were unusable or not satisfactory, but in many of them, my terrified scream and mortified grimace were exactly the content Ted had wanted. These new clips were uploaded, and while none of them went viral like the original "Scared Mary" video had done, Ted's subscriber base grew and he racked up millions of total views. And as he was now able to monetize the videos, he began to generate a small side income, a minuscule comfort to me as I found myself increasingly unsettled and on edge inside my own home.

The wheels in Ted's head were always turning. He knew that in time, his viewers would grow tired of his simple jump scare videos starring himself and his hapless wife. His content needed to evolve and become more elaborate if he wanted to keep his subscribers interested. So he began utilizing props and costumes. Soon, I was screaming as mechanized spiders fell from cabinets, jumping when ghostly moans emanated loudly from dark closets, and recoiling at the sight of severed heads resting atop silver platters on the top shelf of the fridge.

From there, Ted began buying even more elaborate props: giant mechanical clowns that lunged and cackled when I inadvertently stepped on a button on the floor, ghostly little girls whose faces glowed in the dark, their heads spinning as they laughed, and zombies that would spring out from under the bed as I walked by. Ted and I eventually had to sit down together and create an actual budget for the Scared Mary channel, allocating funds for additional props, costumes, lights, and sound effects. We initially cleared out a corner of the wine cellar to store all of these items, and when the Scared Mary inventory outgrew that space, Ted erected a storage shed in the back yard to house it all.

I kept waiting for this phase to pass, just like the internet trend that had inspired it in the first place, but for whatever reason, Ted's channel continued to grow in popularity. He enlisted the help of our boys, Jamie and Jesse, who delighted in helping their father set up each new scare. The three of them had an easy and hilarious screen chemistry that no doubt attracted viewers. Jamie, the more creative of the twins, came up with a logo for the channel – a stylized illustration of my mortified face, mid-scream – and Ted began to sell Scared Mary t-shirts, hoodies, and mugs. As the channel grew, so did the revenue, and one of the biggest surprises was when I began to receive royalty checks for the "Scared Mary" song that featured my auto-tuned scream. The catchy tune had been downloaded so many times that it had briefly become a top 10 dance track on iTunes and its producer – some nameless, faceless music studio geek out of California – had proactively listed me as a performer and co-producer on the song, which entitled me to royalties, a move he had probably made in an effort to keep me or Ted from suing.

Eventually, the revenue from the channel eclipsed Ted's salary at work, and we had the conversation I had suspected for months was coming: Ted wanted to quit his 9-to-5 and focus solely on being a You-Tuber. Methodical as always, he had mapped out a six month, one year, and five year plan for the channel that included additional merchandising avenues, licensing opportunities, and ideas for further content. He presented his plans to me as if we were in a board room and I was his CEO. Already Ted had been contacted by a toy company that wanted to make a Scared Mary doll ("Pull the string – *she screams*!"), and on the kitchen table was an ever-growing stack of screenplays and treatments for a possible *Scared Mary* movie. A new one arrived seemingly every week. Ted read a few of them, all of which were garbage, but I knew that ultimately Ted wanted to write one himself.

Of course I consented to Ted's career change. The money spoke for itself, but even more compelling was the absolute delight he derived from this new endeavor. Instead of spending countless unrewarding hours imprisoned in a cubicle, he was curating a channel that brought laughter to himself and his growing subscriber base. Instead of dreading Mondays, he worked tirelessly on "Scared Mary" while also admitting it felt like he wasn't working at all. There was a vibrancy behind Ted's lightning blue eyes that I had only witnessed twice before: on our wedding day and on the day our sons were born.

But as I sat across the table from Ted, holding his hand as he concluded his proposal, nodding my blessing that he could give his two-week notice, I suddenly burst into tears. It caught us both by surprise.

Ted's face fell. "What is it?" he asked, and I saw fear wash over him: fear that I might change my answer.

"Ted, I'm… I'm just *so tired*. My nerves are shot. I can't…" My voice hitched. "I can't go on being afraid to live in my own house. Every waking moment I'm on edge. Every time I turn a corner, or open a door, or flip on a light switch, I don't know what might jump out at me. My nerves are shot."

Ted, still holding my hand, sat back in his chair. Realization dawned on his face. He had been so wrapped up in the channel, so invigorated by its success that he had not realized his good fortune had come at a price. It was a price that I had been paying for months but had kept quietly to myself because I didn't want to crush his enthusiasm.

"Oh Mare," he said, squeezing my hand. "You always end up laughing along with me in the end. I never even thought… I'm so sorry."

And so Ted promised to change direction. He began producing videos that did not include me. Sometimes he would frighten the boys. He also set up scares along public walkways and recorded the reactions of startled strangers. Sometimes these pranks nearly resulted in fist fights, but usually the scared-then-relieved passersby were more than happy to appear in a video on the Scared Mary channel. He started doing horror movie reviews along with the boys. And he attended pop culture and horror conventions, setting up a table with Scared Mary merchandise where he sold caps and buttons and even DVD compilations of his video clips.

Eventually he asked me to go along with him. "I know it's not your scene," he said, "but nine out of ten people who come to the booth ask where you are. You *are* the star of the channel, after all."

I was reluctant to go and told him as much.

"Most of the people there are really cool," he said. "And how many times in your life have you had a crowd of people asking for your autograph?"

And so I went with him. Twice. And both times were a terrible mistake. People would approach the booth, some of them in pedestrian clothes, some of them wearing the most horrific costumes and make-up imaginable. They would ask for an autograph on a small poster or t-shirt, and while I was in the midst of signing, they would scream or yell or lunge at me, capturing my reaction on their cell phone, which had been recording me clandestinely. Sometimes I was so startled that the autograph would be ruined, but that seemed to delight them all the more. There seemed to be a competition to see who could walk away with the most illegible autograph of all. The clips would hit the internet with the hashtag, "IScaredMary". By the end of both conventions, I was completely strung out.

Ted stopped asking me to come with him. But since I stopped coming to the fans, the fans started coming to me. I received a handful of glitter bombs in the mail, innocent-looking packages that exploded with confetti when opened, equipped with video cameras that caught my startled reaction. #IScaredMary. More than once, fans of the channel hid in our bushes or behind our trees, jumping out when I exited the house. #IScaredMary. I told Ted that I was beginning to fear what extremes one of these anonymous fans might go to in order to record a great "Scared Mary" video of their own. We eventually had to unlist our phone numbers and home address.

That should have been the end of my affiliation with everything Scared Mary. And were it not for that stupid name, I probably could have turned my back on it forever and left it completely in Ted's hands.

But because of that name, that name that Ted had picked in a moment of sheer unoriginality, I was forever linked with Ted's unexpectedly lucrative side-project-cum-career. So while he agreed to divert the bulk of his output to other creeps and scares and things that go bump in the night, he explained to me that every once in awhile he would need to create a new, authentic "Scared Mary" video. "Give the people what they want," he said. "It's right there in the name."

We tried faking a few, staging the scares so that I knew what was coming. But the results were no good. I don't think I'm a terrible actress, but there was simply no pulling off the kind of reaction that spontaneously happened when I was genuinely frightened. And so, very reluctantly, I had agreed: Ted could scare me once every three months, meaning that the channel could have a total of four new and genuine "Scared Mary" videos per year.

He was delighted.

But of course, Ted couldn't just rest on his laurels. Each new video had to outdo the last. He didn't like repeating himself creatively.

All of this history came flooding back to me as I stood in my dark kitchen, nothing but the sound of grinding glass under my feet as I shifted my weight.

"Ted!" I yelled out again, tossing my keys on the kitchen table. "Not tonight. I am *not* in the mood. So wherever you and the boys are hiding, come out. I'm tired and I'm hungry and…"

As if on cue, the door to the walk-in pantry opened, slowly. It creaked on its hinges. I turned my head in the direction of the sound, my heart both sinking and somehow feeling completely numb at the same time. But the kitchen was dark and so was the pantry, so as the door opened, I couldn't see anything beyond it.

I could hear raspy breathing and a sinister giggle. There was a clicking sound as the string was pulled on the pantry's lone light bulb. And there, standing amongst the shelves of canned goods and boxed pasta, was Ted. He was wearing a nondescript blue jumpsuit. He had also donned a white mask, one of those featureless portraits that are calm and benign but also unsettling. His hair looked oily and disheveled, and the light from the bulb above reflected off the long knife he held down at one side. I estimated the price of his entire ensemble to be somewhere around $75 unless he had managed to get it on sale a Spirit Halloween some year prior. He giggled again, the noise a stark contrast to the mask's unsmiling face.

I walked to the nearest wall and turned on a kitchen light before putting put my hands on my hips and regarded him straight-on. Now bathed in more light, I noticed that his jumpsuit was covered in fresh blood, the mask spattered with it, the knife dripping it on the other-wise clean linoleum.

Ted stared back at me, unmoving.

"You need a haircut," I said.

He said nothing. His breathing was loud and raspy.

Frustrated, I picked up my keys from the table. The ring held pepper spray. I pointed it at him. "You know, I would give you a face full of this right now but I don't feel like helping you wash it out afterwards," I said.

He didn't react.

"Whatever," I said, tossing the keys back down on the table. "I told you I'm not in the mood. I'm getting some wine. You and the boys decide what you want for dinner."

I walked past the pantry door. Ted watched me go, turning his head slowly in the direction of my path, the mask an expressionless slate.

I opened the cellar door and flipped the switch at the top of the stairs. Nothing happened. "Nice. Once again you thought of every-thing." Undeterred, I fished my cell phone from my pocket, activated the flashlight, and proceeded with caution down the dark steps.

What I saw down there at first gave me a bit of start, but I willed myself not to scream. It was Jamie, hanging by his neck from one of the beams overhead. His face was swollen and had a sickly purplish hue. The sight was unsettling, especially when illuminated by my cell phone light. No mother wants to see her teenage son like that, not even in my current land of make-believe, but it wasn't the worst condition I'd ever found him in. I'd definitely seen him more dead and bloody before.

I stared at him. He stared back at me, swinging slightly, unblink-ing. His shadow swung on a far wall. I didn't bother trying to locate the fishing wire that was actually holding him up there.

"Impressive make-up job," I said, pushing him aside slightly as I made my way past him to the wine racks. "You and Jesse are getting really good at that."

I scanned the bottles with my cell phone light. "I don't feel like cooking, so you and your father and brother need to decide what you're going to pick up. Sooner rather than later, thank you. I'm starved."

Jamie was a silent pendulum.

Bottle in hand, I turned away from him and back toward the stairs.

Ted waited for me at the top, a dark silhouette against the bright lights of the kitchen, knife by his side.

I didn't hesitate. I pounded up the steps.

"Move," I said when I was about halfway up.

He didn't budge.

At the top, I planted one elbow in his stomach, gently but firmly, and pushed him aside. My arm sank deeply into the flesh of his belly. He stepped back.

"Do a sit-up every once in awhile," I said as I walked past him, immediately feeling childish and remorseful for the comment. Ted ran as often as I did; he didn't deserve the snark. But I wasn't about to apologize, either.

I located a corkscrew in a drawer and popped the cork from the bottle more effortlessly than I ever had before. Ted watched me silently. He barely shifted. He fidgeted with the knife, picking at one pant leg with the sharp tip.

"Cut, that's a wrap," I said as I plucked a wine glass from the cabinet. I filled it near to the rim and took a tiny sip. I sucked in a breath. "Do we need some kind of safe word or something?" I asked. "Something that signals that the jig is up and we're done playing Scared Mary?"

He didn't move. Or speak.

I dropped the bottle loudly on the counter. "Whatever. I give up." Wine glass in hand, I brushed past Ted and through the living room door.

I flipped on a light switch. This one worked.

I didn't react to what I saw. Instead, I walked across the room and plopped down on the sofa, wine glass still pinched between the fingers of my right hand. I crossed my legs and shook my head defiantly. My suspended foot bounced with frustrated energy.

Ted, having turned, watched me from the doorway. The mask made him look dull.

Jesse was at my feet, face down on the carpet in front of the sofa. I'd had to step over him to sit down. He was totally still. He might have looked like he was napping there, except that his face was facing directly down, uncomfortably so, nose buried in the fibers, and all around him was a large, red, wet stain.

"Hold your breath, Jesse," I said, taking another sip. "Don't let me catch you breathing." I chuckled, but it really wasn't funny. "I cannot imagine what the carpet cleaning bill is going to be."

Ted continued guarding the doorway.

"Look," I said, putting the wine glass down on a side table with enough force to threaten breaking the stem. "When I'm done, I'm done, Ted. How many times do I have to say it?" Irritation rose in my voice, and I felt a thrumming in my chest. I had never felt so angry with him before.

He didn't move or respond.

"*Go!*" I yelled, planting both feet on the floor but forcing myself to remain seated. "Either go get dinner, or go start cleaning up the mess you made, I don't care which. Just *go!*"

To my surprise, he did. After a long pause, his shoulders slumped a little. Slowly, he turned from the doorway, back into the kitchen and out of sight. Momentarily, I heard the front door open and close again with a quiet click.

I took a deep breath. The house was completely silent. I sat back on the sofa and exhaled, crossing my legs once again. Picking up the wine glass once more, I drank deeply. It was difficult to swallow.

Distantly, I heard a vehicle door open and close. Then an engine started, rattling and throaty. It roared and then faded into the distance.

I shook my head. Looking around the room, I wondered where Ted might have hidden the cameras for this particular episode of "Scared Mary." I couldn't find them. But that didn't mean they weren't there.

I sipped. The house was now unsettlingly quiet. There was no sound from the basement. No sound from upstairs. I wondered what I might have found if I had gone up there.

With one foot, I nudged Jesse's leg. It rolled away from me and back again. "Get up, sweetheart. It's over now. Get up."

Another sip. Another nudge.

"Get up."

something else entirely

The conference would take me away from home for only two days, but Amy remained stubbornly nervous about it. This would be the first time since the night of our wedding that she would be sleeping alone, and the house was still new enough to us to carry that slightly unsettling air of unfamiliarity. It didn't help that the move had taken a city girl out of the city, leaving Amy to long for the comforting sounds of traffic and the chatter of nearby neighbors. We had traded those familiar surroundings for a rancher in the middle of the woods, its front yard spotted with looming pines and bisected by a narrow dirt driveway, nearly half a mile long, that ended in a winding gravel road yet another mile or so away from our closest neighbors, whom we had yet to meet in person, but had left a pie and a card ("Welcome to the neighborhood – Bryan and Becca") on our doorstep a couple of days after we moved in.

"It's only two nights, babe," I reminded her as I straightened my tie in the mirror. She stood behind me, apprehensively, intentionally or not blocking my exit from the bathroom. She was trying to guilt me into staying, even though she knew I had no choice, and I smiled at the sight of her pouty lower lip. That lip had worked its magic on me more than once in the past, but on this morning I was resolute to resist.

"I know," she said.

I turned around and gave her peck on the lips. She pulled me close, kissing me more deeply, forcing me to be the one to break our embrace. "You said you were looking forward to some time to yourself to decorate," I reminded her.

"That's what I said," she responded.

"And if it gets too quiet you can raise the roof with some Adele and I won't be here to complain."

She rolled her eyes and smiled, but just barely, and retreated just far enough for me to squeeze through the bathroom door. She shadowed me to the kitchen, where I reached down to pick up my briefcase. Sybil, our long-haired white cat, rubbed her cheek against the back of my hand, and with one finger I gave her an brief scratch behind the ears.

"Plus you've got Sybil to keep you company. Our vicious attack cat."

Amy, still dressed in a white terrycloth robe she had donned after her shower, scooped up the cat and held her close to her chest. I could hear Sybil purring loudly and I scratched her again. The feline gazed at me lazily with shining green eyes.

"You have the phone number at the hotel."

"Yes," Amy said.

"Call me anytime, ok? And I'll call you when the plane lands."

"Call me when you get to the airport," she insisted.

I stepped forward and kissed her again, the cat between us, and I could feel Sybil's motor vibrating against my chest.

I stepped through the door connecting the kitchen to the garage. "Bye, babe," I said over my shoulder as I tapped the button to raise the garage door. As it ascended, morning sunshine sliced into the room, light bouncing off the surface of my car. As I reached for the door handle, I caught sight of something just outside, crouched in the driveway. It was only a silhouette in the blinding light of the low sun, but best I could tell it was a rather large rat or perhaps a possum. Its back end was raised up, head low, its fur raised in gleaming black spikes.

I didn't have much time to consider the animal, because Amy let out a loud gasp that startled me, and immediately I saw Sybil, sailing through the air beside me as she leapt from Amy's arms. The cat made silent contact with the concrete floor of the garage and was out the door before I could even react. The other animal – the rat or the possum of whatever it was – darted away, and Sybil disappeared after it.

"No!" Amy cried out, and the two of us walked quickly together onto the driveway. It took a moment for my eyes to adjust to the sunlight. A rustling of leaves and branches betrayed where the animals had disappeared into the woods on the north side of the yard. We stood and stared.

"Sybil!" Amy cried out, small panic in her voice, and I stifled a chuckle. Never had the cat responded to the sound of her name. Nor did we often use it. We were more likely to call her "kitty" or "Sybs" or "fuzzy butt" or, in my case, "idiot" than we were to ever call her Sybil.

Amy looked at me pleadingly.

"She'll come back," I said. "Don't worry." I might as well have asked Amy not to breathe.

"But what if she doesn't?" she asked.

"Cats always do," I said, making my way back into the garage and toward the car.

"Eric," she called after me.

I looked at my watch. "I have to go, babe. I'll miss my flight."

I gave her another quick peck on the lips, which were dry and pressed tightly together. She looked defeated. I cursed the cat's terrible timing.

Climbing reluctantly into the car, I started the engine and rolled down the driver's side window. Amy leaned over to look inside, her arms crossed. "She'll come back," I said again. "Love you." I began backing the car out of the garage.

"Love you too," she responded quietly, and stepped back from the car.

* * *

An hour later, at the airport, I called Amy.

"Hey," she said.

"I'm at the airport. I have about 20 minutes until departure and everything's on time."

"Good," she responded. Her tone was soft.

"Any sign of the idiot?" I asked.

"No," she sighed.

"She'll come back."

"So you said," she responded.

"Babe, it'll be fine," I said, adopting a lighter tone. "Just try to distract yourself for awhile. If you stand around thinking about it, she'll never return. Just dive into something and the next thing you know, she'll be at the front door."

She sighed again. "You're probably right."

"I know I'm right."

"Okay," she said. "Call me when you land?"

"Will do. Love you."

But I didn't call Amy when the plane landed. I was met at the gate by an engineer from the job site. Instead of continuing on to the hotel as planned, I was whisked away to an impromptu meeting with several of my higher-ups, and in the ensuing bustle and stress, I completely forgot to call.

It wasn't until several hours later that I finally opened the door to my hotel room. I threw the briefcase down on the bed and collapsed, face down, beside it. The bedspread smelled musty and faintly of cigarette smoke. My skin felt greasy and I couldn't wait to lose my tie. But first I rolled over, pulling my phone out of my pocket, expecting several missed calls. But there were only two.

"Hey, it's me," Amy said in the first one. "I think you forgot to call me when you landed. So call me when you get this." Her tone was light and surprisingly upbeat.

"Me again," began the second message. "Just let me know you're okay, okay? Sybs isn't back yet, but I have an idea."

I dialed Amy's cell and sat up on the bed.

"Hey stranger," she answered.

"Sorry, babe," I said, loosening my tie with my free hand. "Greg Thompson met me at the airport and took me right to the job site. I literally haven't had a free moment until right now."

"That's what I figured," she said. "It's ok. Everything going all right? You must be exhausted."

"I am," I responded, realizing that I was. Typically a night owl, tonight all I wanted to do was take a scalding shower and fall asleep. "I think I'll call it an early night. Still no sign of the cat?"

"No, but I have an idea," she said, and by her tone I could tell she was smiling.

"Yeah, what's that?" I asked.

"I raised the garage door. Just a bit. Like maybe eight inches. And I put a plate of tuna inside that rabbit trap we found."

It took me a minute to picture what Amy was saying. And then I remembered that among the random junk we inherited when we bought the rancher was a rabbit trap, a small, rectangular cage that would snap shut when a center mechanism was triggered. It was actually a good idea. Sybs would come in, go for the tuna, and be stuck in the cage until morning.

"Do you know how to set the trap?" I asked.

"Yes, I know how to set the trap," she said in an exaggerated tone. "I'm not that helpless."

"No, you're not that helpless." I yawned loudly.

"Go to bed," she insisted. "Wake up tomorrow and be brilliant."

"Will do. Love you, babe."

"Me too," she responded. Our call ended.

* * *

I woke up the next morning sprawled across the bed, my skin cold from sleeping alone. I stretched, my feet poking out from under the covers. A sliver of light was shining from between the curtains, falling right across my eyes like hot iron. I sat up and looked at the bedside clock. It was 7:23 a.m. I had plenty of time to grab breakfast and a shower before I needed to report to the job site. Picking up my phone, I saw that I had a text from Amy.

"Call me when you wake up," it said.

I called. She answered immediately.

"Hey babe," I said.

"Hey," she answered. Her voice was hushed.

"You okay?" I asked. "Did Sybs come back?"

Amy hesitated. "She did," she said softly.

"Oooookay," I responded. "What's wrong? Is she hurt?"

"No, she's…" Amy began, but she didn't finish.

"What is it?" I asked.

I heard a noise from the other end of the phone, and recognized it as the sound of a door being opened. I heard Amy's feet as they scuffled across concrete. I knew she was in the garage. The next sound I heard was hard to distinguish at first, but it grew louder as Amy got closer to it. It was a low mewing sound. Mournful and slow.

"Is that Sybs?" I asked.

"Yes."

"I've never heard her make that sound before."

"Me neither."

"Where is she?"

"She's in the cage."

"In the cage? Is she injured?" I asked again.

"I can't tell," Amy said. There was a long pause and then she said, "Eric, I think something's wrong."

"What?" I asked.

"Just…" she hesitated again. "Well, look."

A second later, my phone chimed with a new message. I opened it up and the screen filled with an image. The trap, situated in the middle of our garage, sat on the floor where my car was normally parked. Sybil was lying in the middle of it, looking directly at the camera. She looked calm, but her wide eyes looked more yellow than green — something I chalked up to a trick of the light — and her mouth was hanging slightly open. She almost looked surprised. Her coat was as white as always, if a little disheveled. I saw no signs of injury.

"Amy?" I asked. "What is it? She looks fine."

"Something's not right," Amy said. "I don't know. Something's not right."

* * *

My morning was one meeting stacked upon another, one of which was mine to moderate. It took a conscious effort to shake Amy and that stupid cat out of my mind. I had reassured her that I would check in with her again as soon as possible, but it might be lunchtime or later before the opportunity would allow. To my relief it only took me a couple of minutes into my presentation to hit my stride, and when it was over I was awarded with several handshakes and pats on the back that momentarily made me forget about any drama at home.

Shortly after noon, I was walking down a hallway to the men's room, relieved to be free of the conference room for the first time all morning. I pulled my phone from my pocket and was greeted with several text messages from Amy. Each one contained a picture of Sybil. The cat was no longer in the cage but inside the house. Sybil on a kitchen chair. Sybil in the living room window. Sybil on our bed. Sybil on the floor. There was nothing at all particularly noteworthy about any of these images, and I felt myself beginning to get frustrated with Amy. But with each successive picture, I felt myself growing increasingly uneasy. In every shot, Sybil was sitting bolt upright, straight as an arrow, looking directly at the camera, her eyes wide and yellow, her mouth ever so slightly open. The images made me uncomfortable in a way that I couldn't rationalize.

I called Amy.

"Did you see the pictures?" she asked, her voice hushed.

"Yes," I answered. "She looks okay to me." It wasn't a complete lie. "What do you think is wrong?"

"Eric," she whispered. "I don't think that's Sybil."

"Don't be silly," I said, internalizing a scoff. "Of course it is."

"No. She feels different. Her fur is too coarse. I don't like to touch her."

"Maybe she's just dirty," I offered. "She did just spend the night in the woods."

"And she sounds weird. You heard her. She sounds off."

I paused, thinking. "I don't know, babe. Do you want to take her to the vet?"

She released a sigh of frustration. "No."

"Why not?"

"Because it's not her."

"Amy," I chided.

"It's *not*," she insisted in a loud whisper. "It's like… someone's bad idea of her."

I was beginning to get irritated. "I don't know what to tell you," I said. "She looks fine to me."

"She doesn't look fine to me," she responded, lowering her tone.

"Why are you whispering?" I asked. "I can barely hear you."

"Because she's *listening* to me," Amy said. "She follows me everywhere. And stares."

* * *

Meetings resumed after lunch. I was seated at the head of a large table, men and women in suits on all sides. My presentation over, my only real duty for the afternoon was to sit and listen, or at least pretend to. My thoughts wandered to home, and I wrestled with concern for Amy, even though deep down I felt that she was overreacting. At the very least I felt sympathetic that she was concerned about her cat and was having to deal with the situation by herself. It occurred to me that we hadn't even thought to find a new vet for Sybil since we had moved to the new house.

When my work day was over, I made excuses to get out of having a late dinner with my coworkers, feigning a headache and promising to see them all again early the next morning. I received a few more handshakes and even an awkward high five, and I did my best to force a smile in return.

I waited until the solitude of my hotel room before looking at my phone again, a tight feeling in my chest as I did so. There was a single voicemail from Amy waiting for me.

"Eric," she said, and her voice was shaky. I couldn't tell if she was crying or scared. Or both. Before she said another word, I heard a sound in the background. A low, mournful mewing in the distance. "Do you hear that?" she asked. She paused, and the sound grew louder. It was awful and full of foreboding. My back and arms broke out in goosebumps as I listened.

"She's outside," Amy continued, and her voice laden with regret. "I couldn't take it anymore. The staring. I pushed her out the door with a broom. That was two hours ago. She hasn't stopped making that sound." Amy's voice hitched, and once again I heard Sybil's cry, unpleasant and low, amazingly loud for it to be emanating from outside.

I called Amy's cell. She answered with a whisper, saying my name. I could hear Sybil's low moans continuing in the background.

"Ames," I said. "Where are you?"

"I'm in the bedroom," she said.

"Is the cat still outside?"

"Yes," she answered. "Eric, I don't know what to do. She's been making that sound for hours. And she's still following me around."

"What do you mean?" I asked.

"I was washing dishes at the kitchen sink, and she was right outside the window, looking at me. Then I saw her outside the living room window when I went in there. Every room I go to, she's just outside the window. Sitting in the grass and looking at me. And making that sound." Amy began to cry.

"Do you want me to come home?" I asked.

I was surprised when she responded with a weak chuckle. "It's so ridiculous, Eric," she said. "It's just a stupid cat." She sniffed. "No, it's stupid. I can't ask you to come home."

"I wish I was there," I said.

"Me too."

"I'll be home tomorrow evening and we'll figure this out, okay?"

"Okay," she said.

"Put in some earplugs and try to sleep. I love you."

"Love you too," she responded, stifling a cry. As I pulled the phone away from my ear to end the call, the last sound I heard was Sybil, moaning.

* * *

I was awakened by a chiming sound that roused me from a deep sleep. The hotel room was so dark and quiet that at first I couldn't recall where I was. My waking mind eventually recognized the sound as an incoming message on my cell phone. I sat up quickly and grabbed my phone, my heart beating rapidly in my chest, my mind fighting through a thick fog of sleep.

The message from Amy was a single picture. It was blurry and almost completely white: a photo taken with a bright flash in a completely dark room. It took me a moment to recognize what I was seeing. Amy had taken the picture while sitting up in bed. The wall of the bedroom was visible beyond the foot of the bed, as was Amy's vanity and one of our wedding pictures on the far wall, all of it bathed in shadow. The white blur in the foreground was mostly comprised of our bedspread covering Amy's legs. And on her lap sat Sybil, her disheveled fur blindingly white, her eyes wide and fixed hard on Amy.

I turned on the light beside the bed and called Amy's cell. It rang three times, then went to voicemail. I hung up and tried again. "Amy," I said, surprised to find myself out of breath. "Amy, call me."

I paced the floor. I sat on the bed. I looked again at the picture Amy had sent me. I grabbed my suitcase from the closet and began throwing clothes into it. I tried Amy's cell again. I closed the suitcase and sat down next to it. "This is ridiculous," I said out loud, and fell back on the bed. I stared at the white ceiling, at a fine crack that made its way from a corner of the room to a spot which ended with a water stain right above my head. For several minutes, my mind and my heart raced, and yet somehow, at some point, my eyes drifted shut and I went back to sleep.

* * *

The gray haired man in the blue suit standing at the far end of the room might as well have been speaking Japanese for all I was comprehending. My mind was far off – at home with Amy – not at this blasted meeting, surrounded by people in suits talking circles around the same discussion points that had been raised countless times in yesterday's sessions. I entertained the desire to upend the table, march across the room, and throttle him. I was allowing my uneasiness to give way to anger, finding some temporary relief in channeling my anxiety at something other than the weirdness happening at home.

I had of course attempted to call Amy again before I had left the hotel, and once more had gotten nothing but voicemail. My schedule for the day was a single, three-hour meeting, followed by a drive to the airport and a flight home. I considered lying my way out of the meeting and getting an earlier flight, but I let better sense persuade me. I reminded myself that I, and my wife, were getting worked up by the odd behavior of a stupid cat. Now I imagined throttling Sybil, throwing her like a beanbag against any available hard surface, and I bit my lip.

My phone chimed in my lap, and I jumped. A few of my coworkers seated nearby cast sidelong glances of disapproval. I picked up the phone, keeping it hidden under the table, and clicked on a new text from Amy. The image was a blur. I stared at it hard, but could make out nothing. It was white and red and brown and shapeless. I furrowed my brow.

Another text. Another image. Amy's foot, out of focus. The toenails painted red. A third image, indecipherable. A fourth image, nothing but a blur of white. A fifth image, this one clearer than the rest. Half of Amy's face, reflected in the mirror of her vanity. A fresh scratch on her cheek. She wasn't looking at her reflection. Her eyes were off to the side and cast downward, the look on her face forlorn.

"Excuse me," I said as I stood up from the table and exited the conference room. In the hallway I called Amy's cell. It rang once and then stopped.

"Amy?" I said.

Silence.

No, not silence. Breathing.

"Amy?" I asked again.

"Eh-RICK?" she said, and my skin broke out in goosebumps. She sounded odd. Almost like she was drunk.

"Are you ok?"

She took a deep breath. "Come. Home."

"Come home?" I asked. I thought for a moment. "Okay, I'm coming home."

"Eric?" she said again. "I killed Sybil."

"Okay, baby. It's okay. I'll be there as soon as I can."

"Come home," she repeated.

* * *

The drive to the airport. The wait in line. The flight. The drive home. All seemed interminable. The sky was black when I finally made the turn into our driveway. The house itself was completely dark, no light emanating from any of the windows, no exterior floods illuminated. I raised the garage door, but stopped short of pulling the car in when I caught sight of the rabbit trap, still sitting in the middle of the garage floor. I killed the engine and exited the car. As I walked past the trap, I saw a white paper plate resting in the middle of it, licked clean.

I opened the door to the kitchen and stepped inside. All was dark and silent. I flipped on a light. "Amy?" I called out. I threw my car keys on the table. They clashed noisily in the still quiet of the house. "Amy?" I yelled again.

I went to the living room and turned on the light. She wasn't there. I ventured room to room, turning on lights in each one, calling out her name. But Amy was nowhere to be found, and the house was unsettlingly silent.

Back in the kitchen, my mind raced. I should try calling her again. I reached into my pocket for my phone, but then I realized I didn't have it; I had left it in the car.

I retrieved the phone from the car and shut the door. Standing there in the driveway, I noted how strangely silent the surrounding woods were. No chirping crickets, no croaking toads. I looked through the darkness to the edge of the woods at the north side of the driveway, to the small open space where Sybil had pursued whatever strange animal had wandered into our driveway two days ago. I imagined that I heard a branch snap. I decided not to linger. I reentered the house through the kitchen door and locked it behind me.

Back inside, I walked into our empty bedroom and called Amy's cell. It rang twice and then connected.

Breathing.

"Amy?" I asked.

"Eric?"

"Where are you?" I pleaded.

"Here," she said, and the call abruptly ended.

I threw my phone down on the bed and ran my fingers through my hair. I was wondering if I should call the police when I was suddenly startled by a sound from outside. I couldn't tell what it was, but the word that immediately entered my mind was *wailing*. Low, slow, mournful wailing. It was loud but also distant. I tried to convince myself that the voice wasn't familiar to me.

Looking out the bedroom window I could see nothing but darkness and the vaguest hint of the tree line behind our house. I fell back on the bed, grabbed one of my pillows and put it over my head, hoping to muffle the sound. My heart was pounding.

I spent the dark post-midnight hours attempting to call Amy again, to no avail. Sometime later, who knows how much time later, in the darkness of the bedroom, in the stillness of the night, and without realizing it was happening, I fell asleep, the continuing sound outside like a distant, horrible lullaby.

* * *

The next morning, as sunlight penetrated the window shades, washing the bedroom in a dim yellow light, I was awakened by the sound of my phone, chiming. I fished it out from the covers and looked at the screen. There was a new text message. From Amy. A single picture.

It took me a moment to decipher what it was, and when I did, my entire body went numb. It was me, asleep in bed. I sat up with a jerk, my entire body an electric wire of fear.

Only then did I see her. Amy, crouched in the far corner of our bedroom.

Only it wasn't Amy.

Her mouth hung open on one side, a string of drool dangling from her lip. One eye was larger than the other and had drifted slightly to one side. Her hair was wildly disheveled and even across the room I detected an odd, earthy smell coming from her.

No, this wasn't Amy. This was someone's bad idea of Amy. She smiled at me, a crooked, hideous expression. I gave her a wide berth as I exited the bedroom, not wanting to get anywhere near her. She followed me with her eyes and then rose slowly to her feet and shadowed me quietly out of the room.

And now, no matter where I go, Amy follows.

nancy

It all started with a whisper.

I was nearing the end of a recurring dream, one in which I was late for class and could not remember my locker combination, a predicament not apparently shared by any of my nearby classmates. I have this dream frequently. If I were to rank my nocturnal reruns, among the greatest hits would be this one, the one where it's finals week and I realize with horror that I haven't attended a single class all semester, and the one where two or more of my teeth randomly begin falling out. Jenna, bless her, claims to never dream, or if she does, she doesn't remember any of them. I envy her that.

The dream always ends with me, alone in the hallway as the other students had successfully departed with their armloads of textbooks, struggling at the combination lock, the next period bell screaming overhead. Only this time, the dream ended differently. Someone stepped up behind me, so quietly that I did not know that they were there until they whispered in my ear. Their breath was not warm on my neck, but icy cold, and their voice was in a strange, sexless register, too high for a man but too low for a woman. And this voice whispered a single word. A name.

"*Nancy.*"

I sat up in bed. Though the voice had spoken softly, I could almost hear it echoing through the bedroom, remnants of it clinging to the walls like cobwebs of sound, and I wondered if in fact I had dreamed what I had heard or if it had been spoken in the waking world, rousing me from sleep. But the room was still and dark and empty of anything, or anyone, unusual.

I glanced over at Jenna, but she was sound asleep, her breathing deep and steady.

It happened again the next night. My fingers were frantically turn-ing the dial on the unresponsive combination lock as the school bell screamed accusatorily overhead. This time, just as the voice spoke into my ear, I felt the pressure of a single finger on my upper back, poking the muscle with uncomfortable force, causing pain, the coldness of the digit just as frigid at the voice itself as it whispered:

"*Nancy.*"

I once again shot up in bed, wide-eyed, a small groan falling lamely from my mouth as I did so. I squeezed my eyes shut and shook my head, shedding the dream.

Jenna stirred. "Are you okay?" she inquired from the darkness.

I sucked in a deep breath. "I think so," I responded as I exhaled.

She placed a hand on my back and immediately withdrew it. My skin was covered with an icy sweat.

"You're soaking wet," she said.

"Bad dream," I said, and fell back onto my pillow. The clock beside me glowed 3:13. I was still awake when my cell phone alarm chimed at 6:15.

***

When I stepped out of the shower that morning, Jenna was sitting on the closed toilet lazily brushing her teeth, her blonde hair stringy and falling over her eyes. Foamy toothpaste threatened to drip from her bottom lip. She gave me a tired, adorable smile that I returned wanly, grabbing my towel from the rack.

"Rough night?" she mumbled over her mouthful of paste and brush.

"You could say that." I walked over to the sink and used my towel to wipe steam from the mirror before wrapping it around my waist. My reflection showed me a face sculpted by exhaustion, heavy bags under my eyes, my lids drooping with sleepiness. I looked terrible.

Jenna joined me, her step springy, and held back her messy hair in one fist as she bent over to spit into the sink.

"Hey, how'd you do that?" she asked my reflection as she stood up again.

"Do what?"

She pointed at my back with a look of concern. I pivoted my right shoulder forward until I could see a small portion of my upper back in the mirror. There was a deep blue, penny-sized bruise there. Round, surrounded by a halo of greenish yellow. My mouth fell open slightly and I furrowed my brow.

"It looks painful," she said. "How did you do it?"

"I have no idea," I answered.

Jenna poked it.

"Ouch!" I protested, but when I saw her playful grin, I couldn't help but smile in return. I moved as if to grab her, and she ran quickly from the bathroom, giggling. As soon as she was gone, my smile disappeared too.

***

There was no dream on the third night. I realized this when my alarm woke me from a deep sleep at 6:15. I silenced it immediately and looked over at Jenna. She turned away from me, placing one pillow over her head to block the morning light slowly infiltrating the room.

I stood and stretched, still sleepy but feeling rested, stepped into the bathroom as quietly as I could, turning the knob so that the door would shut silently. I dropped my boxers on the floor and walked into the shower, shivering under the blast of cold water, allowing it to wake me up as I waited for it to warm.

By the time I was done, the water was piping hot and there was a thick fog of steam filling the room. I grabbed my towel from the rack, dried off, and stepped toward the sink.

There, on the mirror, written in the moisture, was the word: *Nancy*.

My wet skin broke out in goosebumps. I stared at the name dumbly for several seconds. Eyes still on the mirror, I sidestepped to the bathroom door and opened it gently. Jenna remained asleep, or was at least pretending to be, an immobile lump in the near-darkness. The easiest explanation was that she had written on the mirror while I showered, a playful morning prank, but then I remembered that I had never told her the details of the previous two nights' dreams. She had no reason to know that name. I closed the door again.

After another moment's pause, my tired mind still trying to piece together an explanation, I took off my towel and began to wipe the name away.

And in the mirror's reflection, like something out of a clichéd horror movie, I saw someone standing behind me. Someone smaller and more slender than me, someone with jet black hair, pale skin, and black circles around eyes the color of ice, lips upturned in a malevolent, jeering grin.

I let out a low bellow and spun around on my bare heels. My foot slipped on the wet floor and I fell straight down, my back raking harshly against the edge of the sink as I made my rapid descent. My tailbone hit the tile with a thud and I winced, hissing in breath.

When I looked up from my pathetic position, naked on the wet bathroom floor, my body throbbing in about four different places, each one vying for attention, I saw that no one was there.

Soft footsteps rapidly approached the bathroom and Jenna burst in, looking first with panic across the room before lowering her eyes and finding me.

"Are you okay?" she asked, crouching down and placing one warm, concerned hand on my shoulder.

I sat forward, grabbing my towel to cover myself. "Yeah," I responded, groaning out a lie. "The floor was wet and I slipped."

***

There was no dream on the fourth night. I woke on my own and stretched under the covers, my feet searching for cool spots under the sheets. As I stretched, I felt aching in my back and tailbone, reminders of the episode in the bathroom the morning before. I turned my head and looked at the clock on my nightstand. 7:45.

I had overslept.

I sat up quickly, grabbing my cell phone from the nightstand, turning it upright, silently cursing the blasted thing for not waking me. And there, perfectly centered in the dead black screen, was a hole, a hole that punched all the way through the device, surrounded by splintering fingers, a web of cracks extending to every edge of the screen.

Jenna rolled over to face me, and then, seeing the shattered cell phone in my hand, sat up, swiping her hair from her eyes.

"What happened?" she asked.

"I don't know," I answered, fruitlessly pressing the power button on the phone, already knowing it wouldn't turn on.

"Did you step on it or something?" she asked.

"I don't know," I repeated, a note of irritation in my voice. I realized I would rather be irritated at this moment than terrified, so I pivoted my emotions in that direction.

"You don't know?" she asked, skeptical.

I tossed the dead cell onto the covers and slipped out of bed. Jenna picked it up and began mashing the power button. I walked into the bathroom and shut the door.

"Ryan?" she called after me, concerned.

"I'm late for work," I yelled through the door.

***

I got to my office more than an hour late and only twenty minutes before a scheduled presentation with senior staff. Tori, my assistant, appeared at my office door no sooner than I had dropped my briefcase on my desk with a frustrated sigh.

"Is everything all right?" she asked, worry hanging on a face framed by unnaturally red and curly hair. I couldn't tell if she was more worried about why I was late – and I was never, *ever* late – or the fact that I was due to deliver a very important presentation within the hour with no time for our routine pre-game run-through. I didn't mind giving presentations as long as I was both prepared and rehearsed, and at the moment I was barely one of those things.

"Cell phone's dead," I said. "So I overslept. Did you make copies?"

"I made them yesterday," she said in a tone that also communicated the fact that I already knew this. "Folders are on the table in the conference room."

"Projector is on? File loaded?"

"Projector is on. File loaded. Coffee?"

"Please," I said, turning on my computer. Tori disappeared. I loaded my presentation and skimmed through it, reminding myself of the key points, my lips moving as I quickly read each one under my breath.

My heart was pounding. But it wasn't because I had just run up the stairs.

***

Twenty-five people crammed into the conference room. Senior staff took the ten seats at the table. Everyone else was standing at the perimeter. When the door was closed I stood at one end of the table, temporarily blinded as my head intercepted the projector's light. I gave a smile that I hoped looked more self-deprecating than nervous and smoothed out my tie as I stepped aside.

"Good morning, everyone," I said through a mouth full of cotton balls. "I apologize if I appear a little frazzled this morning. Technology failed me."

In spite of the morning's events and my frayed nerves, about three minutes into the pitch I had found my groove. It turned out I had rehearsed enough in the previous days that I was able to kick into autopilot without even realizing it had happened. And as I felt myself calming, I could also feel the room calming along with me. Most of those present, if not everyone, nodded at the salient points and chuckled at the humorous ones. Despite the morning's unfortunate beginning, I was winning the day.

But it all fell apart quickly and with a strange sense of inevitability.

"If you will look at this chart from last year," I was saying, using a laser pointer to shine a spot of red on a colorful pie chart projected on the screen, "you will see that…"

"*Naaaaaaaancy…*"

The voice came from the other side of the room. It was high and light as a feather, and also eerily dry, as if it didn't belong in the room itself. There was no hint of any reverberation, as if instead of bouncing off the walls or furniture, the sound was simply passing right through them.

I stopped talking and turned around. Two dozen faces stared back at me, some of them sporting brows furrowed with confusion or concern, most of them blank, a couple etched with boredom. I cleared my throat. The hand with the pointer hovered pointlessly in the air, the red dot now shining randomly on a poster on the wall. "Teamwork makes it all work."

After an uncomfortable pause, I turned back to the screen and re-aimed the pointer at the pie chart, which took some effort as my hand had begun to tremble awkwardly. I cleared my throat again, though the dryness would not budge. "As I was saying," I croaked, "you will see that…"

"*Naaaaaaaancy…*"

The voice was sing-songy and carried the hint of a barely-concealed laugh.

I turned around again quickly to scan the room, inadvertently taking a step once again into the projector's light. I blinked and immediately sidestepped, a grin of uncomfortable embarrassment on my face as dots of light poked at my vision.

Faces stared back at me in silence. Confused faces. Blank faces. Bored faces. Irritated faces. Tori's face, concerned. And one face, all the way in the corner, smiling. A pale white face with icy blue eyes surrounded by rings of black. Its grinning mouth opened.

"*Naaaaaaaancy…*"

Heart in my throat, I looked around at everyone else. *Do you not hear this? Do you not see this person?* But no one was looking around. No one acknowledged the sound. All eyes were locked on me.

My tie felt suddenly very tight and my tongue like a dry rug. With a nervous chuckle, I picked up a cup of water from the table. I sipped it, my hand shaking, and forced down a swallow. "My apologies, everyone," I said. "Not having a great morning. Bear with me."

I took a bigger swig of water, throwing my head back, and when I looked across the room again, the figure in the corner was gone. I took a deep, steadying breath.

"Okay," I said, putting all my effort into a smile. The corners of my mouth weighed a ton. "How about everyone open up your folders and turn to page three." I set the cup down.

The sound of folders sliding and pages rattling filled the room. I took another unsteady breath, heart pounding, and attempted to calm down. I locked eyes with Tori and raised my eyebrows – a look of camaraderie and desperation. She raised hers in return, her face a question mark.

I continued. "On page three you will see…"

"Who is Nancy?" someone asked.

My heart stopped. "I'm sorry?"

"Who is Nancy?" the voice repeated, and several people began to chuckle quietly.

"I'm sorry, I don't…" I began.

Bob Forrester, CEO, my boss's boss's boss, slapped his folder shut and slid it toward me with force. He was clearly not amused. I stopped the folder before it went over the cliff and threw him a look that I hoped was both grateful and apologetic.

I flipped the folder open. As the chuckling continued, I silently read, "NANCY. Prepared and presented by Nancy Nancy. Nancy 23, 2022. Nancy nancy nancy nancy. Nancy nancy. Nancy, nancy, nancy and nancy…"

***

I was back at my desk, my head in my hands.

"I promise those pages weren't like that when I put the folders together yesterday," Tori was pleading. She stood before my desk, her hands in a knot in front of her chest, her red hair and stick-thin body making her look like a nervous matchstick.

"For the fourth time, Tori, I believe you," I said, lifting my head to make eye contact with her. "Someone is messing with me."

"Who is?"

"I wish I knew."

"Mr. Forrester is livid. So is Walt."

"No doubt," I responded, returning my head to my hands.

"Can I get you anything?"

"A pistol? Some cyanide?"

"That's not funny," Tori scolded.

"Nothing is," I said, and she walked away with a sigh.

I sat in silence.

"Nancy!" a voice shouted, and I jumped.

Jared stood in the doorway, a huge, conspiratorial smile on his face. He knocked "shave-and-a-haircut" on the doorframe even though I was already quite aware of his presence.

"I heard you dropped a massive boner in front of Forrester this morning," he said, walking in. He dropped gracelessly into a chair in front of my desk.

"What do you want, Jared?" I asked, massaging my temples.

He chuckled and shook his head. "I just wish I had been there to see it."

"I'm sure the version being circulated by everyone in the office is far more colorful and interesting than the real thing."

He sat forward suddenly and slapped my desk with both palms, startling me for the second time. I was pretty sure his blood was laced with caffeine. "Do you know what you need, old man?"

"I'm thirty-eight," I said. "You're thirty-one. I'm not—"

"Do you know what every old man needs?" he said, his grin broadening widely. Although he was presently annoying me, he was also the closest friend I had in the office, and, amazingly, I found myself smiling in return.

"What?" I asked. "What does every old man need?"

Jared stood up, practically bouncing on his heels, and pantomimed a swinging gesture.

"No," I said, dropping my smile.

Jared, still bouncing, nodded, his eyes wide, his grin wider, and made a back-handed swinging gesture.

"I said no."

"Racquetball!" he said, only he intentionally mispronounced it, *Rah-qwet-ball.*

I turned away from him and faced my computer screen. "Nope," I said. "I'm working late. They're giving me a second chance at the presentation tomorrow."

Jared backed slowly toward the door, continuing to swing his invisible *rah-qwet*. "Working late is fine," he said. "I couldn't get a court at Lou's until 8:00 anyway. It'll do you some good. Work off some of those nerves. See you there. Old man."

He left. I considered.

***

I worked until 7:30. Stopped at the mall for a new cell phone. Swapped the SIM card. Texted Jenna, who already knew I was working late, to tell her I was meeting Jared at Lou's for racquetball.

"Don't let him wear you out," she texted back. "You're not as young as you used to be."

"Thanks for that," I said out loud but did not text in return.

Lou's was the last independently owned gym in the city. It was ancient, and much of the equipment was outdated, but it had an old school atmosphere and charm that no chain could ever match and a congeniality among the clientele that could never be replicated. And the glue was Lou, a retired Navy seal who was probably in his mid-70s. Tough as nails and armored with old muscle, he was a man who liked to bark insults with thinly-veiled good nature at the sweaty masses. Rumor had it that he had made more than one muscle head cry with just a few sharp but hilarious verbal missiles. He never smiled, even when he laughed.

When Jared and I walked in at 8:00, having first met up in the parking lot, the gym crowd was already thinning out. There were just a couple of people on treadmills and one guy at the weights.

Lou barely looked up at us from his newspaper as we walked in.

"We have the racquetball court at 8:00," I said as we walked by.

"Like I care," Lou grunted.

"Always a pleasure, Lou," Jared said with a smile.

"You have an hour," Lou shouted at us as we entered the locker room, tipping his head back toward a large clock on the wall. "Close at nine. Sharp."

"We'll be done no later than 9:15," Jared shouted back.

"Be a miracle if the old man lasts the hour," Lou called back.

Jared laughed. I shook my head.

***

Lou was wrong. I actually barely lasted 45 minutes.

Jared mopped the floor with me, figuratively speaking, and when we were finished I collapsed on the floor, gasping for breath, every inch of my clothes soaked through with sweat. *I feel like a used rag*, I thought, *and probably look like one too.* Jared bent over, hands on his knees, barely winded and barely sweating. He had a gleeful smile on his face and looked as if he was preparing a verbal barb, but then thought better of it and said, "Good game."

"Was it?" I asked. "I can't remember."

He helped me to my feet and we shambled toward the locker room. We didn't exchange words; I was mostly incapable of speech. The rest of the gym was empty, as was the front desk. Lou must have been in his office. Some of the lights were already turned off.

As we both spun the dials on our combination locks, I had a flashback to my dream from four nights prior. But of course I remembered the numbers, and the door swung open with a loud and annoying creak.

Jared began stuffing his work clothes into his gym bag, then looked over to me. I was still catching my breath, my wet clothes hanging from me like sagging skin.

"I gotta shower first," I said, shaking my head with exhaustion. "I can't drive home in this and I'm too sweaty to change."

"Got it," he said, slamming his locker door. "Good game. See you tomorrow."

"Tomorrow," I nodded, slumping down on a bench as he left the room. I heard him shout a farewell to Lou, which was answered by a grunt.

There was a stack of white towels on a deep shelf near the end of the row of lockers. I stripped and threw my wet clothes on the floor of my locker, which I closed and locked, grabbed a towel, and sauntered over to the showers, my bare feet sticking to the concrete as I walked.

I hung the towel on a hook outside the showers and stepped in. There was a long row of showerheads along the wall with no partitions for privacy. Navy-style. Lou would have it no other way. The water never got above lukewarm. At first it cooled my hot skin, but after a few minutes I began to shiver. The water was also so hard that I could barely make a lather with the soap from the wall dispenser.

As I was rinsing the last remnants of the thin layer of soap from my face, I heard a noise: a distant creaking, metallic like the sound of a locker door opening.

I turned off the showerhead and wiped water from my eyes with my fingertips. "Hello?" I called out. "Lou?"

A locker door slammed shut loudly, and my heart skipped a beat.

I stepped toward the door of the shower room. One foot slipped on soap scum and I jerked, awakening the soreness in my back. I groaned softly and placed a hand on my low back, massaging it as I stepped more carefully. Reaching around the corner for my towel, I found nothing there. I looked. The hook was empty.

"Lou?" I called out again. My voice bounced back from the concrete walls and the metal lockers, and was then swallowed instantly in silence. My body broke out in gooseflesh, my wet skin chilled by the air.

I had a realization. "Jared?" I called out. "This isn't funny, man."
Silence.

I moved toward the lockers, dripping, wet feet clapping on the floor as I walked. The light seemed dimmer and I wondered if Lou had shut some of them off, a way of giving me the hint that he wanted to close up for the day but I was making him wait.

I looked toward the locker I had chosen, expecting my combination lock to be gone or opened, but it was still there, hanging dutifully in its place. I spun the dial, unlocked the lock, and opened the door with a loud creak.

The locker was empty. No, not quite empty. On the high shelf just above eye level were my keys, wallet, and cell phone. But everything else – my clothes, shoes, and gym bag – were gone.

I furrowed my brow in confusion, a nervous feeling creeping its way into my chest. "Lou? Jared?" I called out. The room responded with their names only, and then it was quiet.

I grabbed my things from the shelf and then padded over to the end of the row of lockers where the shelf of towels was located.

It was empty.

I rolled my eyes. "Come *on,* guys!" I yelled. "Not fun—"

In response, all the lights turned off.

The only light was a dim glow coming in around the edges of the locker room door, light that was escaping from the main workout room on the other side.

I walked carefully toward that dim light, occasionally losing it as my eyes had not yet adjusted to the darkness. I stepped carefully, afraid of hitting my toes on a bench or the corner of a locker. The distance seemed endless. My breathing was loud in my ears and shaky, and not only because I was cold.

When I was about halfway to escape, I heard a whisper.

"*Nancy,*" it said.

I felt the breath of it on my wet neck, impossibly cold, sending rapid shivers down my arms and both legs.

I took off in the darkness toward that dimly-lit rectangle, my feet slapping loudly as I went, the sound echoing throughout the dark locker room, and over that sound I could faintly hear quiet laughter.

I slammed through the door and into the gym, panting. The locker door closed silently behind me and I stood there, expecting it to burst open again, expecting someone to come out behind me.

I heard laughter.

There was Lou, behind the desk, sizing me up as I stood there, wet and completely naked, vainly attempting to cover myself with hands that still clutched my phone, keys, and wallet.

***

I drove home wearing a dark blue sweatshirt with cut off sleeves, tattered gray shorts, and a pair of worn-out tennis shoes that were two sizes too small, the best outfit that Lou could throw together from the gym's lost-and-found. I smelled like someone else's old sweat and cigarettes and had to roll the window down.

"Did Jared come back while I was in the locker room?" I had asked him.

"Nope," he said.

"Did anyone else come in?" I asked.

"No," he said.

"Did…" I hesitated. "Did you take my clothes while I was show-ering?" Lou looked at me sternly, and I immediately wished I could retract the question, like a fisherman pulling in a fresh catch, and I dropped my gaze. He didn't bother to respond.

"Sorry," I said. "Just trying to figure out what happened."

He had relented with a rattling sigh. "Someone might have come in while I was in the office. I didn't hear the front door chime. But since they left your valuables and only took your clothes, seems to me some-one just wanted to play a joke on you. No harm, no foul."

"No harm, no foul," I said, although I didn't actually agree. "But how did they know my locker combination?"

Lou fixed me with a steely look. "Gym closed fifteen minutes ago," he said.

***

I got to work early the next day, allowing myself ample time to re-hearse my presentation again. Once Tori arrived, I would run through it a second time with her, and then I would be fully prepared for the meeting at 10:00. I was being given a rare second chance. It wouldn't be good enough for me to not blow it this time; it had to be flawless.

No one else was there. I turned on all the overhead lights until ev-ery early morning shadow was chased away. I left my office door open, humming quietly to myself. I jerked at every distant noise.

As Jenna had kissed me goodbye that morning, she wished me luck and handed me a brown bag. "Breakfast for the all-star," she had said with a smile.

I booted up my computer and dumped the contents of the bag on my desk. A red apple threatened to roll off the desk. I caught it and set it upright. There was also a bottle of water and something wrapped in foil, a bagel with cream cheese from the shape of it. I sat down and unwrapped it without looking, my eyes fixed on my computer screen.

I picked up the bagel and brought it up to my mouth, my eyes scanning the text of an e-mail. The smell hit me just before the bread touched my lips, and I stood up quickly, tossing the bagel to my desk. The backs of my knees struck my chair and it rolled away. There, between the two halves of the bagel and two thick layers of cream cheese, was a dead frog, reeking of formaldehyde. Its back feet protruded from one end, its arms from the sides, and most of its head from the other end, like it was wearing a bagel costume.

I stared at it, my stomach lurching.

There was a soft knock at my office door and I started. It was Tori. She stared at me silently, her look pitying. She didn't look at my desk, didn't see the dead frog masquerading as a bagel that had nearly been my breakfast.

"You're in early," I said to her, attempting to compose myself.

"Have you checked your e-mail yet?" she asked, eyebrows screwed up in concern.

"I was just getting ready to," I said. I grabbed the paper bag, slapped it over the frog bagel, picked it up, and threw everything in the trash. "Why?"

"There's an e-mail from Walt. Mr. Forrester has cancelled the meeting. He said they want to take things in a different direction."

***

I was in the office bathroom, alone, pacing. I was furious. I was disappointed. I was frustrated. And I felt undermined. I ran my fingers through my hair. I put my hands on both sides of a sink and looked into the mirror, studying my pathetic reflection. I wallowed in self-pity, and for a moment I felt like I was going to cry, actually burst into tears, and I shook my head rapidly, denying myself the emotion.

I jerked away from the sink and paced toward an open stall, not intending to enter it, just moving around, trying to shed the negative energy and anger that was coursing through my body. My shoes clicked loudly on the tile with each step.

I stopped in front of the stall door and sighed, my shoulders and head dropping, defeated.

From behind me, a whisper:

"*Naaaaaancy….*" Softly spoken, almost sung, and carried on a breeze of quiet laughter.

I spun around, furious, and for the briefest of moments I saw its face, that very pale and jeering face, but then my stomach caved in painfully as I was kicked hard in the gut. The force of the blow was strong enough to send me tumbling backwards. My back slammed against the stall door, which smacked against the side wall, and I fell, my upper back colliding painfully with the edge of the toilet. My teeth clacked together and I bit my lip.

I slid to the floor, eyes shut with pain. I turned to put my palms on the linoleum, but before I could push myself up, a cold hand gripped the back of my head and slammed my forehead against the rim of the toilet. Bright lights flashed in my vision.

Then I felt myself being lifted. Impossibly strong hands had gripped me by the back of my shirt and I was being lifted until my face hovered above the bowl. I smelled the chemicals in the water and muttered a feeble, "No."

The hand returned to the back of my head. I could feel its coldness through my hair. Fingers gripped my hair, pulling it into a fist, and then my head was shoved down, splashing into the water. My chest was pressed hard into the rim of the bowl and I was forced to exhale, bubbles sliding past my submerged cheeks and ears.

I reflexively inhaled and water filled my lungs, burning them. I choked and convulsed against the hands that held me there. A knee pressed into my spine. I opened my eyes and saw nothing but blurred white porcelain in front of me, the periphery of my vision turning black.

I struggled, my energy waning, feeling consciousness fade even as my panic dully increased. Every fiber in my being wanted to cough, wanted to expel the water that was invading my lungs, but I forced myself to deny the reflex.

The hands that held me down were incredibly strong. Inescapable. *I am going to drown,* I thought with a sudden and eerie calmness. *I am going to die in a toilet.*

And then, suddenly, the weight on my back eased. Not completely, but a little, and there was a loud roar all around me, vaguely familiar. I recognized it: the toilet was being flushed.

As the bowl emptied, I gasped in air, hungry for it, and coughed violently. No longer held down, I placed my hands on the rim of the bowl and pushed myself out. I turned and sat on the floor, letting my back rest against the toilet, coughing repeatedly and then spitting on the floor. Both it and my clothes were wet. My hair clung to my face and dripped.

I sat there, panting, all energy drained from my body, and looked through the stall door. No one was there.

***

The next day was Saturday. I woke up on my own from a dreamless sleep. My cell phone read 7:30. Jenna slept on beside me.

I needed to clear my head. Be alone with my thoughts. Consider how best to deal with this person... this ghost... this poltergeist... this whatever it was that had made the previous week a living hell for me.

I slipped on a pair of shorts, a t-shirt, and my running shoes, and drove to a park only two miles away from the house. There, a running trail surrounded a small playground, and the entire park was framed by overhanging trees that provided a pleasant shade. This early on a Saturday morning, it was deserted.

I began to run.

Where do I start? With Jenna? Tell her everything that has happened? She knows that this week has been a bad one, but I have spared her most of the details, especially the ones that are too fantastical to explain. It would feel good to tell someone, especially someone who loves me and is concerned about me. But she won't know any better than I do how to deal with it. Assuming, of course, that she believes me.

Who then? The police? No. A priest? Maybe. But would anyone actually believe me? Does this sort of thing actually happen to people? Do I believe it myself?

I had made two laps around the park. A light sweat coated my skin, and the morning air was cold against it. One lap was half a mile; on a good day I could make ten laps. But today, my chest was burning. I stopped to cough, my lungs rattling with water, the remnants of yesterday's bathroom incident.

I bent over and placed my hands on my knees, continuing to cough. Each cough prompted another, more painful one. Birds flew out of nearby trees, scolding me for the noise I was making. There was no other sound to be heard except for the very quiet rustling of leaves.

My cell phone buzzed in my pocket. I stood up, making every effort to stifle any further coughing, my lungs fiery. I fished the phone out of a deep pocket of my baggy running shorts and began to walk slowly as I turned it on. I had a new text message from Jenna.

It read, "Who is Nancy?"

I stopped walking and stared silently at the screen.

And then, as if on cue, a voice from behind me: "*Naaaaaaaan-cy...*"

I spun around, seeing nothing but empty trail, a line of tall trees to the right, freshly cut grass and a playground to the left.

"*Naaaaaaaaancy...*"

I began slowly walking backwards, in the direction of the park entrance. My eyes scanned left to right. Where was the voice coming from? There was no one—

But then, I saw it. The figure, half-hidden behind the trunk of a tree about twenty feet away. Jet black hair. White face. Icy blue eyes, staring into my own. Wide, sneering grin. One white hand with black nails gripped the bark.

"*Naaaaaaaancy...*"

I turned and ran. Hopelessness gripped me as I remembered that I was already winded. I could barely run. My lungs buzzed with pain as I gulped for breath. And as I ran, I could hear a second set of footsteps running behind me, scuffing the fine gravel of the trail, getting rapidly closer. I glanced backward and saw that face, grinning madly as it threatened to overtake me. A lightning bolt of terror traveled down my spine. *If I could just get to the car...*

I was shoved sideways so forcefully that my feet left the ground, and I fell. There was no stopping the momentum. I collapsed to the side of the trail, and my cheek met the protruding root of a tree, splitting the skin there, a stinging sensation surging into my left eye, blackening my vision, pain traveling to the top of my head like the worst migraine I'd ever had.

I tried to get up, but I was pushed down again, a cold hand pressing against the side of my head. My head was pulled up, turned so that I was facing the ground, then shoved down again violently, and as my mouth hit the tree root, I tasted blood and felt my front teeth break. The pain was everything.

A knee was placed on my back, right in the center of my spine, and while it was placed gently, the weight of it kept me pinned in place. I spat out blood and struggled to breathe as my face was pressed down into dirt.

Then, I felt breath, frigid against my ear. I shivered and began to cry.

"Don't kill me," I begged, sobbing.

"You told," the voice spoke into my ear. It was whispering, but full of anger. "You *told*. But they can't help you here."

***

Jenna took me to the hospital after I dragged my broken body back to the car and drove myself home. Three stitches above my eyebrow. Four on my cheek. Two on my upper lip. An ER dentist was called in to extract what was left of my front teeth and stitch up my gums. I would need implants or a bridge, but I my mouth would have to heal first. For now, I would have to live with a broken smile. If I ever smiled again.

I told the police I had been assaulted. No, I didn't get a look at my assailant. No, I have no idea why he didn't take anything.

Jenna and I walked into the house silently. I had an ice pack pressed up against my mouth. Sometimes I placed it on my eye, sometimes my cheek.

She walked ahead of me into the kitchen and dropped her keys on the table, right beside a copy of one of my high school yearbooks. 2002, my senior year.

"What's that?" I said. Except because of my swollen lips and missing teeth, it came out, "Whuthz tha?"

"It was here on the table when I got up this morning," she said. "I assumed you put it there?" Her last statement was a question, full of concern.

I shook my head feebly.

"Ryan, what's going on? I feel like you're not telling me something." She chuckled morosely. "I feel like you're not telling me *anything*."

I looked at her, then dropped my gaze. I didn't know where to start.

"And who is Nancy?" she asked. Before I could respond, she reached and flipped open the the yearbook. It landed on a random page. There, scrawled in the margins, filling every available white space in red ink was the name: NANCY.

I stepped toward the book and flipped through it. Every page: NANCY. NANCY. NANCY. NANCY. It was even written across my forehead in my senior picture.

I pulled out a chair and slumped down. I looked up at Jenna, defeated. She sat down softly beside me.

"What is it?"

Ice pack pressed against my lips, I turned a few pages until I found the freshman class. I scanned the rows of juvenile faces until I found him. I pointed with one dirty fingernail at a boy: a boy with white skin and jet black hair. Even though the picture was black and white, his eyes still looked crystal blue and were framed by dark eye makeup. As a freshman, he would've been around fourteen or fifteen years old, but he looked much younger. Eleven or twelve, maybe.

"Evan Michaels," Jenna read, a question in her voice.

I nodded.

"Who is he?" she asked.

And even though it was very painful to talk — for more reasons than one, I realized — I told her everything.

Evan Michaels was a freshman when I was a senior. He was one of those kids who just randomly showed up one day, appearing as if out of thin air, probably on the first day of the school year, but who really knows or cares. All that mattered was that he immediately became the target of ridicule.

Even by freshman standards, he was small. Puny. His voice was still as high and flute-like as a prepubescent boy, an androgynous trill that was rarely heard but always mocked. He had dyed his hair black. He frequently wore mascara and painted his nails a glossy black.

He was a loner. He barely spoke to anyone. When he walked down the hallway between classes, he folded his shoulders inward in an effort to shrink, and kept his head down low, hair hanging over his eyes. He concentrated all of his efforts into being invisible, and so of course we singled him out.

Actually, *I* singled him out. My friends just followed my lead.

It started with name-calling. He was small. Frail. Bad at sports. Not very masculine. So we'd hang out by the lockers and wait for him to walk by, and we'd call out a name.

Nancy.

He wouldn't react, but I knew he heard. After awhile, that got boring. So we… I… would walk up behind him at the lockers and whisper in his ear to see if I could make him jump. Then we started doing physical things. Poking him. Tripping him. Nothing too painful or damaging. Not at first.

There was an art teacher, Mrs. Jones, who took him under her wing. He was a gifted artist. Even then I knew it. He could draw in ink like nothing I had ever seen before. And he was really good at photography. Mrs. Jones recognized this and put him on the yearbook staff.

"Most of these pictures," I said, flipping through the yearbook, "were taken by him."

He had his own camera that he'd brought from home. An expensive one with a powerful lens that allowed him to capture an image without having to get close to it. Once he was on yearbook staff he wore it around his neck every day like a medal. I could see that it gave him more confidence, as well as something new he could hide behind. As he walked around the hallways or hovered around the perimeter at ballgames, he seemed more self-assured.

So one day I brought one of my dad's chipping hammers to school and kept it in my pocket until I saw Evan set his camera down for a moment. One of the guys distracted him, and I casually walked over and punched a hole in the lens with the hammer and put it back down.

We stood by and watched him pick it up, laughing when he went to take a picture and saw the damage. He could hear us. He looked heart-broken.

"Oh Ryan," Jenna sighed.

We looked over his shoulder covertly until we figured out his locker combinations. His school locker and his gym locker. One time we took out one of his report folders and replaced all the pages with papers that just said "Nancy" all over them. He turned it in without looking and the teacher was not amused. I wasn't there to see it, but the other freshmen said Evan turned beet red but refused to give an explanation.

Then one time three of us went into the locker room after fresh-man gym class. Evan took longer showers than the other boys. It was just one of his quirks. I don't think he liked to be dirty. We made the other freshmen leave, and then we took Evan's clothes out of his locker and removed all the towels while he was still showering. We shut off the lights and ran. He screamed from the doorway of the locker room until a janitor heard him.

"And then there was the time I stole a frog from the science lab…"

"Ryan, stop," Jenna said. She had tears in her eyes. She shook her head. "Why did he take it? Why didn't he tell? Why didn't one of the other students tell?"

I explained to her the strange dynamic in our school. Jocks, like me, especially senior jocks, were idolized. By both the other students *and* the teachers. Our school had a reputation for athletic achievement going back for generations. That reputation was sacred. The athletes were almost untouchable. Some of the teachers knew what we were doing to Evan. Some of it, anyway. Not all of it. And they chose to look the other way. They didn't like him much either. They probably thought the experience would man him up.

And we easily indoctrinated the other students. Anyone who told on us would be labelled a tattletale, a squeal. No one likes a tattletale. And the underlying message was that anyone who tattled would be-come the next object of our attention.

Evan, though, was a bit of a mystery. He didn't tell anyone what was happening. And the longer he stayed quiet, the more I wanted to push him. I wanted to find the line where he couldn't take it anymore. And one day I found that line.

The night before we had lost a game. A big game. I had blown it. So the next morning I found myself full of rage, the kind of inexplicable and all-consuming anger only known by teenage boys. I was six feet of muscle and fury in search of an outlet.

I walked out of class that morning without even bothering to ask for a pass. When I went into the bathroom, Evan was there. It was like fate. He looked horrified when he saw me. But I just smiled. I had found my outlet.

I kicked him into one of the stalls and shoved his face into the toilet. I held him there. It was like I could feel all my rage coursing down the arm that was holding his head under the water. The release was sweet.

He struggled at first, but he couldn't move me. I don't know how long I might have held him there, if one of my buddies hadn't walked in. He grabbed me by the collar and pulled me off. Told me to stop. Considered me with a look of shock and disbelief.

"What?" I demanded, straightening my collar.

"You could've killed him, man," he responded.

"I wasn't going to kill him," I scoffed, but I could tell from my friend's face the he didn't believe me. That was okay. I didn't really believe myself at that moment.

This time, Evan told. It might have come down to a matter of his word against mine, but my buddy ended up corroborating Evan's story. I'm not sure why. Maybe because he felt guilty for the part he had played in torturing Evan all year. Or maybe because he was truly horrified by what he had seen me doing.

Once the bathroom incident was revealed, the entire litany of what I had done to Evan was shared as well. It was only one week before graduation. The principal was as lenient as he could be. I wasn't expelled, but instead suspended for the remainder of the school year.

"It's the same thing!" I had bellowed at him.

He remained calm and unwavering. I would receive my diploma, but I wouldn't be allowed to walk with my classmates. And I was under no circumstances to ever talk to or approach Evan Michaels again.

But I knew. School grounds was one thing. But the principal had no authority outside of that building. And so one day the following week, I followed Evan home from school.

**

When I was finished talking, Jenna looked at me with sadness. She shook her head. The look she gave me was one I had never seen before. It was as if her perception of me was, if not completely shattered, fractured in several places. There was still love there, but also deep disappointment.

"Oh, Ryan," she said, reaching across the table to take my hand, but then withdrawing it. "You were… a bully."

"It was twenty years ago," I argued weakly. "I was just a kid. I mostly thought it was funny. And I guess in some strange way I thought that he deserved it."

"No kid deserves what you did," she countered.

"I know," I said, pressing the ice pack against my throbbing cheek. "I know that now."

**

He was easy enough to find.

First I looked for him on Facebook. He had a barely-used profile page. It consisted only of a single picture, but it wasn't of him. It was a black-and-white photograph of a landscape, stunning and beautiful. Artistic. Mesmerizing.

I found him in the White Pages. He was still local. I was surprised that in twenty years we hadn't ever crossed paths. At least, not as far as I knew.

The neighborhood was quiet. His house was small but well kept, the tiny lawn a lush green. I parked the car by the curb. Jenna had come with me, but opted to wait in the passenger seat with the window down.

As I walked toward the door, I spied a pink tricycle alongside a child's bike, cherry red, lying on its side in the grass.

I hesitated, then knocked softly. My heart was pounding. The door opened, and I looked up. There he was.

He was taller than me by a couple of inches. Dressed in a light gray sweater and dark denim jeans, his frame was slender but fit. He was four years younger than me but could easily pass for late 20s. His dark hair was long and wavy, falling casually over his forehead and framing his face. I was struck dumb by the man he had become. I might not have recognized him except for those icy blue eyes that looked back at me, eyes that had momentarily looked welcoming but then fell into cold recognition.

"Evan," I stammered. "You might not remember me…"

"I remember you," he interrupted. His voice was deep and smooth.

I paused. For a moment we silently stared at each other. I realized I was fiddling nervously with my fingers and forced myself to stop. I dropped my gaze and stared at my feet.

"I came here to…" I began. I cleared my throat. "I wanted to apologize to you."

I hesitantly looked at him. *Up* at him. His expression didn't change. It was emotionless. I couldn't tell if he was angry or simply indifferent.

"For… for everything." Suddenly I couldn't find any more words. I considered listing off every offense that I had come to regret, but there was no point. We both already knew them perfectly well.

After a moment, Evan let out a quiet, bitter chuckle and smiled. The smile was broad but didn't reach his eyes. It occurred to me that I had never seen him smile before. Not once. And even though the smile was one of incredulity, it made him even more handsome. His teeth were white and perfect. Teeth, I remembered, that were not all natural.

I suddenly felt incredibly self-conscious of my own appearance. My swollen, stitched up face colored by bruises and abrasions, small Band-Aids failing to fully cover the worst of it. My puffy lips and missing teeth. The way my words were lisped and slurred when I spoke.

"What is this?" Evan asked. "Are you having some sort of get right with God moment, Ryan?" He didn't just say my name. He stabbed me with it. "After twenty years, you want to just show up at my house, say 'sorry,' and make nice? Is that what you think is going to happen?"

I turned and looked back at Jenna, still seated in the passenger seat of the car. She was watching us, but too far away to hear.

"It's just that…" I mumbled. "Something happened. Has been happening…"

"I see that," he said, his eyes wandering over my face. "I looks like someone decided to give you a taste of your own medicine."

I met his eyes. "Do you know anything about…?" I started to ask. But his expression remained set, calm. There was no spark of recognition there, nothing that said Evan had anything at all to do with the events of the past week.

"Never mind," I said. "I just wanted to apologize. What I did to you back then was terrible. Inexcusable. And I am truly, deeply sorry. Please… forgive me."

Evan regarded me for a moment. Took in a deep, steady breath. His features softened ever so slightly. I looked up at him, eyes pleading, feeling like a helpless beggar.

He pursed his lips and looked skyward, thinking. And then quietly he said, "No."

My mouth fell open slowly. A coldness washed over me.

"No, Ryan," he said, "I do not forgive you. And do you know why? Because twenty years ago I had to endure almost daily torture from you. Abuse, both physical and verbal. And the constant fear of what might be coming next. The embarrassment of being harassed in front of other kids. The loneliness of having no one come to my defense. And feeling so ashamed of being so incredibly disliked that I felt like I had to hide everything from my parents and acted like everything was just fine.

"And it doesn't end there," he continued. "You left me with the memories. I can't say I think of you every day, Ryan, but I think about you often enough. Most of the scars might be invisible, but they're still there. And there's nothing you can do or say to take them away. I've carried them for twenty years. And I'll continue to carry them for the rest of my life.

"So… no." He shook his head. "I won't forgive you. But I am ever so glad you came by today. Because whatever it is that's finally pricking your conscience, whatever it is that's now *haunting* you…"

My heart skipped a beat.

"…I'm glad," he said. "I hope you carry that for the rest of your life."

A little girl appeared behind Evan, wrapping her arms around his left leg. "Daddy," she said. She looked up at me and her eyes widened. "Daddy, who's that?" she asked.

Evan casually stroked her dark hair which looked as smooth as silk.

"He's nobody," he answered, his eyes never leaving mine.

I turned away from him and shambled down the sidewalk, head down. I fought back tears. The effort made my eyes and cheek throb.

I was halfway down the walk when Evan called out to me, startling me. I stopped moving but didn't turn to look at him. "Even if I did forgive you, Ryan," he said. "You wouldn't be done. I wasn't the only one, remember."

I heard his front door close.

Looking up, my gaze crossed the distance between me, standing on Evan's sidewalk, and the car, parked by the curb. There, Jenna waited for me, the look on her face one of tired hope. And in the back seat I saw three children, faces pale, eyes glaring at me with anger, lips curled up in malevolent smiles. They were pointing at me and laughing.

I shuffled to the car. Got in. Started the engine. Sighed.

"How did it go?" Jenna asked.

We drove home.

people you may know

Lunchtime. I had gotten up from my desk long enough to shut the door to my office, making a brief stop at the mini-fridge under the window to retrieve a bottle of water and my lunch, a humble brown bag that bulged under the weight of its cargo: half a hero sandwich, a Granny Smith apple, and a granola bar. I plop the sack down on my desk where it bumps against a framed photo of Lynn and Danny, causing the picture to collapse backwards with a clatter. I drop into my chair and right the photo, my wife and son beaming back at me as if grateful to be upright again. I dump the contents of my lunch onto the desk and uncap the water bottle, taking a swig.

The morning was stressful and, thanks to three consecutive meetings that predictably overran their allotted schedules, almost completely fruitless. I need the lunch hour to decompress, take a deep breath, and eat. Maybe then I can better handle whatever the afternoon is winding up to throw at me.

I unwrap the sandwich and take a large bite. The bread is unap-pealingly cold and wet; I grimace but continue to chew. A click of my mouse fills my computer monitor with the home page of Facebook, and I begin to scroll. There is a picture of Lynn, a selfie she took just this morning on our couch at home, Danny sound asleep on her shoul-der, a spot of his drool leaving an oddly-shaped dark stain on Lynn's shirt.

The caption reads, "Is it just me, or does Danny's spit stain look strangely like the *Mona Lisa*? #futureartist." I chuckle through a mouthful of sandwich, then find myself distracted by my wife's familiar face — her skin free of blemish, her teeth perfectly white, her hair care-lessly perfect, her motherly eyes tired but shining. All this without the use of any filters. She never uses them; she doesn't need to.

And then of course there is my little boy, already a bruiser at five months old, toe-headed and chubby cheeked, his closed lids concealing deep blue eyes like his mother's. A future heartbreaker, sleeping like an angel.

I sit back and swallow, pulling in a deep breath. The stress of the morning begins to evaporate as I absorb the photo of my family. After a moment I sit forward again to type a comment underneath the picture, something witty to make Lynn smile and let her know that I had both seen and appreciated it, when my eyes shift to the heading just below:

PEOPLE YOU MAY KNOW

And there, among a row of photos of people Facebook (correctly) thinks I might be acquainted with, is a face I haven't seen in at least ten years: Pepper Lauren. My heart clenches in an explicable way, a mixture of nostalgia and excitement that I would never have anticipated.

Pepper Lauren. She of raven-black hair and porcelain skin. A girl who didn't smile easily, but when she did, time stopped. A girl whose laugh was so hardy and melodic that it immediately rewarded whichever lucky person that had somehow managed to amuse her. She had emerald eyes and a steady, confident gaze. Taller than average and with a physical presence that was feminine yet strong, she was the kind of girl who could probably take down an average man and no one would be surprised, but would also seem perfectly suited to cuddling a kitten or shushing a baby. She had the kind of magnetic personality that easily drew people to her even though you knew deep down she didn't care one lick whether or not she was popular.

Pepper Lauren. A beautiful enigma. In ten years possibly more beautiful now than when I had known her in college.

Slowly, I slide the mouse toward me until the cursor hovers over a button beneath her photo that reads, "Add Friend." Considering, I reach over and absentmindedly pick up the Rubik's Cube that I keep by my monitor. I don't know why I have it. I've never known how to do more than solve a single side of it, and attempting to solve another just messes up the first. Currently, one side is a proud blue and the other five are a jumble of colors.

I put the cube down, take my mouse, and click on "Add Friend" under Pepper's picture and take another bite of my soggy sandwich. The text on the button changes to, "Friend Request Sent," and a drop of mustard plops onto my tie.

***

That night at the kitchen table, I sit in front of Danny's high chair, making voluntary airplane noises and involuntary "open-wide" faces as I attempt to get him to eat pureed carrots that smell sickeningly sweet. Lynn is over by the stove, an assortment of pots emitting both noise and steam as she prepares a meal that smells delicious even though I haven't yet figured out what she is making.

Danny wraps his lips around the spoon I'm offering him and then gives me a wide smile framed by orange goo. I chuckle quietly. Lynn smiles at us over her shoulder.

"Do you remember Pepper Lauren?" I ask her, the question jumping from my lips before I have really contemplated asking it.

"Heh," Lynn responds with a sardonic laugh, flinging a dish towel over her shoulder as she stirs a pot.

"Heh?" I ask, mimicking her.

"I remember her," she says. "Wow, I haven't thought about her in a long time. Blast from the past." She continues to stir, lost in thought.

"You didn't like her?"

"Of course I liked her," she says. "Everyone liked Pepper Lauren. *You* certainly liked Pepper Lauren." She looks up long enough to raise an eyebrow playfully at me.

"Yeah, well," I say, breaking our gaze and scooping up another spoonful of carrot for Danny. As I offer it to him, he blows a wet raspberry that sends tiny droplets of orange spittle everywhere, some of it sprinkling my face coolly.

"What makes you ask about her?" Lynn asks.

"She popped up on Facebook today," I say, picking up a napkin with my free hand to wipe my face, Danny looking quite pleased himself. "You know, suggested friends."

"Hmm," Lynn responds. "I can't think about her without thinking about—"

"Jason Wagner," I interrupt.

"Jason Wagner," she agrees.

"She really dodged a bullet there."

"We both did," says Lynn.

***

College. A decade ago.

I don't remember much about it at all, honestly. In hindsight it's a blur of classes, teachers whose names I no longer remember, lookalike classrooms, late nights studying, and even later nights partying, all in pursuit of an expensive piece of paper that I could later lay claim to in job interviews.

But if there's one thing I do remember clearly, it's Pepper Lauren. I don't recall which class it was, and it doesn't really matter. All I remember is she walked in one day, and the air in the room completely changed. Her long, denim-clad legs carried her across the threshold in a way that made her look like she was already completely familiar with the room even though she was a freshman like me. And when she chose to sit at the desk in front of me, my juvenile heart skipped a beat, foolishly reading meaning into the fact that of all the empty seats available (*of all the beer joints in town, she walks into mine*), she picked the one in front of me. As she spun around and sat in one singularly elegant motion, her long black hair, shining and smooth as corn silk, sent a pleasant wave of aroma across my face, and I breathed it in deeply.

From that day on, it was the only class I was consistently early for. I wanted to be there when she arrived, and every time, my chest tightened at the sight of her. And occasionally, when her eyes would meet mine for the briefest of instants, I would die a tiny death. Partly because she had caught me staring at her, and partly because it felt as though her gaze revealed to her all of my secrets.

She always chose the seat in front of me. For that I was grateful, as any other choice would have ravaged my teenage heart.

And then, one day, three or four weeks into the semester, she talked to me. She simply turned casually in her seat and looked at me like we were old friends, and asked me a question. About the class, about the price of tea in China, about the location of the closest high-end women's clothing store where only the world's most beautiful angels were allowed to shop, I have no idea. I knew nothing in that moment except that she was looking at me and only me, and her question confirmed that somehow I not only existed in her universe, but she was also fully aware of me. I waited for the floor beneath me to crack open and swallow me whole.

Now, let's get something straight here. I'm no slouch. I'm tall. Blonde haired and blue eyed. I have a high metabolism that leaves me naturally trim, and I carry a decent amount of muscle even though working out has never been a consistent habit of mine. In high school I was the star quarterback for my team and I was voted homecoming king my senior year. I likely could have dated any girl I wanted to, but I was picky. Not easily impressed, honestly. "A Ken in search of a Barbie" is the way one of my buddies put it, but that wasn't quite right.

I'm not bragging, although I'm aware that it sounds like I am. I'm just saying that, from a very superficial standpoint, I would be considered a catch, both in college and even now, pushing 30. But Pepper Lauren wasn't just a catch. She was in a totally different body of water. In an alternate universe made of satin and magic.

Whatever her question was, I answered it, my voice probably shaky, grateful to have her requested information readily available to me (if I'd had to answer, "I don't know," I probably would have transferred out of state). She smiled, thanked me, and turned back around. I was staring into the silky blackness of her hair, replaying our brief but groundbreaking conversation and attempting to calm my heart, when she suddenly faced me again.

"I'm Pepper, by the way," she said, offering me a grin before just as suddenly facing forward once more.

"Greg," I said to her hair.

It was important to her that I know her name. I spent the next day spelunking the depths of meaning behind that simple fact, the revelation of her name a gift so priceless, all the while knowing deep down that it meant infinitely more to me than she had ever intended it to.

***

The next morning, the morning after Facebook had thrown Pepper Lauren back into my consciousness, I toss my briefcase absentmindedly beside my desk and hit the spacebar on my keyboard, waking up my computer before I even plant myself in my chair. I sit. I launch Facebook and type "Pepper Lauren" into the search field. Her profile picture comes up, and I click on it with some anticipation, internally chiding myself for the familiar twinge of nostalgic excitement I am trying to deny that I am feeling, simultaneously refusing to acknowledge any sense of guilt that is entwined with it.

Pepper's Facebook page fills the screen, her green eyes staring back at me from her profile picture. But my heart sinks when I see the pale blue button that reads, "Friend Request Sent." She hasn't accepted it yet. Okay. I fidget with the Rubik's Cube without picking it up, rocking it on its edge with one finger until it tips over.

I scroll through her profile. She hasn't bothered to set it to "friends only," and suddenly I am in possession of the highlights of Pepper's life dating back to just after college. Knowing full well that a Facebook profile is never a completely honest reflection of real life (no one posts pictures of their break-ups, their weight gains, or their toenail clippings), I can nonetheless ascertain that Pepper still has a healthy circle of friends, she has traveled a great deal more than I have, and, I note, she has remained single.

She has also remained local.

This is unbelievable. A person like Pepper Lauren does not remain local. A person like Pepper Lauren moves to Los Angeles or New York or Paris. To do what, I have no idea. I have no real recollection of her interests or talents aside from being quintessentially Pepper Lauren. She is the kind of person you could imagine hosting A-list galas or curating a hugely successful art gallery. Maybe marrying a famous athlete while hosting a locally-then-nationally syndicated morning talk show. Wait, no, she's too cool for that. She would look more at home as the lead singer of an alternative rock band than as the host of a show involving coffee and chipper morning banter.

Occupation: bartender. *Are you kidding me?* But digging a little deeper I find that the truth is a little more impressive: she owns a bar. A nice one, from the looks of it, in the heart of the classier end of town surrounded by boutiques, expensive furniture stores, fancy restaurants, and high-end clothiers. It is an area I am vaguely familiar with but haven't frequented in years. Marriage, mortgage, and a high stress job have a way of phasing out that time in life when dinners at fancy restaurants are a weekend norm, as they had been when Lynn and I were dating, had more disposable income, and wooing my future wife was the objective of the day. Anymore, "dinner out" usually means carryout from a chain or even the deli of a grocery store on my way home if Lynn isn't up for cooking.

The reality is that Pepper Lauren's shooting star landed, unexpectedly, in her own home town, and she is now the proud owner of a rather nice-looking (if pictures weren't deceiving) bar that is aptly named *Pepper's*, not ten miles from where I currently sit. Who would have thought?

***

That evening, I pull into the driveway just as the sun is sending its last wink of light over the horizon. As I wait for the garage door to fully raise, I look over at the mailbox at the edge of the yard, its lid hanging open, the words "The Thompsons" in white cursive across the side (Lynn's handiwork). I park in the garage but walk back outside to shut the mailbox. It is empty.

I can hear Danny screaming before I open the door. Lynn thrusts him at me, and I drop my briefcase in order to free my hands.

"Take him," she says. She looks harried, but not upset. Lynn rarely loses her spark. Even on her worst days when she might vent to me in a barrage of verbal diarrhea, there is always a tinge of humor underneath it all. She always has a handle on things, even when she says she doesn't.

"What's going on?" I ask, bouncing Danny against my chest as he wails deafeningly into my left ear.

"I can't deal with *that* right now," she says, waving us away with a gesture that is full of mock resignation. She retreats quickly to the stove, and I realize that something is burning.

"Okay, cowboy," I say to Danny, "Let's give Mommy a break." I take him up to his room, where I discover a blown out diaper that requires not only a change of clothes but also a quick bath in the sink. By the time we are done, all is right in Danny's world again. He is liberal with his grins as we return to the kitchen and intent on making a game of playfully pulling my hair.

"Thank you," Lynn says sincerely. "He's been a bear today."

"Just needed Daddy to help him out of the mud," I say, sitting down at the table and bouncing him on my knee. He begins grabbing for anything within reach – any utensils or books or mail on the kitchen table that he can send plummeting to the floor. I push everything away except a plastic duck that he readily accepts, chews on briefly, and then sends sailing with glee.

Lynn busies herself at the stove. "This will be ready soon. Hope you don't mind a little char on your steak to go with your rubbery green beans."

"Sounds delicious," I say.

A moment of silence passes between us, the only sound in the kitchen coming from the pots and pans on the stove combined with Danny's gurgled cooing.

"Remember how I mentioned Pepper Lauren yesterday?"

A fleeting look passes over Lynn's face, one that I interpret as *her again?*, but it is gone as quickly as it appeared, and Lynn simply responds, "Yeah."

"She owns a bar downtown. Can you believe that?" I continue to bounce Danny on my knee. He begins amusing himself with the sound of his own voice as it fluctuates with each bounce.

"I can believe that," says Lynn.

"It's called *Pepper's*."

"Oh, I know that place."

"You do, do you?" I ask with a chuckle. "Been bar hopping without me?"

"You have no idea the things Danny and I get into during the day."

"Apparently not," I laugh.

"Emily told me about it. Said we should go sometime. She said for tavern food it was actually quite good." Emily is Lynn's best friend, although their relationship since the birth of Danny has become almost exclusively text-based.

"We should go there sometime," I say without thinking, and Lynn shoots me a quick look, one of unmistakable but minor suspicion, and returns to her cooking.

***

After telling Julie, my administrative assistant, that I have an appointment during my lunch break, it takes me only 12 minutes to make the drive from the office to Pepper's bar across town. The building is old and brick, with strung-up lights hanging over an outside dining area, and as I approach the front doors, I catch the alluring aroma of bread and ale.

First I try to convince myself that I am not excited, and when that doesn't work, I tell myself that there is simply nothing to be excited about. She might not even be there, and even if she is, she might be holed up in some hidden office, knee deep in the mundane tasks tied to business ownership.

For noon on a weekday, both the restaurant and bar area are fairly busy. Two dozen or more patrons, most of them in business attire, occupy several of the tables, and two men in suits sit at the bar, deep in jovial conversation. The place is dimly lit, and what light there is reflects nicely off the polished mahogany of the woodwork.

And then, as if by magic, there she is. Behind the bar. Seeing her is like spotting a celebrity out in public. She is wearing a simple yet expensive-looking cream-colored sleeveless top, her straight black hair down over her shoulders. Her nails are lacquered black and she wears dark denim jeans. She looks more like a woman than the girl I met my freshman year and is all the more stunning for it. She also has a nose ring. I don't care for nose rings. But it looks great on her.

I walk up to the bar and take a seat, a stupid smile stretching my face uncomfortably no matter how much I try to subdue it.

"What can I get you?" she asks without looking over at me.

"Hey, Pepper," I say.

She looks over at me and returns my smile. "Hey back," she says. "What can I get for you?"

My smile dies. There is no recognition there. No hint of familiarity. Nothing. Impossible.

"Whatever's on tap," I say.

She turns and begins filling up a mug. She throws a cork coaster in front of me casually and sets the mug down, a little bit of foam erupting from the top and landing on the back of my hand. She starts to walk away.

"You don't remember me?" I ask her.

She turns back and studies my face briefly, even squinting her eyes playfully before offering an apologetic smile. "Sorry, no. Should I?"

"Greg," I say.

Nothing.

"Greg Thompson. Ravenwood U? You used to sit in front of me in… um, I actually don't remember which class."

She shakes her head. "Sorry. Really. College was a lifetime ago. Which class was it?" She is trying to be polite, but with a sinking feeling I realize that not only does she not remember, but she really isn't interested in remembering, either.

"I don't remember which class," I repeat. "But you really don't remember me? Freshman year. We, um… we actually went out once. On a…date."

"We *did*?" she says. "Wow, now I feel terrible. Let me think." She bites down on her lip and looks up, searching her memory. "I'm sorry, I've got nothing. You said your name was Greg?"

"Is Greg. Thompson," I say.

"It's so weird," she says. "Are you sure? I'd like to say something stupid like 'I was so wasted the whole time I don't remember much about college,' but… well. That wasn't me."

She's right. That wasn't her.

"But come to think of it, your name does sound a little familiar," she continues, eyes upward again. Suddenly she smiles and points a finger at me. "Wait a minute, I know!"

For the briefest of moments, my heart leaps. She does remember me after all. Maybe not to the degree that I remember her, but any spark of recognition would be better than having been forgotten altogether.

"Didn't you send me a friend request on Facebook a couple of days ago?" she asks. And even though she is smiling, the question feels like an accusation, or like she is making fun of me just a little, and suddenly I feel like a schoolboy with a stupid crush.

"Yeah, I did," I say, picking up the mug of beer and taking a sip, mainly as an excuse to do something – anything – with my hands and trying to act casual.

"Sorry I didn't accept the request, but, um… I didn't know who you were," and with this statement, she gives me a look that is a cross between apology and pity.

"No big deal," I offer.

"So, uh… how have you been?" she asks with a playful shrug, acknowledging what we both know, that the question is one of rote politeness and not genuine curiosity.

"This is a nice place you've got here," I say, looking around as if I hadn't already done so upon arrival.

"Thank you."

"How long have you—" I start to ask, but then one of the men at the other end of the bar calls out her name.

"Excuse me for a sec," she says. As she turns, a gentle breeze caresses my face in her wake, and I breathe in deeply a familiar aroma.

I exit the bar while her back is turned, leaving behind a twenty and a nearly full mug of beer.

***

It had been, I believe, about three weeks of casual conversation, brief snippets of interaction before and after class and the occasional whispered joke during lectures (likely at the teacher's expense). I thought about her all the time and wondered how much she thought about me. She certainly didn't avoid interacting with me, and any day that I successfully made her smile – or better yet, laugh – was a banner day for me.

I wanted to ask her out, to be able to spend real time with her instead of having a relationship based entirely on stolen moments. But I was suddenly grappling with an emotion I'd never had to deal with before: fear of rejection. Like I said, in high school I likely could have dated almost any girl I wanted to, and some of them made that reality plainly clear on a regular basis, their fawning attraction ironically thwarting whatever chance they might have had with me. And while Pepper and I were physically opposites in a lot of ways – she with her dark sultriness and me with my all-American-boy cream cheesiness – there was no reason for me to think that Pepper wouldn't be attracted to me.

I had decided that today was the day. I would ask her out. I didn't hear a word the teacher said that day, and I'm fairly certain my heart raced for the entire 90 minutes of the class. When we were dismissed, Pepper rose without looking back at me and immediately left the room with the other students, and I feared that I might lose her in the hallway.

I jumped from my desk and sprinted after her, leaving my bag and books behind, behaving as if there would never be another opportunity. I scanned the moving crowd of students outside the door, finally spotting Pepper's long black hair half a hallway away from me.

"Pepper!" I called out.

She – and a handful of other students – turned to face me. She had a surprised but curious look on her face, and she stopped walking. I took maybe one step toward her before she was snatched from behind, a strong arm encircling her stomach and spinning her around. A brick wall of a young man with a brow like a Neanderthal and a cocky smile pulled Pepper toward him. And she, in turn, laughed loudly, a mix of surprise and delight. Then she threw her arms around his neck and they kissed.

My heart seized with a sudden dejected ache. I turned and ducked back into the classroom before their unfortunate PDA was over. Whether or not Pepper ever looked back for me, I never knew.

***

Lynn and I are in bed, reading. Danny is asleep. The house is blissfully silent.

"Did I tell you we had a business lunch today?" I ask Lynn. (*A lie.*)

"Hmm-mm," she mumbles, shaking her head slightly, not looking away from her book.

"We went to Pepper's," I say.

She looks at me over her reading glasses, her "sexy schoolmarm glasses," I like to call them, which isn't a joke. Her look is disapproving.

"Steve's idea," I insist. (*Another lie.*) Steve is my boss.

"Okay," she says, putting her book down.

"Nice place. I should take you there sometime. The food really is quite good." (*Why do I keep lying?*)

A heavy silence passes between us.

"And?" Lynn finally asks. "Did you see her?"

"Strangest thing," I say, and chuckle in an effort to sound casually baffled, when in fact the strange interaction between Pepper and myself is all that had occupied my thoughts that afternoon. "I did see her, just briefly. She didn't remember me."

"Really?" Lynn laughs, a tiny look of victory on her face.

"Really. Not even a hint of recognition."

"That's really weird," Lynn says with sincerity.

"It is, right?"

"Still, it has been what, about ten years?" she asks me.

"Yeah, but… we had a class together. Three days a week. We talked a lot. And we went out that one time." My tone is more desperate than I intend it to be, more insistent. "I can't believe that she could just flat-out forget me."

"I already said it's weird," Lynn says, picking up her book again.

I drop the subject. A few minutes later, when I kiss Lynn goodnight, she doesn't kiss me back.

***

The next couple of weeks after the revelation that Pepper had a boyfriend, I didn't talk to her as much before, during, or after class. We still interacted on occasion, but only when she initiated it. She had a boyfriend – *of course she had a boyfriend, you idiot* – and there was nothing for my ruined heart to do but to move on.

His name was Jason Wagner. I only had to ask around a little to find out who he was from those I knew were friends with Pepper, although most of them didn't call him Jason – his nickname was, no joke, Down Under. ("He was six-foot-four and full of muscles," they explained, *hardy har.*) He was the kind of college guy that you could easily imagine at a frat party chugging beer, laughing loudly at his own obnoxious jokes, and spending most of the evening standing on a table. And with his pale and pock-marked skin, patchy chin hair, and the aforementioned caveman brow, he certainly wasn't good-looking. But he also had the kind of larger-than-life, full-of-confidence personality that inexplicably attracted girls. And he was built like a truck.

It was mostly radio silence between me and Pepper until one day she walked into class – a rainy day if I recall correctly – with none of the self-assuredness that was her trademark. She sank into the chair in front of me and slouched down. And for the first time since witnessing the hallway lip lock between herself and Down Under, I spoke first.

"Everything ok?" I asked. I kept my voice low since other students were walking by, finding their seats.

"No," she said, not turning around.

I considered letting it go. But I mustered up some confidence. "Anything I can do?"

She turned around to look at me, her pretty face etched by sadness, her green eyes dewy. "You're sweet," she said, and I was afraid I may have blushed a little. "I broke up with my boyfriend."

"Oh!" I said, and that tiny almost non-word response carried with it a note of pleasant surprise that she thankfully missed or chose to ignore.

"Turns out he's not such a nice guy," she said. "Why do I do that to myself?" she asked, and the vulnerability in her words, the revelation that Pepper Lauren could be anything less than fully confident, surprised me. I found myself wishing I could hold her. She had her arm draped across the back of her chair as she faced me, and without thinking, I sat forward and put my hand over hers. She surprised me by giving my fingers a quick squeeze.

"Do what?" I asked.

"Go out with bad boys," she said. "It never ends well. Never." She was looking at our hands, mine on top of hers, and with her thumb she casually began rubbing one of my fingers. My chest was fireworks. "I should try dating a nice guy for once," she said, and she looked at me, right into my eyes, our faces only inches apart.

This cannot be happening.

"I'm a nice guy," I blurted, and felt my face turn crimson.

She grinned, a weary smile poking through her sad visage. "Then ask me out," she said.

"Will you go out with me?"

"I will," she said.

***

I knock on Steve's office door. "A bunch of us guys are going out for lunch. Interested?"

It's a situation of my own making. A couple of casual phone calls, a handful of knocks on office doors, and soon enough I have a group of guys game for a bite. "I heard there's this really good tavern across town," I suggest. And so with minimal effort, I find myself crammed into a car with four other guys on our way to Pepper's.

There is no sign of her at first. A friendly young hostess shows us to a table with a frustratingly obscured view of the bar, which is empty.

I am studying the menu while jovial small talk is volleyed across the table when a gentle hand touches my shoulder. I look up into familiar green eyes and am stunned, immediately transported back to those pale wood school desks, 18 years old and full of yearning.

"Hey stranger," she says.

I look back at her dumbly. Has she finally remembered me? I mean college me, not simply the bumbling me from yesterday?

"Pepper!" Steve calls out.

"Hey, Steve," she smiles across the table. Of course, Steve she knows. Steve she remembers. Why wouldn't she? But why *would* she?

"You know that loser?" Steve calls out with a laugh, nodding his head in my direction, his hands clasping a menu.

"Apparently, I do," she says, and gives me a kind pat on the back before walking away. "Anna will be right with you. Hope you fellas enjoy your meal."

I'm not tuned in to the conversation around the table and I barely touch my food. If I tilt my seat back far enough, I can get a glimpse of the bar. There are no patrons, but Pepper is there now, wiping down surfaces, cleaning off glasses, keeping herself busy.

"Men's room," I say as I stand, throwing my napkin over my plate which holds an untouched house salad and a once-bitten burger. None of my coworkers acknowledge me, all of them lost in chatter.

Pepper looks up as I approach and gives me a smile.

"Still nothing?" I ask her casually.

She shakes her head. "Sorry."

I make a gesture with my hand that I hope communicates "no big deal." I sit down at a stool across from her.

"Care for a drink?" she asks. "A cold one for lost memories?"

"It's ok," I say. "I think we're almost done."

"How was it?" she asks.

"Delicious." Not that I tasted it.

She sticks her rag-covered hand into a glass and begins to twist it, polishing the inside. She is looking at me, studying me, a curious look on her face.

"Do you remember Jason Wagner?" I ask her.

Her brow and her smile fall simultaneously. "Oh gosh," she says. "Unfortunately I do. Now why can't *he* be the guy I've forgotten?" She chuckles morosely.

"Sorry," I offer.

"Were you friends with him?" she asks me.

"No," I say. "No, not at all. But I know that you dated him. And I remember when you broke up with him. I was there that night the two of you had that…" I search for the right word. "That fight. At Mickey's."

She cringes. "You were?" She puts the glass down and lets the rag fall from her hand, then holds herself up against the bar, leaning forward toward me just slightly. "What were you doing there?"

"We were on a date," I say.

She puts one hand on her forehead. "I feel like I'm losing my mind," she says. She shakes her head, staring at my face as if she might find the answers written there. "I remember that night. I remember that *fight*. And you were there with me?"

"Yes."

She continues to shake her head subtly. "I'm sorry, I just don't remember you."

I remind her again of the class we shared. The many times we talked. The day she told me about breaking up with Jason "Down Under" Wagner, and how her desire to try dating a nice guy had finally given me the courage to ask her out.

"You honestly don't remember any of that?" I ask her, and in spite of myself, I realize that the cool and casual tone I'd been attempting to maintain was giving way to slight frustration.

"I don't," she insists.

"How is that possible?" I ask her, and I feel myself glaring at her, frustration beginning to give way to an anger I cannot justify.

She pulls away from the bar and takes a small step away from me, regarding me with some caution. "I don't know," she says.

"Greg, you ready?" Steve is calling to me from across the room, my other coworkers assembling near the door. Pepper watches me as I rise reluctantly from the stool, but breaks our eye contact before I do. Trailing my coworkers as they file through the door, I look back at the bar once before exiting the restaurant. But Pepper isn't there anymore.

***

"Honey, I'm home!" I call out as I enter the house, doing my best Ward Cleaver.

"We're in here," Lynn calls back, meaning the kitchen. I find her at the sink, arms elbow-deep in soapy water. Danny is in his high chair, a smattering of Cheerios distributed in equal measures on his tray, his cheeks, and the floor. I tousle his silky blonde hair as I walk past, and he babbles approvingly.

I grab Lynn by the shoulders and spin her around. Suds fly. She begins to object despite the surprised grin on her face, and I plant a kiss on her lips. I'm making an effort.

"Hi to you too," she says.

I squeeze her tightly. "How are you?"

"Good," she says. "And even better now."

At the dinner table, we talk about the water softener in the basement (*it needs replaced*), Danny's wellness visit at the pediatrician's tomorrow, whether or not we will go away to celebrate our upcoming anniversary, and my day at work. I make no mention of lunch at Pepper's or Pepper herself. Tonight, I am going to stay out of that lane.

But then, Lynn takes the wheel. "You know, it's funny you bringing up Pepper this week," she says, and I stop chewing my food. Lynn is distractedly poking at hers. "This time of year, I always end up thinking about Jason Wagner." Her words trail off as she gets lost in thought.

"You do?" I ask, incredulous. "Why?"

"Our anniversary," she says. "We wouldn't have met if it wasn't for him."

I feel a little stunned. "I guess that's true," I say. "I never really thought about it that way."

"I do," she says. "Scum of the earth that he was, at least *something* good came from knowing him." I know she means this as a positive thing, but her words sound forlorn.

"Something *very* good," I assure her, and I grin. She smiles slightly in return. "And let's not forget about *this* little guy," and I poke my thumb in the direction of Danny, who is ignoring me, his attention focused like a laser on the ceiling fan, mouth silently agape.

Lynn laughs quietly.

I raise my glass of water. "To Jason Wagner."

"No," she insists, smile fading. Left hanging, I take a sip of water and put my glass back down.

***

Mickey's was the closest restaurant to campus. For the students of Ravenwood University, it was the go-to place for dates, hang-outs, post-game celebrations, and post-finals decompressions. In hindsight, I should have taken Pepper somewhere else, but originality was not my strong suit. But what a different path life may have taken if I had.

I was both hungry and nervous when we arrived, but when Pepper suggested we play a game of pool before eating, I readily agreed. A game would be a welcome distraction, an easier way for the two of us to interact than plunging immediately into dinner conversation. The thought of extended one-on-one, face-to-face conversation with her both excited and terrified me, and I had the amusing thought that it would be easier for me to talk to her if she turned her back on me instead.

But both the game and the date were over before they had really begun. I was bent over the table, preparing a shot, my eye focused on the cue ball, hoping that I might somehow impress Pepper with my game even though I hadn't played pool in who knows how long, when I heard her say, "Oh no."

I looked up. Then I stood up.

Jason Wagner had walked in. He had stopped dead in his tracks across the room, his eyes focused on Pepper behind me. He wasn't happy. There was a girl with him, a petite blond standing slightly behind him but nearly eclipsed by his girth. Lynn.

"What are you doing here?" he asked, and even before Pepper responded, I wanted to laugh at the stupidity of the question.

"Just leave us alone, Jason," Pepper said with a sigh, raising her voice just enough to be heard over the din of the restaurant.

"And who's this?" he asked, jutting his scruffy chin in my direction. Lynn looked up at him, and then looked at me, a baffled expression on her face.

Pepper circled around to the front of the table, stopping in front of Jason. I stayed where I was behind the table, gripping the pool stick in both hands. "What does it matter to you?" Pepper asked, looking up at him defiantly. But I could see that her hands, down at her sides, were balled into fists and trembling.

Jason looked beyond her and over to me, glaring. "Certainly didn't take you long. This the best you could do?" he asked her without taking his eyes off me.

"How about you just leave us alone?" Pepper said again. "We are not together anymore."

He didn't respond.

Pepper cocked her head sideways, looking at Lynn. "Hi, Lynn," she said without smiling.

"Hi, Pepper," Lynn responded, her face full of uncertainty. She looked again at Jason, then at Pepper, then over to me.

"Listen, how about my friend and I finish up our game, and you two go find a table somewhere, and let's not make a big deal about this?" Pepper asked. Her voice was determined but fragile, her question a cross between a suggestion and a plea.

I swear, Jason's eyes never left mine and his body barely pivoted as he backhanded Pepper across the face, the sound of the slap reverberating through the room. The force of the blow was enough to send Pepper backward and into the table, its corner making sharp contact with her ribs before she crumpled to the floor.

There was a collective gasp in the room and then almost complete silence. Lynn clapped her hands to her mouth in shock. Pepper used the pool table to pull herself back to her feet. She glanced back at me, a rivulet of blood at one corner of her mouth. I stood frozen on the spot, returning her gaze briefly before looking back at Jason, whose eyes still hadn't left mine. I had never seen such rage.

I knew I should move. I wanted to move. But I couldn't. I remained rooted to the spot as Jason landed a second blow across Pepper's face, once again sending her to the floor. Lynn backed away quickly and out the door, her hands never leaving her mouth. Just as I began to finally step forward, there was a sudden mad rush as several males lunged at Jason, and in the loud chaos that followed I lost sight of both him and Pepper.

I was shoved out of the way as more people approached the scene. Before long, there were sirens. As I made my way toward an exit, I realized that Pepper wasn't the only one left bruised and bleeding. Jason's face had been beaten to a pulp by more than one set of fists.

Out in the dark and chilly parking lot, I waited. I realized I still had the pool cue in my grip, so I leaned it against the exterior wall of the restaurant. Eventually, Jason was led out in cuffs. Not much later, Pepper was escorted out as well. She walked right by me, an officer guiding her by the elbow, her jacket over her shoulders, her hands on her face.

"Hey," I called out. "You okay?"

She glanced over at me but didn't stop walking. She said nothing. I watched as the officer helped her into the front seat of his car and then they were gone.

Before I could process fully what I should do next, there was a tap on my shoulder. I turned around and looked down.

"Hi. My ride just got put in a cop car. Do you think you could drive me home?" It was Lynn.

On the drive to her house, we talked, marveling over the surprising events of the evening. Lynn didn't go to Ravenwood; she knew both Pepper and Jason from high school. She hadn't known that they had dated, much less that they had recently broken up.

When I got her home – actually, her parents' home, where she still lived while taking classes at the local community college – I parked at the curb and turned off the car. We continued to talk. And talk. It was easy. It felt as though I had known her all my life. We had an immediate rapport that required no effort on either of our parts. With her, I felt none of the paralyzing if not entirely unpleasant excitement that I felt when I was talking to Pepper. Instead, I felt comfortable. I felt at home.

And she was pretty. Beautiful, in fact. Petite and attractively slender, with deep and friendly blue eyes, a warm and wide smile, a quick sense of humor and an infectious laugh, her hair blonde like mine. The Barbie to my Ken. We matched. And while being in her presence didn't rock my world the way Pepper could with a casual glance, I didn't want our conversation to end. I wanted to spend more time with her.

After more than three hours, Lynn made a reluctant move to open the passenger door. "I should really go to bed," she sighed.

"Okay," I said. "It was really nice talking to you." And I meant it more sincerely than the cliché sounded.

"It really was," she agreed, and beamed at me.

"Is it wildly inappropriate, given the events of this evening, for me to ask for your number?" And I realized that the question came without any hesitancy or fear of rejection on my part.

She laughed. "It really is," she said. And then she gave it to me.

The semester ended shortly thereafter. I never saw Pepper again on campus, and if she did continue to attend Ravenwood, we were never in the same class together. But I never sought her out, either. My focus was on studying and on Lynn. We spent every possible free moment together from that fateful night until I graduated. We married that summer, and I never looked back.

Hardly ever, anyway.

***

Never start an argument – or bring up a sensitive subject – in bed.

"What did you ever see in him, anyway?" I say to Lynn. "Jason Wagner."

"Seriously?" she asks me, putting her book face down on her blanketed lap.

"Yeah, seriously. It never made sense to me. The guy was like Captain Caveman."

She shakes her head, thinking. "I don't know. I mean, he was super confident. Confidence can be very attractive." I try not to read an insinuation in that statement.

"Anything else?" I ask.

"I don't know," she repeats. "Not really. I mean, I knew him all through high school. He was an okay guy, as far as I could tell. He was popular. And he could be really funny. That night at Mickey's was a total surprise to me. I never would have gone out with him if I had known he was capable of that. Or everything else."

That "everything else" is full of meaning that neither one of us desires to rehash. Like Pepper, I lost track of Jason Wagner after the event at Mickey's. I never saw him again, or even thought about him, until Lynn showed me an article in the newspaper maybe three years ago, accompanied by the black and white photo of the bloated and wasted man that used to be known as Down Under.

I won't go into details. But the key words of the article included: Alcoholic. Spousal abuse. Restraining order. Ultimately, a dead wife. A preschool daughter on life support, the full extent of the damage to her brain unknown. A gun in his mouth. The gaps are easy to fill. But this was the bullet that both Pepper and Lynn had dodged. Jason's wife wasn't so lucky.

"Life certainly takes some interesting turns," I say, yawning.

"What do you mean?" asks Lynn.

"Just think. That night, if I had taken Pepper somewhere other than Mickey's. If the four of us hadn't been in the same place at the same time, life would have turned out so much differently. You might have ended up with Jason – heaven forbid, of course – and I might have ended up with Pepper. Life really does turn on a dime."

"And do you think about that?" Lynn challenges me.

"Think about what?"

"Life with her," she says. "Do you think about what your life would look like if you had ended up with her?"

"Yes… *no!*" I say, correcting myself. "No, not really. I mean, nothing beyond a little 'what if' scenario. It's not like I think about it all the time or wish for it."

Lynn stares at me. She is propped up on her pillows, a position for reading. I am flat on my back beside (*below*) her, an uncomfortable position for an uncomfortable conversation. I prop myself up on one elbow to bring my eyes closer to her level. With my free hand, I touch her arm.

"Babe, I love *you*," I say. "I love our life. I love Danny. I wouldn't change a single thing. I'm *glad* I took Pepper to Mickey's that night. I might never have met you otherwise."

She looks away from me, silent.

"Anyway, you've got nothing to worry about," I say, adopting a casual tone. "She doesn't even remember who I am."

Lynn chuckles. "That makes me feel so much better," she says.

"What is going *on*?" I ask.

"I see you two are Facebook friends now," she says.

"What?"

She picks up her phone from the nightstand. Wakes it up. Launches Facebook. Holds the screen uncomfortably close to my nose. "Greg Thompson and Pepper Lauren are now friends," it says.

"You've talked about her all week. You went to her bar—"

"With coworkers," I argue. A true statement, but not the whole story.

"—and now you're Facebook friends. What next, Jason, do you want to invite her over for dinner?"

"Greg," I say.

"What?"

"You just called me Jason."

"Whatever. I just don't get your infatuation with her."

"There is no infatuation," I insist.

Lynn turns her back on me, turning off her nightstand light and sliding further under the covers. "I don't want to talk about it anymore," she says.

"Lynn, babe, c'mon," I say, rubbing her shoulder.

She doesn't respond.

Lynn usually gets up with me in the morning to see me off to work. But when I step out of the bathroom, she is still in bed, her head under the covers. Asleep or pretending to be. I don't disturb her.

At work, I have a message from Facebook. From Pepper. Four words.

"I remember you now."

I fake a stomach bug to Julie, and within a quarter of an hour, I am at Pepper's. It is barely after nine in the morning. The bar is closed, of course, and there are no lights on inside save for a faint one I can see on the far side of the room, beyond the bar. I bang on the glass door.

There is movement in the shadows, and lights come on. Pepper approaches me, meeting my gaze through the glass as she unbolts the door. My heart is pounding. I don't know what I expect or even what I really want, but the feeling of looking into her eyes, knowing that she is in that moment looking at no one else but me, transports me back to college, back into my 18-year-old mind, and my excitement is palpable.

She opens the door, but instead of inviting me in, she steps out.

She considers me for a moment with a look that I try to deny is distain. It is awful, to have her beautiful face regarding me with such contempt. Finally, she speaks. "It's the strangest thing," she says. "For the past couple of days, it's been like trying to remember the words to a song, or the name of an actor in that one movie you saw years ago.

It just wouldn't come to me. And then suddenly, it did." She snaps her fingers.

"I remember you now. I remember everything. I remember how you stood there with your white knuckles clutching that pool stick while Jason laid into me. And you did nothing. Complete strangers came to my defense. Some man I'd never seen before or since handed me a handkerchief because my lip was bleeding. Frat boys were asking me if I was alright. And where were you? Hiding in the parking lot."

I open my mouth, but no words come. The strangest, most unpleasant feeling washes over me. I realize I'm heartbroken.

She shakes her head. "I don't know how I could have forgotten. That part I may never figure out. But this morning it was almost like I stepped through a door. And now that I remember you, I'm going to make every effort to forget you again."

I stare at her. She gives me a moment – a gracious moment, in fact – to say something in response. But when I don't, she makes a gesture. She points down at the ring on my left hand.

"Go home," she orders. "To your wife."

***

I drive around aimlessly for a while. I consider going back to work, but know immediately how pointless that would be. I replay Pepper's words to me and think of the multitude of things I should have said in response, a myriad of words that might have been brilliant in the moment but refused to reveal themselves in a timely manner. I think about going back and confronting her, banging on the door of the bar until she has to face me, has to hear my side of the story, maybe even hear a feeble apology for not being more of a man when I was only an 18-year-old kid.

But I find myself in my own driveway before I even realize I had decided to go home. And also without realizing it, I begin to cry. Behind those doors is my entire world, my entire life. Lynn and Danny. In a few days' time I let a long-dormant attraction resurrect itself in my heart and monopolize my thoughts. And in pursuit of what? Some vapor-like possibility that lived down a road not taken, at the risk of everything I had been given and had worked so hard to build?

Suddenly, I want to see Lynn.

I *need* to see Lynn.

When I press the garage door button, nothing happens. I remove the batteries, flip them, and put them in again. Still nothing.

I stop the car's engine, letting it sit in the driveway, and walk quickly to the front door, which is locked. I fumble for my key, not even sure that I have one on the ring, chiding myself for depending on the garage door opener for access to the house, knowing full well that batteries eventually die.

I bang on the door. My first words are going to be, "I love you" as I take her into my arms.

It opens slowly, and all words are forgotten. Lynn stares back at me. She looks exhausted. She is dressed in a white robe that is too big for her small frame. Her hair is a mess and her face is haggard. She has lines at the sides of her mouth that I have never noticed before, and beneath one eye is a pale yellow-green shadow, the faded remains of a bruise.

Balanced on her hip is a child. A little girl with dark, knotted hair and crusted mucus under her nose. The girl studies me, two fingers in her mouth.

"Lynn?"

"Can I help you?" she asks.

"Who's this?" I say, pointing at the girl. "Where's Danny?"

Lynn takes a step back, fear creeping onto her face, and begins to push the door closed again. My hand shoots out, keeping it in place.

"Baby, what's going on?" I ask her.

"Do I know you?" she says. "Who are you?" Her voice is quiet and trembling.

"No," I say, shaking my head rapidly, denying what I am hearing. "Lynn, this isn't funny. Let me in."

"I don't *know* you," she insists, pushing against the door that I continue to hold open. The little girl abruptly removes her fingers from her mouth and begins to cry.

"Ok," I say, trying to soften my tone, trying to calm her down. "I get it. I've learned my lesson. Let me in."

"I'll call the police," she says. Tears begin to fall silently down her cheeks. The little girl starts to scream.

"Lynn," I plead, raising my voice above the girl's screams.

Then, there is a man's voice, coming from the recesses of the house behind her. "Lynn?" he calls out gruffly. "Who's there?"

"Go," Lynn insists, looking at me desperately. "Go before my husband comes."

The statement drains all strength from my arm, and in that instant she slams the door shut. The deadbolt rams into place. The little girl's wailing increases. I hear shouting.

I back away from the door, my thoughts a scrambled mess of confusion. I nearly fall as I back off the front step into the yard, regarding the scene in front of me. It is my house, familiar but different. The same front door, but the shutters are green instead of black. I recognize the shape of the windows, but the curtains behind them are new to me.

I return to the car and get inside, starting the engine. I back out recklessly, not bothering to check for any oncoming traffic on the street, and nearly take out the mailbox in the process — a black mailbox with white lettering that reads, "The Wagners."

I race down the road, pedal to the floor, the car and my thoughts both racing, no idea where I am going. I run my fingers through my hair, suddenly desperate to remember something, something important. It is like grasping at the details of a dream that seems so vivid and memorable in the first instant of waking, but quickly begins to dissipate like so much smoke.

Remember, Greg, remember. You have a wife named Lynn. You have a son named…

You have a son…

You have…

Three blocks away, the tires squeal when I slam on the brakes at a stop sign, the car skidding two feet into the intersection, the seatbelt holding me fast to my seat. I look around.

Why am I in such a hurry?

And what am I doing here in the first place?

emil bones

Do not read this.

TUESDAY

The only thing really noteworthy about that morning was just how un-noteworthy it was. Nothing memorable had happened the weekend prior; no holidays or anything like that. And I don't recall that I was looking forward to anything special happening the weekend coming up. Everything about the day and the coming week was normal. Routine.

It was a Tuesday in September. I had dropped Benjamin off at school before coming to work. It was his third week in a new school. He had been understandably nervous on the first day, a shy but friendly 8-year-old who thrived in the presence of two or three close friends but tended to subtly fold into himself in unfamiliar settings with unfamiliar faces. But he'd put on a brave face for me, given me a quick but tight hug, and marched through the doors to his new school, casting only a single sidelong glance my way before disappearing.

In my heart I had felt the same tug of trepidation that I knew he was also feeling. After leaving Benjamin at school, I had reported for my first day of work at the local public library. Just like him, I was in a new setting with new faces and new responsibilities to learn, but I was as much excited as I was nervous. Being a librarian had always been number one on my "Attainable Dream Jobs" list. The thought of being surrounded by books on a daily basis was nothing short of absolute bliss for me. Dealing with the book-borrowing, internet-using, forgetting-to-whisper public was just a necessary evil.

I'd never had the opportunity to work at a library before; a librarian's salary was not worth my time, as far as David had been concerned, so I'd set that dream aside for the kind of menial phone-answering, spreadsheet-making jobs that paid little more. But now that David was out of the picture — with the exception of his alimony checks that helped me pay the mortgage and his every-other-weekend visits with Benjamin — I could have any job I wanted. I gladly chose librarian. The elation I felt when I got the job was absolutely unreasonable.

Three weeks later, both Benjamin and I had gotten used to our new surroundings. His teacher, Miss Delaney, told me that he had quickly become very popular among all of his classmates, although he chose to stick close with a couple of other boys from among the smarter and more pleasant members of his class, and his grades so far were excellent, although he was also proving, surprisingly, to be a bit of a class clown. That was his father coming out in him, but thankfully his jokes fell on the harmless and funny side of the line.

I too had managed to make friends with my coworkers and was already on a familiar, smiling basis with several of the library's regular customers. I'd even gotten a little more comfortable around Mrs. Strickland, the branch manager who was the epitome of the clichéd "stern librarian." I knew from my interview that she was no-nonsense (and also had *zero* sense of humor), the kind of boss who would have a very rigid way of doing things and very high expectations of the people she supervised. I had to remind myself that she had been kind enough not only to hire me, but also to delay my start date so that it could coincide with Benjamin's first day of school.

And so it was a Tuesday in September, and it was also the beginning of the end of everything.

* * *

The library parking lot was empty when I arrived. I parked at the back of the lot in the spaces reserved for employees and made the trek to the front doors of the building. It being a late September day, the morning air was cool but not cold. The aroma on the breeze was a mix of dying summer and looming autumn. I love that smell. I took a deep breath and felt peaceful.

The library building was new, relatively speaking, with a concrete square beside the front door with an engraving that simply read,

"1976." Twin oak doors opened up into a small entryway, beyond which was a single door leading into the library proper.

I unlocked these doors shortly before 8:00 a.m. The library would not open to the public until 10:00, and my coworkers would not begin arriving until 9:00. In a welcomed twist of fate, the unwanted responsibility of opening the library each morning always fell to the newbie. While my coworkers seemed to relish the idea of coming in to work at 9:00, I was quite happy to start my day early and spend an hour every morning alone among the books. It was quiet and calm. The tall shelves, blanketed in shadows and silence, gave me the most pleasant of lonely chills. It was easily my favorite hour of the work day. But I didn't let any of my coworkers know this; I liked the fact that something I welcomed doing was seen as slightly sacrificial.

I entered the lobby and locked the doors behind me. I punched a code into a keypad beside the lobby doors, disabling the alarm system. Beside the doors in the library's lobby was a large, padded bin on wheels. This bin collected the books, DVDs, and CDs that customers returned after hours via a slot in the wall beside the doors. I pushed the bin through the lobby, and, after bumping the main library door open with my backside, pulled it into the library proper.

I paused and flipped on the lights before dropping my keys into my purse. The buzz of the fluorescents igniting was the only sound to be heard, and the air was still and slightly heavy with the smell of ink and dust. I swore I would never tire of that smell.

Behind the library's main service desk were two doors; one led to the employee lounge, which contained a small kitchen, a folding plastic table with chairs, and a row of lockers, as well as the entrance to the employee bathroom. The other door led to Mrs. Strickland's office, off-limits unless she invited you in.

I put my purse in my locker and clocked in. As I pulled my name badge from a corkboard ("HELENA") and pinned it to my shirt I probably hummed. Knowing me, I hummed. As much as I loved the stillness of the library in the first hour of the morning, there was something undeniably unsettling about it as well. The tall shelves offered far too many places for someone to hide. Humming was a little like whistling past a graveyard.

After booting up the front desk and public computers, my next responsibility was unloading the bin of its contents so that it could be pushed into the storage room and out of the way. Using both hands, I retrieved books two or three at a time and stacked them on the counter, along with a smattering of DVDs and compact discs of music and audio books.

At some point in this process, I found myself holding a small, thin book with a soft black leather cover. There was no writing on the cover of the book. No author or title. The spine was likewise blank, with no call number. I rubbed my thumb along the bottom of the spine to see if there was any tape residue where the call number might have once been adhered, but I felt nothing but the bare leather.

This wasn't the first time that a customer had accidentally dropped off a book that didn't actually belong to the library. I placed the book on the counter, separate from the stacks, and finished emptying the bin, which I then wheeled into the storage room.

By 8:45, I had checked in all the returned books and stacked them neatly into piles based on their location in the library (adult fiction in one stack, non-fiction in another, children's books in the third, etc.). The little black leather book rested nearby on the counter to my left. I heard the library doors unlock, and I smiled as two of my coworkers walked in, coffees in hand, having what sounded like a typical morning conversation full of inconsequential pleasantries.

"Good morning, Helena," they said in unison as they strolled by the front counter on their way to the break room. One was Beth, a short, round woman of around 45 who had a smile that was almost as wide as her face. Sporadic cat hair clung to everything she wore, and she wasn't much of a dresser, but she had the kind of pleasant, inviting face that convinced me that every person who had ever met her had instantly liked her. The other was Danielle, a tall, lanky twenty-something with a perpetual smirk on her face that made her look conspiratorial but would love to have you join her. Between her style of clothing and straight, long blonde hair, she looked like a model from the late 1960s. She also looked like she belonged anywhere except a library. The two of them together made quite the odd-looking pair.

I said a friendly "Good morning" in return, and as they strolled by the counter, I placed my left hand instinctively on the black leather book and pulled it closer to me, hiding it from their view behind the stacks of books on the counter, a small part of me feeling suddenly and inexplicably possessive of it. Danielle gave me a quizzical look — or perhaps it wasn't a look at all — and the two of them continued into the break room.

I picked up the book and opened it. The first page was completely blank, with no copyright or publishing information. The second page revealed a name, hand-written in black ink: "Emil Bones." I wondered if the book was actually someone's personal journal.

I flipped to the third page, which contained the beginnings of what appeared to be a poem, again hand-written in black ink. I read:

> *There was a boy named Emil Bones*
> *Who would like to be your friend,*
> *But once you let him in your home,*
> *He may never leave again.*

"Good morning, Helena."

Mrs. Strickland's voice startled me, and then I felt my face flush hot as I realized she had discovered me reading instead of working. One look at her stern eyes through her thick, silver-rimmed glasses, and I felt like a school girl who'd been caught passing notes in class.

"Hi… good morning, Mrs. Strickland."

"What's that?" she asked, subtly jutting her chin at the book in my hands as she walked past me and then behind the counter. "That's not one of ours," she added before I could respond. I couldn't be sure if her surmise came from noting the lack of call number on the spine or because, after a good four decades as the head librarian, she recognized all of the library's books on sight.

"No, it's… someone put it in the drop slot last night," I said. "I was checking to see if the owner's name might be somewhere inside."

"Is it?"

"I don't think so."

"Then put it in Lost and Found," she said dismissively before proceeding into her office and shutting the door behind her. I turned and dropped the book into a bin behind me, where it settled among a small collection that included a hideous mustard yellow scarf, a key, a rather ratty-looking plush cat, a green umbrella, a plastic mouse, a necklace, a dead cell phone, and, inexplicably, a hearing aid.

I loaded the stacks of returned books into a wheeled cart and proceeded into the heart of the library, where I returned the books to their proper homes.

* * *

First to work each morning, I was also first to take a lunch break. One of the tiny perks of my job was that a half hour lunch break was included in my eight-hour day, meaning I could work from 8:00 until 4:00 and pick up Benjamin by 4:15, so he only had to endure 45 minutes of additional time at the end of each school day in a study hall with a mix of other students whose parents couldn't pick them up immediately at 3:30. He used the time well and was usually finished with his homework by the time I picked him up each day.

At 11:30, I grabbed my lunch from the break room. Remembering the hint of fall that I had smelled on the breeze on my way through the parking lot that morning, I decided that it would be the perfect day to walk to the park across the street and eat my lunch on a bench under one of the trees.

I strolled from the break room to the counter. Mrs. Strickland was still in her office, door closed, the sound of her voice indicating a phone conversation. Danielle was picking up toys in the children's section, which was to the right of the customer service desk in the center and located opposite the main room of the library, which contained a bank of computers for public use, racks of magazines, a reading area, and the bulk of the library's shelves of books.

Beth was dutifully stationed behind the counter. One of Mrs. Strickland's firm rules was that one member of the staff had to remain behind the counter at all times in order to be at the immediate service of any customers. This rule was particularly ridiculous on mornings like this, when there had been, at maximum, four customers in the entire library at any given time. Beth gave me a look that read, "I don't have anything to do here but grin."

I smiled and held up my lunch bag. "I'm going to eat my lunch at the park," I said.

"That's a great idea!" she said, beaming like a woman who'd just found an onion ring amongst her French fries. "It's gorgeous outside."

"Yes," I said, my eyes dropping to the Lost and Found box behind her. Without thinking, I stopped and reached behind her.

Beth scooted forward awkwardly and said, "Oh, am I in your way?"

"Just grabbing a tissue," I said. "Just in case. I don't think I packed any napkins." I snatched three tissues from a box on a low shelf behind her, and in the same movement plucked the black book from the Lost and Found box. I held it at my side, out of sight, and said, "See you in thirty," and walked out of the library.

* * *

The park was completely deserted. This past summer, it had always been bustling, with children hanging, swinging, climbing, and falling from nearly every available surface. While the small manmade pond and its surrounding walking path were picturesque, I hadn't enjoyed the heat or the noise, but Benjamin had loved the three or four times I'd taken him there on those rare afternoons when I'd gotten tired of unpacking boxes and hanging pictures in our new house. Watching him play from a nearby bench, I had seen a smile bloom across his face, and he was almost unrecognizable to me. It made me realize just how long it had been since he had seemed so genuinely happy.

But now that kids were in school again, the park was quiet. I picked a bench beside the pond, which was occupied by a handful of fat ducks, and plopped down my brown bag beside me, but I didn't open it. I opened the book instead.

> *There was a boy named Emil Bones*
> *Who would like to be your friend,*
> *But once you let him in your home,*
> *He may never leave again.*

He loves to play in shadows,
In voices, shapes, and sounds,
And while you may not always see him,
He will always be around.

He is quite the little prankster,
Who may make you laugh, but then
The jokes stop being funny,
And you will never laugh again.

First he absents things you need
For the collection he's amassed
Then purloins the things you love
Each more precious than the last.

He puts them all inside a room
That light has never known
Where there is no doorway out
And all exist, alone

He will make you suffer far beyond
What any person ever should
And while he may not take your life,
He will make you wish he would.

"That's enough of that," I whispered out loud, and snapped the book shut.

I ate my lunch, taking deep breaths between bites and enjoying the smell of approaching fall and smiling at the fussy ducks swimming aimlessly in the pond before me. I convinced myself that I was relaxing and enjoying the fresh air, but as soon as I was done eating, I returned to the library and clocked in with 10 minutes still left to my lunch break.

* * *

I picked up Benjamin at 4:15 and we went home. We had moved into the house in May, and the newness of it and its neighborhood had not quite worn off on me yet. It was a small, yellow two-bedroom house at the end of a cul-de-sac, one level with an unfinished basement. A couple of small pines dotted the postage stamp-sized front yard, but the fenced-in back yard had enough space for Benjamin to play and some flower beds to satisfy my green thumb.

There were four neighboring houses, two on either side. In the months since we'd moved in, I'd managed to meet the families in all four houses. Two elderly retired couples, one pair of aggravatingly good-looking newlyweds, and a twenty-something couple with a pre-school daughter and a baby boy. All of them were pleasant enough, but it seemed everyone in the cul-de-sac had an unspoken agreement to stay out of each other's way as much as possible.

There was no garage, so I parked in the driveway and we walked together to the front door. Benjamin had already told me about his day, which had included an A+ on a spelling test, a love note passed to him by a dishwater-blonde classmate named Julie (he rolled his eyes as he told me about the note, protesting a tad too much), and his friend Miles who had tripped and fallen on his way to the chalkboard, leading to a moment of uproarious classroom laughter that his teacher quickly hushed, but not without a small grin on her face, Benjamin had noted.

When I opened the front door, I almost tripped over our cat, who snaked her way between my feet, motor running loudly. "Ugh, Mags," I said, frustrated, as I stepped carefully over her and into the living room. I had bought this fluffy, charcoal-gray beauty as a present for Benjamin when he'd turned five. The two were inseparable. Thinking myself quite clever, I'd named her Margaret Catwood, but of course that name had very quickly devolved to just Margaret, then Maggie, then Mags. Benjamin called her kitty.

"Make sure she has food, ok, bud?" I said to Benjamin, after I'd deposited my purse on the floor of the front closet, then made my way through the living room toward the kitchen. Benjamin headed in the opposite direction, down the hallway toward the house's lone bathroom, which also served as the laundry room and the place where we kept the cat's food and litterbox. Margaret Catwood followed close on his heels.

Dinner was fish sticks and macaroni and cheese. Benjamin dutifully helped me clean up the dishes, and then I allowed him to have half an hour of video games, his homework completed at school while he waited for me to pick him up.

Later Benjamin took a bath, and with a little time left before bed, I told him to go play. I was tidying up the kitchen when I heard him banging on something – plastic against plastic – in the living room.

I found him sitting behind a toy workbench. The banging was Benjamin using a plastic hammer against oversized plastic nails. The toy, picked out by his father for Christmas when Benjamin was six, had always annoyed me, and so I had hidden it in the basement after our move. I was not pleased that Benjamin had found it again.

"Really, Benji?" I said, wincing to indicate that the hammering was irritating.

He smiled at me, then reached over and flipped a switch. Lights came to life across the top of the toy, and a buzz saw began to whir noisily. I was further reminded of why I hated the thing. Benjamin beamed.

Then came the electronic voice of a child, speaking above the din of the buzz saw: "Hey, what are we making?" it said cheerfully.

I groaned and retreated to the kitchen while Benjamin continued to play. At 9:00, I ordered him to bed, read him a story (*Where the Wild Things Are* for the umpteenth time, at his request), and kissed him goodnight.

I watched a little television but found nothing worthwhile to watch – it was mostly commercials and disturbing news – and I found myself quickly nodding off, so I decided to turn in early. I checked to make sure that I had locked the front door and found the front closet door slightly open. Hearing a shuffling noise inside, I pulled the door open further and the cat bolted out, upsetting my purse in the process. "Dummy," I said, not sure if I was addressing myself or the cat, and knelt to shove the contents of the purse back inside, amused at how the cat could never resist walking through an open door.

There, on the floor amongst the lipstick, wallet, keys and a couple of random coupons was the black leather book. I didn't recall putting it in my purse. I thought back to my lunch break. I had put the book down on the bench, eaten my lunch, and then returned to the library, brown bag in one hand, book in the other. I had thrown the bag away and then… had done what with the book? I honestly could not remember, but could have sworn I had returned it to the Lost and Found box.

I hesitated. The book had unsettled me, and here in the dark living room at night, it unnerved me even more. But I hadn't finished it. It went against my grain to leave a book unfinished, even ones I didn't particularly care for. I always saw them through to the end.

The book balanced on the edge of the sink as I brushed my teeth. I found myself eyeing it warily. It became a rectangular blur as I removed my contacts. I fished my glasses out of the medicine cabinet, then snatched up the book again.

In bed, I opened the book and continued to read:

> *See Emil was a wicked child*
> *Whose heart was full of sin*
> *Until his mother realized*
> *Emil never should have been.*
>
> *First she crushed him with a pillow*
> *Then she hit him with a club*
> *Tied a cord around his neck*
> *And drowned him in the tub.*
>
> *She bound him up with heavy rope*
> *Put a bag over his head*
> *And then with horror realized*
> *That Emil wasn't dead.*
>
> *She took his body in the night*
> *To the woods behind her shack*
> *Burned him up quite thoroughly,*
> *Placed his ashes in a sack*

Hid the sack deep in the earth
And marked it with white stones
Knowing well that this was not
The end of Emil Bones

That very night she lay in bed
Sad, tired, scared and vexed
When Emil whispered in her ear,
"What game shall we play next?"

What made a mother do this
To a child that she should love?
It's an answer quite disturbing
You may know it soon enough

So now you know the devil child
Whose name was Emil Bones
Rest assured, he knows you too
And won't leave you alone

He's a shadow, he's a whisper,
He's a hornet, he's a pox
For heaven's sake, now heed my words:
Do not answer when he knocks...

A thunderous pounding from the front door startled me so badly that I flung the book into my lap. In in the ensuing silence that fell over the house like a thick blanket, I held my breath, hoping that my stillness would hide me. I started to move, then hesitated. I grabbed my glasses and pressed them onto my face, then looked at my cell phone; the clock said 11:08. No one should be knocking at this hour.

A long pause, and then the pounding resumed, hard and insistent. My bedroom shared a wall with the living room, which was where the front door to the house was located, and I could have sworn the pounding was hard enough to rattle the wall between the two rooms.

Forcing myself out of bed, I opened the bedroom door silently, and crept slowly to the living room and peeked around the corner, my breath held, my hands clutched at my chest. I was unreasonably scared. I stared across the room at the closed front door, willing my eyes to adjust to the darkness.

As they did, I was able to distinguish the silhouette of a boy standing in the room between me and the door, perfectly still, nearly hidden in the shadows, facing me. I put my hand to my mouth and took a step backwards. My blood turned to ice. He shifted.

"Who is it, Mom?" Benjamin asked, and relief swept over me. He wasn't facing me at all, but away from me, toward the door. Awakened by the knocking, he had gotten to the room before me. The front door remained closed.

"I don't know, baby," I said, and I took a step toward him, putting my hand on one pajama-clad shoulder and pulling him toward me. We stepped back from the door together, and I hoped that Benjamin could not feel that my body was practically vibrating with tension as I ushered him out of the living room and toward his bedroom door, which stood at the opposite end of the hallway from mine.

As I tucked him back in bed, Benjamin asked again, "Who was it, Mom?"

I didn't answer at first; I was listening to hear if the pounding would resume. "No one to worry about, pal," I said, and stroked his hair. "Go back to sleep. School night."

He was instantly asleep, and stayed asleep even when his doorway hinges creaked as I shut his door. (*Mental note: oil those.*) I moved as quietly as I could back down the hallway, noting that my feet were damp with the sweat of adrenaline and were sticking to the hardwood floor as I walked. A board squeaked as I got midway to my destination, and I knew that if the knocking resumed, I would likely have a heart attack on the spot.

But it did not. I returned to my room and shut the door behind me. I picked the small leather book off the bed and threw it in the trash. I grabbed another book — a stupid romance novel that was offensive to me both as a woman and as a book lover but was as pleasantly distracting and unhealthy as a bar of chocolate — and read.

My eyes passed over the words, but I didn't register the story. My heart continued to race. Eventually it calmed and I nodded off. When I woke up the next morning, the romance novel was on my chest, my glasses balanced precariously on the tip of my nose, and my bedroom light was still on.

WEDNESDAY

"Rough night?"

Beth had approached the counter, arms full of books that were threatening to spill over her stubby arms, and caught me in the midst of a deep yawn that brought tears to my eyes. "Ugh, yes," I replied, wiping the corners of my eyes with my thumbs.

"Was Benjamin sleepwalking again?" she asked.

"Good guess, but no," I said. "No. It was… it wasn't anything. Just stayed up late with a bad book." I was amused that my little lie wasn't really a lie at all.

"Books put me to sleep," Beth said. "I know, profound statement. But if I only read at night, I'd never finish a single book. Out like a light by the end of the first page."

"That's usually me, too," I replied. "Not last night." I was then distracted by a customer, a tallish man in his mid-30s, who approached the counter and was now standing behind Beth, a hopeful look on his face as he made eye contact with me.

"Can I help you?" I asked.

"Could you help me?" he said at the same time, and we exchanged smiles. Beth tossed me a grin before ducking out of the way and disappearing among the shelves. "Yeah," he continued. "There's a book I'm trying to find. The computer says it's available, but I can't find it." He handed me a small slip of paper. The chicken scratches read, "Men Health Big Book Exercise 613.70449 CAM."

I came out from behind the counter. "Let's go have a look," I said. "Sometimes books just get shelved in the wrong place. We'll see if we can find it."

He followed close behind me as I headed toward the nonfiction books. The section was three long rows away from the front counter, taking us to the center of the library. I looked at the number on the paper again and stopped short suddenly as I realized I had almost passed the section where the book should have been shelved. My quick halt caused the man to gently bump into me. I caught a pleasant aroma that smelled like a mixture of leather and soap.

"Sorry," we both said, and he chuckled. I had to force myself not to smile too widely.

I studied the shelves in front of us, moving an index finger along the upright spines. "It should be right… here," I said, pointing at a gap between two books. "But it's obviously not."

"Yeah, this is where I looked," he said.

"It could still be here," I said, "Just not in the right spot. The game is afoot." I cringed a little at myself, then gave the man a self-deprecating half-wink. He looked right at me and smiled, his electric blue eyes in stark contrast to his short-cropped dark brown beard and hair.

Most of the other books in the section had to do with health, weight loss, exercise, and weightlifting. Together we scoured the titles. He was behind me and to my right, and I had the distinct sensation that he was looking at me as much as he was hunting for the book.

"Aha!" I said, and pulled the book from the shelf, two rows down from where it should have been. An impossibly well-built man with shining skin and paper-white teeth graced the cover.

"Excellent," he said, taking the book as I offered it to him. "Perfect. Thank you."

"You're welcome," I said.

My inclination was to immediately return to the front counter, but the man was standing in my way and seemed to be hesitating. "I'm betting it's muscle heads who usually check out a book like this."

"Oh no," I responded. "Actually the opposite. Fatsos and string beans. Guys who look like they do reps with beer mugs and remote controls. And oddly enough, they look exactly the same *after* they return the book." I smiled up at him, amused with myself, and his face visibly fell.

"Oh *gosh,*" I said, horrified. "Not you! I mean…"

To my relief, he laughed. "It's okay."

"What a horrible thing to say."

"Not at all," he chuckled. "Just brutally honest."

"That's me, especially after a night of little sleep. Like last night. I'm a very light sleeper. The tiniest sound and I'm awake. And I tend to say whatever pops into my head when I'm tired." The man's eyes began to glaze over, but his smile didn't falter. "Like telling perfect strangers about my sleeping patterns and how tired I am and then insinuate that I think they look like a couch potato."

"If it's any consolation," he chuckled, "I *am* a recovering fatso. I've lost about 75 pounds in the past year." He held his arms out in a take-a-look gesture that was somehow not even remotely prideful.

"Really?" I said, sizing him up good-naturedly. He was wearing a brown leather jacket over a white button-up shirt and skinny jeans. He would have looked quite at home on a book cover himself. "Good for you."

"Really. And now that the weight is gone, I figure it's time to try to get myself back into shape. And so…" He held up the book and tapped the cover with his index finger.

"Right. So how did you do it? Lose the weight, I mean."

"Stopped drinking. Stopped eating. Stopped living, really. But I'll look good in my casket." He chuckled. "And I burn calories by making awkward conversations with cute librarians."

"Oh, wow," I said. "You're right, that *was* awkward." I was playing along, and I was playing along well. Go me.

"Sorry!" he said, putting up his hands in surrender, the book clutched in his right. "Former fatso. No skills whatsoever with flirting." His smile was magnetic.

"I should really get back to work," I said, smiling and shaking my head and not at all meaning it. I found it so incredibly easy to keep eye contact with him and secretly hoped that he would keep talking. But he turned sideways so that I could slide past him toward the front counter. I slipped by. Leather and soap. He followed.

"How long have you worked here?" he asked as we walked. My pace was slower than it needed to be. "I don't remember seeing you before."

"Do you come here often?" I asked, hating how much the question sounded like I was making a pass.

"Quite a bit," he said.

"I've worked here a few weeks. Less than a month."

"Do you like it so far?"

"I love it," I said. "Dream job."

"Seriously?" he chuckled, as if he thought I was kidding.

I stopped and turned around to look at him. "Yes, seriously. I've always wanted to work in a library. I'd read books 24 hours a day if I could, but since that's not an option, I think being surrounded by them all day long is a fair compromise. I find it peaceful and comforting to be around all these books." I gave a glance to the shelves around us. "And even a little sad honestly."

"Sad?" he said, his smile fading and his eyebrows curving up inquisitively. I noticed that he was wearing a necklace – a leather string with a foreign symbol made of pewter resting against his chest, barely visible between the open collar of his shirt. I had to resist an incredibly strong urge to reach out and touch it.

"Yes," I said. "All of these stories, waiting patiently to be read. That's all they want. I wish I could read them all and make them happy."

He smiled. "You're an interesting one." Pause. "Helena."

I dropped my eyes down to my name tag. "Shall we?" I said, tilting my head toward the front counter.

The counter between us again, he handed me the book and his library card, which I scanned. The computer informed me that his name was Hugo Denholm, and he read a lot of books. Or at least he checked out a lot of books. Books on woodworking. Weight loss. True Crime. Grilling. Cinema. Poetry. A smattering of DVDs.

I handed him his card and his book. "This is due back in 14 days, Hugo," I said and smiled. "And I expect results."

He locked eyes with me again, and I could tell that he was collecting his nerve. His pause was eternal. "Look," he said, "I'm terrible at this. In fact, you already know that I'm terrible at this. I would love to have dinner with you sometime. We could talk about lonely books and find new ways to insult each other."

I felt my heart literally flutter in my chest, and then was immediately afraid that he could tell. But my smile faded. In the past few minutes I had forgotten that there was anyone else in the world except for me and Mr. Big Book, but suddenly I was very aware of the presence of my coworkers, all within earshot, although by all appearances preoccupied. Or pretending to be.

"Look," I whispered, leaning slightly toward him across the counter. "I'm recently divorced. Very recently divorced. And I have a son."

His expression didn't change. He continued to look hopeful, as if still waiting for the deal-breaking detail I hadn't yet offered.

"Plus I tend to overshare when I'm tired and I sometimes insult library patrons," I added.

"Noted," he said. His smile remained, but it was colored by disappointment. "Well, you have my number," he said, eyeing the back of the computer monitor on the counter between us. "And my full name. Yes, it's Hugo Eugene Denholm and I don't know why my parents hated me. You have my address and my full library history. Any embarrassing titles should be attributed to my roommate, who uses my library card when checking out questionable movies. So if you change your mind, the offer stands. Call me."

I didn't have words, so I just smiled at him and thought about how I wanted to change my answer. He started to back away from the counter, still not breaking eye contact with me. With a small wave he turned toward the door at the library's entrance. He opened it and stood back to let two elderly ladies enter.

I looked down at my hands on the counter, at the indentation that circled the base of my left ring finger, now bare. I felt happy and disappointed and thoughtful and anxious.

"Oh, and Helena?" he called from the door, and I looked up. "I don't have a roommate. I lied. The questionable titles? All mine. Don't judge me." And he was gone.

I chuckled quietly in his wake, and then was startled when Danielle was immediately in front of me in the space where my handsome customer had stood just moments before. She was all straight blonde hair and lanky limbs and scowling face, staring down at me.

"What?" I said, perplexed.

"I used to think you were smart," she responded.

* * *

The evening was pleasant but uneventful. Dinner was a frozen pizza, which Benjamin and I ate on trays in the living room while watching *Kung Fu Panda* on Netflix, Mags curled up on the couch between us, purring though no one was touching her. I was looking at the movie without watching, eating the pizza without tasting, my mind replaying and memorizing my brief but enjoyable encounter with one Mr. Hugo Eugene Denholm. Mr. Hugo Denholm. Hugo. Mrs. Helena Denholm.

I am pathetic.

The sound of Benjamin laughing at the movie awakened me from my daydream. He found the movie uproariously funny no matter how many times he saw it, and the sound of Benjamin's laugh was the sweetest song I'd ever heard. It would never not make me smile, no matter what kind of day I was having. It was the most genuine, innocent sound in the world.

Bath. Bedtime story. Benjamin got lost in the tale in a way that only a true story lover can, his face sometimes making expressions that reflected the emotions of the characters. He had no idea he was doing it. At the story's conclusion, I tucked him in and retreated to the door.

"Mommy?" he called after me.

I stopped. "Yeah, baby?"

"Will Daddy ever live in this house?"

I took a breath and returned to his bedside. I stroked his cheek. "Oh, I don't know, honey," I said. "Daddy has his own house. This house is all yours and mine."

He stared at me. "I wish Daddy could live here too."

"You miss him lots?" I said.

"No," he said, and I was surprised by this answer. "I just want him to live here too."

As I climbed into my own bed a few minutes later, exhausted from the previous night's lack of sleep, I gave a passing glance to the trash can in the corner, the little leather book still resting on top of some crumpled papers and tissues. Trash was collected on Thursday mornings. Tomorrow I would be rid of it for good. Its presence did not bother me in the slightest. Not at all.

I didn't read. I turned out the light, briefly entertained myself with girlish what-if scenarios involving a certain library patron, and was soon asleep. Mere moments or several hours later, I'm not sure, I was startled awake by the sound of Benjamin's door opening down the hall. It's true that I am a terribly light sleeper. The slightest unusual sound in the night causes my heart to leap. The slight rattle of Benjamin's doorknob and the subtle creaking of hinges (*oil those*) had awakened me fully. A moment later, I heard the familiar squeak of a floorboard midway down the hallway, and then the door to my bedroom opened.

Benjamin's shadowy figure entered and he approached my bed, where he stood silently.

"What is it, baby?" I asked. I reached over for my glasses and put them on, and the blurry edges of his dark visage came into focus.

Sleepy, mumbled words came from Benjamin's mouth, none of them intelligible. I could tell that his eyes were only partly open, and he was not awake. He rubbed at one eye with a knuckle of his right hand, then dropped his arm back down as if it weighed 20 pounds. More nonsense words came from his mouth. I thought I heard the word "garden." It was amusing to me how Benjamin's sleepwalking could be simultaneously adorable and frustrating.

I led him back to his bed. He climbed dutifully in and, by the sound of his breathing, was instantly asleep.

I shuffled back to my room and got into bed without even bothering to get under the covers. Sleep enveloped me immediately. Another passage of moments or hours, I do not know, but this time what awakened me was a thunderous pounding at the front door, somehow even more loud and insistent than the night before.

I sat bolt upright in my bed, out of breath as if I had been running. I grabbed blankets and pulled them up to my mouth, trying to cover the sound of my breaths, wanting to hide. A long pause, and then the pounding resumed. Insistent. Loud. Violent. Drowning out all other sound.

I didn't know what to do. I threw on my glasses and looked at my cell phone, face down on the bedside table. My thoughts raced. I reached for the phone, picking it up, and the next round of pounding startled me so badly that I dropped it on the floor where it clattered on the hard wood.

I slid out of bed and crouched down to pick it up. I began to punch in numbers when I heard a terrible new sound: through the wall I could hear the front door being unlocked and opened.

In an instant I was out of my room and around the corner to the living room where I saw Benjamin, standing in his pajamas at the open front door, silhouetted against the dark, starlit September night outside. All was silent. There wasn't the sound of a dog or a bug or a car to be heard. Benjamin's left hand hung at his side, his right hand resting on the doorknob.

"What are you doing, Benjamin?" I whispered, trying not to startle him.

He turned his head toward me without turning his body. He whispered an answer that I couldn't hear.

I stepped closer. I took his hand off the doorknob, backed him away, and began to close the door, giving a quick glance to the yard and street outside, both of which were empty. The night air gave my cheek a cold kiss. The lights were out at every neighboring house. I locked the door and turned to Benjamin. "What did you say, baby?"

His words were nonsense. I placed a hand on his back and pushed him out of the living room, down the hallway and into his bed. With a sleepy sigh, he lay down on his back and clutched his stuffed tiger. I sat by his side until I was sure he was fully asleep.

As I backed away from his bed, he shifted and turned away from me, mumbling more words in his sleep. One of them was "Emil."

THURSDAY

Sleep eluded me for the second night in a row, at least until the wee hours of the morning when I fell into an unconsciousness so thick that I actually slept through the dulcet tones of my cell phone alarm. I was in the middle of a pleasant dream in which Benjamin was running gleefully through the back yard, Margaret Catwood at his heels, while I was elbow-deep in the flowerbeds, the soil pleasantly cool and soft against my bare arms, weeds giving up with the easiest of tugs. I had just grazed something unexpected with my fingertips — buried treasure perhaps — when Benjamin touched my shoulder and said,

"Mom?"

It took effort to open my eyes. Benjamin was standing at my bedside, looking sleepy, his hair a mess. I picked up my cell phone and held the digital display close to my face: 7:29. We should have walked out the door five minutes ago, and yet here I was, still in bed, and there he was, still in his pajamas, unfed, the cat sitting at his feet.

I shooed Benjamin to his room, telling him to dress as quickly as possible. I put on my glasses and dialed a number into my phone, then cradled it against my shoulder while awkwardly attempting to undress.

"Helena?" came Beth's voice from the other end. "Is everything okay?"

"I'm so sorry, I overslept," I said, nearly falling over as I hopped on one foot, attempting to insert the other into a pair of slacks. "It'll be after 8:00 before I can get to the library. I hate to ask you this, but can you open for me?"

"Well, how late are you going to be?" she asked. "It's not the end of the world if you're a few minutes after."

"Really? Mrs. Strickland won't kill me?"

"As long as you're there in time to do the opening checklist, she won't know. Unless she comes in early, but she almost never comes in early."

"Okay," I said, doing some mental clock math. "Okay. I'll do my best."

"Call me again if you need me to come help you out," she said.

"You're the best," I said, and hung up. When I exited my room, cell phone in hand, Benjamin was in the hallway, dressed in yesterday's clothes, his hair only moderately tamed, his book bag in hand.

"What's for breakfast?" he asked.

"Can you go grab a Pop-Tart, buddy? We're very late. I'm sorry."

Benjamin shuffled off to the kitchen. I rushed to the bathroom for a splash cold water on my face and a quick swish of mouthwash. I popped in my contacts. Make-up would have to wait until I got to work. I ran a brush through my hair, confining it to a ponytail, and did a quick mirror check. Passable. But no breakfast for me.

Another quick walk down the hallway, I gave only a passing thought to the fact that it was Thursday, garbage day, but there was no time to gather it, much less put it out. As I swung by my bedroom on the way to the living room and the front door, I glanced at the waste basket in my room. The black leather book was no longer in it.

I opened the closet by the front door and grabbed my purse. Benjamin's voice traveled from the kitchen, a song sung through a mouthful of food. He was easily distracted by his own imagination. If he wasn't off in another world, he was singing songs he'd made up or drawing characters of his own design. He was a well of creativity, a trait I knew he had gotten from me. But right now, I had no patience for it.

I slung my purse on my shoulder and called out, "Let's go! Bring whatever's left of your breakfast." I opened the front door.

Benjamin walked, a little more slowly than I would have liked, out the front door. I locked it behind me and jogged toward the car, passing Benjamin, plunging my hand into my purse. I felt around. No keys.

I stopped moving and stretched the bag open wide. Dug around some more. Benjamin also stopped and stared blankly at me.

"I can't find my keys," I mumbled.

"What?" he said.

"My keys," I said. "They're not in here." I mentally replayed our arrival home the evening before. I had unlocked the front door, dropped the keys into my purse, and then tossed my purse into the closet by the front door. I was sure of it. But the keys were no longer in my purse, and with horror I realized that we were locked out of the house. My heart sank.

I did have my cell phone. I dialed Beth.

"You need me to come in early?" she answered.

"Worse, and please don't hate me," I said. "Can you come pick me up like right now? I just locked us out of the house. I'm a disaster."

"Yeah, sure, of course," she answered, somehow managing to sound both serious and chipper. "Give me your address."

The next hour was a whirlwind: Beth picked us up, we dropped Benjamin off at school (where I realized I was sending him away sleepy and dehydrated, teeth unbrushed and barely a dozen words spoken between us all morning), and together Beth and I conquered the library's opening checklist with about three minutes to spare before Mrs. Strickland and Danielle arrived.

As 9:00 rolled around, I was finally able to stand still and take a deep breath behind the counter, feeling gross and wishing I'd had time to shower. Beth and I exchanged knowing smiles and I said, "Thank you for all of your help."

She wagged a chubby finger up at me. "Don't let it happen again," she said with mock sternness. "And for heaven's sake, buy a hide-a-key."

"Absolutely," I said. Considering how recently I'd moved, I didn't begrudge myself having overlooked that necessary detail, nor even considering giving a copy to my mother, who only lived three miles away. "I had another bad night last night, so I slept through my alarm and wasn't thinking clearly when I got up. Obviously I should've made sure I had my keys before locking the door."

"Was Benjamin sleepwalking again?" she asked, and I realized she had asked me the same question the morning before.

"Yes, he was," I said.

"He's such a cute kid," Beth beamed, and for the second time that morning my heart sank: Beth had never met Benjamin before this morning, and I didn't even introduce them to each other.

"Oh my word. I didn't introduce you to him this morning!" I exclaimed, putting an apologetic hand on her shoulder.

She waved me away good-naturedly. "You had a few things on your mind."

"Yeah, a few. Thank you. Again. I want you to meet him properly sometime."

"Me too," she said. "He looks so much like you."

"Oh, you say that now," I responded, "but if you saw his father you'd know which apple tree he fell from. Spitting image."

"Well, then, his father must be quite handsome," she said, paying the compliment in a tone that acknowledged she was treading on uncertain ground.

"Yes, he is," I sighed with reluctance. "I can't deny that. Too good looking."

I got lost in thought for a moment. Mrs. Strickland emerged from her office and walked, bolt-upright, toward the counter, eyes on me. Beth scooped up a stack of books and walked away.

"Good morning, Helena," Mrs. Strickland said in a pleasant tone without smiling.

"Good morn—"

"Do you have the morning's checklist?"

"I hung it in your office."

She peered at me over her glasses. Obviously, if I had hung it in her office, she wouldn't be asking me for it. I looked around, and then spotted it on a shelf under the counter, a white sheet on a gray metal clipboard. I handed it to her. She took it from me in a move that was slightly gentler than a snatch and gave it a once-over.

"You turned off the library alarm at 8:25 this morning," she said without looking up from the list.

My eyes widened for a moment and then I glanced out toward the shelves trying to spy Beth. I didn't see her. "Yes, I did. I locked myself —"

"Early is on time and on time is late," she interrupted. "And late is inexcusable. Do not let it happen again." She returned to her office without waiting for a response from me. I felt like I was 12.

The rest of the day was a tired blur. I never felt fully awake, in spite of the three cups of coffee I drank from the staff kitchen. Beth only made it one way: strong enough to punch you in the face, which probably explained why she sometimes reminded me of a bouncing rubber ball. I spent my lunch break on the phone with a local locksmith, who agreed to meet me at my house at 4:45. I'd call Uber for a ride to the school and home again, not wanting to overextend Beth's generosity.

That afternoon I hoped for but also feared a return visit from Hugo, although I figured it unlikely that he would be in the library two days in a row. Given the state of my clothes, hair, and makeup, I decided it best if he didn't see me, although I found myself furtively glancing at the library's front doors whenever they opened.

It was with an inexplicable sense of relief that the locksmith opened the front door to my house at 4:50 that afternoon. He left me with a yellow invoice and a few words, among them the advice that I buy myself a hide-a-key. I gave him an impatient "thank you" in return.

While Benjamin ate warmed up leftovers in the kitchen, I turned the house upside down in search of my missing keys. I was on my hands and knees in the living room closet, Margaret Catwood rubbing her body against my face, purring loudly and making my nose itch. I asked Benjamin more than once if he had seen the keys. He insisted that he hadn't. Thankfully there was a spare house key and car key in the kitchen junk drawer, and Beth had somehow managed to provide me with a second library key without alerting Mrs. Strickland to the situation. I'd have to replace the two or three store cards attached to the missing key ring, but would have to say goodbye to the ring itself, a braided brown leather piece that David had made for me by hand. I still treasured it, in spite of everything.

About an hour before bedtime, I let Benjamin turn on a movie in the living room. I kicked off my shoes and curled up on the couch with a book. Margaret Catwood made herself at home on top of my feet. I tugged at her fluffy gray tail and she blinked at me. I barely read a paragraph before I fell soundly asleep.

When I woke up, all was dark in the living room. The TV was off, I was covered with a blanket, my book was resting on the coffee table in front of the couch, and both Benjamin and the cat were gone. I looked at the clock on the wall. It was after midnight.

Slightly alarmed, I walked quietly to Benjamin's bedroom door and opened it slowly, trying to keep it from squeaking. He was asleep in his bed. His back was toward me, but I could see the gentle rising of his shoulder as he breathed. He had never put himself to bed before. In the bathroom, I touched the head of his toothbrush: it was wet. *Good boy.* I smiled to myself in the mirror, proud of my son for knowing to let me sleep.

My stomach grumbled. As I walked through the dark living room toward the kitchen, I stubbed my toe on Benjamin's toy workbench, which he had still not put away. I mumbled and slid it aside.

I flipped on the kitchen light and grabbed a loaf of bread from the bread basket, then took some ham, cheese, and a jar of mayo from the fridge. I didn't even bother with a plate or napkin, figuring the kitchen counter was clean enough for preparing my midnight snack. As I was slathering mayonnaise on a slice of bread, a whirring electronic sound came from the darkness of the living room, followed by the voice of a child, shouting out cheerfully:

"Hey, what are we making?"

I jumped. Leaning away from the kitchen counter, a slice of mayo-covered bread resting in my hand like an offering plate, I peered into the living room. All was dark and quiet.

I slapped the two sides of the sandwich together and took an over-sized bite. "Stupid toy," I said, spitting crumbs. As I ate my sandwich, I felt oddly aware of the kitchen windows and the darkness beyond them. I finished the sandwich in four bites and washed it down with a glass of milk.

I could barely keep my eyes open in the bathroom as I brushed my teeth and washed my face. Sleep would be bliss. I flipped off the bathroom light, gave a passing glance to Benjamin's closed door, and continued down to the hallway in the darkness toward my own.

At my bedroom door, my bare right foot came down hard on something sharp. I withdrew my foot immediately and stifled a curse, a soft moan escaping my throat. I reached into the bedroom without entering it, stretching for the light switch on the wall. But I knew what I had stepped on before the light hit it: my keys.

FRIDAY

Across the breakfast table the next morning, I dangled my keys in front of Benjamin's face. He looked at them sleepily, mouth full of Rice Krispies.

"Do you know anything about this?" I asked.

His face lit up. "You found your keys!" he exclaimed, a little bit of milk spittle flying from his lips.

"They were outside my bedroom door last night. You didn't put them there?"

He paused, staring at me, as if waiting for me to say I was kidding. I could tell he thought the question was ridiculous.

"No," he finally said, almost scoffing.

I withdrew the keys, studying Benjamin's face. He resumed chewing. I relented. "It's Friday," I said.

"Yup," he responded, smiling.

"Want to do something fun this weekend?" I asked.

He raised his eyebrows. "Like what?"

"I have no idea," I said. "We'll figure something out."

"Maybe the park?" he suggested.

"That's an idea," I said. "It's supposed to be nice out tomorrow. I was thinking maybe a movie tonight."

"Yes!" he exclaimed. "Can I get popcorn?"

"We'll see. Finish up. Let's not be late today. Clear the dishes. Feed the cat. Get dressed."

He stood up suddenly from his chair and saluted, "Yes, sir!" and then marched like a soldier with his bowl toward the kitchen sink.

* * *

Mid-afternoon, I was mindlessly scanning book returns into the library's computer system when Danielle came up behind me. She rested her chin on top of my head, her hands on my shoulders, and whispered, "Don't look now, but tall, dark, and eligible just walked in."

I glanced up and made immediate eye contact with Hugo, who was walking toward the counter with a small smile on his face. For some reason I found myself embarrassed, as if the mere act of looking at him betrayed my thoughts.

"You just let me know if you don't feel like finishing this particular novel," Danielle said, "because I'd gladly check it out." I reached behind me and gave her a light smack on the hip and she retreated.

"I'm afraid I have to file a complaint with this particular library branch," Hugo said, smacking a palm on the counter in mock indignation and scanning behind me as if looking for someone in authority.

"What seems to be the problem, Mr. Denholm?" I asked innocently, and he raised his eyebrows, impressed or happy that I had remembered his name.

He put his hands on his hips. "You know that book I checked out two days ago? That exercise book that promises bigger muscles and a whiter smile?"

"I have a vague recollection," I said.

"Well, I read that thing cover to cover, and I don't think I'm even a bit in better shape than I was before."

I smiled but forced myself not to laugh. I wasn't going to let him win. Yet. "Maybe the changes are subtle at first," I said, studying him.

"Maybe you should give it more time?"

"Well, the book says that as you build muscle, your clothes will fit differently. A tighter fit in the sleeves and across the chest and shoulders. But so far, nothing."

"Nothing at all?"

"Well, my shoes feel snug," he said, looking down. "Maybe I'm reading it wrong."

A laugh escaped me, and I shook my head. "I'm sorry, I don't think there's anything I can do."

"Eh, it's okay," he said, throwing a hand dismissively. "The book's not due for a few more days, so I think I'll try sleeping with it under my pillow."

"Let me know how that *works out* for you," I said, nudging the air between us with my elbow.

His smile dropped completely. "That was *terrible*," he said.

"It was," I admitted, "My dad would be proud."

"I wouldn't be so sure," he said. "Anyway, maybe you could help me with something else."

"Sure," I said, secretly delighted.

"Could you tell me where the self-help books are?" he said. "I'm looking for books on loneliness. Dealing with rejection. Or maybe a book on the mating rituals of pretty librarians."

"*Mating* rituals?" I said.

"That sounded forward, didn't it?" he said, genuinely embarrassed.

"Just a tad," I said.

"Sorry," he said, and he was. "Remember, bad at this. But you know what, I'm determined. I couldn't help but notice that it's Friday. How about dinner?"

I paused, thinking. Or at least I tried to think. I had so very many reasons to say no. But every part of me wanted to say yes. My mind was cluttered with thoughts and yet I had nothing to say. And the entire time I couldn't take my eyes off his.

"You want to say yes," he smiled, nodding, trying to influence me.

"I want to say yes," I said.

"Then say yes."

"Yes."

* * *

"Where are we going?" Benjamin asked from the passenger seat. He had noticed that we were on a different route from the normal one we took between school and home. It had taken him a bit longer to realize this than I had expected it to, but as usual, Benjamin had been lost in thought as he looked out the window at the passing trees and houses, the tune of a made-up melody escaping his lips in a hum.

"Mee-maw's," I said.

"Why?" he asked.

"Because you're spending the evening there," I said with a smile, happy to surprise him. He loved his grandmother – my mom – and getting to spend an evening with her, the spoiling escalating by the hour, would be a treat for him. And so I was shocked when he immediately began to cry.

"Wait, what's wrong?" I said, quickly correcting the steering wheel when I realized I had veered too closely to the right shoulder.

"You said we would do something fun," he said, tears of disappointment falling down his cheek. "You said we were going to the movies."

I had completely forgotten. In all of my excitement over spending an evening with Hugo, I hadn't even for a moment given a thought to Benjamin other than wondering if my mother was free to watch him. Guilt poured over me like cold water.

"Oh honey, I'm so sorry," I said. "Really I am, but something came up."

"What came up?" he said, the volume of his voice increasing. He was passing from sad into angry. It was something I rarely saw from him, but whenever I did, it reminded me of David.

"I'm meeting a friend," I said.

"What friend?" he said.

"Someone from work." *True.*

He turned his face away from me. He drew his knees up to his chest, then put his sneakered feet against the dashboard, something he knew I didn't like.

"Put your feet down, Benjamin," I said gently.

He sniffed, but didn't move.

"Benjamin," I said more sternly.

He slowly drew his feet away, pulling his knees into his chest, and then forcefully rammed them against the dashboard. I watched in stunned silence as he did it again, the force of it causing his seat to shift back and then upright again. He wasn't even looking at what he was doing; he continued to stare out the side window while smashing his feet against the dashboard until I heard the slight sound of cracking plastic.

"Stop!" I yelled, and he did, dropping his feet to the floor.

"What in the world was that?" I asked, trying to study him while continuing to drive.

He didn't say a word for the rest of the trip. At my mother's house, he got out of the car before I could say anything, slamming the door behind him, retreating into her house when she opened the door. She gave me a concerned look as I got out of the car and approached the front step.

"Miscommunication on my part," I called out, shaking my head slightly.

"Are you sure this is a good idea?" she asked me, looking into the house after Benjamin, and I didn't know if she meant leaving Benjamin while he was visibly upset or going on a date this soon after the divorce. Or both.

I looked at her. I didn't know the answer to either one. "He'll pep up," I said. "He loves coming here. Just call me if you have any problems." I retreated to the car before she could say anything else. "Talk later?"

* * *

Hugo picked me up at my house at 7:00 sharp. He was wearing dark jeans over sleek black leather shoes, a gray button-down shirt with the collar open, and a dark blue blazer. I nearly matched him in my black skirt, white blouse and gray sweater, my hair pinned up on one side, my make-up just right. I knew we made a striking couple, and the smile on his face when I opened my front door betrayed his pleasure at my appearance.

The restaurant he chose, Pepper's, was new to me. The building was old and brick, with strung-up lights hanging over the outside dining area, the smell of bread and ale floating pleasantly on the evening breeze. It was warm enough to eat outside. Hugo pulled out my chair for me. A single candle flickered between us, and the light gave Hugo's face a pleasant glow. I hoped it was doing the same for me.

When the waitress came to take our order, Hugo asked for suggestions, and she was happy to oblige, more than once placing a hand on his upper back as she looked over his shoulder at his open menu. I did my best not to scowl at her, and she did her best to pretend that I wasn't there. We ordered and I was glad to see her go; I was also glad to see Hugo not watch her as she left.

"Thank you for agreeing to have dinner with me," he said, striking a tone somewhere between flirtatious and genuinely grateful.

I smiled at him. "Thank you for asking me."

"So," he said, running his finger along the rim of his water glass. "Tell me something about yourself, Helena. If you weren't a librarian, what would you be?"

"Hmm," I said, thinking. "The answer is not surprising at all. I wanted to be a writer. I majored in English and minored in creative writing. I love to write."

"Do you still?" he said.

"No time," I answered. "Not since becoming a mom. That took priority. And David… my ex-husband… he thought it was a waste of time. So it's been a very long time since I wrote anything. But I'd like to do it again someday."

"What did you write?" he asked. "Let me guess. Poetry?"

"A little," I said. "I wrote a lot of short fiction. I have a couple of unfinished novels in a box somewhere. I wrote a short story once that won a state competition when I was in college, and a couple of others that were published locally."

He looked impressed. "Good for you. What kind of stories? Romances?"

"Nah," I said. "Who reads that junk? Character studies, mostly.

I like to write about what motivates people to do what they do. How they respond to situations out of their control. I always favor character over plot."

"So, like dramas. True to life stuff."

"I guess so."

"Not a fan of anything thrilling or scary?"

"Not really. You?"

"I like a story that can give me a good chill up my spine," he said. "You know what I mean?"

"I guess so," I said. "Blood and guts just aren't my thing."

"No, me either," he said. "I'm more of a Hitchcock kind of guy, you know? Or *Twilight Zone*. Stories with endings that cut to the bone without literally cutting. Especially if there's some sort of moral justice being served because a character is paying the consequences for their decisions. The whole domino effect."

I sipped my water. "And what about you? What did young Hugo want to grow up to be?"

He laughed, leaning back in his chair and looking up at the sky. "I have this vivid memory from kindergarten. I used to *love* going hiking in the woods with my dad when I was a kid. And for some reason, my pea brain thought people actually did that for a living. Like, *hiked* for a living. And I also thought walking through the woods was called *hitch*-hiking. Don't ask me why, because I don't know. So one day my kindergarten teacher was asking everyone in my class what they wanted to be when they grew up. 'Doctor!' 'President!' 'Fireman!' Me? 'Hitch-hiker!'"

I laughed.

"Yeah, she laughed too," he said. "And of course I had no idea why. It actually hurt my feelings a little."

"Aww," I said. "So how's that dream working out for you?"

"Don't make fun," he said. "It's dangerous work. You never know who will pick you up."

"I just realized I don't actually know what you do," I said.

"Every kindergartener's dream," he said. "Investment banker."

"Oh," I said, and my face fell a little.

"Don't tell me," he said. "Same as the ex?"

"Same as the ex," I said, and took a deep breath and nodded.

"Pretty boring," he said. "Not creative in the least. But I do appreciate creativity even if I'm not creative myself."

"Do you read much?" I asked, happy to steer the subject away from investment banking and back to books.

"I check out and purchase more books than I read. And I start more books than I finish. I'm a wishful reader."

"I get that."

"Plus I'm such a slow reader. Getting 200 pages into a book is a big investment for me. So it feels like a huge waste of time when I get that far in just to realize it isn't any good."

"I get that too," I said. "But I always finish books. Even bad ones. I'm hopeful that there will be something redeeming about them in the end. Sometimes there's not. But I feel like I've let the book down if I don't finish it. It's silly."

"It's cute," he said, and smiled.

Conversation continued to flow easily. Hugo was a good and interesting talker, but he didn't monopolize the conversation, and he listened intently when I spoke, always asking relevant questions when I was done. There were few silences between us except when we were both chewing. The food was delicious, and Hugo continued to deflect the waitress' flirtations. My hero.

"So tell me about your son," he said.

I dabbed at my mouth with my napkin. "His name is Benjamin, after my dad," I said. "He's eight. He's really smart and funny and creative. His imagination is even bigger than mine was at his age. He's probably the most easy-going kid in the world…" My voice trailed off as I recalled the episode earlier in the car. "He makes my job very easy." I dropped my eyes and tore a piece from a roll from an overflowing bread basket between us. So far, Hugo had resisted it in spite of its heavenly aroma.

"And how is he handling the divorce?"

I stopped chewing and stared.

"I'm sorry, was that too direct?" he asked. "It's just… I was about his age when my parents divorced. It was really hard. You never know how a child might respond to it. I went from being a very energetic, outgoing kid to being very withdrawn. I buried myself pretty literally in junk food, and my mom turned a blind eye to it. Little Debbie was my therapy."

"It's hard on him," I said, swallowing. "And it's still pretty new. After the divorce, we moved here. New house, new school, new job for me. We're still adjusting to this new normal. But he sees his dad every other weekend."

"Is that where he is now?"

"No," I said, and sighed, guilt washing over me anew. "He's at my mom's. We moved here to be closer to her so that we could help each other out. She's literally three miles away from the house. She's a big help, but she doesn't drive."

"What about your dad?"

"He died about 10 years ago."

Hugo took a drink of his water and didn't offer an obligatory "I'm sorry" in response.

"What about your parents?" I asked.

"My dad remarried when I was in high school. He's out in California. I see him maybe once a year. I'm still pretty close to my mom. She's only about an hour away. I try to see her at least once a month and help her out around the house. She never remarried."

"That's kind of you," I said.

He shrugged it off. "She's my mom."

"Sure," I said.

"Just… be mindful of him," Hugo said, his face full of concern. "Your son, I mean. I feel for him. Divorce is rough on a kid."

I appreciated his thoughtfulness. "I will."

Hugo sat up straighter in his chair and smiled, trying to lighten the mood. "I can't wait to meet him."

"All in good time, Mr. Big Book," I said.

We talked about food, then diets, favorite vacation spots, the library, and fleetingly of politics, one subject easing into the next without either of us actively searching for a topic of discussion. The time flew, and it was nearly 10:00 when I forced myself to look at my watch and reluctantly told Hugo that it was time for me to get back home. He looked disappointed as he dropped his napkin onto the table.

The ride to my place was quieter, awkward. On the step to my front door, there was some tension between us for the first time the entire evening, accompanied by a loss for words. I knew he wanted to kiss me, and while I wanted him to, I was firmly of mind not to let him.

"Thank you for a wonderful time," I said. "I'd love to do it again soon."

"How about tomorrow night?" he said.

"Tomorrow belongs to Benjamin," I said. "But soon."

"Can I call you?"

"Yes, and you know where I work," I responded.

He continued to hesitate, just as he had when we first spoke at the library. He was staring at me intently, expectantly, so I dropped my eyes, breaking eye contact. A subtle rejection. Between the open collar of his shirt, I saw his necklace again, the leather cord with the pewter symbol. I reached up and touched it with my index finger. It was smooth and cold.

He looked slightly puzzled. "What?" he asked.

"Nothing." I smiled, turning to my door and opening it. "Goodnight, Hugo."

From the living room window I watched him go, folding himself into his car and driving away. The cat sat at my feet, looking up at me intently. Moments later, I left the house again, making the short drive to my mother's house to pick up Benjamin.

My mother assured me that Benjamin had been fine after I had left. He had eaten well, and then they had played two games of Scrabble. He had even played a joke on her by placing a rubber cockroach on her kitchen counter when she wasn't looking. "The rascal," she said with a smile. I had banned toy insects after Benjamin made a regular habit of hiding them everywhere, the worst instance being the time he placed a fake centipede under the toilet seat, eliciting from me a blood-curdling scream in the middle of the night, waking the entire house. David had thought it was hilarious.

Benjamin was asleep in the passenger seat before we got back to the house. I managed to pick him up without waking him, but it took effort, and with slight sadness I noted to myself that before too long I wouldn't ever be able to carry him anymore.

I put him in his bed fully dressed and peeled off his shoes. He turned over, moaning a little but continuing to sleep. I stroked his hair and tucked his stuffed tiger under his arm. He was laying on top of his covers. I gave them a gentle tug so I could wrap them around him somewhat. When I did so, something underneath his sheet shifted and fell to the floor with a plop. It was the little leather book. *Emil Bones.*

* * *

I was awakened by the sound of Benjamin calling for me, distantly. "Mommy?"

I sat up in bed, startled. From the sound of his voice, he was still in his room. He sounded distressed but not panicked.

I started to get out of bed, but then I could hear him opening his bedroom door. The creaking sound of hinges. "Mommy?" he said again. I heard his feet thumping across the floor and the squeak of the floorboard midway down the hallway. "Mommy?" His voice was growing louder as he approached.

The doorknob to my room turned and the door opened. The dark silhouette of Benjamin approached the bed and stopped beside me. "Mommy?" he said again, loudly, as though I wasn't right in front him. It startled me.

I put a reassuring hand on his shoulder. "I'm right here, baby," I said.

"Oh," he said, his eyes not open, a sleepy grin appearing on his face.

"What's wrong?" I said.

"It's just. I just," he said, and stopped. His shoulders fell. He wasn't awake.

I led him back to bed and tucked him in properly. He slept.

Back in my own bed, I was wide awake. I picked up my stupid romance novel (*Who reads that junk?*) and read. In my mind's eye, the novel's hero looked like Hugo, although I had a hard time picturing myself as the protagonist. She was all breathless proclamations, flowing dresses, and heaving bosoms. It just wasn't me. I read until I began to nod off, the book hitting me on the nose more than once before I gave up and put it down.

SATURDAY

When I woke, the room was full of sunlight. It felt good to sleep in. I stretched, my toes poking out from under the disheveled covers. I listened but couldn't hear a peep in the house. I picked up my cell phone from the bedside table, where it had been resting on top of the little leather book. I looked at the screen. No messages. Of course no messages.

I opened the door to my room and glanced down the hallway. Benjamin's door was still closed.

When I stepped forward, my bare foot came down on something cold, wet, and soft. I withdrew my foot immediately, and whatever I had stepped on stuck to it briefly before coming loose and falling back to the floor. It took me a moment to make out what it was: the hind-quarters of a mouse. The floor and my foot were spotted with blood.

"Ugh," I moaned to myself. "Mags."

After cleaning the floor and washing off my foot, I made break-fast for myself and Benjamin. Scrambled eggs with cheese, bacon, and waffles. Benjamin entered the kitchen just as everything was ready.

"That smells good," he said, grabbing a strip of bacon and taking a bite before sitting down.

"Did you sleep well?" I asked.

"Yep," he said, chewing.

"You came into my room again last night," I said.

"I did?" he said, smiling. "What did I say?" Benjamin was always highly amused at whatever strange things he said to me whenever he walked in his sleep.

I dropped my shoulders and let my mouth hang open, imitating him in an exaggerated way. "It's just," I said in a zombie-like voice. "I just."

He chuckled and shook his head. "I don't remember that," he said. He never did.

"Your cat left me a present this morning," I said, plopping scram-bled eggs on his plate, a Thomas the Tank Engine plate that he refused to part with.

"Oh yeah?"

"A dead mouse at my bedroom door. Correction: *half* a dead mouse. I stepped on it."

"Ewwww!" he exclaimed.

"With my bare foot."

"*EWWWW!*"

"Bon appétit," I said, wiggling my eyebrows and eyeing his breakfast. He looked down at his food and smiled.

"She probably caught it in the basement. Time to set some traps," I said.

"Mmm," he said in agreement through a mouthful of food.

I sat down at the table across from him and filled my plate. "I found *that* in your room last night," I said, pointing my thumb at the kitchen counter, where the little leather book rested. Benjamin looked at it but didn't respond. He continued chewing.

"Where did you find that?" I asked.

"In your trash can," he said, swallowing a mouthful of waffle.

"Did you read it?"

"No," he said quickly, and then dropped his gaze. I couldn't tell if he was being honest.

"It was under your covers."

"I didn't read it," he said. "Why did you throw it away?"

"It's not a good book," I said.

When Benjamin finished his breakfast, I reminded him to feed the cat. As he walked down the hallway, the cat close at his heels, he sang, "*Meow, kitty kitty / meow, kitty kitty / your fur so soft and your face so pretty / your tail brings ev-er-y Tom to the city / too bad your litterbox smells so shhhhall weeeeee daaance?*" It was a stupid song that I had made up shortly after we had adopted Mags, and it had never failed to amuse him. Benjamin had quickly memorized it and now sang it habitually whenever it was time to fill Mags' bowl.

Mid-morning, we went to the park across the street from the library, which was closed. No hours on weekends. It was a beautiful day. There wasn't a single cloud in the sky. There were other children enjoying the equipment, and Benjamin played near but not with them, lost in imagination as he swung, slid, climbed and ran. I couldn't tell if he was Superman or Neil Armstrong or a monkey.

I sat on a nearby bench, this one facing the playground equipment, the pond behind me. I had brought along a book to read. Not the romance novel, but something respectable to be seen with in public. I plucked it out of my purse and opened it on my lap, but was quickly distracted from it by Benjamin, by two nearby birds squawking at each other, by the calmness of the day, my bangs tickling my forehead in the warm breeze. I took a relaxing breath and closed my eyes.

My cell phone rang. The number was one I didn't recognize, but I guessed (*hoped*) it was Hugo.

"I don't believe in the wait-three-days rule," he said when I answered. "How are you?"

"I'm fine, stranger," I said. "I'm sitting on a park bench and enjoying this gorgeous day."

"I'd love to join you," he suggested.

"Today belongs to Benjamin," I reminded him. "But you're the most pleasantly pushy man I know."

"Ah yes," he said. "Well, I just wanted to let you know that I think my rigorous workout routine is quickly paying off."

"Oh really, how so?"

"Well," he said, "I went out with this really pretty girl last night, and she could *not* take her eyes off me."

"Oh, get over yourself," I said, laughing.

"I'm not kidding!" he said. "Not long ago, a girl like her wouldn't give me the time of day. This girl is pretty, and smart, and funny, and interesting, and yet she *still* agreed to spend an evening with me. So I must be doing something right."

"You're doing something right," I sighed in mock defeat.

In the silence that followed, I knew he was smiling. "Well, I just wanted to take a moment to remind you of me. Until next time, Helena. Enjoy the sunshine."

I put my phone down, my prior calmness now replaced with pleasant anticipation. *Too good to be true,* I thought, and I smiled and shook my head. How long ago had it been – five months, before the divorce was finalized – that I swore off men? Yet here I was, my heart full of a longing as strong as I had ever felt, even in my high school years when attraction was new and uncharted territory.

But then my revelry was broken when I realized I'd lost sight of Benjamin. I stood up, studying the children running by, trying to pick out his dirty blonde hair. Back and forth the children ran, and I felt a slight edge of panic rising in my chest. I looked behind me, then turned around again and took a step forward.

I opened my mouth to call out his name when I spotted him, leaning against a light post barely five feet away from me, his back toward me, his head down, his shoulders hunched forward.

I wondered how long he had been there. I stepped toward him. Over his shoulder I could see that he had a leaf in his hand and he was looking down at it, twisting its stem between his thumb and index figure, flipping between its dark and light sides. I could hear that he was singing quietly to himself, and the words reached my ears:

"…*want to be your friend… hmmm let me in your house…,*" he sang, as the leaf spun in his fingers.

* * *

On our way home from the park, we stopped at a hardware store and I bought a hide-a-key. The tiny black box opened to reveal dark gray sponge-like material glued to its interior, and a strong magnet covered the entire back side. I slipped a spare house key into it, and Benjamin watched with interest as I attached it to the bottom of the air conditioning unit behind the house, the magnet so strong that the hide-a-key practically leapt from my hand and attached itself with a small *clang.*

Benjamin opted to stay in the back yard and play by himself while I went inside to get some necessary housework done. Wiping off the kitchen counter moments later, I came across the little leather book, which I picked up and studied for a moment. I flipped it open.

> *There was a boy named Emil Bones*
> *Who would like to be your friend,*
> *But once you let him in your house,*
> *He may never leave again.*

I felt something bump against my leg and I jumped, a squeal of surprise coming out of my mouth. It was Margaret Catwood, giving my calf an affectionate head-butt. I reached down and scratched the top of her head.

"Bad kitty," I said. "Well, good kitty for killing that mouse. Bad kitty for not finishing it. No more presents for mommy, okay?"

She purred and rubbed her cheek against my fingers, offering her ears for a scratch. My thoughts turned to dinner.

Through the pantry was the door to the basement. I opened it and flipped on the light. The naked bulb above my head illuminated the plank staircase. Mags passed me down the steps, threatening for a moment to trip me. She reached the bottom first and then disappeared into the darkness beyond.

The floor was concrete, the walls cinderblock. A little light came through two tiny rectangular windows set near the ceiling on the north end, grass outside poking up and obstructing some of the view. I saw Benjamin's sneakers as he ran by in the back yard.

I didn't store much down there because the basement stayed too moist, warping anything made of paper or cardboard and rusting metal. A few plastic tubs of old clothes and other nonessential items dotted the floor here and there, and a single set of tall plastic shelves by the wall under the windows was covered with overflow pantry items: jars and cans of food, mostly. Otherwise, the basement was empty and featureless, a vast space of nothing.

I looked around for evidence of mice but didn't see any. No droppings or nests or anything of that kind. Mags walked around, sniffing at the corners. She was difficult to see in the shadows. She put her paw down quickly on something – a spider or a bug, I couldn't tell – and then ate it.

I didn't like it down there because, in spite of the bright bulbs at the top and bottom of the stairs and the two small windows, the basement was perpetually dark. Its odor was somehow simultaneously dank and dusty, and the ceiling was low. I could reach it without fully extending my arm. Not that I wanted to – the exposed beams above me were covered in cobwebs. And the basement temperature had stayed unnaturally cold all through the summer.

I grabbed a large jar of spaghetti sauce from the shelf and then took a step back, taking inventory and still trying to decide if pasta was really what I wanted to make for dinner. I didn't enjoy cooking. Maybe I would take Benjamin out for dinner, further recompense for ditching him last night.

As I pondered, the light changed in the basement. A shadow fell over my face. There was movement above me and to my right, outside the window. I glanced up.

Benjamin was at the window, crouched down on all fours in the grass, a dark silhouette framed by the bright sunshine above him, his knees and elbows like arrows pointing toward the sky. His forehead was pressed hard against the glass, his head at an oddly tilted angle, his shoulders rising and falling rapidly, his breath fogging the glass at his chin.

I screamed and dropped the jar of spaghetti sauce, which shattered. Cold sauce splashed onto my feet and shins. Mags bolted up the stairs at the sound of it. I staggered backward. Benjamin's head moved as I stepped. Although I could not see his eyes, I knew he was watching me. When I reached the stairs, I pivoted quickly, grabbing the railing, and raced up the steps.

I slammed the door behind me and stepped through the pantry and into the kitchen, out of breath. Benjamin stood there, just inside the sliding doors that opened to the back yard. He stared at me, unblinking, the look on his face one of concern.

"What were you *doing*?" I asked him.

"Looking for you," he said. "Where were you?"

"You scared me," I said, placing a hand on my chest, my heart thrumming against my palm.

"I scared you?"

"Yes, just now."

"How?"

"Looking through the basement window."

"I didn't look through the basement window."

"Don't *lie* to me, Benjamin!"

"I've been inside. Looking for you," he insisted.

"This isn't funny, young man."

"I'm not lying!"

"*GO TO YOUR ROOM!*"

He walked away, his look having changed from confusion to hurt. I could tell he was on the verge of tears. I watched him go, and when he disappeared around the corner, I sat down at the table. I couldn't catch my breath.

* * *

When I went into his room a few minutes later, Benjamin was lying face down on his bed. I sat on the edge and rubbed his back. He turned and faced me. He had been crying. I was reminded of how sensitive he was, and it took the edge off my anger.

I showed him the small leather book. He looked at it, and then at me. "Is there something you want to confess?"

He shook his head.

"You didn't read this?"

He shook his head.

"See, the story is about a little boy named Emil, and he likes to play tricks. Some of his tricks are funny, and some of them are very, very bad."

Benjamin just stared.

"I think you read this book and it gave you some ideas."

"I didn't read it," he insisted.

"Benji," I said with a tone of disapproval.

"I *didn't*."

"You need to know when to stop. It's not funny, Benjamin. You really scared me in the basement. And you scared Mee-Maw with the cockroach."

"She laughed," he argued.

"I know she did, but eventually it stops being funny." I took a breath. "Did you hide my keys too? And then leave them at my door?"

A look of defeat fell over him. "No," he said.

I shook my head at him slowly. "Benjamin," I said. "You won't be in trouble if you just confess."

He sat up suddenly in his bed, full of rage. His face was inches from mine. "I *didn't* hide your keys. And I *didn't* scare you in the basement. And I *didn't* read this book!" With this final declaration, he slapped the book out of my hand and it flew across the room, landed, and slid across the floor.

I stood up. "You stay in here until you're ready to be honest," I said. I stooped, picked up the book, and left his room, slamming the door as hard as I could behind me. A childish move.

As I walked down the hall away from his room, the sound of Benjamin's sobs followed me.

* * *

I was seated on the living room couch, reading a book, Margaret Catwood curled up at my toes, when I heard his bedroom door open. Nearly two hours had passed since I had left him there. He had audibly wept for almost 10 minutes, and it had been silent ever since. I assumed he had fallen asleep.

He came to the edge of the couch and looked at me, but didn't speak. The cat jumped down and slinked around his ankles.

"Do you have something to say to me?" I asked.

He took a deep breath. His eyes left mine and he looked up toward the ceiling, fighting back fresh tears. "I'm sorry I read that book," he choked.

"And?" I asked.

"I'm sorry I scared you in the basement."

"And?"

There was a long pause. "I'm sorry I hid your keys."

"This ends now," I said, and he nodded. "Okay. Go to the kitchen. I know you're hungry."

He turned and walked away from me, and as I followed, I realized that his denials had been more convincing than his confessions.

After dinner, I tried to make light conversation with Benjamin, and even offered to play a game with him, but he remained disengaged. I denied that the ache in my heart was any kind of guilt. He surprised me by volunteering to take a bath and go to bed early.

When I tucked him in, he quietly declined my offer of a story, insisting that he was sleepy. I stroked his hair briefly and he closed his eyes. I told him I loved him and he said the same, but it didn't sound honest.

* * *

I couldn't sleep, and I didn't want to read. I lay flat on my back in bed, my hands folded on my chest, staring into the darkness above me. My feelings conflicted.

I tried to calm myself by thinking more pleasant thoughts. I needed to redeem the weekend. Tomorrow was to be another gorgeous day. There was time for me to give Benjamin the kind of attention he was obviously desperate for. I would ask him what he wanted to do and we would do it if at all possible.

I thought too about Hugo and our wonderful date together, our perfect conversation and the way our personalities clicked so effortlessly. But then my mind replayed the words Hugo had said to me, his concern for Benjamin and his own experience as the child of divorce. My heart ached, and I admitted to myself that I had treated Benjamin too harshly.

From the other end of the hallway, I heard Benjamin's bedroom door open. It didn't startle me. In fact, the sound brought me relief. I wanted to hug him and reassure him and let him know that I would always love him. I sat up in bed.

Footsteps thumped down the hallway, a sleepy shuffle. I heard the squeak of the floorboard. A slight rattle as my bedroom doorknob was touched from the opposite side. And then there was silence.

I turned on the light at my bedside and blinked as my eyes adjusted. "Benjamin?" I called out softly.

No response. I stared at the door, plain and white, and it seemed to loom.

And then, again, I could hear the squeaking sound of Benjamin's bedroom door hinges. *Had he returned to bed?* I listened more closely. There was nothing to be heard. I slipped one foot out of bed and put on my glasses.

Once again I heard footsteps approaching. The floorboard squeaked. The footsteps grew louder and then ended outside my door. My doorknob rattled gently, and this time I could see it move, a slight up-and-down motion. But it did not turn.

I put both feet on the floor but remained seated on my bed. "Benji?" I pled. There was no answer.

Squeaking hinge. Creaking floorboard. Footsteps, faster than before, ceasing just outside my door. The knob rattling more loudly this time, but not turning. Then nothing.

I stood and walked toward the bedroom door. I heard the hinge squeak loudly this time, as if Benjamin's door had been jerked open, and footsteps broke suddenly into a run, growing louder as they approached my bedroom door, pounding on the wooden floor, heavier than they should have been. There was a deafening thud as my bedroom door was rammed from the other side.

I stifled a scream and covered my mouth, taking an involuntary step back and sitting down on my bed. My heart was pounding furiously. Silence fell over everything, somehow just as terrifying as the noise that preceded it.

Clutching my chest, I stood and approached the door. I turned the knob and opened the door slightly, peering around to look down the hallway, holding my breath. The hallway was dark and empty, Benjamin's closed door dimly reflecting the light escaping from my bedroom.

I took a deep breath and opened my door wider, allowing more light to spill forth. There was nothing to see.

The walk down the hallway to Benjamin's was eternal, my footsteps far too loud in my own ears, which were already pounding with the sound of my heartbeat.

When I opened Benjamin's door I found him in his bed, lying on top of his bedclothes, his back toward me, unmoving. By all appearances, asleep.

SUNDAY

A dead mouse – a *complete* dead mouse this time – greeted me outside my bedroom door in the morning. I groaned, but was also happy that I hadn't stepped on it. At least Mags was doing her job, but I needed to find the source of these intruders or call an exterminator. Add that to the ever-growing mental checklist. Menial household tasks like this made me miss and curse David at the same time.

I made every effort at breakfast to be as chipper as possible. I put on a smile and adopted a tone so positive I could barely stand myself, but Benjamin, ever so easily influenced, got my signal and responded in kind. No mention was made of the previous day's events.

It was a sunny, pleasant morning, so I told Benjamin to clean off the table, feed the cat, and then get dressed to play outside. I told him I wanted to do some work in the flower beds that skirted the back of the house, and so I would be joining him outside shortly. Benjamin left the kitchen with an obvious bounce to his step.

"Mom?" he called from the recesses of his house.

"Yeah, baby?" I called, scraping egg remnants from our breakfast plates into the sink.

"Have you seen Mags?" he said. "Her food bowl is full."

I paused, the water still running in the sink. I turned to look at the chairs around the kitchen table. Mags usually sat in one (or tried to force herself into either of our laps), her chin resting on the table, while we ate breakfast, but she wasn't there now. I glanced around the kitchen, then took a step back to peek into the living room.

"No, I haven't," I called out to Benjamin, who returned to the kitchen, a look of concern on his face. At our old house – the pre-divorce house – Mags had managed to escape more than once, but had always returned again in 24 hours or so, sometimes muddy, always hungry. Her infrequent absences were of great concern to Benjamin, who fretted unless distracted. David and I had always attempted to be reassuring, hiding our own mild worry under promises of Mags' imminent return.

But this house was new to Mags, and I couldn't help but wonder, had she actually gotten out of the house, if she would return here or try to make the 60 mile trek back to our old house, the house David now shared with Tricia. I thought of a story I'd read many years ago in *Reader's Digest* about a cat that had somehow made its way from one coast of the United States to the other, a journey that would have required crossing the Mississippi River, in order to get back home after being lost during a family vacation.

Benjamin was looking at me, puzzled. "She's here somewhere," I said. "She just left another present outside my bedroom door this morning."

"Another mouse?"

"Yes," I said.

"*Half* a mouse?" he asked with glee.

"No, a whole one this time. Go get dressed."

* * *

It was beautiful outside. Sunny and pleasant, autumn giving us a warm hello, not a hint of summer's sting in the sunshine. Benjamin ran around the back yard, fighting off unseen foes, a trashcan lid serving as a makeshift shield. I wondered if children in general still played this way – using sticks for swords, fingers for guns, their imagination a limitless playground – or if Benjamin was one of a dying breed.

I found my own joy in the dirt, the cool soil against my bare knees as I worked amongst the flowers. I avoided wearing gloves as much as possible as I loved the feel of the soil against my hands, not caring if the dirt caked under my nails. Not that I had any nails to speak of; I was and had always been a biter, much to my mother's vocal dismay, even to this day.

After awhile I sat back on my heels, wiping scant perspiration from my forehead with the back of one wrist. Benjamin was now standing in the middle of the yard, looking skyward as he tossed something into the air and caught it again, lost in the simple activity. At first I thought it was a ball, but then I saw it was much smaller but with more heft in the way that it fell.

"What is that?" I said.

He caught it and held it up between his thumb and forefinger. It gleamed in the sunlight. "This?" he said. "It's a rock. I found it."

"Let me see it," I said.

He obeyed. The rock was a little larger than a walnut, oval-shaped, smooth, and almost flawlessly white.

"That's really pretty," I said, admiring it. "Where did you find it?"

"Over there," he said, pointing to the flower beds only a few feet to my right. I leaned to the side to see where he was pointing, and when I couldn't get a clear view, I stood and walked a few steps over.

There, between two bushes, were nine more rocks, all nearly identical to the one I was holding. They were placed in a circle in the soil, their line only broken by the stone that Benjamin had removed. "That's odd," I said.

Benjamin said nothing.

"Did you do that?" I said.

"No," he said. "It was like that when I came out here."

I looked at it closer. The soil in the middle of the stone circle was darker, moister, as though it had been recently overturned. It was also mounded in the center, the ground pregnant with something buried underneath. I bit my lower lip and pondered.

Benjamin squatted down beside me. "What?" he said, studying my face.

"Nothing," I said. "Maybe an animal did it."

"An animal did *that*?" he said, and laughed a little.

"Go play," I said, and he did. I continued to work in the soil, but skipped the area between the two bushes. I hummed while I worked, not because I was enjoying myself, but because it calmed my nerves.

* * *

After a few hours outside and a quick lunch, I told Benjamin that he had to choose between playing with toys or reading a book for the next hour – no screens – and he made a nest for himself on the couch with at least four books. I noticed that he looked around briefly for the cat before settling in, but she still had not made her presence known.

In the kitchen, my cell phone alerted me to a Facebook friend request. It was from Hugo. I considered ignoring it in order to allow a few more hours to create the illusion of nonchalance, but curiosity overcame me and I accepted.

I perused his profile. There was no hint of me anywhere, no mention of something new and exciting in his social life, but tiny disappointment quickly gave way to reality. *It's been one date, Helena,* I said to myself before continuing to scan. His most recent status update ("This salad tastes like I'd rather be fat") made me laugh out loud, prompting a "What's so funny?" from Benjamin a room away.

Hugo's posts were consistently funny or thoughtful, his photos proving he had a real eye for photography. He was in very few of them, although he was tagged in several photos taken and posted by his friends. I noticed a dramatic increase in his weight as I scrolled further back in his history. The piercing blue eyes and inviting smile were always there, no matter how heavy he was, but there was no denying his physical transformation had been dramatic, and several of his friends, some attractive girls among them, were consistent in their praise of his progress over time.

A chat bubble lit up at the top of the screen. I tapped it. A tiny picture of Hugo appeared, all toothy smile dark beard, a blue sky behind him, his cell phone reflected in his sunglasses. His message: "STOP STALKING ME."

I laughed. "YOU sent ME a friend request," I returned.

"Only so I could tell you to stop stalking me," he wrote.

"Noted," I replied. "I will stop as soon as I'm finished downloading all of your pictures and making a scrapbook."

"Sweet, yet terrifying," he wrote. "How's your day?"

"Very nice," I wrote.

"I can't wait to see you again."

I paused, then typed, "Me too."

"I have a great idea for date #2."

"Do tell."

"It's a surprise."

"I like surprises."

"You'll love this. Friday?"

Next Friday, Benjamin would be at his father's. There was no reason to say no. But it also seemed so very far away. "Next Friday," I wrote.

A smiling emoticon popped up. "I might see you before then, though," he wrote. "I was just making a grocery list and realized I'm fresh out of books."

I laughed. "STOP STALKING ME," I wrote, excited that I might see him again before Friday. I paused for a second, then followed up with a winking emoticon, just in case.

"Until then," he wrote.

* * *

As I tucked Benjamin into bed that night, he asked for a bedtime story. I picked up *The Horse and His Boy,* a book we had been making great progress through a few weeks ago before we got sidetracked by other, shorter books and nights when Benjamin got to bed too late for any story at all. A bookmark indicated that we were about 35 pages from the end.

"How about this?" I asked, holding it up.

Benjamin answered with a grin, and so I read. I sat in a small chair beside his bed as Benjamin lay flat on his back, his eyes on the ceiling. He moved little, except at those times when I caught him furrowing his brow in anger or widening his eyes in surprise, expressions that reflected the emotions of the characters on the page.

After a dozen pages I felt sleepy, frustrated when my yawns would interrupt me mid-sentence. I put the book down on my knee and rubbed water from my eyes. "I'm falling asleep, baby," I said. "I think we'll stop there."

"Awww," he said, disappointed, turning on his side and grabbing my wrist. "We're almost done."

"There's more than 20 pages left. We'll finish it tomorrow."

He crossed his arms and pouted, and for a moment I feared he was on the brink of a tantrum like the one he'd thrown in the car. "I don't like it when we don't finish books."

"We'll finish it, buddy, just not tonight." I stood up and kissed him on the forehead. I placed his stuffed tiger on his chest and he clutched it tight before turning over on his side.

As I exited his room he called out, "I'm worried about Mags."

I paused at the door. I was too. "She'll turn up. She always does. No worries." I shut the door quietly behind me, then stood in the dark and quiet hallway.

The house was silent and still, and I felt suddenly unsettled. I stood for only a moment, then took a deep breath, swelling my chest with a feeling of determination. *Nothing is wrong*, I thought without actually articulating those words. I marched to the bathroom, where I washed my face, brushed my teeth, and removed my contacts, then moved with confidence to the bedroom, where I changed into my pajamas. I was choosing to behave like the Helena of a week ago. The Helena before missing keys and white rocks and dead mice. The Helena before *Emil Bones*.

I picked up my phone, breaking my personal rule about electronics in bed, and continued to scroll through Hugo's Facebook profile. I learned that he liked being outdoors, he was quite witty in his interactions with his friends, and despite his joking insistence that healthy eating was boring, numerous photos featured attractive dishes filled with juicy meat and colorful vegetables, presumably prepared by him. My mouth watered.

There was no evidence whatsoever of past girlfriends or, heaven forbid, an ex-wife, but I realized that shouldn't surprise me. I had long ago deleted all evidence of David from my Facebook page. My page featured few photos, and if anyone else was in them besides me, it was only Benjamin.

I clicked over to my own Facebook page and scrolled through it, trying to see it through Hugo's eyes, imagining that he might be studying me as well. I was glad that nothing jumped out at me as particularly cringe-worthy or embarrassing, and I hoped that he might come across one particularly flattering shot of me – tan and happy at the shore, wearing a flattering yellow swimsuit. Never mind the fact that David was the unseen photographer.

I clicked through more of my own pictures. Some made me smile, some gave me a pleasant melancholy as I remembered a happier, more settled time. The pictures of Benjamin I found particularly striking. The further back I went, the younger he became (obviously), but also brighter somehow. His smile was always wide, his face a smaller, cuter reflection of his father's handsome portrait, but in the more recent photos, the light diminished somehow. In the scant pictures leading up to and after the divorce, his face appeared almost in shadow, the spark

gone from his eyes. I was overcome with a mixture of guilt and sadness and rested the phone on my leg, turning it off in the process, and
closed my eyes.

When the door to my bedroom burst open, slamming against
the wall, I jerked my legs so violently that the phone fell, smacking
the floor below. Against the darkness of the hallway behind him, I
could barely distinguish the figure of Benjamin as he stood there, head
bowed, his arms up against his chest, still clutching his stuffed tiger.

"Benjamin, baby," I said, breathless, swinging my legs from under
the covers and out of bed. "You scared me to death."

He stood still in the darkness, chin to chest. I retrieved my glasses
and approached him. "Is everything okay?"

He didn't speak or take a step, but swayed ever so slightly just
outside my doorway, a still shadow. When I reached him, I put one
hand on his shoulder and pulled him gently into the room. He took
one heavy step forward and was bathed in the light of the lamp on the
bedside table behind me.

I gasped and stood up quickly, taking an involuntary step backward, a guttural sound escaping my throat. I stifled a scream and
forced myself to take a deep, stuttering breath, my heart pounding in
my chest.

Composing myself as best I could and determined not to wake
him, I stepped forward, placed both hands on Benjamin's shoulders,
and gently turned him around. I walked him slowly back to his room.
He never looked up or, as best I could tell, opened his eyes, yet once we
reached his bed he immediately stepped in, collapsing onto his side, his
back to me.

I stroked Benjamin's hair for a moment. Once I felt certain I had
given him ample time to fall fully asleep again, I reached around him.
Swallowing a moan, I pulled at the animal in his arms. Even in his
sleep, Benjamin's grip was tight. I used my right hand to pry away one
of his arms, and he finally let go. He rolled over onto his stomach and
continued to sleep.

I held Mags by the scruff of the neck in my left hand, as far away
from my body as possible. There she dangled, limp as a rag doll, dead
and covered in dirt.

MONDAY

I spent the remainder of the night on the living room couch. I flipped channels. Infomercials. Commercials. Tired reruns. Commercials. I distracted myself by scrolling through news articles on my phone. Political junk. Pop culture click bait. News. A local man at large after allegedly murdering his two young children, his wife at a press conference looking completely wrung out. *I guess things could be worse,* I thought.

I was still awake as the sun rose. I had placed Mags inside two garbage bags and then left her on top of the washing machine. When the light began to peek over the horizon, erasing the darkness outside, I quietly took the bag out the back door and deposited it in a garbage can, the one with the lid that, just yesterday, had doubled as a shield. Whether I would bury her later or let her go with the garbage was a decision I was too tired to make at the time.

A glance at my flower beds confirmed that the stones and the mound were gone, the soil flat, no sign of disturbance whatsoever. There was a turning sensation in my gut, but it wasn't surprise.

I took a long, hot shower, somehow not entirely awake and yet my mind racing at the same time, so exhausted that I felt I could barely move.

I was sitting at the kitchen table, nursing a strong cup of coffee, when Benjamin entered, fully awake and fully dressed. "Good morning," he said, and plopped down in the chair opposite me.

"Hi," I said, my voice hoarse, and I studied his face. Before he had entered the room I had been mentally laying out a plan for the day, a plan that included begging for a personal day off from work (per the library's policy, I wasn't due for any paid time off until my sixth month, and this was just the beginning of my fourth week) and then getting Benjamin to the doctor as soon as they could see him. Yet here he was, looking rested and awake, the picture of health.

"What?" he asked me, and I realized I had been staring blankly at him for several seconds.

"Are you feeling okay?" I asked.

"Yeah," he said with a small chuckle.

"Are you tired at all?"

"No, I slept good."

"You don't remember getting up?"

"No. Did I?"

"You did," I said, and rubbed the back of my neck. "You came to my room again."

"Did I say anything?"

"Not this time," I said, stretching my back. "Can you get yourself some cereal?"

"Sure," he said, popping out of his chair. I sat and sipped my coffee, my mind too tired to formulate another thought. I rested my head in my hands. Benjamin ate his breakfast in silence, perhaps sensing it best not to talk to me, the sound of his chewing the only noise in the room. He finished his breakfast, slurping the last of his milk, and I heard him rise and place his bowl in the sink.

"Go brush your teeth," I said without looking up.

"Yup," he said, and as he exited the kitchen and walked to the opposite side of the house, I heard him singing quietly, "*Meow, kitty, kitty...*"

* * *

I somehow managed to complete the library's opening checklist in spite of my tired stupor, although at times I found myself standing motionless behind the service counter or out in the middle of the library floor, barely a thought in my head and not at all knowing what I had planned to do next.

Danielle, Beth, and Mrs. Strickland all greeted me on their way in, with only Beth giving me a second, slightly concerned look as she walked by. Later, after all of us had settled into our routines, I was standing at the counter when Beth sidled up beside me and whispered, "Okay, what's going on? You look exhausted."

"I am," I said, "and yes, Benjamin is sleepwalking again, but it's more than that now."

"What is it?"

I rubbed my eyes with both palms and gave a groan of frustration,

"I don't know," I said, dropping my hands. "He's acting out. Doing… odd things. He's not himself."

"Odd things like what?" she said, and I could tell her question was a mix of concern and curiosity.

"Just… he threw a tantrum the other day, which is something he never does. And he's been playing pranks. Not particularly funny ones. He's… not himself," I repeated.

Beth stroked my arm. "What are you going to do?"

"I don't know. I'm too exhausted to think straight. It's been like a week since I've had a full night's sleep. I was considering taking him to the doctor, but this morning he seemed fine. Great, in fact."

"Well, I don't have kids so I'm the last person to give you advice about children," she said. "But he has been through a lot of change recently. New house, new school…"

"Oh, I know," I said. "It's just… there's more to it than that," and my mind wandered to that book, that stupid black leather book, and as much as I wanted to talk about it with someone else, about how I thought it might be influencing Benjamin's behavior, I didn't quite believe it myself and couldn't imagine trying to convince someone else about it.

"Well, whatever it is, I think seeing a doctor might be a good idea. With everything that's happened… he's probably just acting out as an outlet for dealing with what's going on in his head."

"Yeah," I said. "Hugo said the same thing."

"Oooh, are we talking about Romeo over here?" said Danielle, who appeared out of nowhere and slinked up beside us. "Do you think tall, dark and slender might make a cameo appearance today?"

I gave a tired chuckle and shook my head. "Who knows," I said. Yesterday I had hoped he would; today I did not.

"So… how was Friday?" Danielle asked.

"Oh, right!" exclaimed Beth, suddenly brightening. "You went out with him!"

"All right, all right," I said, shushing them both, but smiling in spite of myself, suddenly energized. "It went well. Really well. We had a good time."

"We. Want. Details," said Danielle.

"There's not much to tell. We went out to dinner and talked. It was really nice."

"You're killing me," said Danielle. "We've had our eyes on that guy for months." At this statement, Beth dropped her gaze and blushed slightly. "He went from tall, shy and lardo to biff studly right before our eyes. It was… *magical*," she finished dramatically. "Beth and I have been secretly drooling over him ever since, and the best you can give us is 'It was really nice'? How am I supposed to live vicariously through *that*?"

"Is this true?" I said, smiling and looking at Beth.

Beth simply nodded, still blushing. Danielle continued, "It is true? I tried *all* of my best moves and *nothing*." She wave a hand dismissively. "But then he started that flirt storm with you last week."

I took a breath. "He is very sweet and very funny and smart and I think he really likes me." I felt like I was back in high school, and my friends and I were all a-twitter about the school's star quarterback.

"Are you going out with him again?" Beth asked.

"I think so," I said.

"Did you kiss him?" Danielle asked, grabbing me by the shoulders. "Tell me you kissed him."

Before I could answer, Mrs. Strickland emerged from her office, and Beth and Danielle immediately scattered. Employees in a cluster was verboten, but it did not appear that she had seen us.

* * *

That evening I was emptying the dishwasher after dinner. Benjamin had just finished his homework and had requested screen time. I told him that his bedroom desperately needed to be addressed first, and he dutifully marched out of the kitchen. He had been nothing but pleasant since I had picked him up from school. Me, I was dead on my feet.

I carried a basket of laundry from my bedroom to the laundry room. There I spied Mags' food bowl (full), water bowl (ditto), and litter box (smelly). Through the door and down the hall, I could hear Benjamin singing to himself. I grabbed a garbage bag and tossed the food bowl into it, followed by the water bowl (after dumping its contents down the bathroom sink) and the contents of the litter box. I took the bag and empty box out to back yard, depositing the bag in the trash can (knowing without looking that it was going on top of Mags) and placing the empty litterbox beside it.

Back inside, I threw laundry into the washing machine, then walked with the empty basket toward Benjamin's room, a floorboard creaking below one foot as I stepped. His door was shut, but I could hear his voice through the door.

"I don't want to do that," I heard him say, in a tone that was serious but calm.

Silence.

"I don't know what that word means," he said.

Silence.

"She won't think that's funny."

Silence.

"She *won't*. And I'll get in trouble."

Silence.

"She is? Right now?"

Silence.

Benjamin's voice, louder: "Mom?"

I took a step back from the door, then two more. Attempting to make my voice sound farther away, I answered in a soft tone, "Yeah, Benji?"

"What are you doing?"

"Just getting ready to do laundry," I answered, stepping closer to the door again. "Do you have any dirty clothes in there?"

There was a long pause. Before he answered, I could have sworn I heard him whisper, "Say no." Then he called out, "No."

I opened his door. He was on the floor, surrounded by toys, a pair of action figures in his hands.

"Cleaning your room?" I said, arching an eyebrow.

"I got distracted."

"I can see that," I said. "Who were you talking to?"

He held up the two figures. "Just playing," he said.

I scanned the room for dirty clothes, and in doing so, there among the toys, lying near one of his knees, was the book. *That* book.

I grabbed a few articles of clothing off the floor, then snatched the book as well and threw it in the basket along with the clothes. "I'm not even going to ask," I said sternly, walking out of his room. "Clean up like I asked you to."

* * *

Exhausted as I was, sleep eluded me that night. My ears were attuned to the sound of the house. Every pop and crack as the house cooled caused my heart to jump, bringing me immediately back from the brink of sleep. I waited for the inevitable moment that Benjamin's door would open. But it never did.

I looked at the little leather book, resting on my dresser across the room from me. There it sat, thin and harmless. Taunting me.

I picked up my romance novel, opened it, snapped it shut, and put it back down. Grabbed my phone and checked Facebook. No updates to Hugo's page, and no messages from him either. I read the news. Police had no leads on the missing man who had disappeared after the murder of his children. It might rain tomorrow.

Eventually, I turned off my phone and the bedroom light. I lay on my back in the darkness. I counted sheep. I thought about Hugo. I even tried entertaining myself with some of the happier memories I had from my early days with David, those days of our marriage when our future was uncharted and limitless and we were tethered to nothing but each other. New home, new life. No children.

TUESDAY

At 5:30 I gave up on trying to sleep. When I opened my bedroom door to the hallway beyond, I looked at Benjamin's door: still closed. I looked down at the floor: nothing there. No mouse, whole or otherwise. All seemed to appear as it should have.

* * *

I medicated myself with coffee, both at home in the morning and after I arrived at work, in an effort to wake up my exhausted brain. A couple of times behind the counter at the library, I felt my eyes drifting shut as I stood, snapping suddenly alert with a terrible feeling that I had been caught. Thankfully, I hadn't. I would slap my cheeks with my palms, sneak another sip of coffee, and attempt to be human.

Late in the afternoon, I was pushing a cart of books down an aisle, glad to be moving instead of standing still and fighting sleep, when I spotted a woman at the far end.

She was slightly shorter than me and painfully thin. Her clothes did not look old or worn, but they were terribly disheveled, as was her hair, which was mostly put up in a ponytail, although several strands had come free and hung loosely against her shoulders.

Judging by the thinness of her wrists and ankles and her slightly stooped posture, I assumed she was elderly, but when she turned toward me, revealing more of her face, I realized she was young. Early 30s at the oldest, around my own age. She had dark circles around her eyes and a look that was fretful, even though she stood quite still.

I then noticed that she wasn't looking at the books on the shelves at either side of her. Instead, she appeared to be taking interest in the other people in the library, studying each one as they walked by, following them with her eyes. She took particular interest when Beth passed her, all smiles and chipper tones, leading another customer through the library.

The woman followed them at a distance, and I followed her. She trailed them down one aisle and then another, only stopping when they stopped, Beth too focused on her customer to notice the woman.

The woman continued to stare at them until Danielle walked by, alone, long arms full of books. The woman studied her closely, turning her head as Danielle passed.

Danielle paused, gave the woman a quizzical smile, and asked, "Can I help you?"

I could not hear the woman's response, only the dull tones of her voice. She must have said "No," because Danielle continued on, shaking her head slightly as she walked away.

The woman turned then, slowly, toward me, and I quickly pushed my cart out of the aisle and back toward the counter, hoping that she hadn't seen me.

* * *

When I arrived at Benjamin's school that afternoon, I found him standing curbside at his usual spot. Normally he would have been among two or three friends; this time, however, he was flanked by Miss Delaney, his teacher, a tall Black woman with a kind face and high cheekbones. Both of them watched me as I pulled my car up to the curb. I lowered the passenger-side window, and Miss Delaney ducked down to see me.

"May I have a word with you inside, Helena?" she asked.

Moments later, I was seated at one of the children's desks in Benjamin's classroom, Miss Delaney seated at her desk in front of me. She had pulled a second desk out into the hallway, where Benjamin now sat, focused on his homework.

I hadn't been in this classroom since new student orientation. Giant numbers cut out of colored paper and covered in shiny laminate were taped to the wall near the ceiling on one side, a printed alphabet (upper and lower case) below them. Big windows on one side of the room revealed a playground outside. There were cubbies below the window, stocked with books and tubs full of crayons, pencils and scissors. I spotted the cubby marked "Benjamin," which was written on a shiny paper star. On top of the cubbies, lit by the sunlight, was a large fish tank with at least three large goldfish swimming around. The bottom of the tank was lined with smooth white rocks.

"I need to talk to you about Benjamin," Miss Delaney said.

"Okay," I responded, tearing my eyes from the tank. I found myself messing with my own fingers nervously, resisting the urge to chew at a nail.

"Up until about a week ago, your son had been a model student," she continued. "He was polite, and friendly, and compliant. I never had a worry where Benjamin was concerned. And he was fitting in better and more quickly than any of the other new students this year. He is also extremely intelligent. I had him pegged for a student who could easily skip a grade."

"Okay," I said again, my thoughts swimming, begging for the point.

"About a week ago," she sighed, "that started to change. He started to get edgier with me. Acting up. Sometimes new students take awhile to show their true colors, and I thought maybe he was comfortable enough now to begin causing a little trouble. Trying to get a laugh from his new friends."

She stood up and came around to the front of her desk, leaning against it, towering over me. "I debated saying anything to you. I wanted to give him the benefit of the doubt. Yesterday he snapped back at me and I had to chastise him. Afterwards the class had a math test. When it was over, he handed it in, blank."

"What?" I said.

"He was smiling when he gave it to me."

I sat back in my chair, trying to distance myself from her. Trying to back away from what she was telling me.

"Is everything all right at home?" she asked. "Benjamin does not look well. He looks and acts like he hasn't slept."

"He doesn't. Hasn't," I said. I shook my head. "He sleepwalks. He has for quite some time. Lately it's been almost every night."

Miss Delaney nodded.

"He's been acting up at home too," I continued. "Doing… stuff that's not like him. I've been concerned."

"Well, I'm concerned as well," said Miss Delaney. "I know you are new to the area. And from Benjamin's file I know that you are divorced. Is his father still around?"

"An hour away," I said. "Benjamin sees him every two weeks."

"Do they have a good relationship?"

"Yes," I said. "He's a good father."

"And who is Emil?"

The question caught me off guard. I stumbled for words. "He's a… I guess you'd say he's an imaginary friend. He's from a book that Benjamin once read."

She nodded again, thinking. "As far as I'm concerned, this is either a discipline issue or a medical issue. Obviously you know Benjamin better than I do. If you're saying this behavior is unusual for Benjamin and is concerning to you as well, I would recommend seeking medical help, especially after today."

"Today?" I asked, my heart sinking. I realized I hadn't heard the worst yet.

"This afternoon I stepped out of the classroom for a moment, just into the hallway to speak to another teacher." She picked up her cell phone from her desk, turned it on, and began tapping the screen with her finger. "When I returned, this was written on the chalkboard."

She held the phone toward me, showing me the screen. It was a picture of a chalkboard, the same chalkboard in front of me right now, behind Miss Delaney. The words written on it were shocking. And even more horrifying to me was the handwriting, which was familiar.

"I have never been called that before in my life," she said, speaking more slowly, her voice trembling slightly. She withdrew the phone and shut it off. She took a deep breath and composed herself.

"I don't understand," I said, fighting back tears. "He doesn't even know what that means."

"I had the students line up outside in the hallway, and I called them in one at a time," she continued. "I asked them to identify the student who had written it."

I looked at her, waiting for her to continue, saying nothing.

"All but four said it was Benjamin," she said. "Three of them refused to give an answer. His closest friends."

"Who was the fourth?" I said.

"The fourth was Benjamin," she said. "He said that Emil did it."

* * *

"Hey, Hel."

"Hey, David. How are you?"

"I'm good. You sound tired."

"I am," I said. I was stretched out on my back in bed, the door to my room closed, my cell phone in my right hand, my left hand over my eyes. "I need to talk to you about Benji."

"What's up?" he said, trying to sound casual but betraying a note of concern. For a moment it sounded as though he was walking, and then I heard a door close. He had gone somewhere more private.

"I don't know where to start," I said, and began to cry, the tears rolling over my temples and hitting the sheets with an audible *plop* beside my ears.

"Just… start at the beginning, Snug," he said, and his tone of affection combined with that old nickname nearly broke me down.

I told him about the missing keys, the episode in the basement, the lying, Mags, and the chalkboard, each incident more serious than the last, all of them describing a form of behavior foreign to our son, now asleep in his room. When I was finished, David was silent.

"Are you there?" I asked.

"I'm here," he sighed. "I'm at a loss."

"Me too."

"If I wasn't hearing it from you, I'd be tempted to ask if you were describing the right kid."

"I know."

He took a breath. "Are you going to do what his teacher suggested? Call a doctor? That sounds like the best idea."

"Yes, probably."

"Probably?" he said, an edge to his voice.

"David, there's more. I'm hesitant to tell you because I don't think you'll believe me. I don't know if I believe it."

"What is it?" he asked.

I sat up and reached for the little leather book on my nightstand. I told David about it, how it had come into my possession, and how Benjamin had read it as well. I even recited the first few verses of the poem before snapping the book shut, unable to continue.

"So you're saying… you think this book might be coming true?" he asked.

"No," I said quickly. "I don't know. Is it possible that Benjamin is *making* it come true?"

"Hel," he said, skeptical.

"Just think about it," I said. "He's always been so imaginative. He *loves* to play pranks. And he's so smart. Isn't it possible he's – "

"He's also very sensitive," David interrupted. "He would know when to say when. If this started as a joke, he's taken it too far. And he would know that. I mean… the cat?"

"Yeah," I sighed. "I hear you. But what if he's lashing out at me? At us? Like you said, he's sensitive. We've put him through a lot these past few months. This could be a cry for attention."

"Quite a cry," he said.

"No kidding," I said, and chuckled morosely.

"Look," he said, "I think the first step is a psychologist, like his teacher said. It could be a combination of things. He could be doing this entirely on purpose, or maybe he just snapped, you know?" David said this matter-of-factly, but it made me begin to cry again. "I don't mean that as coldly as it sounds," he said. "In a lot of ways, if it's just psychological, that's a good thing. They can diagnose and treat that. It sure beats the alternative."

"Yeah," I said, smiling through tears. "I guess it does."

"So you'll call?"

"Tomorrow. The school gave me the name of a doctor to call. But they were closed by the time I got home. I'll try again tomorrow."

"If you want, I'll take off work and go with you," he offered. "It just can't be first thing in the morning."

"No, you don't need to do that," I said. "I'll let you know how it goes."

"Okay."

There was a long pause then, laden with unspoken words.

"Thank you, David," I said. "There's no one else I can talk to about this. And my head is so cloudy right now that I can't see anything clearly. You've helped a lot."

"He's my son too," he said, only a minor note of defensiveness in his voice, as if I needed the reminder. He took a breath. "When is the last time you slept?"

"Through the night?" I chuckled. "About a week ago. I feel like I'm losing my mind."

"It might not be a bad idea to see a doctor yourself, Hel," he said. "Things are going to be hard enough for you to handle even *with* sleep."

"True," I said.

"Do you want me to come get him tomorrow evening? I have him this weekend anyway. It would give you a break."

"No, he'll miss school," I reminded him. "They've given him in-school suspension for the rest of the week."

"What does *that* mean?" he asked, a small note of anger in his voice.

"It means he'll be sitting in the principal's office for the next three days."

"That's ridiculous."

"It's not, David," I said, trying to calm him. "Really it's not. I'm surprised they didn't expel him, honestly. They're being gracious. And at least this way I won't miss work. And I'd hate to ask Mom to watch him with… everything that's going on."

"You're right," he said, relenting. "You're right."

"Okay," I said.

From the other end of the line, I heard the soft murmur of a female voice. "I should go," he said.

"Yeah," I said, surprised to find that I didn't want him to hang up.

"I love you, Hel," he said in a low voice.

I blinked back fresh tears. "I know," I said, and took a shaky breath. "I know you do. I love you too."

We hung up. I dropped the phone on the mattress beside me.

Earlier, on the ride home from school, Benjamin and I had not talked. At dinner, he had sat silently at the kitchen table and poked at his food. I didn't ask him any questions. Asking questions would either produce lies or, worse, truths that I didn't want to know. When I asked him to get dressed and go to bed early, he was compliant.

When I hung up with David, it was still fairly early, before 10:00. I left my room and crept silently down the hallway and pressed my ear to Benjamin's doorway. I heard nothing and was relieved. I began to step away when, as if on cue, I heard his voice. His tone was sleepy and muffled.

"I said I didn't want to do it," is what I thought I heard him say. I pressed my ear to the door again.

Silence, then: "It wasn't funny."

Silence again, then, "What do you want?"

The ensuing silence was long enough for me to suspect that Benjamin had fallen back to sleep. But then he screamed, "*WHAT DO YOU*

WANT?"

At this, I opened his door and flipped on the light. Once my eyes adjusted to the sudden brightness, I realized that the bed was empty.

"Benji?" I said.

I could hear him breathing rapidly, somewhere nearby. I scanned the room, stepping inside. "Benji?" I called again, louder. I turned and looked at his closet door, which was closed.

"Mom?" he said, his voice choked with tears. I turned again in the direction of the sound. It was then I realized that his voice was coming from under his bed.

I ran to his bedside and fell to my knees. There was Benjamin, curled in a fetal position, his eyes wide open, staring at me. His face was full of terror. This wasn't happening in his sleep. He was awake.

"Mom?" he said, giant tears falling from his unblinking eyes. "He's in my bed."

* * *

Benjamin slept in my room that night. He was fitful. He tossed and turned, but would settle if I stroked his hair or back. Occasionally he spoke, but none of his words were intelligible.

I spent the night awake, sitting up in bed beside him, sometimes crying, sometimes thinking, mostly so tired that more than an hour would pass without a conscious thought entering my brain, yet I was certain I had never fallen asleep. My eyes never left my bedroom door, which I had locked.

WEDNESDAY

When I dropped Benjamin off at school the next morning, my tired mind registered the presence of the school's principal, Mr. Stockly, standing outside the school. When I pulled up to the curb, I was surprised to see him raise a hand to me in recognition and approach the car. It took a moment for me to remember why he was there. When Benjamin exited the car, neither he nor Mr. Stockly said a word to me. Instead, the principal put an arm around Benjamin and escorted him into the school. Other children watched them go and whispered to each other. I scowled at them from behind the steering wheel.

Approaching the doors to the library a few minutes later, the sound of my shoes on the sidewalk seeming to echo from a mile away, I found myself forcing my eyes to open wider, willing myself to feel more awake.

I unlocked the library doors and punched a code into the building's alarm system. The keypad buzzed at me. The LED display read, "INCORRECT CODE." I groaned and punched it in again. Another buzz, another "INCORRECT CODE." I punched it in a third time, pressing the keys hard enough to turn the knuckle of my index finger white.

The third time was wrong as well, and my ears were filled with the sound of the library alarm, its shrill call piercing painfully. I stepped outside to get away from the noise and slumped down on the curb. I dropped my purse beside me and put my head in my hands. If it wasn't for the muffled but still loud alarm ringing behind me, I almost could have slept.

Moments later, the police arrived, followed shortly by Mrs. Strickland. She glared at me as she marched across the parking lot to the front door, her heels clicking loudly. I apologized to her and said that I thought I had put in the correct code. My voice sounded odd to me, as if I was hearing someone else speak beside me.

Mrs. Strickland spoke with the police. As they talked, she and the officers took turns casting glances at me. I couldn't hear their words, but they looked judgmental, and I wanted to throttle them all. After a few moments, the alarms were turned off and the squad car left.

I followed Mrs. Strickland into the library toward the service counter. She stopped abruptly and I almost bumped into her. She turned to me and said, "Recite the alarm code."

"Three-two-one-seven-four-pound," I said, gesturing as if the answer was obvious.

She shook her head. "That's not even close to correct," she said.

I mouthed the code to myself silently, then out loud again, "It's three-two-one-seven-four-pound," I insisted.

"It's one-one-seven-seven-four-pound," she told me, and my heart sank as I realized she was correct.

"I'm sorry," I said. "I don't know how I screwed that up." I felt myself on the verge of tears and hoped that she could not see it.

She studied me for a moment, her lips holding back words, a dam ready to break. She looked like she was holding a spider in her mouth and was attempting to keep it from escaping. She looked at her watch. "Write it down, keep it in your purse. And for heaven's sake, do *not* label it, 'Library Alarm Code.'" She walked away from me, toward her office. "It's 8:20," she said, not looking at me. "Get your work done." She slammed her office door.

* * *

I somehow made it through the morning. Beth looked at me with concern every time she walked by me. Even Danielle regarded me with curiosity, but neither of them asked me anything. The library was unusually busy for a Wednesday morning, so there was no time for chit-chat anyway, for which I was grateful, though I found myself struggling not to be edgy with the more ignorant customers, of whom there seemed to be more than usual.

At lunchtime, I grabbed my bagged lunch and went to the empty park across the street, away from eyes and ears. It was cool and pleasant and quiet, and for a moment I sat on the familiar bench and closed my eyes. I considered giving in to sleep.

I called the number of the psychologist the school had recommended. When the receptionist informed me that it would be a little more than two weeks before Benjamin could be seen, I erupted into tears that startled me. She asked me if I was willing to be put on hold.

As "Love is Blue" played in my ear, I rested my head in one hand, my elbow against my knee, and cried silently. When she returned to the line, the receptionist said that they could see Benjamin on Monday. It was the best she could do. It was still bad news, but better bad news.

I then looked up the numbers for local doctors. I had not been to see a doctor since we had moved, so I had no regular doctor of my own yet. It took three calls before I finally got one that was willing to see me on my lunch break the next day. When asked what I needed to be seen for, I said insomnia.

I then called Benjamin's school and asked to speak with Mr. Stockly. I not only wanted to find out how Benjamin was doing, but I also wanted Mr. Stockly to know I was being a responsible parent. To his credit, he spoke kindly to me and reassured me than Benjamin was doing fine. He did not offer to let me speak with him.

I dropped my phone into my purse and looked at my bagged lunch. I wasn't hungry. I leaned back on the bench and closed my eyes. The breeze was soothing across my forehead. I may have nodded off for a moment, but I couldn't be sure.

When it was time for me to return to work, I grabbed my lunch and my purse and stood, looking up toward the library across the street. As I did so, its doors opened and a woman emerged. It was the same woman I had seen the day before – young but old, still but fretful, with sunken eyes and a shadow across her face. She shuffled away from the building toward the parking lot. I marveled at how ankles so thin could support her weight. She got into a car and drove away. I watched her go. She did not see me.

When I entered the library a moment later, Beth and Danielle were behind the service counter, whispering excitedly to each other. They both looked over at me as I entered, eyes wide. Beth beckoned me with a hand.

"What's going on?" I asked when I reached them.

"Did you see that woman?" Danielle asked.

"The one who just left?" I asked, pointing a thumb behind me.

"Yes," they both said.

"Yeah, she was here yesterday," I said.

"She was?" said Danielle, and then, remembering, "She *was*."

"What about her?" I asked.

"Do you know who she *is*?" Danielle asked.

"No," I said, looking from Danielle to Beth and back again.

"She's been on the news," Danielle said. "Beth recognized her. Her husband is the one who murdered their kids and then skipped out of town."

I realized then why the woman looked familiar to me, and also why she looked so haggard. I had a mental image of her standing at a podium with the local chief of police, surrounded by cameras and microphones. She never spoke, at least not on the two occasions I had seen her on the news. She just stood dumbly as the police requested any information on the whereabouts of her missing husband, flash-bulbs illuminating her translucent skin.

"Do you know what her husband did to their kids?" Danielle asked.

"No," I said, beginning to walk away. "And I don't want to."

"Well, he's as guilty as sin," she said. "One minute he was mister mournful father, and the next minute he's gone. I hope he fries."

* * *

All afternoon I kept a cup of coffee hidden under the counter, sneaking sips when I knew Mrs. Strickland wasn't watching, and refilling from the lounge coffeemaker whenever my cup was empty. I lost count of how much I had consumed. The caffeine helped, insomuch as it made me feel artificially awake, buzzing yet heavy. The hours moved slowly and I could think of little except how exhausted I was.

I'm not sure what I was thinking about, if anything, when a hand appeared and slid a gift toward me on the counter. I looked up to the smiling face of Hugo, beaming at me. He was wearing the familiar leather jacket over a beige sweater, and he looked flawless to me, alive and vital, the exact opposite of the tired, stressed visage I tried to avoid in the mirror every time I went to the bathroom.

"I'm not sure if you're aware, but today is our one week anniversary," he said, nudging the gift. "And so I got you flowers."

I was puzzled. The gift was quite small and completely flat, about the size and shape of a bookmark, I thought. I picked it up and unwrapped it, giving him a weak smile in return. It was, indeed, a bookmark. On it was a reprint of a painting of roses, a soft crimson tassel dangling from one end. Printed over the image of the flowers was the quote, "What's in a name? That which we call a rose by any other name would smell as sweet."

"The best kind of flowers for a book lover, am I right?" he beamed.

"You're right," I nodded.

His smile faded ever so slightly and he said, "How are you?" The question carried weight.

"I'm okay," I said, then added "just tired" when he gave me a look that read, *I don't buy it*.

"Listen," he said, leaning over the counter and propping himself on his elbows. I got a whiff of leather and mint. "I was wondering what your mother was doing tonight?"

I chuckled. "I'm not sure."

"I know I said Friday, but I don't think I can wait that long. Let's go out tonight." He reached out with one hand and touched mine. The tips of his fingers were rough, the skin warm. My tired heart fluttered.

I blinked at him. He looked so handsome and so happy. I wanted to be nowhere except where he was, feeding off his energy and living in his world, a world that was not cloaked by an ever-following cloud. I was no longer just attracted to him. I *needed* him. He looked like rescue to me.

"I would love to," I said.

He beamed and gave my hand a gentle squeeze. "I'll pick you up at 7:00?" he asked.

"Okay," I said, and my voice was barely more than a whisper.

* * *

Benjamin was seated in the passenger seat, his knees pulled up to his chin, his gaze focused out the passenger side window. We were driving away from his school.

"How was today?" I asked him.

"Okay," he said, not looking at me.

"What's it like spending the day in the principal's office?"

"Okay," he answered. I thought this might be all he was going to give me, but then he added, "He's nice."

"That's good!" I said with a little too much enthusiasm. Benjamin didn't react.

I took a deep breath. "Benjamin, why did you write that on the chalkboard yesterday?"

He said nothing.

"Can you tell me, sweetie?"

"I don't know," he finally said.

It wasn't the denial that I had expected. "You don't know why you wrote it? But you *did* write it?"

"I don't know," he said, and he sniffed. I glanced to see if he was crying, but his face was turned too far away from me. "I don't remember."

"You don't remember?" I asked.

"They told me I did it. Miss Delaney and the other kids. But I don't remember."

"Did…" I hesitated. "Did Emil tell you to write it?"

He didn't answer, but his body twitched ever so slightly. At a stop sign, I paused long enough to give him a longer look, but Benjamin's face remained focused out the window. I couldn't read him at all. I continued driving.

"Do you remember what happened last night, baby?"

"Yes," he responded, and his voice was huskier, slightly louder. "I got in his bed."

My heart rose slowly into my throat. "You mean Emil got in your bed, baby? Do you remember saying that?"

He didn't respond. The silence bothered me in a way that I couldn't explain.

"I'm taking you to Mee-maw's," I said brightly, intentionally changing my tone in an effort to sound upbeat. "She's making your favorite for dinner. And then maybe you can play some games."

Benjamin was quiet. No reaction.

"Maybe when I drop you off I can tell her you've been having a rough week, so you can be allowed to watch as much TV as you'd like tonight. Would that make you happy?"

Benjamin began to laugh, quietly at first so I thought he might be crying. But then the laughter got louder. It confused me.

Slowly, in the corner of my vision, I could see Benjamin turn his face toward me. It took him several seconds to turn away from the window and face me completely. Still driving, I could only steal brief glances, but when I did, I saw his face: his mouth turned up at the corners in a smile so wide that it looked painful, a gleeful grin in stark contrast to his eyes, which were wide with anger, his brows down-turned in a rage. And the entire time, he never stopped laughing. It was like being seated beside a poisonous snake, ready to strike.

* * *

When we reached my mother's house minutes later, my nerves felt frayed. I parked in the driveway and forced myself to face Benjamin, to look at the monster that sat beside me with a face that resembled Benjamin but was like him at all. I was going to tell him to sit still, to stay in the car, while I told my mother that my plans had changed and she wouldn't be watching Benjamin at all.

But as soon as we stopped, the smile disappeared from Benjamin's face. The mask fell off. He grabbed his book bag and left the car. When my mother emerged from the house, Benjamin raced toward her. I cringed and my heart stopped, but Benjamin gave her a hug and disappeared through the front door.

My mom gave me wave, which I weakly returned. We had made all arrangements over the phone; there was no need for us to speak. She hesitated because I was hesitating, her face becoming one of concern and confusion. I put the car in reverse and left. Backing out of the driveway and into the street, I saw my mother enter the house and close the front door behind her. I was leaving her alone with him, and I felt conflicted between a hopefulness that everything would be fine and a fear that he might do or say something terrible.

Ultimately, I chose to leave. To escape, even if just for a little while. Like a coward.

* * *

The shower was as cold as I could stand it. When I was finished, I redid my hair and my makeup as best as I could, considering that my arms felt like lead. I briefly thought about calling Hugo, cancelling, and just going to bed. Sleep would be bliss. But I imagined Hugo's disappointed voice on the other end of the line and talked myself out of it.

I was ready to go before Hugo was due to arrive. I found myself walking into Benjamin's room without consciously deciding to do so.

It was in normal disarray, and in the late afternoon sunlight there was nothing ominous or threatening about it. In fact, it was almost pleasant; the air even felt fresh. But then I looked at the bed and recalled Benjamin cowering under it following what sounded like a whispered conversation.

I had an idea.

I walked down the hallway, through the kitchen and into the pantry. At the top of the basement stairs, I flipped on the lights. The two bulbs illuminated my path down the steps. When I reached the bottom, one shoe crunched on broken glass and I pulled it back. I realized I had never returned to clean up the jar of spaghetti sauce I had dropped. The floor was covered with small shards of glass and sauce that had dehydrated and turned sticky.

I avoided the spill and made my way to the half dozen or so plastic tubs scattered around the basement. One of them had a label made with scotch tape and marker that read, "Baby Stuff." Inside, hidden among the handmade baby blankets, a stuffed yellow rabbit, a pair of knitted booties, and a saliva-worn rattle was the item I was looking for: Benjamin's baby monitor.

Back upstairs, I plugged the monitor into a receptacle in Benjamin's wall, then hid the monitor itself under his bed. I placed a stuffed alligator – already living among the dust bunnies – against the monitor to hide its glowing red light.

I placed the other end of the monitor – the receiving end – on my nightstand, concealed from clear view by a stack of books. I clicked it on. It buzzed to life, and I was surprised that after all these years, at least six since it had last been used, the batteries still had some juice in them.

My little project had distracted me, and so when there was a knocking at the front door, I was momentarily startled. Hugo was on my doorstep, his face a welcoming smile. Without thinking about it, I gave him a hug.

"Hey to you too," he laughed when I let him go.

"Just happy to see you," I said, patting his shoulder and feeling a little embarrassed. He walked me to his car.

We returned to the restaurant of our previous date, with Hugo making an aside comment once again about celebrating our anniversary. The air outside was cooler than it had been on Friday, and so we opted to eat in the dining room this time.

I did my best to look energetic and engaged, but it took a palpable effort. I was so happy to be with Hugo again, and yet I felt exhaustion all the way to my bones.

We placed our orders and surrendered our menus, then had a few awkward moments of small talk before Hugo pried, "Are you sure everything is okay?"

For the briefest of moments, I considered telling him everything, just dumping it all out on the table like so much word vomit. Part of me felt like the exercise would be a relief, a catharsis, but then I realized, no… it was too much. I had known this man for exactly one week – as he kept reminding me – and any hopes of this being a successful second date would be dashed the minute I started down that path.

"You know what?" I said. "Yes, everything is great." I picked up my water glass and held it out to him. "To a wonderful evening."

* * *

After dinner (*delicious*) and somehow managing to hold up my end of another engaging conversation, I was feeling human again. I was full, and I could feel the rich food energizing me. If Hugo noticed that I'd downed three espressos, he didn't say anything. I felt myself forgetting the reality of my situation at home, and I welcomed it. Looking into Hugo's vibrant eyes, it was easy to forget everything else.

"So, about that surprise," I said.

"Yes," said Hugo, wiping his mouth with his napkin and beaming. "Let's go."

We drove for about ten minutes to an older part of town that was unfamiliar to me. We pulled in to a rather full parking lot in front of a large brick building with huge, welcoming windows. A sign above its doors read, "A Novel Idea."

"What is *this*?" I asked.

"You'll see," he said, and he took my hand. It enveloped mine and was comfortingly warm.

The front doors opened into an expansive lobby. In front of me and to my left and right were rows upon rows of books. Looking up, the ceiling was open to a second and third floor above us, and beyond that was a cathedral ceiling, covered in beautiful stained glass.

"Oh, Toto," I said, dropping Hugo's hand, "I don't think we're in Kansas anymore."

He chuckled. "You like?"

"I like," I said, taking a few steps forward. "I don't know where to start."

"Let's start at the very beginning," he sang quietly, borrowing the opening notes from the song "Do-Re-Mi" from *The Sound of Music*, and I was not at all surprised that his singing voice had a tone that was rich and pleasant, even though he was being playful.

I went up one aisle and down another. Sometimes Hugo and I were together, and other times one or both of us would get distracted by a particular volume and separate, and yet somehow we always managed to find each other again without trying.

The store was wonderful. It smelled of dust and ink and paper and leather and smoke and history. Many of the books were quite old, with spines that were threatening to let go. A lovely glass display case was filled with antique first editions beautiful enough to be in a museum. I knew I could get lost in here for hours and not care.

I was standing in one aisle, admiring a dilapidated almanac, when Hugo met up with me again. "Question," he said. "Is it bad form to ask for assistance in the Self Help section?"

I laughed and slapped him on the shoulder. "This place is great," I said. "Thank you for bringing me here."

"We should come on a Saturday morning sometime and just spend the day," he said. "It would take that long just to see everything."

"Wouldn't it be fun to break into a place like this after hours and just wander around?" I asked him.

"Best hide-and-seek ever," he said.

I poked him in the ribs. "You know what I mean," I said, and I smiled, looking up at him. He was suddenly quite close to me. "All these books…"

"Waiting patiently to be read," he winked. He leaned toward me, then looked over my head, down the aisle behind me. Another customer, an older woman with two books under her arm, was watching us, frowning severely, her disapproval almost comical.

Hugo chuckled, taking a step back and pulling me with him into the next aisle. It was empty. He pulled me toward him. Standing there among the volumes of books, stories waiting to be read and characters longing to be known, Hugo kissed me. Leather and soap combined with the smell of the dusty books that surrounded us, and for a moment, everything else was forgotten, lost to a kiss.

We were interrupted by the sound of a man clearing his throat. One of the bookstore employees, a gentleman I had seen near the register when we had entered, was giving us a disapproving look. Hugo pulled away from me, shrugged, and pointed upward. Above our heads, suspended horizontally from a shelf, was a sign that read, "ROMANCE."

The employee laughed, shook his head, and walked away without saying a word. I was still smiling when Hugo leaned down and kissed me again.

* * *

Later, we were standing at my doorstep. The evening was over entirely too quickly and I felt a peculiar awareness of my own house behind me. It was like the feeling you get when you are talking to someone but know that someone else is waiting, impatiently, to speak to you as well, a harbinger of bad news.

"That was easily the best second date I've ever had," he said. "And also the second *best* date I've ever had. After our first, or course."

"I'm totally confused," I said.

"New math," he responded, and kissed me. I could get used to this.

I pulled away from him. I clutched my purse along with a small paper bag with the "A Novel Idea" logo printed on it. Inside was a 1911 printing of *Little Women* (the first and second parts). It was surprisingly pristine for its age and priced reasonably, and Hugo had insisted on buying it for me when he had caught me admiring it.

"Thank you for tonight," I said. "I really needed this."

"You're welcome," he said.

We were both hesitating. Again my eye was drawn to the necklace he was wearing, the foreign symbol resting against his chest. "What is this?" I asked, and touched it with my finger for the second time.

"It's a Chinese symbol," he said. "It means strength."

"It's nice," I said. "Although it looks a little like a lowercase 'h.'"

"I saw it in a beach store once and liked how it looked," he shrugged. "No deeper meaning there."

I sighed and looked into his eyes. "Again soon?" I asked him.

"We're still on for Friday, as far as I'm concerned. I'll pick you up at 7:00 if that works for you."

I nodded.

With a final kiss, Hugo left me on my doorstep and walked toward his car. I watched him go, partly because I liked watching him go, and partly because I didn't want to enter the house, which seemed to loom so very dark behind me, breathing down my neck, staring at my back, like someone was watching me through a window.

Hugo got into his car, started it, and rolled down the window. "Goodnight, Helena," he called out. Suddenly I was overwhelmed with a desire to go with him, to jump in the car and tell him to drive, and when he would ask me where we were going, I would say I didn't care, just drive me as fast and as far as you like, and wherever we end up, we will be together and things will be better. Everything else will be forgotten and nothing will matter except for the two of us.

Perhaps Hugo saw something in my expression, because he hesitated for just a moment, and I just knew he was going to call out, "Come with me," but he didn't. Instead he drove away, and I watched until his car reached the end of the cul-de-sac, turned a corner, and disappeared.

Knowing everything that I know now, I wish I had given in to that desire, that I had run to him and somehow convinced him to whisk me away to somewhere, *anywhere* else. Instead, I turned around, and with a weak hand I unlocked my front door, stepped into the darkness inside, and never saw Hugo again.

* * *

In my exhaustion, I nearly forgot that I still needed to pick up Benjamin from my mother's house. He was asleep on her living room couch when I arrived, and she looked surprised when I asked her pointedly if everything had gone alright.

"Yes, of course," she said, almost offended.

"It's been a rough week," I offered as vague explanation, hoping my tone indicated that further details would not be forthcoming. She didn't press me. I kissed her goodbye and she hugged me tight. Mothers know.

Benjamin did not wake when I tucked him into bed. I pulled off his shoes, covered him as best I could, and rubbed his head. He moaned slightly. His skin felt slightly warm to me, and I wondered if he might be coming down with something.

How horrible it felt to be so incredibly tired and yet dreading my own bed. I brushed my teeth, washed my face, and changed into my pajamas, all the while questioning the value of such rote behavior. It felt like priming the walls for a house that was about to be demolished.

I didn't even attempt to read. Mere moments after turning off the light and resting my head on a folded-over pillow, the soft hiss of the baby monitor not far from my ear, I was sound asleep. It was dreamless, deep, and far too brief.

I woke up to the sound of Benjamin calling out, "Mom!" and was confused as to why his voice sounded so strange. It took a moment to realize that I could hear him twice – both through the monitor and traveling down the hallway. The monitor picked up the sound of his feet hitting his bedroom floor, and then I heard the squeak of his bedroom door.

"Mom?" he called out again, and he sounded both sleepy and distressed. I sat up in bed and turned on the light beside me. I put on my glasses. The floorboard creaked as Benjamin approached my door.

The third time he called for me, he was right outside my door, and even though it was expected, the loudness and closeness of it startled me. I tried to convince myself, as I waited for the doorknob to turn, that I had nothing to be afraid of.

But the doorknob did not turn. I waited. A moment later, when

Benjamin called out to me again, he was no longer outside my door, but farther away. I slipped out of bed. Again he called for me, and his voice was faint.

When I opened my bedroom door, the hallway was empty. "Benji?" I called.

"Mom?" he said, and I realized that his voice was not coming from the direction of his room, but from the kitchen. I hastened through the living room, reaching the kitchen door in time to see Benjamin enter the pantry.

"Benji!" I called out in a harsh whisper. I walked quickly to the pantry and was greeted by the open basement door, gaping and black. Benjamin was descending the steps into the darkness below. I could not see him, but I could hear his fading footsteps and his voice as he called out to me again, his voice trembling.

"Benji!" I called out again, and I felt myself panic. What if I startled him, scared him out of his sleepwalking? He might fall down the stairs. Or he might stumble in the darkness anyway. I put my hand on the light switch and hesitated. I called out to him again, trying to sound calm yet loud enough for him to hear.

"Mom?" he responded, still descending the steps.

I flipped the switch. For less than a second, the basement was flooded with light, blinding me. But then, in an instant, both bulbs exploded with a loud pop. I screamed.

In that brief moment when there was light, I saw Benjamin, his pajama-clad body facing away from me, descending the stairs, one hand holding the banister loosely. And at the bottom I saw the shadow of a child, a boy, reaching up toward my son.

THURsday

"Beth, it's Helena."

"Hey, Helena." She sounded sleepy. "Is everything okay?"

"Not really."

I was still in bed. Benjamin was sound asleep beside me. I had managed to retrieve him from the stairs, without incident, after grabbing a flashlight from the pantry. Whether or not there had been someone else in the basement, I could not say for certain. I had not paused to look, but instead had carried Benjamin as quickly as possible back to my room and locked the door behind us.

"Benjamin is sick." I spoke quietly so as not to wake him. "We've both been up all night. I really think I need to take a sick day."

There was a pause at the other end.

"I know I don't get any paid time off yet," I continued. "I'll just take a day without pay. He's really not well."

"I'm not sure it's a good idea," Beth said. Her voice sounded hesitant. "I mean, you can call Mrs. Strickland and ask her, but…" she trailed off.

"But what?"

"Look, I'm not supposed to tell you this," she said. "Like *at all*, but you need to know. You're on really thin ice with Mrs. Strickland right now."

I felt myself getting angry. "How do you know this?" I demanded.

"She talked to me and Danielle yesterday when you were at lunch," she said. "You're basically on probation with her. She's just waiting for one more reason. To let you go."

"Okay, I was late one day because I lost my keys and then I screwed up the alarm," I snapped. "Do I need to explain to her what's going on with Benjamin? The sleepwalking, I mean."

"No, she knows, I told her," Beth said. By her tone I could tell she was trying to calm me. "I hope that's okay, but I thought she should know what you've been dealing with."

"And still she puts me on probation without even telling me?"

"It's more than that," she said. "You messed up the returns yesterday."

"What?" I said, surprised, and Benjamin stirred beside me.

"Yesterday morning you shelved all the books without checking them in first."

My heart sank. All returned books had to be scanned, alerting the library's system to their return and availability, as well as, most importantly, logging any overdue fees. By skipping that step, there would be absolutely no way of knowing, except for the few titles I might remember, which books had been shelved yesterday morning. I could already picture customers coming to the desk with a book they had just pulled off the shelf, only for the computer to say that this book was already checked out and overdue for return. The consequences of this mistake would revisit me for days, if not weeks.

The money wasn't a huge deal. The library logged maybe $50 in overdue fees per day and would eventually collect only a fraction of that. But the whole disorganization of it all would be infuriating to Mrs. Strickland.

"You've got to be kidding me," I sighed. "I don't remember doing that."

"Look," said Beth. "I'm really sorry Benjamin's sick. But it's really in your best interest to be there today." She paused. "I'm telling you this as a friend."

I sighed. "Thank you, Beth," I said. "I'll see what I can do."

We hung up. Benjamin rolled over to his stomach and draped one arm across my legs, then looked up at me sleepily. He smiled. "Good morning, ama," he said. I touched his face; he still felt a little warm.

"Hi," I said, putting down my phone. "How did you sleep?"

"Good."

"Good? Good. Do you remember why you're in here?"

He shook his head against the pillow, "No," he mumbled.

* * *

Benjamin and I left the house earlier than usual that morning. We made a stop at a Dunkin' Donuts on the way, where I treated him to a chocolate frosted doughnut and a small chocolate milk (and I said a small prayer for Mr. Stockly, who would be spending the day with my sugar-infused kid), and got myself a large coffee with a turbo shot. By the time Benjamin finished the doughnut and most of the milk, he was quite chipper in the passenger seat beside me and actually began singing along to the radio, which I hadn't even realized was playing.

"Bye, Mom," he said as he exited the car at school. Then I heard him call, as he sprinted away, "Thanks for the doughnut!"

I checked and double-checked my work at the library that morning and made sure everything was brightly lit and in order by the time my coworkers arrived. I forced myself to make eye contact with Mrs.

Strickland when she entered and gave her a "good morning" that I hoped sounded equal parts courteous and professional. She nodded in response and did not smile.

When Beth arrived, she gave me a small, knowing nod, but we exchanged no words.

* * *

At 11:45, I was seated on an exam table at Hickman Mills Family Practice. The nurse who brought me to the room had asked me some general questions about my medical history and took notes on a tablet (electronic, not paper). She weighed me and took my temperature and blood pressure, then told me to have a seat on the table and wait until Dr. Mills came.

I checked the time on my cell phone. I needed to be back on the clock by 12:30, and it had taken seven minutes to get here. I noticed that I had unread messages, one from Hugo, another from David. *The men in my life,* I thought, amused for no particular reason. The former was reiterating his appreciation for last night's date; the latter wanted an update on Benjamin.

I kicked my dangling feet and realized I was wired with energy from my coffee. I nearly came off the table when Dr. Mills, an overweight man of about 50 with salt-and-pepper hair, entered the room. He shook my hand and introduced himself.

After a handful of generic questions, most of them repeats of the ones the nurse had already asked me, Dr. Mills said, "So why are we seeing you today, Helena?"

"Insomnia," I said. "I haven't been sleeping well at all lately."

"And how long has this been going on?"

"About a week… or so," I embellished. A week seemed too brief.

"Do you drink a lot of coffee or caffeinated soda?" he asked.

"Not much at all," I lied, and I tried to still my legs.

"Are you sleeping and then waking up, or not going to sleep at all?"

"A bit of both," I said. "Lately I'm just awake all night."

"How many nights in a row?" he asked.

"Three or four," I said. "I can't remember for sure." The past several days and nights blurred together. I couldn't be certain what day *today* was.

"Do you have a history of high blood pressure?" he asked.

"Not at all," I responded.

Dr. Mills regarded me briefly, and he looked skeptical. So I was surprised when he said, "Sleep deprivation is a serious thing. I don't think people realize just how serious. One or two days isn't a big deal, other than a lack of energy and perhaps some memory issues. But beyond that you run more serious risks."

"Like what?" I asked.

"Moments of what they call 'micro-sleep.' Inability to concentrate. Moodiness."

I nodded as a way to communicate that I was experiencing at least some of these symptoms. Dr. Mills noticed.

"In severe cases, patients can experience psychological issues like paranoia, even hallucinations." I thought for a moment about the figure at the bottom of the stairs. But I was certain that it was no hallucination. *Wasn't I?*

"Uncontrollable laughter and crying," he continued. "Your body's immune system can also become compromised. I noticed that you're actually running a slight fever today." He was looking now at my chart.

"I am?" I asked. "My son felt warm to me this morning. Maybe we both caught something."

"Perhaps," he said. "I'm not quick to jump to sleeping pills; they have a plethora of side effects of their own. But I take insomnia very seriously. So I am going to prescribe a drug called Estazolam. You will take one about an hour before bedtime. It will help you fall asleep and stay asleep."

He began writing on a notepad. His scribbles were loud.

"My son sleepwalks," I blurted. I didn't know why I said it.

Dr. Mills stopped writing and regarded me. "How often?"

"Frequently," I said. "Lately almost nightly."

"Is this why you're not sleeping?" he asked. "Because he disturbs your sleep?"

"Not entirely," I said, regretting that I had mentioned it. I looked at his notepad, willing him to continue writing.

He studied me for a moment, then continued with his notepad. "I would need to see your son before I could address his issue. Or you should take him to his pediatrician." Dr. Mills tore the sheet from his notepad and handed it to me. I thanked him.

He opened the door to the exam room. I hopped down from the table. As I walked past him, he pointed to the slip of paper in my hand and said, "That is not recommended for children."

* * *

The library in the afternoon was quiet. There was a young man, college-age, seated at one of the eight computers made available for public use. A gentleman, older, was reading a newspaper in a separate seating area while his wife perused the large print non-fiction books nearby. Danielle was busy straightening up the children's section following the morning's story time, which had attracted about half a dozen preschoolers and their bubbly young mothers. Mrs. Strickland was holed away in her office while Beth stood at the counter, looking simultaneously chipper and bored. Two elderly ladies sat at a table working on a puzzle. Other than their whispered conversation, the library was silent.

I was pushing a gray metal cart full of returned books, all of which, I had made doubly certain, had been checked in. At the far end of the library I looked out a window and noticed it had just begun to rain. The gray skies outside hid the sun completely, which dimmed the light inside the library as well. I entertained the notion of finding an empty corner and taking a nap, soothed by the sound of falling rain. I was aware as I pushed the cart that I was leaning on it quite heavily, using it to support my weight. I was like an old woman with a walker.

As I passed the end of an aisle, from the corner of my eye I thought I saw, at the opposite end, a boy, standing perfectly still, facing me. A shadowy figure. I stopped and looked at him directly, and he was gone. I closed my eyes, hard, in an effort to clear my vision. My eyelids felt incredibly heavy.

My hands on the cool handle of the cart, I pushed it beyond the aisle to the end of the next one. This aisle was empty. I picked up a book and shelved it. The voice of one of the elderly ladies working the puzzle reached my ears. "My arthritis is killing me today, Eunice."

"It's the rain," Eunice sighed.

"Must be the rain," the first one responded, as if the idea was new and her own.

I smiled at the exchange, then knelt to place a book on one of the lower shelves. As I slid it in place, I glanced up and looked directly into a pair of eyes staring at me over the row of books, eyes belonging to a boy who was crouched in the aisle on the other side of the shelves. His glare was malevolent.

Startled, I fell backwards from my crouched position and hit my head on the racks behind me. I moaned and pushed myself up with one hand while touching the back of my head with the other. There was a small lump. I looked through the shelves in front of me to the aisle beyond. The boy was gone.

"It's worse than usual," one of the ladies complained.

"It's the *rain*, Lydia," the other one responded, her voice testing the edges of a true whisper.

I stood, straightened my skirt, and pushed the book cart from the aisle to the end of the next one. My fear had given way to irritation. The aisle was empty. I stood still and stared.

I left the cart where it would be out of the way and walked toward the service counter, passing the ladies and their incomplete puzzle on the way. "My arm hurts worst of all," Lydia said. "The left one." She was rubbing it.

"You sure are whiny," Eunice responded, not even looking up from the puzzle.

As I walked toward the desk, my pace quick, from my left I sensed the boy again, looking at me from where he stood behind the man reading the newspaper. I looked over quickly. He wasn't there.

Beth looked at me oddly as I approached. "Everything okay?" she asked.

"Yes," I said, and I circled to the other side of the counter, re-trieving a water bottle from a low shelf and taking a long drink. "Just thirsty."

"Hey, can you stay here a minute?" she asked. "Nature calls."

I made a gesture with my head that was partly a nod and partly a dismissal. Beth left.

I scanned the library. College boy at the computer. Old man with a newspaper. I couldn't spot his wife. A younger couple that I hadn't seen enter were perusing the shelves of DVDs. For a moment, I thought they had a child with them, but when I looked again, they were alone.

The elderly ladies at the puzzle table were bickering, their voices getting louder. "This isn't fun if you're just going to complain the whole time," Eunice said.

"Well, it *hurts*," said Lydia, still rubbing her arm. Neither were bothering to whisper anymore.

"So you've said," Eunice responded.

I continued to scan the library. "Where are you?" I whispered.

I heard Mrs. Strickland's voice coming from her office behind me, talking on the phone. The fluorescents buzzed loudly overhead.

"I'm done," said Eunice, standing up from the puzzle table, raising her hands in a gesture of dramatic surrender. "I'm done."

"No, you're not," said Lydia. She gestured at the table. "There's still pieces left."

Eunice picked up a book in front of her. "No, I mean I'm going to check out and we're leaving. We'll come back when you stop complaining."

Lydia looked offended. "It's the *rain*," she called after her friend as she walked away from the table.

There was a noise to my right as someone approached me. I turned with a start. It was Beth.

"Just me, jumpy," she said.

There was a sudden noise as Eunice slammed her book on the counter in front of me, clearly miffed. She slapped her library card on top of it. I picked up both.

"You don't have to be so insensitive," I heard her friend say as she approached her from behind.

I scanned the library card. The woman's name was Eunice Platt. I gave her a small smile as I handed her card back to her. She barely returned it. Her friend stood behind her, rubbing her arm.

"I'm done talking about it," said Eunice, not even turning around.

"It really hurts," said Lydia, and I noticed that her tone had changed from one of mild discomfort to genuine concern.

I scanned the book. "This will be due back in two weeks," I said as pleasantly as I could, and handed the book to Eunice, who took it from me. She turned away from the counter, giving me a full view of her friend behind her.

Lydia stood quite still, her head bowed, her face drawn up in pain. She had her right hand on her left arm, which hung limply at her side, rubbing it above the elbow. Beside her was the boy, his head turned sideways, his teeth clamped across her forearm, gnawing. He was looking directly at me. His wide eyes were full of violence and glee.

I heard myself scream, the sound echoing through the library, bouncing off the walls.

All eyes in the library turned to me. I heard the door to Mrs. Strickland's office open. In the brief moment that I looked behind me and then forward again, the boy had disappeared.

"I'm so sorry," I said, looking around. Beth looked at me with disapproving concern. I didn't even dare look at Mrs. Strickland, whom I could feel looming behind me. "I thought I saw something." I could feel my heart pounding in my throat, making it hard to breathe.

The two women left the counter and walked toward the library's front doors, Eunice in front, Lydia walking feebly behind her. She continued rubbing her limp arm.

"It has to be the rain," she said, and they left.

* * *

That evening, at dinner, Benjamin barely touched his food. While he shoved baked beans around his plate, his face fallen, I retrieved the thermometer from the bathroom and took his temperature. It was 102.

"You're sick, kiddo," I said.

"I don't feel good," he said, and dropped his fork, which hit the table with a *tink*.

"Go put on jammies and get a blanket. You can watch a movie on the couch." He obeyed, shuffling slowly from the kitchen.

I cleared the table. On the counter by the sink was a white paper bag from the pharmacy, my sleeping pills inside. I plucked the bottle from the bag and removed the lid. I took out one pill, placed it on the counter, and split it with a butter knife. One portion was slightly larger than the other. I crushed the smaller portion with the flat end of the knife, then brushed the powder into a small glass, which I filled with orange juice from the fridge. I set the glass down on the counter.

I went to the bathroom. Washed my face and brushed my teeth. Took out my contacts. Changed my clothes. By the time I walked through the living room, Benjamin was already on the couch, curled up, a cartoon playing on the TV.

I retrieved the orange juice from the kitchen. "Drink this," I said, and Benjamin sat up slowly. He took the glass from me and drank it without ever taking his eyes off the television. He turned up his lips slightly, as if the juice didn't taste quite right. When it was empty he gave the glass back to me and lay back down.

I set the glass on the coffee table and squeezed in beside him on the couch. He raised his head enough to put it in my lap. I could feel heat radiating against my legs. I rubbed his back. He mumbled something I didn't understand.

I watched the television for a few minutes but could not focus on it. It was a monumental effort just keeping my eyes open. Before long – a half an hour, at the most – I could tell from Benjamin's breathing that he was asleep.

I slid out from under him and, with much effort, I picked him up and took him to his room. He was hot, limp, and heavy. I had already pulled back his bedclothes, so I put him in his bed as gently as I could and covered him up.

Back in the kitchen, I picked up the bottle of sleeping pills. I opened it and pulled another pill from the bottle, popped it in my mouth, and washed it down with water from the sink that I cupped in one hand. I then saw the remainder of the other pill, still sitting on the counter. I swallowed that as well.

Lying down in my bed felt like sinking into a cloud. I picked up my new-to-me copy of *Little Women,* a book I had read more times than I could count, the bookmark with the printed roses already tucked behind the front cover. The baby monitor hummed quietly beside me. Before I had finished the second page, before I had even noticed the sleeping pill beginning to take effect, I was asleep.

In my dream I was at my mother's house. I was sitting at the kitchen table at breakfast, a giant bowl of cereal in front of me. My mother was at the sink, her back to me, washing dishes, singing something that was making me giggle. Her hair was brown like it used to be, not gray as it had become since my father had died.

Even though I was a child, it was my mother's current house, not the house from my youth. I looked around me. Morning sunlight poured through the kitchen windows, so bright that I could not see anything outside but light.

"What are you doing here, sweetie?" she asked, never turning around to face me.

"I live here," I giggled, then slurped the drop of milk that had fallen over my lower lip.

"No, honey," she said, "You should go home."

"But I am home!" I insisted.

"Come with me," she said. "Let's call your mommy." She stepped sideways toward a door to her right. A pantry door. *My* pantry door. She had left the sink running, and water was beginning to overflow its edges, splashing onto the floor. It was steaming hot.

"Where are you going, Mommy?" I asked.

"To get the phone," she said. "I left it in there. With Emil."

"He's in the pantry? With the door closed?" I asked, and for some reason I laughed. I covered my hands with my mouth, dropping my spoon, which hit the table with a *tink*.

"No, not the pantry," she said. "The basement."

She opened the door. Beyond it was not a pantry or a basement but a void, nothing but darkness beyond, no walls, no ceiling, no bannister, no stairway. Nothing.

She stood in front of the void, her back still toward me. She was still. The air that was coming out of the darkness was dreadfully cold. I could feel it creeping across my face. It was blowing my mother's hair very gently. Suddenly I knew what she was about to do.

"No, Mommy!" I said, and stood up at the table. I climbed on top of it, crawling across it, one knee upsetting my cereal bowl. "Don't!"

She turned her head only slightly toward me. "Let's call your mother," she said, her voice soft and pleasant, and stepped forward, her body immediately plunging into the nothing. A moment later I heard a sound, a sound like glass shattering. I screamed.

* * *

I sat up in bed, took a breath, and immediately lay back down. I tapped the screen of my cell phone, which was resting on my nightstand. The screen told me it was 3:20 in the morning.

I could feel myself drifting away again almost immediately, the drug stealing away my consciousness. I closed my eyes and willed myself not to dream, as if it was something I could control. Sleep had almost overtaken me again, like a dark blanket being pulled over my head, when I heard Benjamin's voice over the monitor.

"Mom?" he said. His voice was raspy and weak.

The familiar pattern followed: his door opened ("Mom?"), the floorboard creaked ("Mom?"), and my doorknob rattled, then turned. The bedroom door opened.

I could see his blurry silhouette at the doorway, and he approached my bed. When he reached my side he said my name again. He was rubbing his eyes and his head hung down sleepily.

"What is it, baby?" I said.

He didn't respond.

I sat up and reached for him. I put my hands under his arms and lifted. It took all my strength. Limp as a rag doll, he let me pull him into the bed, his feet dragging across my legs as I pivoted, placing him on the other side of the bed beside me. I put my hand on his forehead: it was shockingly hot and completely dry. I did not bother trying to cover him up.

I turned away from him and closed my eyes. The bed trembled as Benjamin turned toward me, moaning, and pressed himself against my back. I could feel his heat through the bedclothes, his breath against my neck, smelling of sickness.

I wondered momentarily if I could ever go back to sleep like this, uncomfortable with the heat of Benjamin's body against mine, when I felt myself beginning to drift. I was almost asleep when I heard the murmur of Benjamin's voice: "Mom?"

It wasn't coming from behind me. It was coming from the baby monitor.

FRIDAY

I awoke at the kitchen table, my head on my arms, a butcher knife in one hand. I had no idea at first where I was, and once I realized it was the kitchen, I had no idea why I was there.

Then I remembered.

I stepped from the kitchen to the living room, peering through it to the doorway of my bedroom. It was closed. I approached it and turned to look down the hallway to Benjamin's door. Also closed.

Was it all a dream?

I had the vague memory of a dream. My mother at the sink. The pantry door. But the more I tried to recollect it, the more it slipped from my memory, like sand through my fingers. Had Benjamin (*or someone else*) gotten into my bed last night? Had I then also heard his voice through the monitor?

I looked at one door, and then the other. Ultimately I opened neither. I returned to the kitchen and began making coffee. I felt hung over from the sleeping pill, but I realized at least I had slept. For several hours in fact. But I still felt exhausted.

I returned to the kitchen and shivered against a damp chill. I realized then that the back door was open, the morning air creeping into the room. I got up, closed it, and locked it. I peered through the kitchen window into the back yard, but there was nothing to see. The ground was wet and glistening in the morning sunlight. A bird sat in a tree.

I was seated again at the table, drinking coffee, knowing that I needed to make some decisions about the day but unable to put together two thoughts. I heard a door open from the other side of the house and my heart gave a feeble leap, startled and yet too exhausted to properly react.

I heard feet shuffle down the hallway and through the living room, and then Benjamin was standing at the kitchen door. He looked pale and sleepy. His pajamas looked big on him, the sleeves hanging down to his fingers, the hem of the pants touching the floor. They were also wet. Benjamin's feet were dirty, and I spied blades of grass sticking to his toes.

I said nothing, and after a moment Benjamin approached me. I put a hand on his forehead; it felt cool.

"How are you feeling?" I asked.

"Okay," he said. "Just...*really* sleepy still."

"Are you well enough to go to school?"

"I think so," he said.

"You sure? I can call Mee-Maw and you could stay with her today."

"Nah, I was just there," he said, and sat down in the chair beside me and rested his chin on his arms.

"Sure, but you like going to Mee-Maw's," I reminded him.

He shrugged as if unconvinced.

I let it go. "Hungry?" I asked, and he nodded. I got up and poured some cereal and a glass of orange juice. Made toast.

"Aw, no Dunkin' Doughnuts?" he asked sleepily. *He must be feeling better.*

"Not today, kiddo," I said, putting his breakfast in front of him. He began to eat. "I'm going to go take a shower, okay?"

He nodded.

I reached the hallway and looked from one bedroom door to the other. Both were open.

* * *

I was so used to being tired that I did not consider whether my lethargy was lack of sleep, a hangover from the sleeping pill, or both. Either way, focusing on my work took effort. Standing behind the counter at work, I experienced what Dr. Mills had described as "micro sleep." I found myself shifting between unconsciousness and wakefulness, my chin at times hitting my chest. I would awaken with a start, horrified that I might have been seen.

Whenever opportunity would allow, I would go into the employee bathroom and splash cold water on my face. I hardly recognized the woman in the mirror. I had purple circles around my half-lidded eyes, which were bloodshot. My skin was patchy, pale and gray, and I had done a horrible job disguising it with makeup. My cheeks were oddly sunken in.

It was around 11:00 in the morning, and I had just stepped out of the bathroom and into the employee lounge. I had been rubbing my eyes, and when I looked up, there was a figure standing in the doorway ahead of me. I started.

It was her – the woman from the news. From the look on her face I could tell that she had been waiting for me. She approached me, studying my face. She looked even more fragile than before, like a stiff breeze would blow her over, yet at the same time she appeared heavy, laden with the weight of the world. She looked hard into my eyes.

I had to resist an urge to back away. "Can I help you?" I asked, attempting to smile but failing.

"You read it," she said.

"I read…" I didn't finish my statement. I knew what she meant.

Her features softened, and she looked like she was both sorrowful and afraid. "I'm so sorry," she said.

"The book is yours?" I asked.

"No!" she said, almost yelling. Then, more softly, "No. Not any-more."

I had so many questions but I didn't know where to begin. "Did you write it?"

She shook her head quickly. "I don't know who wrote it. One day it was in my mailbox. No address or postage. Just there. It was so peculiar to me. I read it. I showed it to my husband and he read it. We thought it was a horrible poem but nothing more. But there was a knock at the door. And then things began to happen." Her eyes trailed away from me. She was remembering.

"We tried to dismiss it at first," she continued. "The noises. Things disappearing. We blamed each other. We fought. We blamed our children. For so long we denied that anything was seriously wrong. But then it got much, much worse." She stopped speaking. I wanted her to tell me more, even though part of me I was afraid of what she would say.

"Do you think he is real?" I asked, not wanting to say the name.

She hesitated. "There is part of me that still denies that he is real. It can't be possible. This sort of thing does not happen. It just *doesn't*. But there is no other explanation, unless I am crazy."

She looked deep into my eyes. "My husband did not kill our children," she said, and she was pleading with me, her eyes begging me to believe her. She began to cry. "We loved our children. We had a boy and a girl. Michael and Micaela. They were twins." Her voice broke off and she began to sob. I wanted to console her, but I kept a distance between us.

When she collected herself again, she said, "I regret so much what I said to them. What I did to them. I thought they were acting up. I thought they were doing some of the things that were happening in the house. But I couldn't sleep. I couldn't trust anything I thought I saw. Even now I'm not sure, the things I thought I saw them do with my own eyes. Michael talking to me in my kitchen, just as pleasant as could be, casting two shadows. Or Micaela speaking to me in a voice that wasn't hers. I thought I was losing my mind.

"And then, one morning, they were gone. We woke up and they were gone." Tears began to flow again. "We looked everywhere. We called everyone. The police asked us so many questions. I could tell that they thought we were lying to them. And we were. We couldn't be completely honest with them because the truth wasn't believable. So we lied, and we knew they suspected we had done something horrible to our children.

"And then John was gone too. I woke up one morning and he was gone. So were some of his clothes, his keys, and his truck. All gone. But he didn't leave. He didn't *skip town*," she spat, bitterly. "He wasn't running away from the police. He was taken, just as they were."

She wiped her nose, took a breath, calming herself. "Are you married?" she asked.

"No," I said. "I'm divorced."

"Do you have any children?"

"I have a son."

She closed her eyes, pushing out new tears. "I am so sorry."

"Then why did you do it?" I asked her. "Why did you leave that book here?" I wanted to take her by the shoulders and shake her.

She hesitated.

"*Excuse me!*" It was Mrs. Strickland. She had just entered the employee lounge and was standing behind the woman. "This area is *employees only*," she said. "Please excuse yourself."

The woman looked at me, bowed her head, and backed out of the lounge, squeezing past Mrs. Strickland. I began to follow her. "I'm very sorry, Mrs. Strickland."

"*Helena*," she said, and I stopped. The woman disappeared out the door. "You have left the front counter unstaffed for more than five minutes. Are you aware of this?"

"No, ma'am," I said.

She glared at me for a long moment, as if trying to bore holes through my head with her eyes. *This is it*, I thought. *She's going to fire me.*

She took a deep breath and said, "Get back out front right now."

I walked past her, legitimately afraid that she might strike me as I walked by. Back at the service counter, I scanned the library, but the woman was nowhere to be seen.

* * *

Afternoon. I have no idea what time. I have no recollection of the events of those hours except for a woman, a customer I don't recall having seen before, approaching the counter. I did my best to appear awake and welcoming, even attempting to smile at her.

"Yes, I have two books on hold," she said, not returning my smile but jutting her library card toward me.

I took the card and ran it under the scanner. The scanner beeped at me negatively. *Card not read.* I scanned it again. *Card not read.* I groaned a little and gave the customer a pleasant shrug. Scanned it again. *Card not read.*

Danielle was beside me. She took the card from me, flipped it over, and scanned it. The customer's information filled the screen. Danielle handed the library card back to the customer. "Ah, there it is," I said, embarrassed. I read the screen, squinting because the letters were blurry. "Yes, you have two books on hold."

I squatted and looked under the counter, where we kept any books that were being held for customers. It was dark under there and I was having trouble making out the titles on the spines lined up in front of me. I also felt very heavy against the backs of my own calves and unsteady as well. I put one hand on the floor to keep from tipping.

I couldn't find either of the books that the computer said were on hold for the customer. I looked through the titles again. I then looked up for help, but Danielle was gone.

I stood up unsteadily. "I'm sorry," I said, smiling at the customer, who frowned in return. "I can't seem to find them."

"I received an e-mail this morning," she said, "Saying that the books were waiting for me." She began tapping her library card on the counter. *Tap-tap-tap.*

"I understand," I said. "Let me just check something." I looked at her account on the screen, verifying the titles a second time. I backed up and looked under the counter again, knowing I would not see them.

The customer sighed impatiently. *Tap-tap-tap.*

"Let me just check over here for a second," I walked to another area behind the counter and looked beneath. Reams of paper. Files. A mug full of pens. No books.

"I made a special trip out here," the woman said. *Tap-tap-tap.*

"I understand," I said. I looked beyond the counter into the library, hoping to find Danielle or Beth. I did not see them. I returned to the computer and looked up both book titles individually, which took longer than it should have because I kept missing keys.

"This is unbelievable," the customer said, looking at her watch dramatically. *Tap-tap-tap.*

The computer said that both titles were checked in and on hold. "I don't know what to say," I said to her. "I'm very sorry. I have no idea where they are."

"And I'm sorry you can't do your job," she huffed. "If those books are not here then I should *not* have received that e-mail. I went *out of my way* to stop here today."

"Again, I'm very sorry," I said, trying to remain calm, but I felt my smile fade. "There's nothing I can do. When we find them I will make sure to let you know."

"Don't bother!" she said, shoving her library card into her purse. She began to walk away and muttered, "What should I expect from a trash library at the trash end of town?"

"Trash customers," I responded.

I had a moment to cherish the white-faced shock of the woman, who stopped and looked at me as if I had just slapped her across the face. But then Mrs. Strickland said, "Helena. My office."

* * *

Benjamin's school. 4:20 p.m. I had pulled up to the curb. I reached over and removed a cardboard box from the passenger seat and set it in the back. It contained everything that had been in my locker at the library.

I put my head on the steering wheel and willed myself not to cry. Several feelings battled for dominance. Anger. Rejection. Sadness. Embarrassment. Exhaustion. At the moment, sadness was winning.

If he wasn't already waiting curbside, it usually only took a moment or so after my arrival at school for Benjamin to come bursting out of the doors, but today he did not. I put the car in park and let it idle while I got out and approached the building.

Children who were picked up late at school every day, like Benjamin, were assembled in a classroom near the front doors, where they played games and did homework under the supervision of one or two teachers until their parents arrived.

I pounded on the front doors, which were locked. I pulled out my cell phone to make a call when a woman approached, a teacher whose name escaped me, and opened the door. She looked confused.

"Hi," I said. "I'm Helena… Benjamin's mom?" I'm not sure why I made it sound like a question.

She shook her head slightly. "Benjamin left already," she said, and a chill crept up my spine. "Your … husband picked him up?"

I closed my eyes and thought. *What day is this? Friday. Fourth*

Friday of the month. This is David's weekend. David always picks him up from school when it's his weekend. So Benjamin is with David. I felt a wash of relief. *Did Benjamin even pack a bag this morning? He has clothes at his father's house, but he still usually packs a bag of things that he wants. I didn't remind him because I hadn't remembered.*

"Yes, of course," I said. "I'm sorry to have bothered you." I backed away from the door with an embarrassed smile and walked toward the car. I called David. The phone rang. And rang again. It was ringing too much. I stopped walking. *He isn't going to answer.* I felt my heart begin to pound.

He answered. "Hey, Hel."

"David!" I said. "Is Benji with you?" I realized my voice sounded panicked.

He let out a small chuckle and said, "Yeah, of course. He's right here."

I let out a sigh. "Good," I said. "Sorry, I got my days crossed."

"S'okay," he said. "Listen, can't talk. We're on the road. Enjoy your weekend." And he was gone.

"Enjoy my weekend," I said to myself, and got back in the car. I sat there for several minutes, the car idling, and sobbed.

* * *

The house was quiet – oppressively quiet. No kid, no cat. As much as I loved Benjamin, I secretly relished the weekends he was with David. It gave me time to reboot and recharge, and I appreciated that time alone. (Well, actually I typically enjoyed the first 24 hours, after which I began to miss Benjamin and started counting the minutes until his return.)

Tonight, though, was different. I had never been fired from a job before, much less a job I loved, and with it came an overwhelming sense of loneliness. It felt as if everyone else in the world belonged somewhere, yet here I was, rejected, no longer welcome in the place where I wanted to be.

I walked through the house, my purse still slung on my shoulder. Everything appeared as it should be, albeit covered in quiet and in the shadows of a late September evening. Nothing was out of the ordinary, and only Benjamin's room gave me a sense of unease, but that was simply because Benjamin was not in it.

In the kitchen I dropped my purse on the table, then poured myself a glass of wine. I checked my cell phone for messages. I hoped to have a missed call from either Beth or Danielle (or both), a message expressing their dismay over my firing, maybe something encouraging like how they planned to speak to Mrs. Strickland and beg her to give me a second chance. But there was nothing from either of them, and it made me sad. I hadn't even been given the opportunity to say goodbye to them.

I dialed my mom, knowing that her voice alone would be some comfort to me, although I dreaded telling her my news. The sound of her voice on the answering machine brought inexplicable tears to my eyes. I asked her to give me a call and hung up.

I next called Hugh.

"Hey," he answered, his tone warm.

"Hi," was all I could manage in return.

"What's wrong?" he asked.

"I'm sorry," I said. "I need to cancel our date tonight. Rain check?" There was a rattle in my voice that I could not disguise.

"What's wrong?" he repeated.

"I'm just…" I trailed off. "I don't feel very well. I wouldn't be good company."

"Can I bring you anything?" he asked. "Chicken noodle soup? I promise I won't stay."

"No, it's okay," I said. "I just need to sleep." *You have no idea.*

A few more pleasantries exchanged, we hung up.

I spied the sleeping pills on the counter and picked them up. "Not to be consumed with alcohol." I looked at the clock on the microwave. 6:20. It wasn't even fully dark outside yet. I popped two pills in my mouth and washed them down with wine. If nothing else, I was going to sleep.

* * *

The pounding was quiet, distant at first, and as I regained consciousness, I at first reasoned that I had heard it in my dreams. But no, the sound was real. It was coming from the front door: great, thunderous bangings that had roused me from a very deep sleep.

I sat up in bed and felt dizzy. I remembered my dinner of two sleeping pills and a glass of wine.

It was completely dark in my room; there was no light at all outside my windows. I reached for the bedside lamp, aiming for the switch but hitting the shade, almost knocking it to the floor. I turned on the light.

Bang bang bang bang BANG!

My eyes felt dry; I had fallen asleep without removing my contacts. I reached for my cell phone only to find that it wasn't there. I always put it on my bedside table at night since I used it for my morning alarm. I looked around me in the bed, turning back sheets and blankets. I leaned over and looked on the floor. It was nowhere to be found. I got on the floor and crouched down, looking under the bed. Nothing.

From my squatting position on the floor, I listened. The pounding had stopped, and there was a new sound. The front door had just opened.

I was so overcome with fear that my body went cold and I lost all feeling in my fingers and toes. I looked around the room. I had nothing to defend myself – no bat or knife or gun. I considered hiding under the bed or in the closet.

More silence. Then footsteps.

What followed next was a cacophony of sound: a door slamming shut. A dull thud against the floor. A scraping against the wall. Glass shattering. A voice, deep and angry. A deafening cry.

I put my hand over my mouth, trying to put a stopper on the scream that wanted to escape. With my other hand I reached up and turned off the light, plunging the room into darkness. I then lay flat on the floor and pushed myself under the bed.

The violent noises continued. There was another shattering sound, and then a loud, echoing crack followed by a moment of silence, as if the house was taking an agonizing breath. And then there was a scream.

I reached up to the hanging bedspread and yanked it down in front of me, blocking my view of the room, hiding me. I covered my ears. There I waited, panting and out of breath, my eyes on the crack at the bottom of my bedroom door, barely visible to me. It was nothing but darkness.

Eventually, I don't remember how long after, the sounds stopped. Well, almost stopped. There was a scraping sound, like an object was being dragged across the floor, accompanied by the tinkle of glass. And then were was nothing more. For several long minutes I waited for the silence to be broken yet again.

Eventually, I began to fall asleep. I knew it was foolish, but I could not fight it.

SATURDAY

I awoke in bed. I had no way of knowing what time it was, but judging by the brightness of the sun outside, it was mid-morning.

Another dream? It had been a particularly vivid one, if so, but my bedtime cocktail had almost guaranteed I would have at least one.

I got out of bed and walked to the door, my body a sack of bricks. My head ached. I exited the room and began to walk toward the bathroom, my bladder screaming for relief. But then I glanced toward the living room.

Two pictures that had been hanging on the wall were now on the floor, the glass shattered and twinkling in the sunlight coming through the living room window. There was a dent in one wall, near the floor, with cracks shooting off in all directions like bolts of lightning. The couch was overturned and resting on its back.

I retreated to the bedroom and threw on clothes – jeans and a sweater from the floor of my closet – as well as shoes. I walked through the living room, carefully avoiding the sparkles of glass. I looked at the front door and was surprised to find it not only closed, but locked.

I didn't know where my cell phone was, so my best option was to get my purse and either drive somewhere or go knock on one of my neighbors' doors. It was a Saturday morning (*right?*). Surely someone would be home.

My purse was there on the kitchen table where I had left it, but so was something else: my cell phone. It was not near the edge or anywhere that I might have casually placed it. It was sitting square in the middle of the table, as if placed intentionally.

I snatched it and turned it on. I saw that I had voice messages. Four of them. All from Hugo. All from yesterday evening.

6:41 p.m.: "Hey, it's me. I know you said don't come over, but I'm coming over. Persistent, remember?"

7:02 p.m.: "Me again. I'm here. Are you here?" [Message ends.]

7:04 p.m.: "Wake up, little Suzie, wake up…" he sang. [Message ends.]

7:05 p.m.: "Your neighbors are gonna call the cops on me if you don't open up. Your car is here, so… [Sound of pounding.] Ah, never mind. There you are." [Sound of the front door opening. Message ends.]

I dropped the phone. It landed by my feet with a clatter. I covered my face and cried heavily, gasping for breath. I pulled out a chair and attempted to sit in it, missed, and crumpled on the floor, sobbing, the sound of my sorrow travelling dully through the empty house.

* * *

I was sitting up in my bed. I could not cry any more. I had cleaned up the living room as best I could, righted the sofa, swept up the glass, and pitched the shattered picture frames.

I had contemplated calling the police, but to what end? There was nothing they could do to help. Instead I called Hugo, several times. He never answered.

And so I sat in my bed, my head hung low, my upper back aching, my throat sore from crying, my eyes puffy. I dabbed my nose with a tissue. A drop of liquid fell from me – a tear or snot, I didn't care – and fell on the little leather book in my lap. I opened it up.

> *There was a boy named Emil Bones*
> *Who would like to be your friend,*
> *But once you let him in your house,*

He may never leave again.

"You want to be my friend," I said out loud, and shook my head slightly. I almost wanted to laugh.

> *He loves to play in shadows,*
> *In voices, shapes, and sounds,*
> *And while you may not always see him,*
> *He will always be around.*
>
> *He is quite the little prankster,*
> *Who may make you laugh, but then*
> *The jokes stop being funny,*
> *And you will never laugh again.*
>
> *First he absents things you need*
> *For the collection he's amassed*
> *Then purloins the things you love*
> *Each more precious than the last.*
>
> *He will make you suffer far beyond*
> *What any person ever should*
> *And while he may not take your life,*
> *He will make you wish he would.*

I started to cry again, softly. *I'm almost there*, I thought. *I'm almost there.*

> *See Emil was a wicked child*
> *Whose heart was full of sin*
> *Until his mother realized*
> *Emil never should have been.*
>
> *First she crushed him with a pillow*
> *Then she hit him with a club*
> *Tied a cord around his neck*

And drowned him in the tub.

She bound him up with heavy rope
Put a bag over his head
And then with horror realized
That Emil wasn't dead.

She took his body in the night
To the woods behind her shack
Burned him up quite thoroughly,
Placed his ashes in a sack

Hid the sack deep in the earth
And marked it with white stones
Knowing well that this was not
The end of Emil Bones

That very night she lay in bed
Sad, tired, scared and vexed
When Emil whispered in her ear,
"What game shall we play next?"

What made a mother do this
To a child that she should love?
It's an answer quite disturbing
You may know it soon enough

So now you know the devil child
Whose name was Emil Bones
Rest assured, he knows you too
And won't leave you alone

He's a shadow, he's a whisper,
He's a hornet, he's a pox
For heaven's sake, now heed my words:
Do not answer when he knocks…

I thought back to that night, when was that? Tuesday before last? Eleven days ago? It felt so much longer. The night that Emil Bones had first knocked on our front door. I was sure of it now. *It hadn't been Benjamin knocking from the inside, had it? No.*

How many hours I had I slept in those eleven days? Not enough. Not nearly enough. I absentmindedly flipped the page and was startled. There was more.

I hadn't finished it.

"*...I always finish books,*" I heard myself saying to Hugo. "*Even bad ones. I'm hopeful that there will be something redeeming about them in the end. Sometimes there's not. But I feel like I've let the book down if I don't finish it.*"

That night, eleven days ago, when the knocking had begun, it had startled me and I had put the book down. I assumed it was finished and had never continued.

> *It does not matter where you go*
> *For you are his to haunt*
> *For days and nights unending*
> *'Til you give him what he wants*
>
> *The answer is quite simple*
> *In fact, it's very plain*
> *For Bones and those just like him*
> *What they want is all the same.*

"What he *wants*?" I said out loud, and flipped back to the first page. *There was a boy named Emil Bones who would like to be your friend.* I read it out loud, slowly and with purpose, but it revealed nothing new to me. "He wants to be my friend?" *What does* that *mean?* I thought, and threw the book across the room. It hit the wall and fell to the floor.

* * *

I didn't remember lying down, but at some point I had fallen asleep in my bed. When I woke the sun hung low in the sky and my room was full of shadows. I sat up and arched my back in a stretch. The book – *that book* – was lying face down and open on the floor where I had thrown it.

It took me a moment to realize why I had woken. There was knocking at the front door.

As quietly as I could I left my bed and crept to the living room. I walked past the door and pulled back the curtain enough to see outside without being seen.

Two men – police officers – were standing outside the door. Confusion gave way to realization: *Hugo*. Missing. Dead. Perhaps a friend knew that Hugo had been on his way to see me.

I opened the door.

The officer closest to me spoke. "Helena Boyd?" he said.

"Yes," I said.

"I'm Officer Hamm," he said, then tipped his head backward. "This is Officer Shields. May we speak with you for a moment?"

I stepped back and let them inside. Walking through my living room, I saw Officer Hamm glancing at the dent in my wall as he walked by, then giving a look to Officer Shields behind him.

"Rambunctious son," I offered, even though they didn't ask.

The officers sat on the couch. They both removed their hats. Officer Hamm indicated that I should sit down, and I did so in a chair opposite them.

"I'm afraid we have some very bad news," he said.

I nodded, bracing myself for what I knew he was about to say.

"Your mother is dead."

The floor dropped out from under me. My throat tightened.

"A neighbor became concerned when she hadn't seen your mother since Thursday," he continued. "She couldn't get an answer on the phone or at the door yesterday. This morning she called the police."

Don't say any more, I thought.

"They found her at the foot of the basement stairs," he said. "It appears she fell and broke her neck…"

"I can call Mee-Maw and you could stay with her today," I had said.

"We think this happened sometime yesterday morning or the night before."

"Nah, I was just there," Benjamin had replied.

I covered my face with my hands. All I could see were Benjamin's dirty feet.

"We are very sorry for your loss."

* * *

I was standing in the back yard, hovering over the trash can. The lid was off, and I was forcing myself not to acknowledge that the odor assaulting my nose was Mags. On top of the accumulated garbage was the book. That little black leather book. *Emil Bones.*

In my hand was a long match, unlit.

It won't burn, I thought. *It won't let you destroy it. It will stay with you forever. Like a cat that keeps returning, no matter what you do to it. It'll cross the country, traversing the Mississippi in the process, to get back to you.*

I struck the match and held it to the book's edges.

It wants to live, I thought.

But it began to smoke, then flame. The cover lifted open in the heat, and I saw those words, *There was a boy named Emil Bones…* and then the words burned away. Flaming bits of paper floated up into the air and were carried away in the breeze. I watched until there was nothing left but a smoldering pile of ash, and then I closed the garbage can lid.

* * *

That night, I sat on the couch. I didn't bother with changing into my pajamas, or brushing my teeth, or washing my face. I hadn't eaten anything all day. Every light in the house was on.

My phone was beside me. It hadn't rung all day. I didn't hear from David. Or Beth or Danielle. Or Hugo or my mother because they were both dead.

I sat facing the TV, which was off. I could see my reflection in it. I was sitting bolt-upright, legs crossed, hands in my lap, palms upturned. My hair was a mess and my face felt sore from crying. I couldn't cry anymore.

I passed the night this way. I did not move and I did not sleep. I did not take a sleeping pill. I wanted to be awake. I wanted to hear.

There were sounds: the house creaking as it cooled. A car passing the end of the cul-de-sac. An owl hooting. The refrigerator turning on and off again. Innocuous sounds. Normal sounds.

But there were other sounds as well. A basement step would occasionally squeak. A popping sound, right behind me, identical to the sound Mags' claw would make when she got it caught on the back of the sofa. Something that sounded like a door opening ever so slightly. A creaking floorboard in the hallway.

I sat there, hearing everything and nothing, until the sun came up.

SUMDAY

It really shouldn't have worked. I did a Google search for "father disappears after killing children" and got several results. The family's name was Callahan. The mother's name was Joanna.

I then Googled their telephone number and was surprised when I got a result. Then again, I don't suppose a woman in the midst of public tragedy would think to unlist her phone number or necessarily have reason to do so. More likely than not, she just wasn't answering her phone right now.

I dialed the number. She answered after the first ring. I recognized her voice. It sounded exhausted and worn.

"Hello?" she said.

"Is this Joanna Callahan?" I asked.

"Yes," she said.

"This is Helena Boyd. We met," I paused, wondering if that was the right word. "We met at the library."

There was silence at the other end. I could hear her breathing, which was soft and shaky.

"I'm so sorry," she finally whispered. At first I wondered if she knew about my mother, or Hugo, or both. But I decided she knew about neither; she was simply apologizing, again, for putting that book in my life.

"It's … it's okay," I said, not meaning it. "I just… I have so many questions."

"I wondered when you might call," she said.

"Is the story true?" I asked. "Was Emil Bones a real boy?"

"I have no idea," she said. "I don't know who wrote it or who left it with me. I don't know anything more about him than you do. I wish I did."

"Okay," I said, and took a deep breath. "Why did you leave the book at the library?"

There was silence. And then: "To give him what he wanted," she said.

"I don't understand," I said.

"It took me awhile to figure out," she said. "It says you have to give him what he wants. I didn't know what that was. I read that book so many times trying to understand. And then I finally did. I don't know if it matters whether or not Emil was ever a real boy. What matters is what he has become: he's a character in a book."

I ran my fingers through my hair, frustrated. "I'm sorry," I said. "I still don't understand."

"He wants what every character in every story wants," she said. "He wants to be read."

All of these stories, I had said to Hugo, *waiting patiently to be read. That's all they want. I wish I could read them all and make them happy.*

"That's all?" I said, and I felt both relief and confusion. And frustration.

"Maybe," she said. "I don't really know. But it was the only thing that made sense to me in the end. I felt like maybe, if someone else read the book, he'd leave me alone. But I felt horrible about it. If I was right, I was passing on my curse to someone else. I couldn't bring myself to do it directly, and so that's why I left it at the library. I left it up to chance.

"But then, I had to be certain. That's why I came back. I realized after thinking about it awhile that it was probably someone who worked there who would've picked it up first. And I was right. As soon as I saw your face I knew you had read it. And I'm so sorry."

"But did it work?" I pleaded. "Once you'd passed on the book, did Emil leave?"

"I don't know," she said, and started to cry. "Sometimes I think he's still here. I think I still hear him. Sometimes something seems out of place. Something will go missing. I still see things that shouldn't be there. I hear…," she paused. "But I don't know if it's him or if it's me. I haven't slept in so long…" she trailed off, softly crying. After a moment, she sniffed and continued. "In the end, what does it matter?" she asked. "Whether he's here anymore or not, what does it matter? He's taken everything from me. There's nothing left. But maybe it's not too late for you. Maybe you can pass it on before… anything else happens."

"My mother is dead," I said, and it was my turn to cry. "So is my… a friend."

"And your son?"

"He's with his father right now," I said.

"Maybe it's not too late," she said. "Pass it on to someone else."

I felt a chill throughout my body, a sense of inevitability and doom. "I… I burned it yesterday. The book. It's gone."

* * *

The only thing noteworthy about the rest of that day was how often the phone rang. I believe the coroner called once. Something about my mother's body. I don't remember what he asked. I do remember I started to cry again, and then laugh. I couldn't stop. I'm not sure which one of us hung up first.

The phone rang again, later. A woman who identified herself as Hugo's sister. He was missing. Hugo had told her about me and she thought I might know something. I told her I didn't know where he was (*true*), and after we hung up I realized I probably sounded neither surprised nor concerned.

A third phonecall, from Beth. She didn't let me speak. All the familiar friendliness was gone from her voice. She insisted that I lose her phone number and never call her again. She said something about inappropriate messages and calling at all hours and how much she had tried to help me and this is the thanks she gets. When she finally took a breath and I had an opportunity to speak, I hung up.

The fourth phonecall came as the sun was beginning to set. It was David's number.

"David?" I answered, my hands shaking.

"It's Trish," said the voice on the other end. She sounded upset.

I didn't respond. It occurred to me that we had never spoken before. All I knew of her was the physical description Benjamin had given of her (young, pretty, smiles a lot) and the e-mails I had discovered, the ones she had exchanged with David when we were still married.

"Helena?" she asked.

"*Yes?*" I responded.

"Do you know where David is?"

"No," I said.

"He's gone. Him and Benjamin. I got up this morning and they were both gone. He left his phone here, so I can't call him. Have you heard from him?"

"No," I said.

She continued to talk, but I stopped listening. At some point I dropped the phone beside me, hanging up in the process.

* * *

I took three sleeping pills that night. My body would have no choice but to sleep.

As I climbed into bed, I noticed how unusually quiet the house was. Not a creak nor a stir. It was an unnatural silence, like the way birds will cease singing when a predator is nearby.

I shut the door to my room and locked it. I'm not sure why. Given everything that had happened, a locked bedroom door was certainly not an obstacle. And regardless, I was no longer afraid. My nerves had died. No longer scared nor sad, I was nothing. Numb, perhaps. Mostly just tired and ready for an end of some kind.

Still, I had brought a knife with me into the bedroom and slipped it under my pillow. One other option to explore. Could Emil be killed? Likely not. Consider what his mother had done to him, and yet he survived.

Worth a try, however. And if it couldn't be used on him, it could be used on me.

* * *

In my dream, I was sitting in an open field. The blanket under me was white with red checkers. Trees covered the mountains that loomed gorgeously in all directions. A breeze stirred the grass around me and blew through my hair. Benjamin played nearby. He was giggling, tossing a ball to Hugo, my husband. Hugo smiled at me, that 100 watt smile that lit up the world. Something brushed against my hand, and it was Mags, purring loudly and butting up against my arm. It was the cruelest dream I had ever had.

It ended with the sound of Benjamin's door opening at the other end of the hallway with a bang, frightening me enough to make me sit up in bed before I even knew I was awake. My limbs felt heavy with the chemical sedation coursing through my veins.

The next sound was not of shuffling footsteps nor a creaking floorboard, but of running feet, rapidly approaching my bedroom door, my bedroom door which was no longer closed and locked, but standing wide open, nothing but darkness beyond it and the sound of approaching feet, the sound of someone coming closer, someone coming for me.

I slid out of bed onto the floor, collapsing onto my knees. I stretched out my arms, relenting, welcoming whatever the waking nightmare had in store for me. I gave myself over to the exhausting inevitability. The pounding footsteps approached for an eternity, running for longer than the length of the hallway should have allowed, until finally a small shadowy figure burst out of the darkness and into my room, the silhouette of a boy, his hands stretched out toward me, his fingers curled into claws.

He hit me so hard that I fell over backwards, my head ramming into the bedside table. But instead of fighting him, I pulled the shadowy figure toward me, embracing him. He pulled at my hair and scratched at my shoulders. He bit at my chest.

I reached up for the knife, but the bed was too far away. I grabbed at the bedclothes, but they could not hold my weight and instead slid toward me where I was pinned to the floor.

I held him close to me. He continued his assault against my skin. He was hot and his breath was foul. Somehow I managed to sit up, my back against the bedside table. I pulled him closer to me, drawing up my knees. I held him there tightly, one arm around his back. With the other hand I held the back of his head and pressed his face against my chest.

His arms flailed. "Shhhhh," I said. And I began to rock. "It's okay," I said. "This will all be over soon." My weak and heavy arms somehow found the strength to hold him tighter. Eventually, he stopped struggling and went limp, limp like a sleeping baby. I hummed a lullaby.

I cradled his body and slept.

MOANDAY

I awoke on the floor, alone, sometime after noon. My bedroom door was closed. I stood and looked under my pillow. The knife was still there. I picked it up.

I unlocked and opened my bedroom door. All was quiet and dark in the hallway. There was something on the floor in front of me, a sliver of white against the hard wood. It was a tiny scrap of paper, burned around the edges. On it were the words,

> *What made a mother do this*
> *To a child that she should love?*

I let it go and it fluttered back to the ground, where it lodged in the crack where the floor and the wall met.

* * *

I woke up on the couch. I didn't remember lying down in the first place. It was evening. When I stood, rubbing my eyes, I felt something cold against my chest. It was a necklace – a leather string with a foreign symbol made of pewter. I couldn't take it off fast enough.

My phone rang a few times that evening. I never answered it.

At bedtime, I poured a glass of wine, then went to take some sleeping pills. I planned to take several of them. I would finally sleep a dreamless sleep and never wake up again. I had never had a more sane idea.

But of course the pills were gone. "You think of everything," I said out loud.

THUESDAY?

Since I'd stopped answering my phone, there came a constant knocking at the door. Sometimes it was people. Sometimes it was no one. Either way, it was interrupting my sleep, which still came to me at all hours in spite of the lack of pills. It felt as though my body was shutting down. I welcomed it.

The police came. Benjamin and David had been reported missing. Eventually the press would begin comparing it to the Callahan case. They had no idea how right they were.

The police brought a social worker. Between my mother's death and my son's disappearance, they thought I shouldn't be left alone. I refused to go with them. Why bother? Emil would come with me.

They looked at me suspiciously. Dead mother. Missing ex-husband and son. Perhaps they also knew my connection to Hugo, also missing. Who knows and who cares. Either way, I knew they would never pin any of this on me, no matter how suspicious the circumstances. Emil had made sure of that. He wanted me here. All to himself.

They pleaded with me, but somehow I convinced them to leave. Perhaps it was because I wouldn't stop screaming at them until they did.

???day

There was a pile of dead rats outside my bedroom door this (or yesterday) morning. I think I'll sleep on the couch from now on.

* * *

I'm almost out of alcohol. But I don't want to go out. Going out means acknowledging that the world continues to exist outside these walls. I'd rather pretend that it has stopped for everyone and not just for me.

* * *

Three gleaming objects on the coffee table when I awoke from a nap. Three wedding rings: David's. My mother's. And a third that I could only assume was my father's, but I couldn't be sure. I hadn't laid eyes on it since the day of his funeral.

* * *

I remember at one time I believed that the sound of Benjamin's laugh was the sweetest song I'd ever heard, how it would never not make me smile, no matter what kind of day I was having. It doesn't make me smile anymore, not when I hear it coming from his room at night.

Last night I went to his room and begged him to stop. There on his bed was *A Horse and His Boy,* face-down, open to the page where Benjamin and I had left off. "I hate it when we don't finish books," he had said. I collapsed on the floor and sobbed.

When I was done, I stood, wiped my eyes, and walked out of the room, shutting the door behind me. I will never go in there again, no matter what he says.

But Benjamin's isn't the only voice I hear. Sometimes I hear my mom's. It comes from the basement. Sometimes I hear Hugo's, outside the front door. Hugo says it is dark where he is; Mom says it is so very cold.

* * *

The most recent gift that Emil left for me was my typewriter. That doesn't sound sinister at all, does it? You can laugh. I did. It was there on the kitchen table when I awoke from either a nap or after a night's sleep, who can tell? Either way, there it was, beside a stack of blank sheets.

It had been tucked away in a closet for years, no longer of use once David had convinced me to give up my fruitless writing. I sat down at the table and pulled it toward me. It was heavy, as were my eyelids and my fingers. But my mind was suddenly clear. I knew what he wanted me to do.

"Let's make a bargain," I said to the empty kitchen. "I'll tell your story if I can tell mine as well."

I placed my fingers on the keys. *It was a Tuesday*, I typed, then paused. The question was, when I got to that part, the part where I opened the book for the first time, alone on a park bench in a different life, would I remember the poem in full? If I didn't capture it word-for-word, would Emil still be satisfied?

In the end, it didn't matter. When I reached the part of the story where it was time to tell his tale, to recite his poem, the words came to me. I remembered them exactly. Either that, or they were being whispered in my ear. I couldn't tell either way.

When I finished, hours and days later, I laughed. Emil had turned my life into a nightmare, but he had made one dream come true: I had always wanted to write a book. Helena Boyd, author. Non-fiction. If only my friends could see me now.

* * *

I wonder if this will work. If I pass on Emil's tale, will he finally leave me alone? And, like Joanna said, will it even matter? And once he goes, who will I have left to talk to?

TODAY

Before I close, I need to say something to you. Yes, you. I don't know where you got this book. Perhaps someone who hates you gave it to you. Or maybe it came into your life anonymously, almost innocently, like a book placed in a mailbox or in a library book return, on a beautiful day when life was good.

Either way, I am sorry.

But I told you not to read this.

Do not answer when he knocks.